PRAISE FOR A MAN LIES DREAMING

"Stunning . . . very funny . . . remarkably poignant . . . [Tidhar] reminds us that even—especially—under the most terrible of circumstances, stories are all we have. And in the right hands, they can be a formidable weapon." —*The Washington Post*

"Bold and unnerving . . . A Man Lies Dreaming is a book of big ideas, from the pathological origins of racist ideology to the way humanizing and dehumanizing those we love or loathe are flip sides of the same coin." —NPR

"It's caustic. It's risky. The unexpected thing about the book is this: It's good. It's damn good." —Jewish Book Council

"[*A Man Lies Dreaming*] blends two venerable genres—alternative history and noir mystery, with Hitler playing the gumshoe. Though this seems like a stretch, Tidhar makes it work. In keeping with the conventions of the genre, his writing is clipped and precise, but colorful enough to reinvigorate familiar tropes." —The *Forward*

"A daring work, briskly paced and impossible to set down." —*ALIVE Magazine*

"Quite literally took my breath away." —*Cleaver Magazine*

"Everything in this genre-bender works; intriguing historical characters are worked into expertly managed plots, and the visceral noir atmosphere is juxtaposed nicely against the drawing-room world of London's political scene." —*Booklist*, starred review

"A wholly original Holocaust story: as outlandish as it is poignant." —*Kirkus*, starred review

A MAN LIES DREAMING

LAVIE TIDHAR

A MAN LIES
DREAMING

A NOVEL

◆ MELVILLE HOUSE
BROOKLYN · LONDON

A MAN LIES DREAMING

First Melville House Hardcover Printing: March 2016

First Melville House Paperback Printing: May 2016

Melville House Publishing   8 Blackstock Mews
46 John Street   and   Islington
Brooklyn, NY 11201   London N4 2BT

mhpbooks.com   facebook.com/mhpbooks   @melvillehouse

Library of Congress Cataloging-in-Publication Data
Tidhar, Lavie.
   A man lies dreaming : a novel / Lavie Tidhar.
      pages ; cm
    ISBN 978-1-61219-504-9 (hardback)
    ISBN 978-1-61219-505-6 (ebook)
   1. Auschwitz (Concentration camp)—Fiction.   2. World
War, 1939–1945—Prisoners and prisons, German—Fiction.
3. Imagination—Fiction.   4. Authors—Fiction.   I. Title.

PR9510.9.T53M36 2016
823'.92—dc23

2015031072

Design by Marina Drukman

ISBN: 978-1-61219-560-5

Printed in the United States of America

10 9 8 7 6 5 4 3 2 1

He had gone beyond good and evil, and entered a strange landscape where nothing was what it seemed and all the ordinary human values were reversed.
—HUGH TREVOR-ROPER, report for the Secret Intelligence Service

Clichés, stock phrases, adherence to conventional, standardised codes of expression and conduct have the socially recognised function of protecting us against reality.　　　　—HANNAH ARENDT, *The Banality of Evil*

A MAN LIES DREAMING

In another time and place, a man lies dreaming.

1

EXTRACT FROM WOLF'S DIARY, 1ST NOVEMBER 1939

She had the face of an intelligent Jewess.

She came into my office and stood in the doorway though there was nothing hesitant about the way she stood. She gave you the impression she had never hesitated a moment in her life. She had long black hair and long pale legs and she wore a summer dress despite the cold and a fur coat over the dress. She carried a purse. It was hand-threaded with beads that formed into the image of a mockingbird. It was French, and expensive. Her gaze passed over the office, taking in the small dirty window that no one ever cleaned, the old pine hatstand on which the varnish was badly chipping, the watercolour on the wall and the single book-shelf and the desk with the typewriter on it. There wasn't much else to look at. Then her gaze settled on me.

Her eyes were grey. She said, 'You are Herr Wolf, the detective?'

She spoke German with a native Berliner's accent.

'That's the name on the door,' I said. I looked her up and

down. She was a tall drink of pale milk. She said, 'My name is Isabella Rubinstein.'

Her eyes changed when she looked at me. I had seen that look before. In her eyes clouds gathered over a grey sea. Doubt—as though trying to place me.

'I'll save you the trouble,' I said. 'I am nobody.'

She smiled at me. 'Everyone is somebody.'

'And I do not work for Jews.'

At that the clouds amassed in her eyes and stayed there but she remained calm, very calm. Her hand swept over the room. 'I do not see that you have so much choice,' she said.

'What I choose to do is my own damn business,' I said.

She reached into her handbag and came back with a roll of ten-shilling notes. She just held it there, for a long moment.

'What is it about?' I said. At that moment I hated her, and that hatred gave me pause.

'My sister,' she said. 'She is missing.'

I had two chairs for visitors. She pulled one to her and sat down, crossing one leg over the other. She was still holding the notes between her fingers. She didn't wear any rings.

'A lot of people are missing nowadays,' I said. 'If she is in Germany I cannot help you.'

'No,' she said, and this time there was tension in her voice. 'She was leaving Germany. Herr Wolf, let me explain to you. My family is very wealthy. After the Fall our assets were seized, but my father still had friends, some even amongst the Party, and he was able to transfer much of our capital to London. I myself, and my mother, were both allowed to leave the country legally, and my uncles continue the family's continental operations in Paris. Only my sister remained behind. She is young, younger than me. At first she was beguiled by their ideology; she had joined the Free Socialist Youth before the Fall. My father was furious. But I knew it would not last.' She looked up at me, with a half-smile. 'It never does, with Judith, you see.'

All I could see was the money she was holding between those long slim fingers. She moved the roll of notes back and forth, idly. I had been penniless before, and poverty had made me stronger, not weak, but that was in my former life. My life was different now, and it was harder to be hungry.

I said, 'So you arranged for her to leave.'

'My father,' she said quickly. 'He knew men who could smuggle people out.'

'Not easily,' I said.

'Not easily, no. Not cheaply, either.' Again that half-smile, but it flickered and was gone in a flash.

'How long ago was that?'

'A month. She was meant to be here three weeks ago. She never appeared.'

'Do you know who these men were? Do you trust them?'

'My father did. As much as he could be said to trust anyone.'

Something jogged my recall, then. 'Your father is Julius Rubinstein? The banker.'

'Yes.'

I remembered his likeness in the *Daily Mail*. One of the Jewish gangsters who grew rich and fat on the blood of the working man in Germany, before the Fall. His like always survived, like rats abandoning a sinking ship they fled Germany and re-established themselves elsewhere, in clumps of diseased colonies. They said he was as ruthless as a Rothschild.

'Not a man to cross,' I said.

'No.'

'Your sister . . . Judith? She could have been captured by the Communists.'

She shook her head. 'We would have heard.'

'You think she was brought to London?'

'I don't know. I need to find her. I *must* find her, Herr Wolf.'

She put the roll of notes on my desk. I left it there, though whenever I looked at her the notes were in my field of vision. The Jews are nothing but money-grubbers, living on the profits of war. Perhaps she could see it in my eyes. Perhaps she was desperate. 'Why me?'

'The men who smuggled her here,' she said, 'are old comrades of yours.'

There was nothing behind her eyes, nothing but grey clouds. And I realised I had misjudged Fräulein Isabella Rubinstein. There was a reason she had picked me, after all.

'I do not associate with the old comrades any more,' I told her. 'The past is the past.'

'You've changed.' She said that with curiosity.

'You do not know me,' I said. 'Do not ever presume to think that you do!'

She shrugged, indifferent. She reached into her purse and brought out a silver cigarette case and a gold lighter. She opened the case with dextrous fingers and extracted a cigarette and put it between her lips. She offered me the open case. I shook my head. 'I do not smoke,' I said.

'Do you mind if I do?'

I did mind and she could see it. She flicked the lighter to life and wrapped her half-smile around the cigarette and drew deep, and blew smoke into the cold air of my office. A draught came in through the window and though I was dressed in my coat I shivered. It was the only coat I owned. I looked at the money.

I looked at her face. She was nothing but trouble and I knew it and she knew I knew. I had no business hunting for missing Jews in London in the year of our Lord 1939. I once had faith, and a destiny, but I had lost both and I guess I'd never recovered either. All I could see was the money. I was so cold, and it was going to be a cold winter.

When the Jewish woman departed, Wolf sat there for a long moment staring at the money. The smell of her cigarette hung in the air, rank and nauseating. He could not abide the smell of tobacco. Outside the window it was already dark. The cold clawed at the windowpane. Below he could hear the market shutting, the sound of whores sashaying into the night. His landlord's bakery on the ground floor had already closed for the day. He stared at the money.

He pushed the chair back, stood up and took the roll of notes and put them in his pocket. He set the chair back and went round the desk and stood looking at his office. The painting on the wall showed a French church tower rising against the background of a village, a field executed in a turmoil of brushstrokes. Three dark trees grew out of a tangle of roots rising in the foreground of the church. On the bookshelf, a personally inscribed copy of *Fire and Blood*, Ernst Jünger's memoir of the Great War, sat next to J.R.R. Tolkien's *The Hobbit*, Madison Grant's masterpiece of racial theory, *The Passing of the Great Race*, a collection of Schiller's poetry, and a row of Agatha Christies.

There was no copy of Wolf's one published book. He stood looking at the shelf. He had saved only a handful of the collection of books he had amassed before the Fall. Their loss ate at him. But he had already lost so much. He went to the hatstand and put on his hat. His shadow fell on the wall like a dirty coat. Wolf opened the door and went outside.

*

Berwick Street, Soho, on a cold November night. Electric lights cast the pavement in a gloomy glow. The dirty bookstore was open. Whores loitered outside. He stood under the awning of the bakery when his landlord came out of nowhere like a Jew in the night.

'Herr Edelmann,' Wolf said.

'Mr Wolf,' Edelmann said. 'I am glad I caught you.'

He was a short, pudgy man with hands and a face as pale as flour. He had a furtive manner. 'What is it, Herr Edelmann?' Wolf said.

'I hate to bother you, Mr Wolf,' Edelman said. He wiped his hands at his sides as if he still wore his apron. 'It is about the rent, you see.'

'The rent, Herr Edelman?'

'It is due, you see, Mr Wolf.' He nodded, as though confirming something to an unseen audience. 'Yes,' he said, 'it is due some days now, Mr Wolf.'

Wolf just stood there and looked at him. The baker hopped from leg to leg. 'Cold, isn't it,' he said. Wolf watched him in silence.

'Well,' Edelman said finally, 'I hate to ask, Mr Wolf, really I do, but it is the way of things, isn't it, it is the nature of the world.' His whole stance seemed apologetic, but Wolf wasn't fooled. There was a flash of steel underneath the baker's quivering exterior. Wolf didn't deign to reply. He reached into his pocket and pulled out the wad of money and peeled off two ten-shilling notes, watching the baker's eyes all the while. He returned the rest to his pocket. He held the money in his hand. The man seemed hypnotised by the money. He licked his lips nervously. 'Mr Wolf,' he began.

'Will this do, Herr Edelmann?' Wolf said. The man made no move to take the money, waiting for it to be offered. 'It is the nature of the world that evil exists,' Wolf said. 'It is not money that is evil but the means to which it is put to use. Money is an instrument, Herr Edelmann, it is a lever.' He held the money steady in his fingers. 'A small lever to move small people,' he said. 'But give me a large enough lever and I would move the very world.'

'That's very interesting, Mr Wolf,' Edelmann said. He was still looking at the money. 'Do you wish to pay for a month upfront?' Wolf handed him the notes. The baker took them and secreted them about his person.

'I would require a receipt,' Wolf said.

'I will put one through your door.'

'Make sure that you do,' Wolf said. He touched the brim of his hat, lightly. '*Guten abend*, Herr Edelmann.'

'Good evening to you, too, Mr Wolf.'

Wolf walked off and the baker disappeared into the darkness like a shadow. There had been too many dark streets and too many shadows, melting into the night, never to be seen again. Wolf thought about Geli. There had not been a day gone past when he had not thought about Geli.

The whores were gathered in Berwick Street. They stood light as shadows, mute as stone. Wolf hesitated as he passed nearby. With his approach the girls grew lively, and raucous laughter welcomed Wolf's approach. In a passageway between buildings a fat whore was squatting with her back to the brick wall, crapping. He caught a glimpse of her pale loose flesh, her garments round her ankles. 'Looking is for free,' someone nearby said. A girl no older than sixteen flashed him a smile. Her lips were red, set in a white, made-up face. Her teeth were small and uneven. 'Hey, mister,' she said. 'You want a quick one?' She spoke English with an accent he knew well and with a vocabulary learned from reading cheap novels.

Wolf said, 'I've not seen you here before.'

The girl shrugged. 'What about it,' she said.

'You are Austrian,' he said, in German.

'What about it.'

In the alleyway the fat whore farted loudly and laughed as her bowels emptied steaming onto the cold flagstones. Wolf averted his gaze.

'You should find another line of work,' he told the girl.

'Go to hell, mister.'

Underneath the streetlights a few johns were already passing, eyeing up the girls. In a few hours trade would be brisk. Another whore approached them. She was someone Wolf recognised, Dominique, a half-caste girl. 'Pay no attention to him,' she told the new girl. 'It's just Mr Wolf's way with us. Isn't it, Mr Wolf?' She smiled at him. She had light brown skin, red lips and cool eyes. The new girl looked at Wolf uncertainly. He knew the expression in her eyes. Trying to place him. When he had first come to London many had known his name. Now there were precious few who cared. 'Fräulein Dominique,' he said, politely.

'Mr Wolf.' She turned to her sister in trade. 'Mr Wolf never goes with one of us.' Her smile was mocking. 'Mr Wolf only ever looks.'

The Austrian girl shrugged. There was a dull look in her eyes. Wolf wondered how she had come to London, what she had escaped from. He could imagine it well enough. He bore the scars of such a departure himself. 'What is your name?' he said.

'It's Edith.'

He touched the brim of his hat. 'Edith,' he said.

'You can fuck me for ten shillings,' the girl said.

'What Mr Wolf wants,' Dominique said, 'it would take more than a ten-shilling whore to satisfy.'

Wolf didn't answer back. There was never a point, with prostitutes. In Vienna before the War he had seen them on the Spittelberggasse, each girl behind a lighted window, some young, some old, some sitting, some standing, some doing their hair or smoking cigarettes. For a long time he had walked past the low one-storey houses, with his friend, Gustl, watching them, and the men who came to use their services, how the lights in the rooms would be turned off once a deal was concluded. One could tell by the number of darkened windows how trade was going.

The fat whore—her name was Gerta—had emerged from the alley-way pulling up her undergarments. She waved at Wolf cheerfully. He repressed a shudder of revulsion. The young girl, Edith, had lost interest in him. A couple of men on the other side of the street were looking at her with interest, cattle traders examining livestock. They called to her and she was gone, into the shadows. The half-caste Dominique was suddenly very close. She was taller than Wolf. Her lips were by his ears. Her breath warm on his skin. 'I know what you want,' she said. 'I can give it to you.'

There was a strength about her; he feared and desired what she could sense in him. Her hand reached down and pressed painfully on the front of his trousers. 'Yes,' Dominique murmured, 'I know. And I would enjoy doing it to you, too.'

For a moment he was frozen; she had snared him with lust; what the Jews called the 'evil inclination', the *yetzer hora*. But he was stronger than her; stronger than that. He removed her hand. 'I'll thank you not to touch me again,' he said. Dominique looked him down and up. Her lips curled and then she too was gone, into the night. Wolf walked on.

WOLF'S DIARY, 1ST NOVEMBER 1939—CONT'D.

At night the fruit and vegetable market closes and a different type of market springs beyond my office window. Whores. How I hated whores! Their bodies were riddled with syphilis and the other ills of their trade. The disease was but a symptom. Its cause was the manner in which love itself has been prostituted.

I did not feel pity for the young girl, Edith. No. Instead I felt a cold anger, the sort of anger that had once driven me to oratory, when it had burned bright and strong. To see a Germanic girl prostituted in this way, in a foreign land, was a reminder to me of my own failure, of the way the land itself had been prostituted. Once Germany bled like a soldier; now it bled like a whore. It was

13

a slow death; it was a death of love. I walked past the girls and in the night I felt unseen eyes watching my passing; but there are always eyes watching in the night. A mystery is not when one's action goes unobserved. Rather it is an action to which no witness is willing to come forward.

I know what Isabella Rubinstein feared. I made my way down through Walker's Court onto Rupert Street, passing the White Horse and the Windmill cinema onto Shaftesbury Avenue. Theatreland. The lights burned bright here and theatregoers strolled along the avenue mingling with pickpockets and dollymops. At the Apollo Theatre on the corner the electric signs advertised Patrick Hamilton's *Gaslight*. A pair of coppers I knew by sight went past me, eyeing the whores openly. I nodded to them and went on.

Gerrard Street was full of little clubs and dusty alcoves. At this time of night gentlemen were heading out to supper with their wives, and young men of a literary bent were debating the merits and faults in the poetry of H.B. Yeats, Ezra Pound and Modernism in general. On the corner with Dean Street I saw a group of Blackshirts standing together in a dark mob, eyeing the passers-by with sullen hostility. On a wall I saw a placard for Mosley's election campaign. Oswald's handsome British face stared out at me with its dapper moustache and ironic smile. I saluted him, crisply. Then I went into the Hofgarten.

It lay at the bottom of a narrow staircase behind a grey wooden door that bore no plaque. It was not a members-only club but then it was not *not* a members-only club, either. It was a place for like-minded people to meet and talk of the past. I abhorred it for all that it represented and all that it wasn't, and couldn't be. I pushed the heavy door at the bottom of the stairs and went in.

It was dark and smoky inside. The smell of heavy Bavarian

beer hung in the air like a peasant woman's thick skirts hanging to dry. I could hear laughter, men's drunken talk, the tap-tap-tap of chess pieces against a chessboard. A small piano stood in the corner, but no one was playing. It was too early and years too late for anyone to be playing the Horst Wessel Song.

I could feel eyes on me. Heard the pitch of conversation change. In years past I would have revelled in it. Now I set my jaw and bore it. I hung up my coat and my hat and made my way to the bar counter.

'What could I get you, sir?'

'I would like a herbal tea,' I said.

He was a big ugly brute of a man; a fine Aryan. The face he turned on me began to open its maw in a display of mockery or outrage, revealing a wealth of gold. He truly was a man who carried his valuables on his person. He never did finish, though. He took me in and his face changed and his mouth closed without voicing whatever wisdom it was he had been about to impart.

'Tea, sir?'

'If you would be so kind.'

'But of course. Of course. Herr—'

'Wolf,' I said.

He rubbed his hands together, as if he were cold. 'Wolf. Of course.'

'Has Herr Hess come in yet?' I said.

At that he all but stood to attention. 'Not yet, sir,' he said.

I gestured to an empty table in the corner. 'I shall be sitting over there,' I said. 'Please be so kind as to bring me the tea when it is ready.'

He nodded that great big head of his. A farmer boy from Austria, of the kind I had grown up amongst. Salt of the earth. I wondered if he was smarter than he looked. I made my way to the empty table and sat down. I was glad of the darkness of the room. Too many familiar faces, too many reminders of a past the world had already forgotten and I was trying to. I fingered the roll of money in my suit pocket. I had not been to the Hofgarten in three years.

'Our fight is for the soul of this country, and the soul of the world. We must struggle, for nothing comes easily to men such as us, who will change the world. We, the Blackshirts, have been called, and we shall lead this nation to a new and higher civilisation. There is a cancer growing in our midst, the cancer of Judaism. This is our revolution. We shall be baptised in fire. Remember, you have a voice. You have a vote. Vote Mosley. We shall triumph in adversity—'

'Turn the God damned radio off,' someone said.

His shadow fell on the table before I saw him. I may have dozed off. The cigarette and pipe smoke hurt my eyes. My tea had been cooling on the table for some time.

'Hess,' I said. He had thick wavy black hair and thick black eyebrows. His smile was genuine but cautious. I didn't blame him.

'Wolf,' he said. For a moment, I thought he might try to hug me. I rose from the chair and shook his hand, formally.

'It is good to see you again,' he said.

'You, too,' I said. I looked at him. He bore up well. London had been good to Hess. His hair looked luxurious and shiny. His jacket was styled in black with the lightning bolt of the Blackshirts on the lapels. It looked tailor-made. He wore riding boots and a paunch. Hess had grown fat in this foreign city, after the Fall.

'You are doing well,' I said.

He patted his belly. 'I get by,' he said.

I gestured at the chair opposite and sat down again. He followed. 'Can I get you anything?' he said. I shook my head. 'You never come to the Hofgarten,' Hess complained. 'Never come to see me. I wish you'd let me help you, at least. Money—'

'I do not want your money.'

He sighed. 'I know,' he said. He signalled to the barman. The lad brought over a small brandy and placed it at Hess's elbow. Hess swirled it around, sniffed it appreciatively, and sipped.

'Good?' I said.

'Wonderful.'

I slapped the glass out of his hand and it smashed to the floor, the brandy spilling on Hess's hand. I heard chairs scraping back, saw three men rise and marked them. Hess shook his limp hand then sucked on his fingers. He stared at me mournfully. 'Bring me a napkin, please, Emil,' he said. He gestured at his men and they sat down again. 'You have an escort these days,' I said.

'These are dangerous times,' Hess said. 'A man needs must take precautions.'

The big barman brought over a silk handkerchief. It was embroidered with RH. Hess wiped his hand clean fastidiously and gave it back. 'Thank you, Emil,' he said.

I stared at him across the table. 'I meant no disrespect,' he said.

'I'm sure that you didn't.'

'What is it?' he said.

'I need information.'

He nodded. 'I heard you were working as a private investigator,' he said.

'You heard correctly.'

His eyes grew as soft as his face. 'They called you the Drummer,' he said.

'I have always fought,' I said. 'But I have always fought for order.' I took a sip of my cold tea. 'There must be order in all things.'

'Yes,' he said. 'Of course.' He loosened his tie. 'What do you need to know?'

'I am looking for a girl. She would have been coming from Germany, to London.'

'I see. Without papers, naturally.'

'Yes.'

'Such a thing is not impossible, for a price,' he said. 'Tell me, Rudolf,' I said. 'Do many people disappear, en route from Germany?'

'Disappear how?'

I said, softly, 'She was a Jewess.'

He stared into my eyes. 'Wolf . . .' he said.

'Don't.'

'For the sake of my love for you,' he said. 'Don't ask me.'

'I need to know.'

'There are doors which are best left closed,' he said. He pushed his chair back and stood up. 'For the sake of our friendship.' He looked at me curiously. 'What do you care what happens to a Jew?'

'I don't.'

'Come and work for me,' he said, impulsively. He saw my face. 'With me, I mean. There is money to be made, power. I am someone here, Wolf. I am a man of influence.'

'Hess,' I said, 'you are a pimp and a thief. You have traded your honour for cash.'

'Don't use those words.'

'What words would you have me use?'

He laughed at that. 'Perhaps I've merely outgrown you,' he said.

'You have been reduced,' I said. 'While I remain the same. My integrity cannot be purchased so cheaply.'

'You are a shadow of what you once were. A ghost.' He laughed again, a sad, bitter sound. 'You died in the Fall; what is left of you makes a mockery of what you once were.'

I stood up too. He was taller than me, but he had always been the smaller man. 'Please,' he said, again. 'Do not go asking such questions, mein freund.'

'Give me a name,' I said.

Hess sighed. He reached into his breast pocket and threw down on the table a *carte de visite*. I picked it up. Printed on thick, expensive paper, it contained an address in the East End and nothing more. On the back, a symbol I had not seen in some time: it was a swastika.

The night was full of eyes, watching. Wolf made his way out of the Hofgarten. At the end of the street the same group of Blackshirts was beating a man lying on the pavement. The man had curled in a foetal position, his hands uselessly covering his head. The Blackshirts wore thick-soled boots and they were kicking the man savagely. A pair of policemen were watching from the sidelines without expression. The air was scented with the smell of men's sweat and blood and violence. It was a smell Wolf knew well, had in fact delighted in. Two white teeth lay on the ground beside the victim. Wolf paused as he walked past them. One of the Blackshirts wiped sweat from his face with the hem of his shirt. 'What are you looking at,' he said. Wolf shook his head. He walked on. Behind him the victim was whimpering in a broken voice. Oswald Mosley stared down at Wolf from the public walls, smiling winningly. Wolf walked on.

There were eyes in the night, watching. He felt shadows gathering about him and he stopped and started, dawdling in front of shop windows, trying to catch a reflection, a clue as to the unseen watchers' identity.

Perhaps there was no one there. But he could scent them, hunters in the night. He had used the name Wolf in the 1920s and now he used it again, in London. He had always felt himself to have an affinity with wolves.

The *carte de visite* was in his suit pocket. He did not like seeing Hess again, did not like being reminded of what had passed. How Hess had risen while he himself fell. There was a dull ache in his left leg. It had broken in the camp and never healed properly, and ached in the cold. He had been there three days short of five months when he escaped. Sometimes he missed Germany with a powerful ache, with every fibre of his being. He knew he was unlikely to ever see her again.

The '40s were coming. Christmas was in the air and along Charing Cross Road early decorations were already going up. A man behind a cart was selling roasted chestnuts. He had the swarthy complexion of a gypsy. The city was filled with refugees from the Fall, but the borders were closing, and tensions were mounting everywhere. Wolf bought the evening edition of the *Daily Mail* and glanced at the headlines as he walked. 'Duke of Windsor in Support of Mosley' said the front page. Well, no surprise there. The abdicated king had been a keen supporter of Wolf's own politics, too, back when Wolf still had politics. He was a fool to marry the American woman, though. Love was a weaker force than hate, and Wolf could not help but despise the former monarch for that.

There. Was that a shadow moving behind him? Wolf ducked into an alleyway. A man in a black suit with an unremarkable face. But the man continued past, seemingly oblivious. Wolf emerged from the alleyway. He found himself by Collet's Bookshop, still open at this hour, coffeehouse revolutionaries conspiring amidst leftwing pamphlets and communist propaganda. The man in the black suit had disappeared. Wolf walked on, stopped by Marks & Co. to browse the books outside. Popular fiction, books thumbed and marked. Dashiell Hammett's *The Maltese Falcon*. A row of P. G. Wodehouse novels. Another copy of *The Hobbit*. A review copy of Anthony Powell's *From a View to a Death*. But Wolf had little love for the weakness of the English tongue. German had a martial tune; it was neither tarnished nor afraid. He walked on.

Oxford Street coming up, Wolf walking aimlessly, checking his reflection in shop windows. He had black hair receding at the temples, a high forehead, a strong chin, ears sticking out slightly. No moustache. He could no longer abide the moustache.

There!

He turned suddenly and rapidly and began to walk with purpose the way he'd come. A second youngish man in a black suit and tie like an underemployed undertaker had begun to turn the other way, too late. In moments Wolf was on him, grabbing the man by the lapels, slamming him against the brick wall. He pressed his face close into the stranger's. 'Who are you?' he said, speaking low. 'What do you want?'

The man didn't struggle. 'Excuse me, pal,' he said, 'I think you got the wrong idea there.'

Despite his diction his accent came across loud and clear and American. Wolf released him. The man had not struggled though he looked like he could have put up a fight, had he wanted to. Under the cheap suit was a body kept trim and in shape. 'Why are you following me?' Wolf said. The man looked embarrassed.

'Do you know the way to the British Museum?' he said. 'This damn city can be confusing. I think I lost my way somewhere.'

'Yes, you did,' Wolf said. He stared hard at the man. 'The museum is closed.'

'It is?'

There was a twinkle in the man's eyes. Wolf's hands tightened on the man's lapels. The man still didn't struggle. He seemed to regard Wolf with some irony. It was not a quality Wolf possessed, or much appreciated.

'Where is your friend?' Wolf said.

'Excuse me?'

Wolf spat. His phlegm hit the brick wall over the man's shoulder and slid down, slowly. 'I won't give you and yours a second warning,' he said. He turned just as abruptly and walked off. He did not watch to see if the other man was following him still.

•

In Berwick Street the whores were busy at their trade. The watcher in the dark had seen the detective exit his office and speak to the young German whore and to the coloured one, and seen him leave, but he remained behind. He had time. All the time in the world. He eyed the whores.

He was wrapped in shadows. He was like a ghost, or H. G. Wells's invisible man. In his invisibility there was power. He felt the knife under the coat. The smoothness of the grind versus the sharpness of the point and edge. How good it felt. He watched the whores, watched a sailor talking to the young German, or was she Austrian, he understood only hazily the difference but it didn't matter. The sailor took her by the hand and they vanished into the shadows. He felt the knife, stroking the metal. They couldn't see him, nobody could. All he had to do was choose. He felt so hard, painfully so, but it was a good pain: it was a pain of anticipation. Soon. He had no need to rush. Waiting was half the pleasure, though perhaps he did not see it that way. It was just a fantasy. He wouldn't do anything. Not yet. But he could imagine it, standing there, watching the women, holding his knife. The things he would do to them. They didn't even see him. But he saw them.

Later he saw the detective come back. A small figure, so unremarkable. But you couldn't be deceived by appearances. It was for the detective that he was doing this. He watched the man's weary steps. The detective passed so close to him, nearly brushing against him, and he held his breath, but the detective didn't even notice him. No one ever did. Once the detective was past he pressed his back against the bricks and watched the whores again, his hand in his pocket. He was so hard and then he was soft and there was a pleasant warmth. He wasn't going to do anything. Not yet.

But soon.

●

In another time and place Shomer lies dreaming.

2

When Wolf returned it was late. He climbed the steps slowly. He rented a small bedsit next to his office. When he pushed the door open he found an envelope on the floor where it had been pushed through under the door. It was a heavy cream paper. His name was written on the back in a beautiful hand, in black ink. He picked it up and hefted it. There was no postmark. It must have been hand-delivered. He thought he knew the handwriting. He carried the envelope across the room.

Wolf's accommodation consisted of a bed and a desk and a kitchenette. The only decorations were the books. They lay everywhere, on the floor, on the windowsill, on the desk. A sea of books, their pages like waves. Sometimes he thought he would drown in words, all those words.

Wolf set the envelope on the bed and went to boil water for tea on the hotplate. The room had a gas heater operated by coins. He inserted money into the device, willing it to work. The room was cold and when he exhaled a fog rose from his mouth like a shroud. When the tea was ready he carried it with him and sat hunched on the bed as close as he could to the radiator. His leg ached dully. He sipped his tea. His eyes were still irritated by the smoke from the club. The money from the Jewish woman was still in his pocket. He kept his coat on. He set the tea on the windowsill and reached for his letter opener. Inside the envelope was a card printed on expensive paper. *Sir Oswald and Lady Mosley request the pleasure of your company.* The address was the Mosleys's house in Belgravia. The date was for two days hence: a Friday. Wolf fingered the worn hem of his coat. He could not afford to hire a suit, and his clothes sat uneasily on him.

He turned the card over. On the back, in the same rich black ink and impeccable handwriting, Diana had written: *My dear Wolf, it has been so long since we had the pleasure of your company. Oswald will be so happy to see you as, of course, will I.* She had signed it with her name, and Xs and Os. Underneath, a P.S.: *Unity may also be in attendance.*

Wolf slid the invitation card back into its envelope. He drank his tea. He rose and washed the cup in the sink thoroughly and left it to dry. He hung up his coat. He sat on the bed and then stretched out on his back, staring up at the ceiling. The past was re-emerging, threatening to catch up to him. He had not seen Oswald and Diana since their wedding, in '36. He had been their guest, but no longer an honoured one. Things were different, after the Fall.

What did it mean, to be invited, now? What did Oswald want with him? Wolf was under no illusions. Oswald wanted something. They were the same in many ways; though he, Wolf, was strong and Oswald was weak. Had always been the weaker man.

Briefly, he thought about Unity. He lay on his back and stared at the darkness beyond the window and listened to the voices of the night until he fell asleep.

In my dream I was back in the trenches in Neuve Chapelle, in the dugout we called Löwenbräu, after the brewery. In my dream it was nighttime, some days after the battle that had raged over the 9th and 10th of May 1915. The battle was not significant enough to be named, though I suppose it was significant enough for the dead.

In my dream I stood half-crouched in the trench during inspection. In the night beyond, mortar fire bloomed and in the no-man's-land the cries of the dying could be heard. Hundreds of dead British soldiers littered the barren ground and the stench of their death filled the night. When we had first arrived at the front the land had been filled with orchards and fields and the hum of bees could be heard. Now it was a wasteland. The British soldiers lay rotting in the sun during the day. At night their bloated corpses lay ripening as flies laid their eggs on the entry points of the bullets that killed them. Beetles crawled inside them, feeding, and the stench of the rotting corpses filled the warm spring air. Worse yet were the ones still, miraculously, alive; the ones who took so long to die. Their moans were unholy sounds. We wished them dead so we would be spared their horror.

In my dream Ziegler, the commander of the Tenth company, was walking down the line of inspection, slapping the soldiers he deemed slovenly or disrespectful. As he approached me I saw him as a being of great shadow, his face invisible behind a pool of darkness, the shadows lengthening behind him in the light of the moon like the wings of a great beast. When he reached me he stopped, and I could smell the rank odour of alcohol on his breath. He leaned towards me, into the light, and I saw his face, but it was not Ziegler's face but my father's, Alois. I cowered from him, his small eyes set in a fleshy face, the smell of wine on him. I saw him smile with unholy joy as he raised his fist and swung and hit me. The impact threw me back against the sandbags and then he was on me, kicking and cursing my name.

It is my habit to read a book a day. When I woke it was early and the sun had not yet risen. I washed my face in the sink, and the cold stung where my father had hit me in my dream. I made myself an infusion of camomile tea and set it on the windowsill. Soho at this hour is as close to silent as it ever gets. Even the whores were asleep. From down below came the smell of freshly baked bread. I picked up a book, Harold Laski's *The Grammar of Politics*, published some years back by Allen & Unwin. I spent the next two hours thus quietly occupied. Then I rose, donned my coat and my hat and went into my office.

The morning passed uneventfully. I paid bills, caught up on paperwork. I have always loved working at my desk. From behind a desk, a man can force an order on things. From behind a desk, I once believed, I could rule the world. Now other men sat behind other desks, in offices grander than mine, and told the people what to do and how to think. In the afternoon my telephone rang.

'Wolf Investigations, this is Wolf.'

'This is Isabella Rubinstein speaking.'

'Miss Rubinstein.'

Her voice sounded brisk on the phone. 'Have you made any progress yet?' she demanded. I pictured her in a vast London residence in Mayfair or Belgravia, somewhere anyway where they let Jews move in. Talking to me on the phone while her father's chauffeur washed the Rolls and her father's gardener pruned the rose bushes and her father's chef prepared their Jewish meal in a kitchen with two separate sinks in it. 'You only came to see me yesterday,' I said.

'I expect results, Herr Wolf,' she said.

I held on to the phone for a long moment, watching how the blood drained from the tips of my fingers where I was gripping the receiver.

'Hello?'

'Yes, Miss Rubinstein.'

'Well?'

'I have met with one of my . . . old associates. He has given me the address of a club. I shall be visiting it tonight.'

'What sort of club?'

'The sort nice society girls shouldn't go to,' I said, and she laughed, a little breathlessly.

'You'd be surprised what nice society girls do,' she said.

'When they have the mind to do it.'

I let that go. 'If that would be all, Miss Rubinstein . . .' I said.

'No,' she said.

'No?'

'I want to come with you.'

'That is entirely out of the question.' I think I was shouting down the line. She got me that way, did Isabella Rubinstein.

'Where is this club?' she said. I could hear steel sheathed in her voice.

'Miss Rubinstein, you hired me to do my job. So let me do my job.'

'I hired you for who you once were,' she said. The intensity of her voice changed. I pictured her on the other end of the line, lying on her bed, the window open, a warm breeze wafting into the room (it is always spring, for the rich). Was she playing with the cord? Running her long slim fingers up and down the shaft of the receiver? 'They used to scare us with your name. Did you know that? My mother told me if I misbehaved the big bad wolf would come and get me. I would lie in my bed at night in the dark and picture you, creeping into the house, climbing up the stairs, softly pushing the door to my room . . .'

'Yes?' I said. My mouth was dry.

'You'd stand over my bed and I'd know you were there but pretend that you weren't,' she said. 'You'd reach down at last and lay your claws on my bare shoulder and slowly push the strap of my nightie down, peeling it off, but gently. We all hated you. Your voice was everywhere, on the wireless. I used to hear it as I fell asleep.'

'Yes?'

'Like now,' she said, and she suddenly laughed, gaily. 'And now you work for me,' she said. There was unholy glee in her voice, and something else, syrupy and sickly-sweet.

'Yes . . .' I said.

'You will do what I tell you, won't you, Wolf?' she said.

I shifted uncomfortably in my seat. How dare she presume to order me about! I hated her and wanted to punish her and yet I wanted to be punished, too. Something to do with violence a long way back, no doubt, or so some hack like that Jew, Freud, would tell you.

I pictured her on the four-poster bed with the gardener outside watering the damned roses. Pictured her slowly lifting up her dress, her fingers trailing along the smooth whiteness of her leg. 'No,' I said, almost moaned. 'No.' I waited for her to say something, but all I could hear was her heavy breathing down the line and then abruptly she hung up and the line went dead. I swore and shifted in my seat. How I hated all Jews! They were a parasitic race, preying upon the honest portion of mankind.

Power. It all came down to power. To control. I thought of Geli.

I missed her every day. At seventeen she was such a beautiful creature, vivacious and alive. With Geli I had found what I had sought. All women have a will. With Geli I had thought I could control that will, mould it to my needs. We had lived together, uncle and niece, I took her to the opera, to the picture houses in Munich. I had loved her and she had betrayed me with my own gun.

When I stood up the pressure had eased but a dark wet patch stained the front of my trousers. Men should never excuse their needs but subordinate them to a greater cause. But my cause was gone, shot down in flames when I was betrayed by the people, and now Ernst Thälmann presided over Germany, the fat loathsome prick. And so I went and got changed before setting out.

Wolf had decided to walk, though the day was cold and occasional lashings of rain stung his face. He drew his fedora low over his head, hunching his shoulders as he pressed against the wind. Outside the British Museum he saw a group of Gurkhas, each wearing a curved kukri knife. They passed close by, their faces alien to him. They marched in a unit. Wolf remembered them on the battlefield, the black devils they used to call them, these Nepalese soldiers serving the British king. In the trenches during that war he had been a dispatch runner, serving with the Bavarian List Regiment. As the warm spring turned to bitter winter, the rains flooded the trenches and the men lived in eternal damp. Liquid mud covered their faces and ran down their eyes, its taste was in their mouths. It was cold and their blankets were as wet as they were: they could not get warm. The walls collapsed, their bread was wet and inedible. Wolf remembered men who shot themselves in order to escape the front. Remembered one man who, on capturing a British prisoner of war, calmly cut the man's throat with his knife. When challenged, the man had said, 'I just felt like it.' As was the practice, the PoW was reported as having died of heatstroke.

He remembered the winter of 1914 and the Christmas Truce. Nighttime, Christmas Eve, and a sky shining with cold stars like frost. Across the no-man's-land the English troops of the Devonshire regiment began to sing carols and from the German side rose hymns in response. A soldier from RIR 17 stepped out of the trench and shouted in English, 'You no shoot, we no shoot! It is your Christmas. We want peace. You want peace.'

The next day was cold and bright and the men from both sides met in the middle, shaking hands, exchanging hastily written Christmas cards, even dancing. Dancing! The others were overjoyed but how he had resented them! He had been enraged by the men, by their betrayal. Wolf did not participate in the truce and on the 27th the rains returned and with them the mud, and lightning flashed in the sky, etching indelible scars in the skin of night.

Wolf walked past the company of Gurkhas. As a young soldier he had admired them in battle. Later, as a leader of men, he had often wished he had a company of such men in his service.

Right now, as a down-at-the-heels private eye, Wolf just couldn't give a damn.

He walked down Museum Street past the offices of Allen & Unwin and turned left on High Holborn. Already it was growing dark and the streets were filled with Londoners of all stripes. London reminded him sometimes of the Vienna of his youth, a godless city of sin and corruption. Here there were lawyers striding about in their robes, clerks hurrying at their sides; insurance men and bobbies on the beat; labourers grimy with dust; housewives returning late from market and society wives from their shopping; orthodox Jews arguing the Torah and the rising price of gold; newspapermen with cigarettes in their mouths congregating outside the Cittie of York pub; churchmen and pickpockets and here and there an early-rising prostitute; and the businessmen not in their offices yet.

When he reached Leather Lane, night had fallen and the air was fetid, rank with the smell of cooking and waste dumped openly into the street. Wolf began to hear German spoken, and saw in the people the lost gaze of the eternal refugee. These were his people, mostly: Austrians and Germans displaced by the Fall, rejected by the nations of Europe until they had made their way, in one secret form or another, across the Channel into England. They were people without papers, without hope. Their clothes were shabby and their habits frugal, and the women did not walk alone in the night and the men congregated in small furtive groups on the steps of their tenements, smoking thin cigars and drinking home-made schnapps that was little better than rotgut, but it was all they had.

They were a sign to him of how far he had fallen.

Running adjacent to Leather Lane was Hatton Garden, and here there were still Jews. Shuttered shops held behind them jewellery of gold and diamond, silver and sapphire and rubies, yet here too rubbish collected in the street; the fronts of the buildings were dirty and the brickwork exposed. Wolf walked slowly, his hat pulled down low. He walked the city and the darkness welcomed him as its own. Down Hatton Garden to the noisy thoroughfare of the Clerkenwell Road, where Wolf saw signs in the language of his birth and rowdy bars lit with electric lights that yet reminded him of Vienna and Berlin. The smell of bratwurst and sauerkraut wafted in the air from covered stalls and men, already drunk at this hour, walked with arms linked together singing of the glories of the Fatherland. Wolf averted his gaze and walked in the shadows, west along Clerkenwell and back down Leather Lane. Receding in the distance he could hear the Horst Wessel Song.

Wessel had been an SA-Sturmführer in Berlin, only 22 when he was murdered by a communist assassin, shot in the face when he answered a knock on the door. It was gimp-leg Goebbels's idea to turn the young idiot into a hero, his song into an anthem for the Party. Wessel had lived with a young prostitute, Erna, and had probably acted as her pimp. It was just as likely that he died over her affections as for not paying the rent. Strange, though, how the song had caught on, that men were singing it even now, years after the Fall.

In Munich in '31 he never would have imagined the coming of the Fall. He was living with Geli then, the daughter of his older half-sister Angela. He was so taken with the child; she was like a bright butterfly. Wolf liked his women cute, cuddly and naïve, or so he liked to say at his more expansive moments back in Munich: he liked little things who were tender, sweet and stupid.

Geli was all that and more, she was young and she was powerless and she was malleable. He could be like a god to her, he could fashion her in the image he desired. Geli had depended on him, wholly and utterly.

And yet she had tried to rebel. When he found out about her affair with Emil, the chauffeur, Wolf was incensed. But he had loved her, too. Had loved her perhaps more than any other woman in his life, more than Eva, who he was also seeing at the time, lovely Eva who was such a simple creature, as comfortable as slippers.

Then came that fateful night. Strangely it was Hess who had rung him. Wolf had gone to Nuremberg for a meeting. Geli had used his own pistol against him, perhaps that was what had hurt most of all. His trusty .22-calibre, the No. 709 made by Messrs. Smith & Wesson of America. The pistol he had left in the apartment, loaded, in the middle drawer of the nightstand. He pictured Geli's small hot hand enveloping the inlaid metal of the handle, her index finger with its manicured nail hesitating on the trigger. It was the ultimate betrayal. Frau Winter, his housekeeper, had found her. Geli had missed her heart and punctured her lung. It must have taken her hours to die, alone in the room. He imagined the sounds she made, the hoarse breathing, the whistle of air, the grunts and whimpers like a slaughtered pig.

Frau Winter had called Hess, and Hess had called Wolf. By the time he arrived in the apartment, the police had already been and gone.

Wolf took a breath of night air. He had failed so many times since Geli; and each failure was worse than the last.

Before him was a plain door set into a thick brick wall. It was the right place. He knocked on the door, three times.

A metal shutter he hadn't noticed slid open at head height, revealing an iron grille. Glittery black eyes regarded him through it. 'Yes?'

Wolf pushed the card Hess had given him through the iron grille. 'Herr Wolf,' he said. 'Herr Hess sent me.'

The shutter slid shut. After a moment the door opened noiselessly. Beyond it he could hear a piano playing and the sound of laughter and conversation. The man in the doorway looked vaguely familiar but Wolf couldn't place him. He had a boxer's round face and a scar on his left cheek and his hair was cut short. 'Have we met before?'

The man shook his head, unsmiling. 'No, but I have seen you.'

Wolf shrugged.

The man said, 'I am Kramer, sir. Josef Kramer.'

'You work for Hess?'

At that the man did smile. 'Not Hess,' he said. 'Though Herr Hess has a share in this club. Please, welcome.'

'Thank you.'

Wolf stepped through into the hallway and Kramer shut the door behind him. It was a thick oak door on oiled hinges. It allowed no sound to escape.

'Please, follow me.'

Wolf listened for sounds. Muted conversation. Faint music. The hallway was thickly carpeted.

'I joined the Party in '31,' Kramer said. 'The SS in '32, sir.'

'Good for you.'

If he was offended Kramer didn't show it. 'Through here,' he said, leading Wolf into a large sitting room. Wolf stopped in the doorway. A man in a tuxedo sat at a grand piano, playing Beethoven. All around him were comfortable sofas and chaise longues, and men with ties loosened sat with drinks in their hands. Along one wall ran a walnut-coloured bar and behind it a barman was polishing glasses. 'Can I get you a drink?' Kramer said.

'I don't drink,' Wolf said.

The air was thick with the smell of expensive cigars. Wolf recognised several of the faces in the room. He had thought some of them dead. Around the men, shimmering through the room in their too-short sequinned dresses, were the girls.

They were an upscale version of the streetwalkers of Soho, Wolf thought. They were dressed like brazen flappers, in costumes that revealed more than they hid. He noted their diversity. He saw Slavic features and Aryan faces and a black girl who reminded him of Dominique. He eyed the girls and they eyed him back, but there was a vacancy in their eyes. He had seen such an expression before, in the eyes of a doped-up horse before a race. He saw the men look up at his entrance. He kept his face blank and watched them turn away.

'Please, Herr . . . Wolf,' Kramer said. His hand swept around the room. 'You may have your choice of the girls. It is on the house, sir,' he added.

'I am looking for this girl,' Wolf said. He drew the little sister's picture from his breast pocket. Isabella had given it to him before she had departed his office. Now he and the man Kramer studied it together. The girl was thin-faced and mousy, her features almost mannish. 'A Jew?' Kramer said.

'Do you stock any Jews?'

A slow, unpleasant smile broke across Kramer's crater-moon face. 'Yes, sir,' he said. 'This is just the antechamber.' He nodded his head as if some things had become clear to him. 'Please,' he said. 'Follow me.'

Wolf followed him, leaving the men behind to the attentions of their whores. He half-expected Kramer to lead him upstairs, to the rooms that no doubt waited there, beds and mirrors and perfumes and lace, a wardrobe for a gentleman to hang his coat in, a washbasin for when his sordid business was done. Instead Kramer led him through a second door and locked it behind him. They were in a corridor in marked contrast to the pleasant sitting room they had vacated. Here bare light bulbs hung from the ceiling and the walls were plain cold stone and so was the floor. There were scuff marks on the stone. He could hear faint sounds, cries and a scream cut short. Kramer led Wolf down a stone staircase, down below ground. Wolf's fingers itched, and for one irrational moment he wished he still had a gun. But he no longer carried one.

It was cold in the basement, and the air was scented with a familiar tang: a mixture of blood and semen and shit. It was the smell of the camp they had kept him in, before he escaped, the smell of captivity and hope-lessness and fear.

They stood in a wide corridor and to either side of the corridor were the metal doors to locked cells. Pinned to the wall like billiard cues were black leather whips. 'Come,' Kramer said. He reached for a whip, lashed it through the air. The sound was like a gunshot. Each door had a sliding metal shutter. Kramer slid the first one open and Wolf looked through. In the cell beyond a white girl no older than fifteen lay naked on a mattress, a worn one-eyed teddy bear held in her arms. Her ankle was chained to the wall. The room was bare but for a hook on the wall for a gentleman's hat and, in the corner, an old-fashioned chamberpot to piss in. The girl was asleep.

'No?' If Kramer seemed disappointed he didn't show it. He slid the shutter back. Wolf took a deep breath.

In the next room two lithe women lay back to back on the same mat-tress. 'Identical twins,' Kramer said, with some pride. 'Prime specimens. The Marshall always makes sure to keep the cellars well stocked.'

'The Marshall?' Wolf said. 'Göring, sir?'

Wolf nodded as some things became clear. 'The fat oaf always did like to give himself a grand title,' he said.

Kramer shrugged. In the next cell Wolf saw an elderly man hunched over a dwarf woman, his pale quivering buttocks rising and falling steadily.

Wolf shook his head. Kramer shut the window. 'This one's occupied,' he said, unnecessarily.

'All Jews?'

'What?'

'Are they all Jews?'

'Yes. Of course.'

'You said Göring sends them over from Germany?'

'The Marshall? Yes. There's good money in people smuggling, these days,' Kramer said.

'And these ones?'

Kramer shrugged. 'Jews,' he said, as if that explained everything. 'Who will miss a Jew?'

'This girl,' Wolf said. He brandished the photograph again. 'Where is she?'

'I've not seen her,' Kramer said. He seemed hurt. 'I thought—'

'You thought,' Wolf said.

'I thought your tastes ran into more . . . I mean, when you said Herr Hess sent you . . . Herr Wolf, I did not—'

Wolf grabbed the whip out of the man's unresisting hand. He felt the familiar rage rise inside of him. 'You dare?' he said. He lashed the whip. It caught Kramer on the cheek and left an angry red welt. Kramer screamed. 'You cavort with filthy animals, you, an Aryan, you deal in the flesh of Jews? What perversion is this?' He was screaming, spittle was coming out of his mouth in long strings that hung from his lips. He was lashing Kramer with the whip, behind the cell doors the drugged specimens were whimpering and the copulating man could be heard banging on the metal door demanding to know what all the God damned ruckus was about, he was trying to finish his business.

'Herr Wolf, enough!' Kramer had half-risen and grabbed Wolf's wrist in a painful grip. His coarse peasant face rose over Wolf. 'I beg you.'

They stared at each other, motionless. Wolf saw Kramer's eyes open wide at something behind Wolf's back. His mouth opened, his lips beginning to form words. 'Please, don't—'

Wolf didn't have time to turn. He felt something cold and sharp sting his neck. It penetrated his skin. His fingers opened. The whip dropped to the floor. His neck felt numb. The numbness spread, fast. His vision blurred and the last thing he saw was Kramer's face blooming in a silent explosion of blood and bone.

•

In another time and place Shomer lies dreaming. In his blessed half-sleep he can pretend if only to himself that he does not hear the other men sleeping below him and the ones pressed against him so that when one wants to turn they must all turn. In sleep Shomer is not aware of Yenkl beside him shitting himself and the liquid shit dribbling down from their bunk onto the sleepers down below, and he can also pretend that it is not at all freezing cold, that it is in fact a lovely warm day and that this isn't Auschwitz but some tropical beach, perhaps some South Seas paradise and that his belly is full and when he smiles his grin is a dazzling white and full still of all his teeth.

In his half-dream which he had begun some time ago on the train on the way here and continued through the selection process and the cleaving of his family, in that murky half-world which was once his novelist's mind, there is a detective and a damsel in distress; there always are. He shifts and murmurs, instinctively trying to pull away from Yenkl. He feels lice crawling inside his striped prisoner's pyjamas but he pretends that he does not. It becomes easier by the day.

Instead Shomer, this once upon a time purveyor of Yiddish *shund*, that is of cheap literature or, not to put too fine a point on it, of trash, dreams of a dark city and of dark deeds, and of a watcher in the dark: for in the camp there is always someone watching.

On Berwick Street Edith could feel the watcher, the way his gaze lingered on her body, and paid particular attention to her breasts, and then down to her inguen, where it lingered further. She had grown used to the attentions of men, wanted and unwanted both, since the moment she and her family had fled from Bregenz into Switzerland and the border official who had helped them claimed her for himself as part of the overall price. He had been her first and she remembered how he had buckled his belt afterwards, not his face but only for some reason his buckle; it was shaped like an iron eagle. They had made it to England at last, smuggling themselves across the Channel in a fishing boat, on a moonless night, with no lanterns or lamps. It was a miracle they hadn't drowned. By then she had grown accustomed to her body being her currency. The fishermen each took their turn to fuck her, as her mother and baby sister sat huddled at the bow. Her mother never mentioned it. Perhaps she had no words with which to speak. Maybe there was nothing to say. It was just one of those things you did to survive.

But she could feel him out there, though no doubt he thought he was invisible, the watcher. He was back a second night in a row. None of the other girls saw him but Edith did. She knew he was there and she knew he was watching her.

At first she thought he was just shy, that he was watching in an effort to gather his courage and approach her. Many men were like that, requiring drink or darkness for their base natures to emerge, their desire to be made manifest. But after a while she did not think this was the case. The watcher disturbed her, though she could not say why. He wore the darkness too comfortably, as though he never intended to emerge from the shadows. A watcher—a *voyeur*, as the French girls said. Sometimes they got men like that, sad pathetic things with one hand twiddling away in their pocket, masturbating as they watched the whores. But the watcher was not like that, either. He got his thrills another way, she was sure.

She was busy that night, going first with a sailor off a Royal Navy ship docked in Greenwich, then with a proper gentleman whose En-glish was as sharp as cut glass, like the King's or the BBC man on the wireless. Lastly with a young Jew, a yeshiva boy with curly peyos, dressed all in heavy black, who thrust against her quickly but enthusiastically, against the wall of the alleyway they used as combined brothel and latrine. Now she was smoking a cigarette with quick inexpert jerks, stamping her feet against the cold, when the watcher came to her.

She saw him emerge across the road. It was late, and the other girls were all either working or had gone home and she was alone. She smiled at him. Her mother had always told her to smile.

There was nothing much very remarkable about him. His suit hung on him a little uncomfortably. It looked like a hand-me-down. He had good teeth, and the smile he gave her back was surprisingly charming. 'You want to fuck?' she said.

His hand was in his coat pocket. He didn't take it out. He looked ner-vous and excited. 'Where can we go?' he said.

'It's ten shillings,' she said. He agreed with a nervous jerk of his head. 'In there,' she said. The alleyway was empty, a fresh pile of shit against the wall where that fat pig Bertha had taken her evening constitutional. They wouldn't be disturbed.

'The money first,' she said.

He took his hand out of his pocket, and she felt strangely relieved. He was holding a note. He passed it to her and she took it and tucked it in her brassiere. She took him by the hand. It was warm and dry. 'Come on,' she said.

He followed her meekly into the dark alleyway.

3

I woke up in pain. I was not lying down and yet I couldn't move. I tried to shift my hand but it was held fast. It was dark but I was still in the club, I could tell; the smell of fear and shit was the same and there was blood and fragments of bone and brain on the front of my suit, which would cost me a fortune to clean. My vision swam in and out of focus. It was a warm room and a flame came alive as a dark figure lit a match and applied it to a large wax candle, and then another candle and another. In the light I could see the chains that were holding me upright. I was secured to the wall, arms and legs spread. The figure turned to face me. It was a woman. She was not an attractive woman. She had a peasant's wide face and a petulant expression as if life had never failed to disappoint her. She wore black leather with the SS insignia on her armband, for all that there was no more SS. She wore thigh-high boots and black leather gloves and in one hand she held a horse whip.

'I am so sorry, Herr Wolf,' she said. 'For the unpleasantness.'

'I'm afraid you have me at a disadvantage, Fräulein . . . ?'

41

'Koch, sir. I am Ilse Koch.' She gave a simpering little curtsey. She had a Dresdener's accent.

'What happened to Kramer?' I said.

'Josef?' she shrugged. 'He was remiss in his duties. He shall be replaced.'

'And I?'

A small, cruel smile briefly illuminated her ugly face. I felt a sudden rising panic. Ilse Koch tested the whip. The crack it made filled the small hot room. I looked around, seeking escape. Instead, what I saw in that room were implements of torture.

Her gaze followed mine. 'Yes . . .' she said. Her smile again, like a deformed butterfly. She lashed the whip with a flick of her wrist, missing my face by inches. She came and stood close to me. I could feel the warmth of her body, the press of her soft heavy breasts against me. She reached out a gloved hand and ripped my shirt open, buttons popping. Her hand grabbed my jaw, her fingers digging into flesh. Her face was close and hot on mine, her breath sour with drink. 'I know what it is you want, Herr Wolf,' she said. Her other hand reached down and grabbed me painfully. Her smirk etched itself into my face. 'You are a hard man, Herr Wolf.'

'Let me go, you filthy whore!'

She slapped me. The sound rang through the room. My cheek burned. My eyes narrowed and my mouth opened and I licked my lips, tasting blood. Her hand was down below grasping me and moving with a certain rhythm.

'I can stop whenever you want,' she said. 'Just say the word.' Her smirk told me she understood. She reached beyond my vision and returned with a vulcanised rubber ball on a studded leather strap. She fitted the strap on my head but left my mouth free. 'Well?' she said.

'Don't stop,' I whispered.

Ilse shoved the ball in my mouth then yanked a lever and suddenly my body was jerked from the wall and I hung suspended in the air before her. She pulled roughly at my trousers until they dangled around my ankles. I dangled there like a mounted butterfly, bare to her. She swung me round. I faced the wall. I felt her behind me, looming. My breath came short and sharp and I was stiff as a boy. I felt her gloved hands on my bare behind. She stroked my cheeks, first one and then the other, before she slapped me, hard, and I cried out. Her hand on my back, rubbing softly . . . 'I will please you, mein herr,' she whispered. I felt the weight of her against my back. Her lips against my ear. She pushed her finger deep inside me. Her other hand came round and took hold of me and stroked as she kept up a rhythm. A second finger joined the first, violating me. I shuddered with pleasure, hating her and all women, and thinking of Geli and the things I had taught her to do.

When Wolf re-emerged onto Leather Lane it was early morning and the market was already being set up with vegetables and fruit and bright materials and cloths. He made a sorry sight, and he wrapped his coat tightly around him and hunched his shoulders and drew the hat low over his face. In the old days he had Emil to chauffeur him around, men to do his bidding, a comfortable apartment to return to and his library and, after Geli, there was Eva, sweet good-natured Eva of the blonde hair and pleasant disposition and soft white flesh.

Now he had to trudge through early morning mist, on foot, in order to return to a cold unfriendly room rented out to him by a Jew.

'It's on the house,' Ilse Koch had told him, before he left, refusing his offer of payment.

'Is it Hess?' he asked her, the same question he had asked Kramer before her. She shook her head. 'Who is it?' he had said and she shook her head with finality and said, 'It is better if you do not come back here again, Herr Wolf.'

But Kramer had been indiscreet, that much was clear. The Marshall, he had said. Wolf remembered Göring, a fat ruthless man with a great many appetites, who had built the storm troopers from a ragtag collection of misfits into an efficient paramilitary organisation in the '20s. A decorated air-force pilot, a flying ace in the Great War. Wolf did not trust pilots; they changed course with the wind. Last he heard, Göring had survived the Fall and even thrived, changing allegiances once again. Now he was Comrade Göring, working for the communists he once despised, and trading in human flesh on the side. The hero of the skies had become a simple pimp.

The Jew girl, this Judith Rubinstein, could have been smuggled out of Germany by this same network. Her father, the banker, would have paid dearly to take his only daughter out of the communists' grasp and bring her to the relative safety of London. But then, why would she disappear? The women in the cells were disposable; no one would be looking for them. But the Rubinstein girl would be valuable cargo. Unless there was someone willing to bid even more for her . . .

He was deep in thought, calculating possibilities and avenues of inquiry, and wincing slightly as he walked. So when, at last, he approached Berwick Street he did not at first notice the presence of policemen all about until they stopped him. They crowded Walker's Court holding sausage rolls and steaming mugs of tea, as if they were at a picnic.

'You can't go through here, sir.'

'What happened?' Wolf said.

'Police matter, sir.' The policeman took in Wolf's rough appearance, paused with a bacon roll halfway to his mouth. There was brown sauce on the ring of his lips. 'Is that blood on your shirt, sir?' he said.

Wolf was aware of the other policemen's attention all turning to him. He began to back away. 'This is a misunderstanding,' he said. 'I live here.'

'Would you mind coming with me, sir?' the fat policeman said. The tea and roll disappeared from his hands to be replaced by a nightstick. Wolf looked around. He was surrounded by the policemen. His shoulders slumped.

'This is all a misunderstanding,' he said.

'I am sure it is, sir,' the policeman said. 'I am sure it is.'

A second policeman grabbed Wolf; he did not resist. The first one placed handcuffs over Wolf's wrists and called out, 'Inspector! I have something for you.'

A man in a worn suit appeared. He had a thick moustache and short thinning hair and there was a light scattering of dandruff covering his shoulders. He took one look at Wolf and shook his head. His eyes were brown, soft and mournful, as if he had already seen all of the evil that men can do to each other. 'Not here,' he said. 'Take him to the station.'

'Hear that, precious?' the fat policeman said. 'You're nicked, my son.'

'Go to hell,' Wolf said. The policeman just smiled. He led Wolf to a waiting car, and then they took him away.

•

In another time and place Shomer is no longer sleeping.

The guards raise them for roll-call with their usual charm and rubber truncheons. Yenkl won't move and the guard roars until Shomer and another prisoner carry his inert form outside and leave it in the snow, where he lies as fat and peaceful as a snowman, with his eyes closed and his hands like twigs. At roll-call they stand in the cold in their wooden clogs and striped pyjamas as the guards entertain themselves until such time as an SS officer arrives to take count of the living and the dead. At last the ordeal is over and the boys of the Sonderkommando take Yenkl away, and Shomer is assigned to a work unit: today they are digging graves. 'Lovely weather we are having,' he remarks to Yenkl. Yenkl is beside him now, smiling and looking at ease. 'Fresh air and physical labour,' Yenkl says and rubs his hands together, 'what's not to like, eh, Shomer, old friend?'

Shomer nods enthusiastically. 'Just what the doctor ordered,' he agrees. Shomer and the other prisoners are given shovels and dig in the hard ground while Yenkl walks around quite at leisure, his hands behind his back as he pontificates.

'What is a man!' he says. 'What is a man but mended cloth, hastily worn and discarded?'

But it is a rhetorical question. He does not expect an answer. 'What makes a man?' he ponders. 'What makes a hero, Shomer? Is it simply to live when there is nothing left to live for, when all you knew and loved is gone? Is it, simply, to survive? For like the threads of an intricate shawl, we have been pulled at and torn, Shomer. We have been unravelled.'

A great barren sky, in which the sun is distant, spreads above Shomer's head. And he closes his eyes against the glare.

'Invigorating!' Yenkl says, and rubs his hands again. And to Shomer he seems suddenly transparent, and through his friend's outline he sees the chimneys belching soot, black soot and ash, flakes of black snow falling.

'For what is a man,' says Yenkl, 'if not ash? And did not Rabbi Akiva say—'

But Shomer doesn't hear what Rabbi Akiva, God rest his soul, ever said, for the overseer at that moment shoves his boot in Shomer's ass and Shomer falls flat on his face on the hard ground the better to amuse the SS guards. And so Shomer returns to the twilight world which is the writer's mind and in which, though he has no pen or paper, he is nevertheless concocting another shund, a cheap little tale for amusement and a little elucidation, for did not Rabbi Akiva say—

But the guard is screaming, 'Get on with work, you filthy little Jew!' and Shomer digs, he digs for all the dead: those that are and those who are yet to come.

They brought me down to Charing Cross nick and took my blood-soiled clothes and gave me woollen slacks and shirt instead and left me in a cell and locked the fucking door.

My head throbbed and my mouth tasted of vulcanised rubber. I lay back on the bed and stared at the ceiling. I had been incarcerated before, in Bavaria in the '20s. Hess had been with me then, he was as close to a friend as I had ever come to having beside Gustl.

Did they think they could intimidate me by incarcerating me in a prison? Childhood is a cell. The happiest day of my young life was the 3rd of January 1903: my father on his last morning visit to the Gasthaus Wiesinger for his last glass of wine. I was not there; later, I could only imagine it, his face turning red, the breath growing faint in his throat. Did he gurgle? Did his hands reach to his neck in incomprehension? Did he feel his last breath departing from his lungs with none to follow, ever again?

His last breath; a key to my freedom. Do not threaten me with jail cells. And I held my mother that day the way a man, not a child, would. I held her, my mother's delicate loving flesh that no young boy could protect, as she cried, the way she had held me when he came home and the drink was upon him and he took to the belt and the boot. My mother looked after the household and lovingly devoted herself to the care of her children. I respected my father, but I loved my mother.

I will give him this, though: the old man looked after his books.

But I did not wish to think just then of my poor dead mother, nor of other cells in other times. What were they holding me for? That was what had me worried. I had done nothing wrong.

I must have dozed off for when I came to, the cell door was

open and the same fat policeman was standing there, smiling his greasy smile. He said, 'Detective Inspector Morhaim will see you now.'

I followed him without comment. Down a corridor busy with the cries of drunks and the thud of policemen's boots and into a small interview room with a large desk and the plain clothes policeman I had last seen on my approach to Berwick Street. He gestured to me civilly. 'Please. Sit down.'

From somewhere he brought forth a meerschaum pipe and became busily engaged in the ritual of such men with such things, stuffing it with foul tobacco. At long last when all was to his satisfaction he lit a match and applied it to the pipe's bowl. 'Sit!'

The fat policeman pushed me into the chair. I sat with my back ramrod straight. 'Tea? Coffee?'

'I drink neither.'

'That must be satisfying.' He motioned to the fat policeman, who withdrew and shut the door behind him. We were alone. 'Morhaim,' I said. 'Isn't that a Jew name?'

'It can be. In this case, it is. Does that bother you?'

'Many things bother me,' I said, and he laughed. 'Tell me,' he said. 'Where were you last night? You were not at your flat.'

'Is that a crime?'

'Not yet,' he said. He puffed on his pipe. The smell of it filled the room. 'You are an alien here, Mr Wolf.'

'I have been granted asylum.'

'From Germany.'

'Yes.'

'All such asylums are by their nature temporary.'

I said nothing and he nodded, to himself. 'I see that after the Fall you were kept for some time in a communist konzentrationslager.'

'Concentration camp, yes,' I said, enunciating it clearly for him in English. He smiled. 'You escaped?'

'Eventually.'

'You are a lucky man, Mr Wolf.'

'What is this about?'

'First things first, Mr Wolf. Where were you last night?'

'I work as a private investigator,' I said. 'I was out. On a job for a client. Surely you can appreciate the need for discretion in my line of work.'

'That's a curious line of work for a man such as yourself.' 'It requires an orderly mind and a keen sense of justice.' He was biting the stem of the pipe, blowing smoke rings into the air from the side of his mouth. A hard trick to master, I would have thought. Also, without use. 'Your old associates seem to prosper. You don't.'

'So you know who I am.'

'I know who you were.'

That one hurt, but I let it go. 'What is this about?'

'Do you have an alibi for last night, Mr Wolf?'

'Do I need one?'

He sighed and sat back in the chair. 'Why did you kill her?' 'Who?' I almost shouted in frustration. My fist hit the desk. 'What is the meaning of this? I am an innocent man! I demand to be released!'

'You used to have a moustache,' he said suddenly. 'A funny little moustache. We used to see a lot of you on the newsreels, but this was all a while back, wasn't it?'

'I do not see why we need to discuss one's choice of facial hair, surely.'

He shrugged. 'Perhaps it was merely the interest of one man with a moustache in another.'

I knew their tactics. Did he think I had never been interrogated before? He would give me nothing, and he would take his time in trying to break me.

'I would like a solicitor,' I said.

His pipe seemed to have gone out. He fiddled with it distractedly. 'Do you have one?'

'No.'

'We can certainly appoint one for you. You haven't been charged yet, Mr Wolf. Would it make you feel better to confess?'

'Confess to what?'

'To the murder, of course.'

I stared at him, no longer willing to talk. Perhaps he saw it in my stance, for he put down the pipe and reached into a drawer and returned with an envelope, which he opened carefully. He slid out a set of photographs and laid them neatly in front of me.

I stared at the photographs.

•

The watcher in the dark truly *was* invisible. Wasn't he? He felt so calm now, so different from the way he'd felt the night before. Then he had been eager, almost frenzied with desire. She didn't understand, no one understood. It wasn't lust, it wasn't *sexual*, he was not a monster.

It was *ideological*.

How trustingly she had taken his hand and led him into the dark! He shifted uncomfortably in his hard chair, wetting his lips in concentration. He had so much work to do, paperwork to get through, but no one paid him any attention: no one ever did. The office he worked in was grey like the light outside. Had he made mistakes? He had planned so carefully, had thought about it for so long and then it just happened. It felt so natural, the way they always said it should. He had not wanted to hurt her. On the contrary. He had wanted to set her free.

I stared at the photographs. They were stark black-and-white. The Austrian girl I had spoken to, Edith, was lying on the ground. The photographs were from different angles. In one I could see a pile of human shit against the brick wall, not far from Edith's blonde hair, which was made near-white by the photograph. Edith was situated in rest, on her back, her arms carefully crossed over her abdomen. Blood matted her hair. Her shirt had been ripped open and her breasts, full and wholesome, lay exposed. Carved into her chest was a swastika. Her face had been battered and her eyes were bruised and open to the sky. Beside her head stood a little toy figure. I leaned forward and drew one of the pictures close and studied it.

It was a little wind-up toy.

A tin drummer.

'Who did this?'

Inspector Morhaim studied me levelly. 'Did you know her?'

'I live on Berwick Street, Inspector. It is hard not to see the whores.'

'So you did know her.'

'I spoke to her, last night. Briefly. She propositioned me. I do not like whores.'

'Is that why you killed her?'

'I did not kill her!'

'Do you recognise that symbol?'

'It's a swastika.'

'Why would anyone carve a swastika into a woman's chest before killing her?' He saw my look. 'Yes, she was alive when he did it, though probably unconscious.'

'I hope you find this man and hang him,' I said.

'But what if we *have* found him?'

I sat straight in the chair. One did not see the swastika much, any more. In Germany it had been banned by the new communist regime. In England it was irrelevant. One saw Mosley's lightning bolt enclosed within a circle in its place, instead. Mosley, who had tried to copy Göring. It was the fat man's initial idea to adopt the swastika as a symbol.

They used to call you the drummer . . .

Did Morhaim just say that? Was it my imagination?

I raised my head and looked the Jew straight in the eyes. 'I did not kill her,' I said.

'Your coat was covered in blood.'

'It wasn't hers.'

'Then whose?'

'I am being set up.'

At that Morhaim laughed. 'Set up?' he said. 'Why? You're nothing but a washed-out dick. You're nobody, a nothing. I don't like you, Wolf. You have the face of a cockroach. Is that why you killed her? To reassert yourself, what you once were?'

'I did not kill her!'

'Then where were you?' he said. The door opened and the fat policeman came in carrying a tray with tea and biscuits on it. He set it down before Morhaim.

'Thank you, Constable Keech,' Morhaim said. He picked a sugar cube with small silver tongs and dropped it into his tea. 'No, Constable. Stay, please.'

'Sir.'

I knew what was coming. It didn't hurt any less. Morhaim pinched a second sugar cube and held it aloft above the tea. I felt Keech move behind me. Morhaim looked at me sadly. 'A confession would go such a long way in your favour,' he said.

'Fuck you, Jew.'

'Such a long way.' Morhaim dropped the cube into the tea. Keech's fat pig's hand slammed into the side of my head, sending me sprawling to the floor. Then he was on me, a sadistic smile on his face, his fists and his boots speaking volumes. I curled up into a ball as best I could, covering my head with my arms. His boots caught me in the ribs, the side of the head, the back of the legs; his huge hands slapped me, his fists rained on my body. Through all this, Morhaim sat behind his desk and stirred his tea and took delicate little sips and looked down on me sadly.

'Stop,' he said, after a while. Keech lifted me up, onehanded. 'For what it's worth, Wolf, I do not think you did it. Only a fool would return to the scene of the crime when it is riddled with policemen, and I do not think you are a fool.'

'That's the nicest thing anyone's said to me all day.'

'I think you're a despicable rat of a human being, a shit I would wipe off my shoe on the pavement, an anti-Semitic bully and leech who should have been left to rot in a communist konzentration-slager. I think you're a murderer and a psychopath.'

'You're too kind,' I said. I spat blood on the floor, hoping to catch the fat copper's shoe, but I missed.

'You're all that, Wolf,' Morhaim said. 'But I don't think you killed Edith Griesser. And while I would have no problem having you thrown in jail for the rest of your unnatural life, it occurs to me that, if you are not the killer, the real killer will still be out there, and that he may well kill again. And I do not want that on my conscience.'

'How admirable,' I said. 'For a Jew.'

Keech grunted above me and slapped me on the side of the head, hard. I blinked back tears of rage. Morhaim looked at me with those sad brown eyes.

'I will ask you one last time,' he said. 'Where were you last night?'

I hung loosely from Keech's enormous hand. Stared into the unsettling brown eyes of Inspector Morhaim. Lowered mine.

And told him.

4

*In the dream he was standing on a high podium in a town square in Nurem-
berg. It was a beautiful day and the sky was bright and blue and before him,
below him, were thousands of people, men and women and children, their
faces raised to him, their lips slightly open, adoration in their eyes. He spoke,
and it was like an angel speaking down from Heaven, and the festivities below
ceased, little boys with yellow and red balloons and women in their Sunday
dresses and good German men who worked hard and went to church and paid
their taxes, and the sausage sellers and the candyfloss sellers and the beer sellers
and the SA men in their uniforms like a guard of honour and all for him. He
spoke, with passion and intensity, raising his fist in the air, slamming it on the
stand, shouting, spittle coming out of his mouth, but easing them in, at first,
then rising, rising, rising until they were all a-frenzy—shaking, some of them
were. He pictured the women wet under their dresses; it was said the power of
his voice alone could bring them to a shuddering climax. The men with their*

fists raised, ready to follow him, the boys and girls watching wide-eyed as history was made. Higher and higher until women fainted and men grew berserk, ready to march now and fight and fulfil his orders, for it was the future he promised them: a glorious one.

Higher and then lower and gently until they rose blinking as if they had been sleeping and were now awake and looking all about them in wonder and awe, at a world remade anew. They had called him the Drummer, then: and it was said that all of Germany marched to his tune.

●

In another time and place Shomer rises blinking. Shomer rises energised and refreshed from the bunk he shares with nine other men and he makes the bed exactly to specification and puts his feet into the wooden clogs with illicit paper padding them and the sores on his feet rubbing and pussing. With the others he shuffles to roll-call, with the others he stands in rows as they wait, and Yenkl stands beside him, puffing on his pipe.

They wait for two hours in the cold before the SS officer arrives to take their numbers and tally the figures of the living and the dead. Shomer's *kommando* once again marches to the same frozen piece of ground to continue the digging of the graves. The routine does not vary, and the graves do not end. At last Shomer is allowed to go to the latrines and Mischek, the scheissbegleiter—that is, the toilet companion or timekeeper—comes with. The latrines are cesspits divided into partitions for the Jews and the non-Jews: the common criminals and the politicals and the prisoners of war. Shomer goes into the Jews' latrine and Mischek, the dirty little Russian Jew, keeps time.

'Have you read my latest review?' Shomer says to Yenkl, sitting beside him on the shared latrine and opening up the latest broadsheet from Berlin. He lets out a loud fart and laughs. 'I must stop eating such heavy meals,' he says, patting his stomach.

'Soup!' Yenkl says. 'What is more wholesome than soup, with a slice of bread, to keep a man's spirit up?'

Shomer's stomach rumbles but he pretends to ignore it. A ration of bread and margarine with a ladle of watery soup must serve: the bread is currency, with bread one may buy and sell and trade, but not in futures. There are no futures here.

'I was mistaken for Freud, once, you know,' he tells Yenkl. 'Do tell?'

Shomer shrugs. 'It was at a literary party, I forget who for.'

'Which means you remember exactly but resented their success?'

Shomer laughs. 'I had been to the washroom and stood pissing next to a young boy not long out of cheder, a young poet who blushed when he saw me and addressed me as Herr Freud. Of course I set the little blighter straight. Did he not know who I was?'

'Did he not?'

'Do you think yeshiva boys do not read shund?'

Yenkl laughed. 'I imagine they do, in secret.'

'He apologised profusely when I told him who I was. Would have asked me to sign something if his pisser wasn't in his hand. I told him to watch where he aimed and washed my hands and returned to the party. Half an hour later, I ran into Freud. "Hello!" I said, civilly. "Someone just thought I was you, which is really stretching credibility to the limit!" '

'You said that?'

'Sure I did.'

'And what did Freud say?'

'He said, "He managed to insult both of us in the same sentence"!'

Yenkl laughed. The Russian, Mischek, popped his head in and told Shomer in broken Yiddish to hurry the fuck up or the kapos will punish both of them.

'Did I tell you about the time I was mistaken for Freud?' Shomer asks Mischek, but Mischek shakes his head miserably and says, 'Freud? Who is this Freud.'

'Some people can't take a joke, can they,' Shomer says to Yenkl but Yenkl is no longer there and the other prisoners look away from him as though he is mad: do they not know who he is?

He gets up and contemplates washing his hands in the foul water and at last does so, his belongings held tight between his thighs, rubbing his hands together to wash off, at least, the worst of the shit. Then back he goes across the camp with Mischek at his side, back to digging graves— 'And what after all should we be digging for?' he says to Yenkl, 'turnips?' and Yenkl laughs and so, with renewed spirit, Shomer returns to work, while his mind conjures up a different kind of cell and a different prisoner; one who, unlike Shomer, does not have a blue number tattooed on his arm.

•

Wolf woke from a deep dark sleep, and dreams in which he fled from booted Jewish hordes, ugly and screaming, with hooked noses and yellow stars, and looking like a caricature from Julius Streicher's *Der Stürmer*. He, Wolf, was running, but run as he might the Jews like the living-dead were relentless, and they pursued him across a map of Europe, like in the pictures from America in which a dotted line grows across a map to symbolise flight. He sat up on the cot in the cell as the cell door swung open.

The fat policeman, Keech, was standing there, no longer grinning. 'Rise and shine. The Inspector wants to see you.'

'It's about time.'

Wolf stood up. Outside it was growing dark. Once again he trod the corridor to the Inspector's office. Morhaim was inside sitting behind his desk. 'Sit down, Wolf.'

'I prefer to stand.'

'Keech?'

The big policeman grinned. Wolf sat down.

'Did you find it?' he said.

'Find what?'

'The club. The body in the basement.'

Morhaim rubbed his eyes. He looked tired, and mean. 'My men and I have indeed visited the address you mentioned in Leather Lane,' he said.

'Full of them filthy foreigners,' Keech said. 'Quite,' Morhaim said.

'Them German refugees and whatnot.'

'Indeed. Keech?'

'Sorry, sir.'

'So?' Wolf said—demanded. 'You know I was telling the truth!'

'We found nothing.'

'What did you say?'

Morhaim shrugged. 'We found an empty house. There were scuffmarks on the floors, as if furniture was hastily removed. A door opened onto a cellar like the one you described. However, there was no one there, and the cell doors were open and empty.'

'They moved them . . .'

'Who are *they*, Mr Wolf?'

'I don't know.'

'You're lying,' Morhaim said, and smiled a small, bitter smile. 'But it does not matter. On the cellar floor we found marks, stains. Possibly something has happened down there, but what?'

'I told you. She shot the man, Kramer. For . . . for taking me down there.'

'A man named Josef Kramer is indeed on our list of alien residents,' Morhaim said. 'His occupation is listed as market porter. His whereabouts are unknown.'

'No body,' Keech said, and grinned. 'No body, no crime. No crime, no nothing, shamus.'

'But that's—' the reality of his situation sunk home for Wolf. They had cleaned up, and in a hurry. Moved the white slaves, the furniture, the still-cooling corpse. He couldn't help it: he felt just a touch of pride. His people had always been efficient.

But that meant he could not prove his innocence. He looked at Morhaim. 'Are you going to charge me?' he said.

He saw the fat policeman look to the Inspector; look away. Morhaim was jittery, distracted. The silence lengthened in the room.

'No.'

'No?'

'Mr Wolf,' Morhaim said. 'You are free to go.'

'I am?'

'Get this piece of shit out of here,' Morhaim said.

Keech said, 'Yes, sir,' and picked Wolf up.

'Get your hands off of me, you fat pig.'

The copper's ugly face froze in a snarl. 'You want more of what I've got?' he said.

'Leave him be, Keech.'

'But Inspector—!'

'We'll be keeping an eye on you, Wolf.'

'You do that,' Wolf said. He half-turned and smiled. Touched the bruise on the side of his face. He felt like a piece of meat chewed by a giant angry dog. He leaned close to the fat policeman. 'I'll get you back for this, precious,' he whispered. 'That's a promise.'

Keech beamed at him. 'I'd like that,' he said. 'I'd like to see you try.'

'I said get him out of here!'

'Yes, sir!'

Keech pushed Wolf out of the door. Back into the corridor.

Shut the door behind them, gently, as on a sickroom. 'Tetchy, isn't he?' Wolf said.

'He's in mourning.'

'For what?'

'For you walking the streets free and all.'

'You know I didn't kill her.'

'You're guilty of something, Wolf. People like you always are.'

'What are you, a Jew lover?'

'No. Just someone who knows the difference between right and wrong.'

'Are you sure you're in the right line of work?'

'Enough wisecracks, shamus. Get dressed.' They were back in the cell. The door was open. Wolf's blood-spattered clothes lay on the bed, neatly folded.

'Can you turn round? I'm shy.'

'Just do it already, will you, Wolf? You have guests and we don't want to keep them waiting.'

Wolf did as he was told. He folded the clothes they had given him, neatly, and put on his suit and his coat and his hat.

He assumed they'd gone through his clothes: it was just a shame no one had bothered to clean them after.

Lastly he put on his shoes; they were good English shoes.

He followed Keech out and Keech opened a door and though they merely transitioned from one room to another room it was a transition from captivity into freedom; and he felt the need for air and drew it in, in a big shuddering inhalation. Somehow the air tasted different this side of the door: more sweet and more pure.

Behind the reception desk a bored policeman was reading *Black Mask*, an American pulp Wolf himself was fond of. The lurid cover showed a woman lying in a pool of blood, a faceless assassin standing over her with a knife. Wolf scanned the people waiting patiently, eternally, on the benches beyond the desk. They were lined with whores and drunks and thieves: the people he now lived amongst.

One who stood out was unfamiliar to him. It was a man decked out all in black leather with black boots and black gloves and a black peaked cap. He marched up to Wolf and gave a Prussian click of the heels.

'Herr Wolf?'

'Ja?'

'I am your chauffeur.'

'My chauffeur.'

'Yes, sir.'

'But I do not have a chauffeur.'

The man almost smiled, but not quite. 'Please, sir. You are tired. I have been instructed to take you to your flat, where you will no doubt wish to wash and change. Do you have the invitation?'

'The invitation?'

'To tonight's soiree, sir.' The chauffeur sounded almost reproachful.

'Mosley's soiree?'

'*Sir* Oswald would be delighted to see you, mein herr,' the chauffeur said. 'As will Lady Mosley. It promises to be quite the night, sir.'

'Did . . . did *Oswald* have me released?'

'I am sure it is not my place to comment, sir.'

Wolf kept a calm expression. You had to, when dealing with the help.

'Let's go,' he said.

'Sir.'

Wolf followed the chauffeur out of the police station and into the night.

WOLF'S DIARY, 3RD NOVEMBER 1939—CONTD.

I was furious, though I tried not to show it. The chauffeur drove me the short distance to my apartment. Outside, the whores were at trade as usual. It would take more than a murder or two to stop them.

How I hated whores!

I well remembered, as a young man, the prostitutes of Vienna, walking one night with Gustl along their Sink of Iniquity, after the opera. How I loved the opera!

And yet worse was the time we had been approached in the street by an older man, on the corner of Mariahilferstrasse-Neubaugasse. Well-dressed and prosperous-looking. He spoke to us pleasantly, asked us about ourselves. When he learned that we were students he invited us to dinner. I was studying architecture at the time, while Gustl studied music. Sometimes I miss Gustl. He had been my only friend.

The man took us to the Hotel Kummer. I was very poor at the time and he let us order whatever we desired. I must confess I had at the time a predilection for pastries and tarts and I had sated myself at the man's expense. He was a manufacturer from Vöcklabruck, in town on business. Over dinner he told us of his indifference to women. He wanted nothing to do with them, for they were all gold-diggers. He and Gustl discussed music. Towards the end of the meal, as Gustl was stuffing his face obliviously, the man slipped me a *carte de visite*. At the end of the meal we thanked him and then left. Gustl was entranced, the infantile. Charmed by the man. 'Did you like him?' I said, as we were walking home.

'Very much,' Gustl said. 'A very cultured man, with pronounced artistic leanings.'

'And nothing else?'

'What else should there be?'

I took out the *carte de visite* and showed it to him. 'That man,' I said, calmly, 'was a homosexual.'

Poor Gustl! He had never even heard the word. I had had to explain it to him, in some detail. His poor little eyes opened up in horror. The idea of two naked, sweaty men engaging in unnatural copulation, grappling with each other, muscles straining, their hard bodies rubbing against each other, fingers and tongues working over buttocks and nipples, a hard thrust and I . . .

It disgusted me. The card went into the fires of our oven.

If it were left up to me all homosexuals, along with communists and Jews, would be sent to specially built camps for their kind.

But the world I had once envisioned was not to be. The future I had envisioned had been robbed from me.

I washed, wincing with each movement as my bruises began to turn dark. I dressed carefully, in my one remaining suit. There was this, too, about Gustl: he was a compulsive masturbator. At any given opportunity, in his bed, in his wash, behind his piano, sometimes at his desk in class or even on the corner of the street, his hand in his pocket, Gustl would relieve himself the way I had denied myself. He was a sweet, innocent boy; I wondered how he fared under communism.

Germany was lost to me. I put on my tie and my hat. Touched my face. My eye was swollen. I was angry. Not at Keech. He was a mindless thug, and mindless thugs I understood. Not even at Morhaim, the Jew. He only did what was his nature, as the personification of the devil, the symbol of all evil, assumes the living shape of the Jew. No—I was angry at being obliged to Mosley. I refused to be in anyone's debt, and least of all an inferior man's.

I took a last look in the mirror. An old, broken man stared back at me. I took a deep breath and felt the hatred fill me, animating me. I would not be broken that easily. I raised my hand, fingers outstretched, in the old salute. I straightened my shoulders. Then I went downstairs to the waiting car.

It was a black Rolls-Royce and it fairly glided through the London streets, heading for Belgravia.

Wolf sat at the back and schemed, thinking furiously. He had not given the girl's murder enough consideration. The location of the attack, the swastika carved into flesh, and the final insult: that damned wind-up toy.

The little tin drummer.

How *dare* he!

Somewhere out there, beyond the car's window, out there in the dark city, there was a man not unlike himself. Wolf did not want to admit it but it was true. And Wolf was a man who seldom deluded himself. He knew who he was; he was always true to himself.

He felt hatred, yes. But it was hatred in service of a greater power: of destiny. Wolf had been shaped into a weapon by the circumstances of life. But a weapon did not kill indiscriminately. It was used for a purpose.

What, then, was the killer's *purpose*?

He was talking, Wolf realised. He was *communicating*, but his communication was not meant for the police.

No. It was meant directly for Wolf himself.

They were driving through St James's Park. Wolf rested his head on the glass and looked out of the window at the dark trees as they passed. He had made little progress with the missing Jewish girl, though it was early days yet. Did his former associates hold her? And which of them owned the club he had visited? He determined to have another little chat with Rudolf Hess. He tried not to think of that woman, Ilse, and her cellar. He winced and shifted in his seat and his thoughts were as dark as the night.

The drive went smoothly. The driver spoke little; Wolf appreciated that. At last the chauffeur indicated and pulled onto Ebury Street. Wolf had been there once before, shortly after his arrival, a landless, penniless refugee on this cold and foreign island. Then, Sir Oswald and Lady Mosley had owned a flat in the building. Now, Wolf saw as they approached, they must have owned the entire bloody thing.

Torches were burning outside. Wolf wound down the window. The air smelled warm and scented as though he had crossed some invisible meridian line by coming here and was now in another country entirely, some tropical land divorced from both space and time. The flames of the torches reflected in the neighbours' windows across the road. In their light Wolf saw Blackshirt foot soldiers standing to attention like an honour guard, and the flags of the lightning bolt that was the symbol of the British Union of Fascists waved in the breeze to either side of the grand entrance with its faux-Doric columns. The driver stilled the engine. Spilling from the house Wolf heard music, laughter, the tinkling of glass and the hum of conversation. The Mosleys's party, it seemed, had been going on for a while.

The chauffeur came round and opened the door for Wolf and Wolf stepped out. He straightened his tie, brushed his hair to one side of his forehead.

'Thank you,' he said.

'You're welcome, sir.'

Wolf nodded. Then he took the invitation out of his breast pocket and marched to the entrance of the house.

'Help you, sir?'

They were fresh-faced boys, really. They wore the Union's futuristic uniform—high-waisted black trousers and black tight-fitting tunic tops that showed off their pectorals, and the whole thing set off by a wide black belt with a large square silver buckle. They looked like they belonged on a rocket ship from one of the American pulps. Most of them sported a pencil moustache, aping their leader. They looked like bulls: well-fed and aggressive. On the left breast of their tunic tops was the jagged lightning bolt of the BU.

'My invitation.'

'Of course, sir.'

The boy scanned the card and stepped aside. Wolf nodded to him civilly enough and went in.

Inside, a pungent cloud welcomed him: eau de toilette, eau de cologne, eau de parfum. Full-bodied cigars and slim ladies' cigarettes and lawyers' fragrant pipe-tobacco: it made his eyes water. 'Wolf!' It was almost a shriek.

He turned and there, descending the grand staircase, was Lady Mosley in a fetching Parisian dress. Jewels sparkled on her wrists, at her neck. She came down to his level and hugged him.

'Diana,' he said.

'It is *so* good to *see* you!' Diana Mosley said.

'Thank you for inviting me.'

'But of *course*! My dear *Wolf*—it *is* Wolf, still, isn't it?'

'It is, yes.'

'Wolf. How *romantic*.'

'I'm sure.'

'It's been so *long*!'

Wolf nodded his head in silent acquiescence.

That night in '34 he had been welcomed to their apartment like an exiled prince—valued, sympathised with, even admired—yet one whose power had waned, whose time had come and gone. He had come like a beggar, limping with the wound in his leg that he had sustained in the concentration camp, and they had spoken of what had passed and what was to come, but it was obvious to all of them, by then, that Germany was lost.

He had left. He would not take charity. Since then he never went back. Mosley then was a minor figure in British politics, almost a figure of ridicule. In the intervening years, with the dark shadow of communism growing ever longer across the Channel, he too had grown, in both power and status. And Wolf had not been invited back; there was that, too, to consider.

Until now.

'You poor *dear*!' Diana continued on, in that prattle British society women were so well-practised in. Wolf knew better than to underestimate her. None of the Mitford sisters were entirely stupid, though one of them, Jessica, *was* a devoted communist. Diana touched Wolf's cheek, lightly. 'What happened to your poor *face*?'

'I fell.'

'Did the police do this? How utterly *dreadful*. Things like this will never happen when Oswald is in power.'

When, Wolf noted. Not *if*.

'I'm sure it was just a misunderstanding.' Still, he was angry: the anger was never far from the surface. 'There was a Jew inspector—'

'A Jew! How *ghastly*!'

'Well, it is of little significance.'

She squeezed his arm. 'Oswald is just *dying* to see you,' she said. 'But he can wait. Come. Let's get you something to drink.' She led him into a large room with high windows. Guests milled about and he saw familiar faces, politicians and film stars, the usual assortment of trash one could find at any such gathering. A buffet ran from one wall to the other, every manner of beast and fowl represented, and Wolf realised just how hungry he was. Diana Mosley, *née* Mitford, brought him a tall glass. He took it from her. 'Fresh orange and strawberries,' she whispered, smiling. 'We have them shipped over, darling. I made sure we'd have something waiting especially for you. Come. You must be *ravenous*!'

One buffet table, Wolf saw, was covered in vegetarian dishes, from an Indian-style curry to Italian lasagne and British shepherd's pie. Diana took a plate and began to heap food onto it. 'Here you are.'

He took it from her. Put his drink down on the table. Picked up a fork. Delicately sampled the curry. Diana watched him like a wife. 'Eat!' she said.

Wolf ate. The assortment of foods all blended together. He barely tasted any of it, the hunger was so strong. He ate with quick strong strokes, like a swimmer—like that good Aryan boy Johnny Weissmuller, who played Tarzan in the pictures.

When he was done he put the plate down and in seconds a waiter whisked it away. Wolf picked up his drink and took a sip. 'You look well,' he said.

'I feel well,' Diana said, and laughed. She touched his arm. 'It really *is* so good to see you, Wolf. You have always been *such* an inspiration, to both of us, you know. Oswald values you highly.'

'Is he here?'

'He's around. He would be delighted to see you.'

'And I, him,' Wolf said, politely.

'Good!' She clapped her hands. 'But do let me show you around first, Wolf! It's not often we get such distinguished company.'

'You're too kind, really.'

Wolf found himself dragged along in her wake. Her hand on his arm was surprisingly strong. She had always liked him more than she should have, he thought. The way her sister had. Now he was her prize, for one night. She was determined to show him off, the way she did her jewels. But unlike gold, Wolf's value had not gone up in the intervening years.

'Ah, Lady Mosley. What a delightful party.'

'Thank you *so* much! Wolf, this is Mr Fleming. He's a stockbroker.'

The man was handsome, with the bearing of a military man. 'Call me Ian, please.' He had a strong grip when they shook hands. 'Mr Fleming almost bought our old flat from us, do you know!' Diana said. 'In the end we bought the whole place and did it up instead.'

'A great gain for all of us,' Fleming said, smiling. He looked at Wolf. That same look he always got. 'You remind me of someone.'

Wolf shook his head. 'I get that a lot,' he said. 'You are German!'

'Austrian, actually.'

'I studied in Austria. Kitzbühel.'

'Did you,' Wolf said. It was not exactly a question.

'I'm sure you look like someone.'

'Believe me, I am no one.'

Fleming peered at him closely. 'Have you been in a fight?' he said.

'Really, Mr Fleming!' Diana turned to Wolf, apologetic. 'Mr Fleming was a journalist, you see. He was in Moscow, in fact, in '33. At the time of the . . .' she hesitated.

'The Fall?'

Wolf noticed that the Fleming fellow had lost his smile. His eyes took on a cold aspect. Wolf knew that look, too.

Recognition.

'Excuse me,' Fleming said. He turned rather abruptly and went to join a group of City men by the half-open windows.

'How rude!' Diana said. 'I am so sorry, Wolf.'

'I take it he is not a supporter of the BU, either?'

Diana shrugged. 'This is a private party, not a political one.'

'I see that is Lord Rothermere of the *Daily Mail* there, talking to the writer—Williamson?'

'Henry Williamson, yes. Wonderful writer. *Wonderful.* Have you read *A Chronicle of Ancient Sunlight*? No, well, anyway, of course yes, both of *them* are supporters, naturally.' She looked at him steadily. 'Was that your point?'

'I was just curious.'

'Do you know,' Diana said, whispering mischievously, 'It is rumoured Mr Fleming is sleeping with Baron O'Neill's wife? While not knowing meanwhile that she, at the same time, is also having an affair with Lord Rothermere's heir?'

'A busy lady.'

'Busy *indeed*!' And Diana burst into laughter. 'Poor Fleming,' she said. 'But he's young.'

Wolf was rescued at that moment with the arrival of a young man as grey and unremarkable as his suit. Clearly, not a guest, but an employee. The man—a boy, really—whispered in Diana's ear.

'Yes, thank you, Alderman,' she said. She turned to Wolf, apologetically. 'Oswald is in his study, upstairs. He wishes to see you. Would you . . . ?' She gestured with her palm.

'Of course.'

'Just follow Alderman. It is *so* lovely to see you, Wolf.'

'You too, Lady Mosley.'

'Diana, *please!*'

Wolf took her hand and kissed it, gallantly. 'Diana,' he said. 'Oh, Wolf!'

She fanned herself and laughed. Wolf took his leave, following the taciturn Alderman.

Up the stairs through more festive people, the men in suits and the women in dresses, and all expensive and expansive and all laughing gaily, and drinking and smoking, and chattering and parting before Wolf, like the Red Sea at the approach of Moses and the Israelites.

'Please, sir,' the boy said.

'Yes, yes? What is it?' Wolf said, impatiently.

'I'm a big admirer of yours, sir.'

'I see,' Wolf said, who didn't. 'What of it?'

The boy reached into the breast pocket of his suit and brought out a small rectangular object and began to say, 'Could you perhaps sign this—' but Wolf wasn't paying attention. 'Mosley?' he said, crossly, if only to the air. 'Mosley, are you there? Blasted man.'

'Here, sir,' the young man said, with some obvious regret. Whatever it was he wanted to show Wolf had disappeared. They had reached the top floor. Oswald Mosley's private office was in what had once been an attic. Alderman knocked, waited and pushed the oak door open. Beyond was a small, comfortable-looking room, with bookshelves and an antique desk and bronze lamps. It was warm and well lit. Behind the desk sat Oswald Mosley, perusing papers.

'Mr Wolf to see you, sir.'

Mosley raised his head. He was a good-looking man, with thick black hair slicked back and a pencil moustache that made him look a little like a screen villain. He was dressed in a Savile Row suit rather than the BU uniform he had himself designed. The smile he gave Wolf was genuine, and beaming.

'Sir Oswald,' Wolf said.

'Wolf!' Mosley rose, his arms outstretched. 'You may leave us, Alderman.'

'Sir.'

Mosley advanced on Wolf as the door closed with a soft snick, leaving them alone in the room. Wolf bore the hug stoically. Before the Fall, no one would have dared greet him so informally.

'It is so good to see you, my friend.'

'And you.' He was relieved when Mosley released him. He looked around the room. 'You have come up in the world.'

Mosley shrugged. 'I worked hard for it. There is much work before us. You of all people know—'

'You are running for prime minister,' Wolf said. He looked more closely at Mosley's face, searching for those telltale signs of age since the last time they'd met. But it was strange. In recent months he had grown used to Mosley's face, wherever he turned, looking down on him from billboards and posters glued to the city's walls. At first no one had taken the British Union of Fascists seriously; now, the Blackshirts were everywhere and Mosley's image, larger than life, haunted the dark city.

'Yes,' Mosley said. Shrugged with his palms open, disarmingly. 'I am.'

'Can you really afford to go to war with Germany?'

It was the question people were asking. Mosley ran on a platform opposing Marxism. He claimed a coming war was inevitable.

Mosley said, 'Can we afford not to?'

'A war with Germany is a war with Russia,' Wolf said. 'With Stalin and all his power.'

'Marxism must be destroyed,' Mosley said. 'It is the poisoned ideology of the Jewish race.'

Wolf rubbed the bridge of his nose, feeling a headache coming on. To see Mosley, that clown, with such power! It filled him with irrational rage. Even the man's words were second-hand.

'But I am sorry to go on,' Mosley said. 'Please, sit down, my friend. Can I get you anything?'

'Thank you, no. Your wife has been most kind.'

'Diana is a loyal woman.' Mosley re-seated himself behind his desk. Wolf had heard of the man's little indiscretions. When Oswald was married to his first wife, Cynthia, he was also having an affair with her younger sister Alexandra, *and* with their stepmother. Sometimes Wolf wondered how the man ever found the time to be a Fascist. But then didn't Mussolini carry on as if he were single-handedly responsible for repopulating the entire Earth after a holocaust?

Whatever the case, he knew they were weak men, where he was strong. And yet their hearts were in the right place for all that, as the English said.

'So,' Wolf said. He watched Mosley, who sat back in the chair and folded his hands in his lap.

'So,' Mosley said.

They regarded each other across the desk.

At last Mosley sighed. 'Unfortunate business with that young prostitute,' he said.

'Nothing to do with me,' Wolf said.

'Of course. Of course. Nevertheless . . .'

'Yes?'

'It's bad publicity, Wolf. I am fighting for my political life here! For the very future of this country, if not the world! I cannot afford even a whiff of scandal. Not now.'

'What are you suggesting, exactly?'

Mosley raised his hands. 'I am not suggesting you are embroiled in all this,' he said. 'This . . . murder and what have you. But the signs are all too clear. The swastika most of all. Not many would understand the clue of the tin drummer. Not any more.'

It was a stark reminder of how far Wolf had fallen.

'Yes.'

'I cannot afford to be linked to these murders.'

'You invited me to your home.'

'Diana did that.'

'I see.'

'I had asked the driver to bring you directly to me. Perhaps he misunderstood.'

Wolf thought of the chauffeur and his Munich accent and his veteran's poise. A loyal man, he thought. But not to Mosley.

'What is it you want?'

Mosley lowered his hands. He looked tired suddenly, older than his years. 'I want to hire you,' he said.

'*Hire* me?' Wolf had not expected that. 'To do what? To disappear?'

'No, no.' Mosley shrugged. 'Look, I apologise. The murderer will be caught. So far I have managed to keep the details out of the newspapers. It is a problem, but it is a matter for the police. As for that Jew, Morhaim, I shall make sure he is dealt with. We do not want Jews in our police force, do we? But these are critical times, and I cannot be seen to interfere directly. Not yet.'

'So you would do nothing.'

A hurt look entered Mosley's eyes. Then he smiled.

'You were always the most astute of us all,' he said.

I was always your superior, Wolf thought, but didn't say. 'Thank you for getting me out,' he said.

'It was the least I could do.'

'Something is troubling you.' He adopted his detective's voice. The voice of a confidant. 'Tell me what it is.'

'Someone is trying to kill me.'

'Oh?'

'Three nights ago an assassin opened fire on my car as I was driving to a rally in Derby,' Mosley said. 'I lived. The assassin escaped. We had kept the news from the papers.'

'You must have been shaken.'

'I was certainly bothered, yes,' Mosley said. Wolf thought, You pompous coward. I bet you all but pissed yourself.

'You were very brave.'

'I serve a greater purpose,' Mosley said.

Yes, your prick, Wolf thought.

'Sorry? Did you say something?'

'Oh, nothing.'

'And two weeks ago there was an attempt on my life as I stepped out of a soiree in Kensington. My men found a suspicious package taped to the undercarriage of the car. It turned out to be a bomb. Only by luck it did not go off.'

'So you are suggesting an orchestrated campaign?'

'I am afraid, Wolf. I am afraid that next time they will succeed. I am afraid not for myself, but for the world I shall leave bereft of my leadership.'

Wolf would have been happy at that point to kill Mosley himself. But he brought himself under control. He always did.

'Do you know who they are?' he said, calmly.

'Who do you think?'

'Jews?'

'Who else? They call themselves the Palestinian Liberation Front. The PLO.'

Wolf said: 'Palestine?' The word left an unpleasant taste in his mouth.

'They want it for themselves. A land for the Jews. They demand Parliament cede it to them. Just imagine! Next thing you know the Indians will be demanding independence, or the blacks in—' he waved his hand vaguely, 'Bongo Bongo Land. Can you imagine, Wolf?'

'It is a way of, in the first instance, removing the Jews from Europe,' Wolf said. Such a plan had been put forward before, by Himmler, Göring, even Julius Streicher. 'Surely that should be the main objective?'

'Our problem in Britain has never been a large population of Jews,' Mosley said. 'Until recently, at any rate. The Fall and the influx of immigrants is rallying the country round to my way of thinking, at long last.'

'But they are blaming all immigrants, not just the Jews.'

As an alien in Britain he had experienced his share of hostility, but he was not going to mention that to Mosley. He had his pride.

'The Jews are behind it. They are behind everything. And is communism not just a Jewish ploy? But this is getting us nowhere, Wolf. The point is that the Jews have formed in recent years—no doubt emboldened by the rise of their kind in the communist East—several covert military groups even as they engage in illegal immigration to Palestine—very much *against* British Mandate law, I should add. They buy ships! They purchase false papers! And Palestine is a lawless land, a Wild West—we can hardly spend the resources to administer it properly.'

Wolf sighed inwardly. No doubt Mosley saw conspiracies under the bed—that is, if he was not himself hiding under it, having been surprised by the unexpected arrival of a lady friend's husband.

'I assume they have communicated with you.'

Mosley laughed, a short bitter sound. 'Do you know the number of threats I have received over the past few years?' he said. 'They are all after me, Wolf!'

'The cost of power,' Wolf said, coolly.

Mosley subsided. Reluctantly, he smiled. 'You are right. I am letting their tactics of terror affect me—but the danger *is* real, Wolf. I want you to work for me.'

Wolf clenched his fists, his short nails digging into his palms. How much he resented those words.

'I want you to find them. Money is not an issue.'

'What about your own MI5?'

'They're working on it.' He lowered his voice. 'To tell you the truth, sometimes I think the intelligence services don't take me quite as seriously as they should.'

Wolf suppressed a rare smile. 'Is that so.'

'Please, Wolf! You I can trust, implicitly.'

Wolf said nothing. Mosley opened a drawer with some force and took out a cheque book. He tore out a cheque and wrote down a number and handed it to Wolf. Wolf looked at the cheque.

'Well?'

Wolf was still looking at the cheque. Then he folded it, neatly, and tucked it away in his pocket.

He nodded, tight-lipped.

Some offers you just couldn't refuse.

5

HERR WOLF—

Did you like her? She was so pretty. When we
went into the alleyway her hand was warm in mine.
It reminded me of going to Spitalfields with my
mother shopping for vegetables, cabbages and peas.
She was taken by God when I was very young. We
have so much in common, you and I. Your mother,
too was taken. But we are soldiers, we soldier on.
Be brave, my mother said, she held my hand and it
was moist and warm, she was lying in bed and she
was running a fever. I don't know what she died
of; a doctor never came. Be brave, he needs you.
I thought she was talking about my father but now
I know the truth of it, and she must have known
one day I would meet you. I took the whore into
the alleyway and my knife came out all slick and
sharp and she tried to cry, but I put my hand
over her mouth and pressed my body against hers,

against the wall, and put my lips close to her ear and said, Shut up you whore, or I will kill you. I put the knife to her throat. How she trembled! Her neck was so white and I could feel her heartbeat, I could cup it in my hand like a flame from a match. I kissed her.

It was so romantic. I remember the sky spread out above us, and the stars and the smell of pines—for some reason I could smell pines, and freshly cut grass, and her cheap perfume. I remember the taste of her lips, and the heat of her body against mine, and the sky all above, and thinking what lay beyond it, beyond air and the sun: did they have other worlds up there, like ours and yet unlike, where lovers met in secret in the strange byways of an alien city?

I stuck the knife in her. She dropped in my arms and I held her, tenderly, and looked deep into her eyes and saw the suffering ease and at last she was at peace, like my mother was at peace. I laid her down on the ground. The blood gushed out of her. I had the irrational desire to taste it. I stroked her hair. She was so blonde and so pretty. The front of me was wet. I knelt over her like a priest at prayer. I gave her benediction. Can't you see that? The knife was in my hand and I delicately etched the sign on her. I had to make it deep. I was so excited that my hands shook. I arranged her properly. I made her beautiful again. Innocent. She wasn't a whore now; she was like a new bride. I folded her arms

on her belly, and finally I reached into my coat
and took out the little toy. The little drummer. I
was going to wind it up. I wanted to see it march
across the ground of that alleyway, march along
her body, march like I would have marched for you.
But I heard voices and I was suddenly afraid. I
left it by her head. I touched her one last time.
I was shaking when I stood up. I wore a raincoat
for the blood. The voices came closer, and so I
went the other way and no one saw me.

The problem, Wolf reflected, was Balfour. Arthur James Balfour and all
the other Jew-lovers in His Majesty's government. Long dead now, the
old fool—but promises hastily made are nonetheless remembered, especially ones made by the Foreign Secretary of the greatest empire in the
world.

Wolf was only a young soldier then, serving with the First Company of
the List Regiment in the Bavarian army, but he could still remember his
outrage when news of Lord Balfour's promise reached the front. Back then,
of course, Jews were still a part of German and Austrian society. Jewish of-
ficers served in the war against the British, just as on the British side Jews
fought against the Kaiser.

But already the Jews were agitating for *emancipation*. An insidious form of nationalism took hold of the Jewish people, a desire for a
homeland. They had called their movement Zionism, and they had been
spurred on by the vision of one Theodor Herzl, an Austro-Hungarian
journalist Jew.

In 1917, Lord Balfour wrote a letter to Baron Rothschild, in which he
asserted British support for the establishment of a Jewish homeland in
Palestine (then still in the possession of the Ottoman Empire, though it

fell to British forces shortly after). Of course, Wolf thought, no one had *actually* intended to commit to such a disastrous course of action, but the Jews persisted, and were becoming increasingly more militant in their nationalist aspirations.

But it was absurd, Wolf thought. Try as he might he could not take the threat to Mosley seriously. The Fall had changed things. Communism was a Jewish sickness and Austro-Germany had become a Jewish paradise in which their thinkers and their scientists flourished—did not Freud found and radically expand his very own Sigmund Freud Institute in Vienna, with branches in Berlin and even Moscow itself? Was not that clown Albert Einstein now Chair of the Max Planck Institute in Berlin? It seemed nearly every day his famous image, with that wild unruly hair and smirking face, stared out at Wolf from the dailies or in the newsreels, an icon used by the communists as a threat of terrible weapons to come, should war ever be declared.

Marx, Freud and Einstein: the three corners of the evil that was international Jewry, Wolf thought.

If only *he* had been in power . . .

But then reality, of course, sank in. He was not in power. He was a nobody, a grey man in a cheap grey suit, and his only reason for being at Mosley's party was that they wanted to hire him. As the *help*.

Scheisse!

He left Mosley's office and started down the stairs clutching a large brown envelope containing—or so Mosley said—all of the communications he had received from the Palestinian terrorists. He intended to dump the file as soon as was convenient. There would be nothing useful in the anonymously mailed threats.

'They have influence, still,' Mosley told him. 'The Jews. They've worked themselves into British public life, insidiously, and with money. The Rothschilds have been funding Jewish immigration to Palestine for decades. Don't underestimate them, Wolf.'

Implicit in the words: *Like you have before.*

Now he went down the stairs and all he wanted to do was get away. He was beat-up and tired and old. In his pocket, Mosley's cheque was a reminder of everything he had once been and would never be again.

Not looking, he bumped into something soft and full that smelled of expensive perfume. A squeal of delight followed and a familiar female voice said, 'Wolfy!'

He raised his head and found himself staring directly into the adoring eyes of Unity Mitford.

'Valkyrie?' he said. He had always used her middle name.

'Don't you recognise me?' she said, laughing.

Wolf winced. He found he could not draw away from her, his eyes kept searching that sweet, smooth face, the full red lips, the mischievous eyes. She had not changed. Her delicate perfume tickled his nostrils. 'You haven't aged a day,' he said.

'Always so gallant,' she said, laughing. 'Did my sister not say I would be here? I've been looking for you *everywhere*.'

Wolf took her hand in his. 'It is very good to see you again, Valkyrie,' he said.

'And you, too. So, so much.' She slipped her arm through his. In her other hand she was holding champagne. 'Oh, Wolf!' She looked up at him with those adorable, adoring eyes, a sad look just like the one Wolf remembered, so fondly, from his German Shepherd, Blonda. Leaving his dog behind had been one of the hardest things he'd ever done. 'Oh, Wolf, where did we go wrong?'

'You were too beautiful,' Wolf said, 'and I was a penniless prospect. A cat may look at a king.'

'But you hate cats!'

He grinned, a wolf's grin, and didn't speak again.

'Come,' she said. 'Let's get some air.'

'I should get back.'

'Not yet you don't.' She led him and he followed. Down the stairs and out to the garden in the back. It was a beautiful night. The rich never live in winter; only the poor.

Music was playing, Glenn Miller's big band tunes, and couples were dancing in the garden. Tall torches set into the ground cast shadows from their flickering flames, like snakes shedding their skin. Unity took Wolf's hand in hers. 'Do you still think of me?'

'Always.'

'You lie.'

'In every great lie there must be a kernel of truth,' Wolf said.

'Always the cynic.' She sighed and leaned against him. 'Do you remember?' she said.

Wolf said he did.

There are all kinds of truths and most of them are uncomfortable.

1933: the last of the Nuremberg Rallies.

Wolf, bitter in defeat. But not yet defeated.

It was an unofficial war and it had raged over the Roaring Twenties and early thirties, across Germany and in particular Berlin. Brownshirts and communists, SA men and KPD comrades fighting for control. That poor dumb fuck Horst Wessel was an SA-Sturmführer when a communist assassin shot him in the kisser. People were predicting civil war, though there was nothing civil about it. Germany was a powder keg, as the saying goes. Wolf was the match. Then came the elections and the communists, the KPD, came to power, shocking everyone but especially Wolf.

1933 and he still thought he could win. The commies were still consolidating their unexpected authority. It was time for a last, desperate push.

The Reichstag burned.

And Wolf marched in Nuremberg. Not in victory but in defeat, but he marched all the same. It was then that Valkyrie and her sister Diana came to see him. He had been taken with Valkyrie. She was only nineteen. In a way, she reminded him of Geli.

He was keeping Eva at the time. She was a pretty, uncomplicated little creature. At twenty-one years old she was two years older than Valkyrie but less mature. He had first met her at the photographer's where she worked as a model and assistant. She had been seventeen then.

He often wondered what had happened to Eva, after the Fall. Did she die in the camps? Or did she, a simple creature not much given to politics, get by? Did she find herself a handsome young commissar to marry and did she bear him children? Wolf supposed he could have tried to find out, but he never did.

Valkyrie came into his life when his life was all but over. She was a precious thing, and she doted on him. Those puppy eyes, just like Blonda's. He took her to balls and rallies while Eva was left behind in the apartment he had bought her. Valkyrie looked good on Wolf's arm.

It was the last ever of the Nuremberg rallies. He remembered the flags waving in the wind, the people standing down below looking up at him with heavy, veiled eyes. Remembered the heat, the sweat, the feel of the woollen suit against his skin, chafing. The smell of defeat was the smell of a homeless soldier back from the war, the smell of gangrene and sour alcohol.

'Do you remember?'

Two months later the KPD thugs came and arrested him. The organisation had been broken, mass arrests were made, and Wolf was sent to the camps. Some of the others fled: Hess, the coward, took a private plane across Europe and into Britain. Göring joined the communists. Julius Streicher was killed in a shoot-out in Nuremberg. Even Wolf didn't mourn his passing. The man was a menace, a rapist and a drunk, but he had been effective. Streicher's newspaper, *Der Stürmer*, was shut down.

National Socialism was dead.

'I remember,' Wolf said. His teeth were clenched. All around them ghostly couples danced in the light of the burning torches. Valkyrie was close against him, her warmth like a promise, her perfume an invitation.

Her lips by his ear. 'Remember when we were alone. I could do those things for you again, that you like.'

He pushed her away, but not roughly, more with a sense of loss and regret. And tried not to think of the monstrous woman, that Ilse Koch as she had called herself, and her torture chamber under that now-abandoned club on Leather Lane.

'I am no longer that man.'

'Oh, Wolf.' There was so much sadness in her voice it made him ill. 'People don't change. You are still who you were! A leader, a visionary. You are what poor deluded Oswald could never be.'

'You're young,' he said. 'And I am not. And time comes upon all of us, like a thief in the night.'

'Oh, how I hate the Jews who did this to you!'

'You were always steadfast in your hatred of them, Valkyrie.'

'No one says my name like you do.'

One memorable night in Nuremberg, he and the two Mitford sisters . . . but no. He would not think of that.

'Diana still worships you as I do,' Valkyrie said.

Wolf smiled. 'No one does it like you do,' he said.

'Come with me. Back to my flat.'

There was such naked need in her voice. Wolf shook his head. The past had a habit of catching up with you. 'I had better go,' he said. 'I think Oswald would have preferred me to use the servants' exit.'

'The man is a buffoon.'

'He *is* your brother-in-law.'

Valkyrie shrugged. 'Let Diana warm his bed for him,' she said.

'He might be the next prime minister.'

'Is that what this is?' Valkyrie said. 'Is it about *power*, Wolf?'

'It is *always* about power,' Wolf said.

'Do you think I love you less for having lost your power?'

An ugly word: *love*.

Perhaps sensing she had made a mistake Valkyrie, too, withdrew. 'I'm sorry. I didn't mean—'

'Did you not?' Wolf said, darkly.

'Please, Wolf.' As if she couldn't but move closer to him, a moth to his banished flame. Whispering in his ear, 'I will fuck you the way you like it.'

He pushed her away, roughly this time. 'Whore,' he said.

'I will be your whore, if you'd only let me!'

People were looking at them now. 'Lower your voice,' Wolf said, and his own voice was distant and cold.

The woman was close to tears, he saw. Wolf touched his fingers to the brim of his hat. *'Auf wiedersehen*, Valkyrie.'

'Wolf, no!'

But already he was going, walking away, and the English people parted before him, as though they could sense the lethal mood he was in. Unity didn't follow. She remained standing there, alone, with people staring and then looking away and murmuring amongst themselves. 'Damn you, Wolf!' she shouted. 'And damn you too, you nosy bastards—' pointing a finger at the assembled guests, who studiously avoided eye contact.

'Come on, pet.' It was that young broker, Fleming.

'Oh, Ian,' Unity said. She let him lead her away. She leaned her head on his shoulder. 'It's all so very *beastly*,' she said, miserably.

WOLF'S DIARY, 3RD NOVEMBER 1939—CONT'D.

That stupid bitch Valkyrie had made a miserable ending to a miserable day and I suspected it was not yet over. I did not like women trying to assert an authority over me. The Mitford girl was too unpredictable, too *independent*. I liked my women the way I liked my dogs, obedient and devoted, like Catholics suddenly confronted with their maker.

I did not make a good Catholic. My father hated the clerics and I had hated both the clerics and my father. My mother was devout, and I remembered as a boy going to church and waiting on my knees, as God in the form of a priest stuck his flesh and dribbled his blood in my mouth. My mother had so much love to give, to her Lord and to me. Even to my father. And I remember, too, as a young boy, hearing the sounds coming from their bedroom, at night, my father's grunting, my mother's soft sobs and sighs. Perhaps it was as early as that that my dislike of my father began, with the sounds of his nightly assault.

But though I loved them, women always betrayed me. First and worst, Geli, of course. How dare she escape me, and using my own gun as the key to her freedom! But she was only the first of them.

I met Eva when I came to visit Herr Hoffmann's studio in Munich. It was a place I frequented regularly. The first time I saw her she was climbing a ladder in the shop and I saw her pretty ankles and the rising hemline of her dress and I was smitten, I will admit that I was smitten. She was a model of Aryan womanhood and at seventeen she glowed with good health, her eyes were innocent and clear and yet unspoiled. Whenever I came in to see Hoffmann I would take her hand and kiss it with decorum and call her my lovely siren from Hoffmann's. I would make her blush. She knew me as Herr Wolf, which was the nom de guerre I was using at the time. No doubt she thought of me as that politician who was in prison. Her language was plain. There was no guile about her. Later I would take her on holiday to Berchtesgaden where she would sun herself in the clear air, as naked as the day she was born. She was Eve before the fall. We would go rowing on the lake together. Such a simple, delightful creature she was.

In Munich I would take her out to the opera or to my favourite restaurant, the Osteria Bavaria. I would buy her presents—the first thing I ever gave her was a yellow orchid. It was the first flower a man had ever given her. I had given the whore everything! And yet she, too, tried to escape me.

I had found her diary, the pages of which I had not destroyed but kept, as proof of her guilt. She was a silly girl! All she could speak of was of my taking her away from the shop, of perhaps giving her a little house of her own. At first she was jolly but as the days went by her distress grew. One Sunday, for instance, I had promised to see her. She had phoned the Osteria, left a message with Werlin to say she was waiting to hear from me. I was not there, of course. I had gone to Feldafing, and when Hoffmann invited me to coffee and dinner I told him where to stuff it. The silly girl waited for me all through the night. The Hoffmanns had even given her a ticket for the Venetian Night that evening, but she didn't go.

Her diary became increasingly confused. I am utterly miserable, she wrote, the little slut, as if she could know true misery! *I* had been on the Front. Eva threatened to buy more sleeping powders.

He only needs me for certain purposes, she wrote.

Later I invited her to dinner at the Four Seasons. At the end of it, I gave her an envelope with some money.

A few days later the stupid whore Frau Hoffmann told Eva I had found a replacement for her, called Valkyrie.

On 28th May she took thirty-five sleeping pills and tried to kill herself but she failed.

The stupid whore! She could not even kill herself suc-cessfully.

The whole thing was a pathetic ploy, a cry for my attention. Well, I suppose she did get it, after all. I have always had a soft spot for a plump bit of dumpling and no mistake.

•

In another time and place Shomer lies dreaming and tries to forget.

In memory there's no escape.

He remembers them fleetingly, in jumbled fragments. Avrom's dark curls gleaming in candlelight, Bina's laughter as he made faces at her and she snorted like a certain treife animal; their smell when they were babies, in those sleepless days when he sat by his typewriter morning and night churning out tales of Yiddishe gangsters and chaste girls with a wild heart hidden within, of bloodied murders and anti-Semite conspiracies and of detectives who walked the cold streets in search of a justice they knew to be an illusion—in those early days when the babies cried and Fanya feeding and the shouts of merchants outside silenced by snow, and a fire burning, and his fingers on the warm hard keys, and the smell of milk, of babies, everywhere in the house, and in everything he touched, and in his clothes—those were the happiest days of his life, he realised, and you only learn that too late, when they are vanished like smoke.

Those are the moments he wishes to burn like the pages of a manuscript. To see them consumed by flame so he would never have to see them or remember them or how they were, their smell eradicated for ever. He resents Fanya when she appears to him, unexpectedly, in unguarded moments; he resents her for leaving him. He wants her gone from his mind the way she had left this world, so abruptly: one moment they were together a family, and the next the man severed them with his horsewhip, they to go one way and he the other. They to the ovens, he to the work units. And he didn't know, they didn't know, Fanya held Avrom and Bina's hands and looked back at him as they parted, and her lips tried to form a smile. 'You will see each other again, they are only going to the showers, to be washed,' a soldier said, a voice lacking in emotion, and an old man masticating toothless gums said mournfully, 'Auschwitz, Auschwitz, what is this Auschwitz?'

He is angry at them not for leaving him but for coming back. They come from a world that no longer exists and has no right to intrude upon his present. Auschwitz, Auschwitz: there is only Auschwitz.

'Do you remember?' is a sentence never spoken, it is *verboten*, a transgression against the now. There is only now, no past, no future, there is only Auschwitz, an island floating on the Polish ground. The dead rise in black ash into the sky, day and night the ovens burn, day and night the trains come laden. And Shomer's mind retreats into itself, the way it had when he was still a man. For he had been a writer of *shund*, of pulp, for *Haynt* and other publishers. He had made his living with his hands, at his desk, writing lies for money.

He had had some success. He was read by yeshiva boys in secret, passing his books from hand to hand; by young Zionists filled with ideological fervour, who would have denied it stoutly were they challenged; by the rabbis who confiscated the books from their wards, by the women who picked them up for a few kopeks along with a bag of onions in the shop, by intellectuals who railed against this prostituting of literature, by wealthy merchants and farmers and cobblers and clockmakers, carpenters and engineers: they all knew the name Shomer, which means guardian, or watchman, and was his nom de plume, for it was not respectable for a man to be writing *shund*.

For it was hopeless. His life had been erased like his books, set alight, reduced to ash and scattered. It no longer existed. But then, all lives were ultimately extinguished, and in their passing nothing remained of the person who'd been—their dreams, their thoughts, who they loved, what they hated—from Neanderthals and Cro-Magnon and down the ages to Jews.

And yet Shomer lives still.

He'd met Fanya at an open-air showing of a film about Palestine and the work of the pioneers there. She wore white. He was in his best suit, he had only recently begun to write: stories about detectives and dames, with no redeeming literary value. He'd sported a thin moustache at the time (Fanya made him shave it off before the wedding). In the film, men and women no older than he were tilling stony fields and sleeping in tents and picking oranges. They looked like Biblical peasants reborn in distant Palestine; he couldn't imagine why anyone would want to live in this way. But he only half-saw them, anyway. All he really saw was Fanya, more real than anything the screen had to offer, like a woman out of the pages of one of his stories.

Of course, in hindsight, he realised that she wasn't. She was not cut out of cardboard like the dames in the stories. She had an internal life he would never see (and now never could), irrational likes and dislikes, moods he could not interpret, times she was happy for no reason he could tell and times she was sad and he could do nothing to change it. But she loved him, he loved her, and they were happy for a while. Even in the ghetto they could still make each other happy, even on the train here he was still telling her and the children stories.

Stories, stories, he is sick to death of stories!

Yet they are all he has.

WOLF'S DIARY, 3RD NOVEMBER 1939—CONTD.

I was in a foul mood when I left the Mosleys' party. The taciturn driver waited outside. He hailed me but I refused his offer of a ride, foolishly perhaps. I walked away, though I walked with a slight limp from my old injury. The night was dark and quiet but I was not fooled, for it is in the night that one comes most alive. To know the light you must understand shadows. I walked through Belgravia though I had the feeling I was being watched, and often I turned abruptly but there was no one there. Nevertheless the feeling of being watched persisted.

In this manner—that is to say, furtively—I traversed the city in an easterly direction. My mind was busy like a rat's.

Vicious, dirty creatures, rats. Julius Streicher's genius with *Der Stürmer* was, firstly, the graphic caricatures he ran: the long-nosed rat-like Jew, always lusting after German maidenhood. It was a magazine appealing to the lowest common denominator, glorying in gruesome tales of sex crimes and murders, all naturally blamed on the Jews. He was rat-like himself, was Julius Streicher, vicious and dirty and oh so effective. His magazine was all but porno-graphic; it put the English *Daily Mail* to shame. I didn't know why I was thinking about him again after all those years. The past was threatening to catch up with me.

My mind returned to the symbol carved on the dead woman's chest. I had thought the swastika forgotten. A red star rose over Germany now. In my preoccupation, I was tired and footsore, and perhaps not as cautious as I should have been. I had failed to pick up the signs of danger.

The approach through Walker's Court in Soho was quiet. Too quiet. I did not see the whores. Of the murder scene there was no sign, but then again it was only the death of a whore, and the police had other matters to engage themselves with. My footsteps echoed lonely in the abandoned street. I took off my hat momentarily and passed my hand over my damp hair and replaced the hat over my head. I took out my keys and opened the door and went up to my room. It was dark but the stairs were familiar. I had traversed them up and down so often I sometimes thought that I knew them better than I knew myself. I opened the door to my office. I seldom bothered to lock it. I had nothing to steal. Nevertheless, I was sure I had locked it on my departure. I was too slow, too tired. I was not yet alarmed.

I stepped through and switched on the light and saw the damage.

The desk was lying with its legs in the air like a corpse, its drawers open, their contents tossed out at random. The painting was torn off the wall. The books were scattered across the floor like the pearls off a broken necklace. Someone had taken a shit on the floor and used Ernst Jünger's *Fire and Blood* as toilet paper. The two visitor chairs were broken into pieces. For some reason my own chair was left standing, as though someone had calmly sat watching while the destruction was being wreaked. The phone was pulled off the wall and the typewriter lay on its back like a drunk.

I won't mention what they did with the hat rack.

I heard footsteps behind me but by then, of course, it was too late. They must have waited in the next room, my room, waiting for me to return. I began to turn but all I could see were shadows and then something smacked into the side of my head, near breaking my jaw, and I fell, the pain searing through me hot and bright. I tried to crawl away and for a moment they let me, just watching. My face was against the floor and the smell of piss was overwhelming. They had urinated on my effects and I would have killed them if I could.

A voice said, 'That's enough. Pick him up, boychiks.'

I tried to get away from them but they reached for me, two big men, one on either side, and lifted me up, as easily as if I were a doll. I dangled uselessly between them. 'Stay away from my daughter, you fucking anti-Semite.'

He wore an expensive black wool coat and a black fedora and his shoes were polished to within an inch of their lives. He had big hands and hairy knuckles and a single item of jewellery, a plain silver wedding ring. He was older than me and heavier and he was unshaved, not out of worry but because he didn't give a damn.

'Put him in the fucking chair.'

'Yes, Mr Rubinstein.'

They dropped me into my desk chair, not gently. My head

was throbbing and blood was gushing from the wound they had inflicted on me. One of them held a blackjack and it was stained with my blood.

'Who the fuck let you in?' I gasped.

'Watch your language. Moishe?'

The big brute on the left raised the blackjack and tapped me on the knee and I thought I would die from the pain.

'Yes, Mr Rubinstein.'

'Ready to be civil, now, Mr Wolf?'

'I'm sorry?' I said. 'I don't speak Yiddish.'

He sighed, now. 'Moishe . . .'

'Yes, Mr Rubinstein.'

This time I thought I was ready for the pain but I wasn't. He boxed me on the ear, nearly tearing it off. His hand came back covered in blood and he wiped it on my coat distastefully.

'You're Julius Rubinstein,' I said. 'The banker.' I spoke with difficulty. My lips found it hard to form words and my tongue felt sluggish

'I'll say it again, shamus. Stay the fuck away from my daughter.'

'Which . . . one?'

'Dovele?'

'Yes, Mr Rubinstein.'

The brute on the right picked me up, one-handed. Then he tossed me against the wall. I fell down on the pile of books, my cheek coming to rest on the big brown heap of shit they'd left for me there. It stung my eye. 'You . . . filthy animals,' I said. It came out as a moan.

'Pick him up.'

'Sir, he's got shit all over him.'

'I said pick him *up*!'

'Yes, Mr Rubinstein.'

94

They picked me up, grimacing, and deposited me back in the chair. I tried to wipe the excrement off my face but only managed to smear it around.

Rubinstein paced before me, his hands behind his back, as though delivering a lesson of the Torah to an errant yeshiva boy.

'My daughter,' he said, 'can be headstrong.' He turned to me abruptly, studied me with his pale eyes, then continued pacing restlessly. 'It is not easy having daughters. You never married, did you, Wolf?'

'No.'

'Wise, perhaps. You never had children?'

'No.'

He sighed. It was a long-suffering sigh. 'Daughters,' he said. 'They'll break your heart and laugh as they do it. Boys I can understand, boys know where their duties lie. But God never saw fit to give me boys.'

I kept my mouth shut. I had nothing to gain by antagonising him further. 'What did she want?' he said.

'Who?'

'My daughter.'

'Isabella.'

'Don't use her name, you piece of shit. You're not worthy of speaking her name.'

'She told me your other daughter went missing. She wanted me to find her.'

'Judith?'

'You have another one?'

'Moishe, please!'

'Yes, Mr Rubinstein.'

This time he slammed my head into the wall. I think I blacked out. When I opened my eyes again he was still there, silhouetted against the open door. I blinked, tasted blood. 'Don't give me lip,' Rubinstein said. It seemed redundant to reply so I didn't.

'Did she say why?'

'She told me . . .' I licked my lips. Moved my mouth but no sound came.'Dovele, give him a drink.'

'Yes, Mr Rubinstein.'

Dovele pulled out a hip flask and unscrewed it and put it to my lips. He forced my head back and forced me to drink. The alcohol hit me like an uppercut from Max Schmeling.

'*Scheisse!*' I said, when I could speak again.

'It's the good stuff,' Dovele said.

'I don't drink.'

'You do now.'

'Go to hell.'

Rubinstein smiled. 'This *is* hell,' he said. 'But this is your hell, not mine.'

'Where is your daughter?' I said.

'Which one?'

'The one I was hired to find.'

'That is not your concern. And Isabella should never have approached you. You will not see her again. I very much recommend that you don't try to either.'

None of it made much sense to me but then at that point I could barely make sense of my own face if I had a mirror. 'Did you pay to smuggle her out of Germany?'

'That is not your business.'

And yet he did not cease pacing, nor did he stop answering my questions. If I had to venture a guess at that point, I may have said I was looking at a very worried man.

And worried men are often angry.

'You don't know where she is, do you,' I said.

'Listen to me, *Wolf,* or whatever you call yourself these days—do you think I don't *know* you? You are nothing, you are less than nothing; you are the shit beneath my shoe.'

'Göring,' I said—throwing it out to him.

He stopped and stood stock-still. That was enough for me. 'You paid him to get her out of Germany, didn't you,' I said. 'But she never made it out the other end and now you're panicking.'

For a moment he looked murderous, then abruptly he subsided and shrugged. 'So you still have some contacts with your old comrades,' he said. 'You think they value you? One thing that can be said for Nazis, Wolf, they make shitty sen-timentalists.'

'One thing that can be said for Jews,' I said, 'is that . . . no, I've got nothing.'

Unexpectedly he laughed. 'You used to have plenty to say.'

'I can help you find her. If you let me go.'

'You?' He gestured at the room, the broken furniture, my broken face. 'You can't even help yourself, you schmuck.'

I had a moment of clarity, then. Perhaps it was the whiskey.

'You don't think they did it, do you? You don't think they did it because you work with them.'

Again he went still. This time, I had the feeling I was on thin ice. He was a man always in control, but it must have cost him, and inside he was coiled tight. The wrong pressure could set him off and then there'd be no telling what he'd do. 'How can you, a Jew, work with—'

'Nazis?' He laughed. 'Cock-sucking opportunists,' he said. 'That's all they are. Rats growing fat having jumped a drowning ship.'

He kept mixing his metaphors or perhaps it was the whiskey and what it was doing to me. I felt so drowsy, drowsy and warm. 'How much did you pay Göring?'

'Comrade Göring is a good communist now.'

It was hard to believe that fat Göring had once been a decorated flying ace: he often boasted of having shot down twenty-two Allied airplanes during the Great War. He had even been awarded an Iron Cross, First Class: but then I had one myself.

'You stay away from my daughter,' Rubinstein said again. He sounded less sure of himself, somehow.

'Whatever you say.' I was too tired to argue, and I sensed he didn't know any more than what he'd told me. It must have driven him mad, not knowing where his daughter was, what had happened to her. Did she lie dead even now in some Alpine fissure, or worse, was she even now being made to pleasure some rich old man in barbarous Egypt or Hindustan, another slave amongst many? Whatever he said I knew he didn't truly believe in Göring's innocence. You lie down with dogs and you're liable to get up with fleas, as my mother used to say.

Though I loved dogs.

'What did he say?'

'He mumbled something about dogs,' Dovele said.

'Huh.'

Rubinstein stopped pacing. He leaned towards me, putting his face close to mine. I could smell his expensive cologne. His voice was quiet and lethal like a stiletto. 'I want you to remember what I told you.'

I nodded, or at least my head fell on my chest. 'I'll remember . . .'

'You will,' he said. And then he smiled, and it was a smile that brought me suddenly wide awake. It was the coldest and meanest expression I had ever seen on a human being. 'Hold him, boychiks.'

'Yes, Mr. Rubinstein.'

'Let's do this.'

'Do what?' I said, but they ignored me. I tried to struggle against them but I was too weak.

'Take his trousers off.'

'What? Stop!'

I fought them. Panic gave me strength I thought lost.

They knocked me about and then they pulled down my trousers and my underpants and I was lying there with my trousers round my ankles and my private parts exposed.

'Cold, Wolf?'

His men obediently laughed. 'Pick him up, pick him up! We haven't got all day.'

They picked me up and righted the chair and sat me down again.

'Dovele, you hold him still. Moishe, spread his legs.'

'You fucking animals, you dirty fucking Jews—!'

'Put a sock in it.'

'Yes, Mr Rubinstein,' Moishe said, though it had been addressed to me. He took off my left shoe and peeled off my sock and scrunched it up into a ball and shoved it into my mouth. My teeth bit down on cheap cotton soaked in sweat and I gagged and almost choked. Dovele held my body secure while Moishe took hold of my legs.

'Don't fucking struggle,' he said. He sounded almost compassionate.

'Tie his legs to the chair.'

'With what?'

'God damn it,' Rubinstein said. 'Just hold him still, will you?'

Moishe slammed his fist into my face. I felt my legs go limp.

'Don't knock him out!'

They had me the way they wanted me. I was too weak to struggle, and the men were too strong. My legs were spread wide, my private parts exposed to Rubinstein's scrutiny. He leaned in, studied them dispassionately, like a scientist examining an insect. 'Thought you'd have a bigger dick,' he said, conversationally. 'Saw you in Munich, once, you know.' He mimed, his hand waving between his legs, near dragging on the floor. 'Thought you'd be swinging like a bloody elephant, almost, the way you carried on,' he said, and his men laughed.

I couldn't speak. I could barely breathe. I was hyperventilating, flooded with fear. He didn't rush, Rubinstein. He savoured the moment. Outside the window I thought I saw the first rays of dawn, but I could have been imagining it. It was so very quiet.

In the silence the flick of his knife was as loud as the strike of a clock.

•

In another time and place Shomer lies dreaming. He tosses and turns on the upper bunk he shares with two other men, an emaciated ginger-haired Jew from Slovenia and a short once-fat Transylvanian trader whose folds of skin flap like loose sails in the wind. All around him are the groans and snores and murmured cries of the other inmates, hundreds of men crammed into this block.

Shomer dreams of women. Big busty Austrian girls with breasts as white as cream, nipples like dark chocolate truffles, girls who smile with saucy eyes and press close against him, murmuring filthy words, enticing him to touch, to feel, to experience their inherent goodness. Shomer dreams of small dark Jewish girls with bright clear eyes, whose modest dresses hide their lithe bodies and wanton desire.

Shomer dreams of gypsy girls moving in the light of torches, sweat glistening on their skin, a dancing bear sitting forlornly with its back to a tree, chewing on bark. The girls dance and clash their cymbals and their dresses rise and give him a flash of ankle, even of thigh. Shomer dreams of Viennese housewives waiting for the milkman all alone with their husbands and children out of the house, dressed in nothing but a shift they wait by the door, touching themselves through the thin material. He dreams of posh English girls and society ladies, slowly unlacing their elaborate dresses to reveal sheer nakedness underneath. He dreams of the women held prisoner in the Joy Division, the camp's brothel explicitly prohibited to Jews, where the spoils of war wait every night for the other prisoners to come and rut with them like the animals they are. And out of nowhere comes the image of his wife Fanya, her small serious face and her dark eyes that could nevertheless twinkle so mischievously, and the smell of cholla bread fresh out of the oven and the sweet taste of kiddush wine and the candles burning on the windowsill and Avrom and Bina his children looking up to him as he breaks the bread and dips it in salt and passes it to them, on a Friday night dinner not that long ago. And he tosses and turns, fighting off the dream for he does not want to see their faces, does not want to hear the sound of their voices or their laugh, their baby smell, their love, and moreover and most of all he does not want to think of the day they had arrived here, in Auschwitz, and at the gates were parted, he to go one way, they the other, never to be seen again.

And all around him the men toss and turn and cry in their sleep ten to a row, dreaming of loved ones, and their dreams turn to ash in their mouths and they turn and they dream of food, masticating in their sleep, hollowly, that endless sound of hundreds of men all chewing food they would never chew again.

And Shomer is awake, his bladder pressing painfully, and so he climbs down cautiously from the bunk pushing and fighting his way and down to the ground and makes his way in the darkness of the block to the bucket, this big monstrous iron bucket full of piss, and he pulls down his prisoner's pyjamas and holds his penis in his hand and stares down at it in wonder, this alien appendage, unfamiliar and awful strange. He urinates painfully, and the piss slops off the rim of the bucket and he knows he has lost to-night's lottery, it is his lot to carry the bucket outside to be emptied, but something inside him almost welcomes the humiliation and pain. For a long moment more he stands there, listening to the camp and the sound of nightmares made literal and given voice. He shakes his penis sadly, with resignation, and folds it back into the uniform pants. At last he picks up the bucket and carries it with careful pained precision into the cold outside but the piss still slops onto his feet and soaks the bottom of his pants but at least he's no longer thinking of Fanya and the children and the night so full of ghosts; there is that at least.

●

'Hold him still, damn it!'

Wolf was struggling in the chair, his eyes bulging, the veins standing out on his forehead, pulsing with blood. He made strange, animal-like sounds.

Rubinstein knelt between Wolf's legs with his knife in his hand. Wolf's penis dangled uselessly, his stomach was knotted with revulsion and fear. Rubinstein grabbed Wolf's penis in his hand. Dovele looked on, impassive, as Moishe turned his head away, in disgust or sympathy it was impossible to tell. Wolf was screaming, screaming through the sock stuffed in his mouth, the sound muffled but no less terrified for all that. Rubinstein, almost gently, pulled on Wolf's cock, drawing forth Wolf's foreskin until it protruded beyond the tip like a monk's cowl. He pinched the foreskin, pulling it still, with Wolf shaking and shaking above him and the two men holding him down.

'Filthy thing,' Rubinstein said, dispassionately. He pulled, sharply, then with almost the same smooth easy movement, almost as though he had had plenty of practice, he brought the knife up to the penis and sliced neatly through the foreskin.

Wolf screamed.

On his knees before Wolf, Julius Rubinstein regarded the slice of human skin he held between his fingers.

'Huh,' he said.

'Mazel tov!' Dovele said. 'It's a boy!'

Still, for a long moment Rubinstein remained where he was, an almost puzzled expression, it seemed, clouding his face. He stared at Wolf's foreskin like a scientist confronted with evidence; but evidence of what, he didn't seem able to say. Slowly he raised his eyes, regarded Wolf's withdrawn and shrunken penis. At last, with an almost contemptuous gesture, he tossed the shred of foreskin to the floor and stood up. 'Who's the fucking Jew now,' he said.

He made a gesture with his head. His two men released their hold on Wolf and stepped aside. That head movement again, so slight as to be almost missed. Moishe kicked the legs of Wolf's chair as Dovele back-handed Wolf across the face. The chair collapsed and Wolf was sent sprawling on his back, his pants down, his newly-circumcised penis flopping sadly.

Rubinstein took two steps that brought him directly over Wolf. He looked down on him, like Moses looking down on the people from the heights of Mount Sinai.

'Stay the fuck away from my daughter,' he said. He pulled at his belt buckle. Untied himself. His member loomed above Wolf, dark and foreboding. Rubinstein was built like an ape.

'No, no,' Wolf tried to say. It came out muffled. Rubinstein grunted. A stream of hot piss burst forth from his member, hitting Wolf. It was in Wolf's hair, on his face, in his mouth soaking the gag until Wolf thought he would choke to death. Wolf moaned and tried to crawl away. No one said a word. It was silent in the room but for the hiss of urine. It seemed to go on and on. Wolf closed his eyes. For a moment it seemed to him it was his father standing above him, that this was just a repeat of the nightly ritual of childhood. Then Rubinstein grunted again and the stream trickled to a halt and Rubinstein buckled his belt. He bent down and, almost gently, pulled the sodden sock out of Wolf's mouth. 'Sweet dreams, sunshine,' he said—whispered. Then he kicked Wolf viciously in the ribs. Wolf screamed and this time the scream was not muffled.

'Let's go, boychiks.'

In moments, like silent shadows, they were gone; like they had never been. Wolf lay on the floor for a long time. The only sound in the room was the sound of his sobbing.

6

WOLF'S DIARY, 4TH NOVEMBER 1939

. . .

WOLF'S DIARY, 5TH NOVEMBER 1939

. . .

WOLF'S DIARY, 6TH NOVEMBER 1939

. . .

In my dream I was alone in the house upstairs.

It is a big old house, and when I was a boy I believed there were ghosts living in it. My mother said ghosts are mean old people who don't go away even after they die, and that is all there is to it. My father said, he served in the Great War and he'd seen no ghosts, but he had seen plenty of the dead. Like my father, I do not believe in ghosts.

In my dream I was alone in the house upstairs, and I could hear the floorboards creaking. It is an old house and it breathes as if it were alive, grunting and farting, but it is only the water in the pipes or the rats in the attic or the floorboards contracting and expanding with the weather. That's all there is to it.

In my dream I felt a great dark presence in the house. It stalked from room to room, but quietly, like a parent, and I hid in my room. It was coming close to my door and still I knew there was no one else in the house, and that I was truly alone. I called out, Father, Father, but he was not there. When I was born he had touched me with his calloused fingers and traced my face, so he could see me: God took his eyes in the Great War with gas. Let me look at you, let me look at you. I cried, No, and the presence at the door huffed and it puffed and I became so frightened that I cowered in the corner of my room with my hands over my head, and the floorboards creaked and creaked.

No one can see me, but it saw. In my dream I

looked through my pockets but the knife was not
there, and it is my only friend. At last I became
too frightened to cower and I went to open the
door and see the face of my tormentor, but there
was no one there, and the house was silent; there
was no one there at all.

On the Tuesday the telephone rang and this time Wolf picked it up. The
voice on the other end was cool and collected. 'Well?' she demanded.

'Miss Rubinstein.'

'Have you made progress?'

'I met your father.'

That gave her pause.

'Oh?'

'He is a violent man.'

Her voice changed, became soft and concerned and rushed.

'Did Daddy hurt you? What did he do to you?' Wolf didn't answer.

'Stay right there. I will come over.'

'I do not think that is a very good idea.'

The line went dead. Wolf stared at the receiver before placing it back.

He set to tidying the office. It would all have to go. After the assault he had
at long last dragged himself upright and tottered to his bedsit. The room was
relatively undisturbed but in the middle of the small bed there lay a human
shit. On Sunday Wolf's landlord, the baker Edelmann, came and knocked on
his door, but Wolf called him vile names and the baker withdrew.

The phone rang twice on Saturday and three times on Sunday and
had begun to ring at half-hourly intervals on Tuesday until Wolf finally
picked up.

After the call he dragged himself to the communal bathroom on
the landing. He shared it with an ageing prostitute named Martha, a

corpulent old crone who now made ends meet by selling seeds to feed the pigeons in Trafalgar Square. She had once confessed to Wolf that the seeds were poisoned. In her own small way Martha was a mass murderer, working in secret and without need for fame or acknowledgement of her deeds. She sold the seeds, the visitors to the capital fed the birds, and she watched them die with a sense of quiet achievement. 'One day,' she said to Wolf, 'there will be no more pigeons in London, then the world. Then at last we will all be free.' Wolf never knew what she had against the pigeons, which she seemed to view with the same hostility and suspicion as she did people who lived south of the river, immigrants, sailors, stone angels, moss and Wolf himself. He tended to avoid her after that.

He stared at his gaunt face in the mirror. Some of the bruises were fading. Others had turned a nasty shade of black and green. He shaved, though his hand shook from hunger and fatigue. Grey and black hairs stuck to the surface of the washbasin. He rinsed them off.

He washed himself. Scrubbed himself with soap. The water was lukewarm to begin with, then cold. He emerged shivering, dried himself and dressed awkwardly. He was still aching all over, and his cock burned. Wolf gritted his teeth and carried on. He went back to the room and put on his coat and his hat and then he went out.

WOLF'S DIARY, 7TH NOVEMBER 1939

Just a short hop to Gerrard Street. Down the stairs to the Hofgarten. The same dark atmosphere, the same brutish barman. Emil, I remembered Hess calling him.

'Herr Wolf.'

I ignored him. I saw Hess at a corner table. He was beginning to rise as I came to him. Without stopping I slammed my fist into his jaw. He fell back against the wall, surprise and blood mixing on his face. His bodyguards were rising, coming for me. I saw the flash of gunmetal.

'Wait.'

He shook his head and coughed. 'I would not do that again, Wolf, if I were you.'

'You set me up.'

'How?' He looked tired. He sat down again. 'Please, Wolf. Sit.'

'Who owns the club you sent me to?'

'Does it matter?' He shrugged.

'Who controls the trafficking?'

'Why do you care?' His anger surprised me. He looked at me wanly. 'Why do you care,' he said again. 'You're not involved. You didn't want to be. You could have led us.'

'To be like common criminals?' I barked a laugh.

'For the cause. For Germany.'

'Germany is lost, and you are a fool, Hess. Do not lie. Not to me.'

Old pain in his voice. 'Wolf . . .'

'You cheapen yourself and your race,' I said.

'Wolf! Enough!'

His open palm slammed on the table. Abruptly I sat down, opposite him. 'No more lies,' I said. 'Who works the trafficking network this end?'

'I tried to warn you,' he said. 'You didn't want to listen.'

'I heard you loud and clear.'

Thinking of that nameless club, the man Kramer with his face blown off, Ilse and her whip. 'Give me a name.'

'You should leave, now.'

Movement behind me. I stayed sitting down, looking straight. 'You sold yourself for thirty pieces of silver,' I said. 'Oh, Rudolf . . .'

'We are no longer your disciples!'

I stared into his eyes and saw nothing but craven greed there. Who was he so afraid of?

'Where do they operate? Give me a name!'

He sighed. 'Try Petticoat Lane,' he said. 'Ask for Barbie.'

I nodded. There was that movement again behind me. Hess's agonised face stared at me. 'Don't come back here again, Wolf,' he said. 'You put me in danger as well as yourself.'

'The Jew,' I said, in hatred. 'Rubinstein. You work with Jews now, Hess?'

'This is out of my hands, Wolf. I've given you all I can.'

'How much did he pay you to bring his daughter out of Germany?'

'Wolf!' He rubbed a weary hand over his face. 'This is bigger than me, bigger than all of us. Don't go poking your nose into business that doesn't concern you.'

'But it does concern me, Hess. It concerns me very much,' I said. My groin burned with a pain I could barely keep under control. 'What happened to her?' I said. 'What happened to the daughter?'

'I am sure I don't know what you're talking about,' he said. 'Now go. We shall not see each other again.'

He motioned with his head and the big barman, Emil, loomed behind me. I nodded, ceding his warning—or perhaps it was a premonition.

I stood up. 'I'll leave on my own,' I said. Emil's ugly mug of a face stared at me without expression.

'Very good, Herr Wolf,' he said.

Wolf left the Hofgarten, his shoulder blades tense, half-expecting a cosh to the back of the head, a knife between the ribs. Nothing happened. Hess had always been a follower, not a leader.

So who was he trying to protect?

Or perhaps more cynically he was wringing his hands and protesting, all the while steering Wolf in the direction he wanted him to go. You could trust Hess to be untrustworthy, Wolf thought. You always knew where you were with an ex-Nazi.

He had no intention of staying off the case; not for Hess's warnings, not for that murderous Jew gangster Julius Rubinstein and his assault. For did not the Jewish Bible itself say, 'a man who inflicts an injury upon his fellow man, so shall be done to him: fracture for fracture, eye for eye, tooth for tooth. Just as he inflicted an injury upon a person, so shall it be inflicted upon him.'

His thoughts were murderous as he hopped on a bus going to the East End. The advert running along the side of the bus proudly proclaimed that Swan Vestas Were The Smoker's Match. Wolf sat towards the back, sandwiched between the window and an elderly woman carrying a woven basket filled with something that stank: rotten fish or something even more vile. She was talking all the time, mumbling with a soft, emaciated mouth. 'Bloody foreigners, coming over here, taking our jobs, taking our homes, pissing in the streets don't they, the filthy buggers, selling their women cheap, the dirty whores, and their thieving children, a woman isn't safe any more, not anywhere—' She clutched the basket to her chest as if afraid Wolf was going to steal it. 'Nasty buggers the lot of them, things like this would never have gone on in my grandmother's time, we had proper law and order then didn't we, not let any Tom, Dick and Kraut into the country, if it was up to me I'd gas the lot of them I would, put them in camps and gas them or chuck them in the sea.'

'Jews?' Wolf said, interested despite himself.

'Germans,' the woman said, and gave him a nasty, beaming toothless grin.

'Disgusting old witch.'

'Witch! Did you hear what he called me!' the woman shouted. Heads turned, then turned away. No one wanted to be too close to that smell. 'Witch! You people make me sick, you do! That Mosley fellow has the right idea, you just wait, coming over here, taking our jobs, pissing everywhere, bums! Bums!' and off she went again, in a repeating cycle, while Wolf stared out of the window and breathed through his mouth and tried to ignore her.

Was that what Mosley was doing? he thought, uneasy. Mosley was right. He could not shift blame to the Jews in England, not easily. But was he really cultivating European immigrants as a whole to take the brunt of the British's hatred? There were Jews amongst the refugees from the Fall of Germany, but there were also honest, respectable men and women, good Germans!

He was relieved to escape the bus at last, when it stopped outside Liverpool Street Station. The fresh air revived him, and it was raining in a thin drizzle that stung his face but brought with it relief for his bruises, if not for the fire in his groin where the bastard Jew had circumcised him. He went past bagel shops and pickle vats taller than a man, past black-clad children playing with stones and chalk, and yeshiva boys congregating in murmured conversations, past women with their shopping bags laden with food, apron-clad butchers with naked turkey birds displayed in their windows, fishmongers calling out in Polish and Yiddish, shoemakers and cloth merchants and fences and thieves, and amidst this population of Jewish Londoners the new arrivals, gentiles like Wolf, the refugees of Germany and Austria and of a once-bright dream that had burned to cinder and ashes. He made his way through the narrow crammed streets and pulled his hat low against his forehead.

He'd first met Jews in large numbers while living in Vienna. In his first few, heady weeks in the city he hardly noticed them. The Jews were a minority, after all, and at the time Vienna was, to the young Wolf, the very centre of the world. There amidst the politicians and artists, rabble-rousers and architects and operagoers and poor young students not unlike himself,

Wolf barely cared about Jews. One day walking down the street he saw one of their number in the black Hasidic garb and he was plain bemused: was this a Jew?

And yet the longer he resided in that city the more he saw them; wherever he turned, like an alien entity forever embedded in the Germanic population; and more than that he thought them dirty; their very odour made him sick.

Besides all of which, the Jews were everywhere; manipulating all behind the scenes; and no doubt they were the reason he had been rejected from the Academy of Fine Arts, to boot—was it a wonder that he hated them?

He had begun to perceive the great conspiracy behind all things; perhaps even then, so early, he knew it was his destiny to fight it; and yet in the final tally, he had lost. The Fall had made a mockery of Wolf. Imagine only if he had succeeded; if Germany was his, its military and its citizens, to wield as he saw fit: what would have happened to the Jewish people, then?

But Wolf had given up what-ifs long ago. And so he made his way amongst the throng of Jews in this alien city, the way he had once walked through the Jewish ghettos of Vienna; and the same hostile alien faces stared back at him. He came to a fishmonger and stopped and said, 'I am looking for a man named Barbie.'

The man pursed his lips and shook his head and Wolf moved on. He came to Petticoat Lane where all the Jewish cloth merchants congregated at one end. It tapered slowly towards vegetables and fruit, fish, crockery and badly made toys, and various and sundry merchandise which had happened to fall off the back of carts only to wind up here.

'Barbie. I am looking for Barbie.'

More heads shaking, lips pursing, Jews cursing: the name resonated but no one wanted to talk. He was almost on the Whitechapel Road where the market became more unruly and the wares more decrepit and less legitimate and for a moment he stopped and admired a gold watch.

'Palestine for the Jews!' The man was wild-haired and wild-eyed, swarthy and thin, and he was holding an armful of pamphlets and offering them like a priest offering the flesh and blood of Christ. 'Palestine for the Jews, comrade! Take one!'

Without having time to reply the man shoved a grubby pamphlet into Wolf's hands and moved on. 'Respect the Balfour Declaration! A homeland for the Jews!'

Wolf stared after him thoughtfully, his eyes cold. He looked at the pamphlet. The cover showed healthy-looking men and women, the men in khaki work clothes, the women in white dresses, against the background of a clear blue sea and distant mountains. Orange trees grew around them and a group of laughing, happy children stood in a circle, holding hands. Some sort of electric train, brightly coloured, vanished into the distance and high overhead, above the blue-chalked mountains in the distance, there hovered a bad artist's impression of an airship. *The Old-New Land*, the cover said, *by Theodor Herzl*.

Wolf crumpled the pamphlet into a ball and dropped it on the ground.

'You a Jew?'

Wolf turned again. The gold watch he had been admiring lay on a none-too-clean blanket on which sat various items pilfered who knew where. There were watches and rings, bracelets and necklaces, silver- and gold- and pearl-handled letter-openers and their like. The man was squatting behind his wares, on the ground. The look he gave Wolf was neither hostile nor friendly; it just was.

'Do I look like a fucking Jew,' Wolf said.

'Can't say as I could tell, mate.'

The man was speaking German. He spat on the ground. 'Jews,' he said. 'Don't mind them, myself. Sure got a lot of them around, though.'

Wolf nodded.

'Live and let live,' the man said. 'I come from Dortmund, myself. Got in trouble with the commies, had to make a run for it, didn't I.'

'Political?'

'Nah. Got caught with some things what didn't belong to me. You?'

Wolf shrugged, vaguely. 'You know how it is.'

The man nodded. 'Times are hard for everyone,' he said. 'You want to buy that watch?'

'I'm looking for a man. Name of Barbie?'

'Oh, you mean Santa Claus?' the man said.

'Excuse me?'

The man grinned, a little sheepishly. 'It's what they call him, around here, the English. The Jews don't like him much.'

Understanding dawned. 'His name is Klaus?'

'*Ja*, Klaus. You can find him down that end.' He gestured towards where the market met the Whitechapel Road. Kept his voice low. 'Deals in this and that, if you know what I mean.'

Wolf threw the man a shilling. The man caught it deftly and made it disappear. 'Cocky looking devil, if you know what I mean,' the man said. 'You can find him in the bicycle shop down there. Can't miss it.'

'Thanks.'

'Go in peace, my friend. By the way–' the man jerked his head sideways, 'did you know you're being followed?'

Wolf didn't turn to look. 'How many?' he said. 'Two.'

Wolf nodded. 'Black suits?'

'Sure. Friends of yours?'

Wolf shrugged. 'Who isn't,' he said. The man smiled back but he didn't look convinced. Wolf walked on.

The bicycle shop was indeed there. The window was dark and dusty and the bikes seemed to have been sitting there for at least twenty years. A faded poster on the wall showed a young black boy riding a bike while being chased by a lion. *Raleigh: The All-Steel Bicycle*, the poster proclaimed. Wolf pushed the door open and went inside. It was dark and dusty and smelled of aniseed. There was a wireless on the counter, tuned to Radio Luxembourg, playing the *Horlicks Tea Time Hour*, which changed into a spirited advert for Brown and Polson's custard powder as the door clanged shut.

'Waiting for the racing news, see.' Two men stood in the gloomy interior leaning against the counter. One was tall; one was short. Both had pencil stubs behind their ears. Both turned as Wolf came in. They regarded him with puzzled curiosity. 'Who's your money on?' the tall one said.

Wolf said, 'Me.'

The tall one laughed, dutifully. The short one scowled. 'Everyone's a clown,' he said.

'Maybe he's a copper.'

The short one scratched his head. 'You a copper?' he said.

'No.'

'Didn't think so, mate. Didn't think so.'

'Well what does he want?'

'Yeah, what do you want?'

'Is this a betting shop?' Wolf said.

'Is this a betting shop, he says,' complained the tall one. 'Well, what does this look like to you, friend?'

'Maybe he's in the wrong place,' said the short one. 'Are you in the wrong place, mate?'

'I'm always in the wrong place,' Wolf said.

'He's a smartarse isn't he,' the tall one said.

'German, isn't he.'

'Austrian,' Wolf said, stiffly.

The tall one waved a hand vaguely. 'All the same,' he said. On the radio a woman was trying to convince them of the benefits of Life-buoy Soap— *More than a Good Soap, it's a Good Habit!*

'I only got bad habits, me,' the short one said. 'So what do you want, kraut?'

'I'm looking for a man called Barbie. Klaus Barbie.'

'Oh, *him*.'

'Santa Claus, eh?'

'You know him?'

'Sure we know him. But does he know you?'

Wolf saw a shadow move on the other side of the counter. And he was ready when the short man pulled out a nasty looking shiv and made a lunge at Wolf. Wolf grabbed his hand and twisted, breaking the small bones of the fingers with vicious pleasure. The man screamed. The knife clattered to the floor. Wolf kneed him between the legs and kicked him when he was down. He felt much better now. The tall man watched them mournfully. 'Everyone's a clown,' he said. 'Come on.' He knelt and tugged at his friend, who cried with a soft whistling sound.

Wolf came round and helped him drag the man outside. At the door he stood and watched them both, the tall one and the short. The tall one pulled out a note from his pocket. 'Put a tenner on Bogskar for us, will you?' he said.

Wolf took the money and they walked off, the one tall, the other limping and hunched. On the corner of Petticoat Lane and Whitechapel, Wolf saw a man in a black suit he thought he recognised. The man raised his hand and smiled in apparent greeting. He had very even, white teeth; like an American's. Wolf went back inside and shut the door.

'You Barbie?'

The man was good-looking with sharp Aryan features and a cruel sensuous mouth. He leaned on the counter. His sleeves were rolled up. He said, 'You're not good for business.'

'You know who I am?'

'I know who you were.'

Wolf had to hand it to him: the man was cool. He said, 'I hear you can get things.'

'What sort of things.'

'Girls,' Wolf said. Barbie shrugged. 'Sure,' he said. 'Plenty of girls all about.'

'Young girls.'

Barbie looked at Wolf. His eyes were clear and he didn't blink much. 'Never had you pegged for one of those.'

'What did you have me pegged for?'

Barbie shrugged. 'What do I know,' he said.

'Sell many bicycles?'

That made him smile. 'Sometimes,' he said. 'You'd be surprised.'

'Who owns the betting book?'

'A man.'

'Has he got a name?'

'Sure,' Barbie said. 'Everybody's gotta name.'

'Do I know his name?'

'If you did, you wouldn't be asking, now, would you?'

Wolf didn't like the man's attitude. 'So what can you get me?'

'It depends. You got money?'

Wolf took out a roll of notes. 'I don't suppose you'd take a cheque.'

Again the man smiled. 'I don't suppose you're wrong, at that,' he said.

'I'm looking for a Jewish girl.'

'Jews,' Barbie said. 'The world's got too many damn Jews in it.'

'And Jewish girls?'

'Sure. Girls, boys . . . whatever you like.'

'This one would have been out of Germany a few weeks ago,' Wolf said. 'Family paid to have her delivered safely. She never made it.'

'All families pay,' Barbie said, and shrugged. 'Who cares if a Jew goes missing.'

'I care.'

'You want to fuck her? I can get you a Jew girl to fuck six ways from Sunday.'

'I want this girl.' Wolf took out the photograph Isabella had given him. Laid it flat on the countertop. 'Know her?'

Barbie was still looking at Wolf. 'Don't seem familiar,' he said.

'You're not looking.'

'I've seen all I need to see.'

'Look at her,' Wolf said. The man was staring at him. 'I said, *look at her.*'

Barbie looked down. Wolf grabbed Barbie's head and slammed it against the countertop. There was the *crunch* of breaking bone. Wolf lifted Barbie's head and slammed it down again, and again, until the man's face was a mess of blood and snot and the photo of the girl was unrecognisable with blood. At last Wolf released him and Barbie slid slowly down to the floor. Wolf went and opened the hatch in the counter and passed to the other side. He pulled up a chair and sat down.

'You're just a fucking follower,' he said, though Barbie couldn't hear him. Wolf looked through the man's clothes. He found a set of keys and a little black book. He opened the book. It was full of lists, numbers in an ascending serial order and amounts next to each one. 'You supply them,' Wolf said. 'Clubs like the one on Leather Lane, or men who come to you wanting something special, little girls, little boys. But you're still only a middleman. You're a nobody.' He straightened up and then kicked Barbie hard in the ribs. There was something thoroughly satisfying about the sound of breaking bones. Barbie didn't make a sound. Wolf rather expected that he would choke on the blood. Eventually. He kicked him in the head just for good measure and then went to the back of the store. There was a safe and one of the keys opened it. Inside was a fat brown envelope. Wolf took it out and put it in his coat pocket and closed and locked the safe again. There was a door and it too was locked. He tried the keys until one worked. He opened the door and saw steps leading down to a basement. He had a sense of déjà vu. He switched the light on and went downstairs.

There were no cells this time, no mattresses, nothing of the luxury afforded the slaves at the club. There, consideration was made for the clients. Here it was just the holding pens.

It must have been a warehouse, once. The door was securely locked but there was a grille and he could look through it. Inside the large room there were some sixty to a hundred women. They wore nothing but undergarments. They were crammed into the space. The place smelled: of unwashed bodies and piss and shit. The women stared up at him with eyes as dull as cattle. The light was dim inside. He saw that they had been tattooed, a blue number, a serial corresponding, he assumed, to the numbers in Barbie's little black book.

'Hey, you,' he said. Some of them turned to look at him. 'I am looking for Judith Rubinstein. Is there a Judith Rubinstein here?' A slim black-haired girl roused herself from a pallet. 'I'm Judith,' she said. She approached him cautiously, like a wounded animal. Wolf squinted at her. Could it be that easy? He tried to compare her to the photograph. The girl in the photograph had been healthy, happy. This one was just a number. He didn't know.

'Come closer,' he said. 'Let me take a look at you.'

The girl shook her head, this way and that. She looked unsure of where she was, now that she had spoken.

A blonde girl stood up. 'I'm Judith,' she said.

'I'm Judith—' from an old grandmother.

'Take me, mister, I'll be your Judith!'

'Does she fuck you like I would? Does she take it in the ass?' One of them was yelling curses in Yiddish. Another tried to shush her, fearfully. Wolf rapped on the bars. Immediately all the girls fell silent.

'You,' he said, pointing at the first one. 'Come here.'

'I didn't do nothing, mister.'

'Come here.'

The girl was shaking. 'Don't make me, don't make me,' she said.

'I said come here!'

The other girls were pushing her. 'You have to go, otherwise he will come back—' Wolf assumed they were talking about Barbie. He could imagine how Barbie liked to amuse himself, when business upstairs was quiet. He said, 'I won't hurt you. I just want to ask you a question.'

The girl stumbled forward, pushed from behind. Her face was pressed to the bars of her prison. Her hair was dirty and lank, Wolf saw, her face pale and drawn. She had a dark bruise under one eye. He said, 'Did you know Judith Rubinstein?'

'She's not here, mister. Honest.'

'Do you know where she is?'

The girl lowered her voice. 'If you let me out, my father is a rich man, he could pay you, whatever you asked. Just let me go.'

'Who is your father?'

The girl said a name. Wolf shrugged. The affairs of Jews did not interest him. 'Tell me about Judith.'

'We went to school together in Berlin.'

'Before the Fall?'

'Before, during.' The girl shrugged. 'Her daddy wanted to leave. So did my daddy but he couldn't get us out. And the Party confiscated everything he had. We were poor.'

At least she was being honest now, Wolf thought. 'And Judith?'

'She wouldn't leave. She wanted to be a revolutionary.' The girl laughed. It was a terrible sound, in that room. 'The stupid cow,' she said.

'But you were still friends.'

'Sure. And she still had money. Her daddy kept her safe. He had contacts, people high up. I joined the Party too. We all did. We had to, after the Fall. I remember once our Youth Group was sent to Unter den Linden, some squat hellhole in a crumbling old building that used to be a nice hotel. It was full of Brownshirts, you know, ex-Nazi boys. They'd formed into gangs after the Fall, ran wild, robbed and killed to stay alive. We went to school with some of them.' There was a bitter sort of wonder in the girl's voice. 'They had a man on watch but he was only one and the rest of them were asleep. Judith was scout. She went up to the watchman as quiet as a *fledermaus*. He never saw a thing. Didn't even see her when she pulled out her knife and cut his throat. We went inside then and killed them.

121

Every single one of them boys lying there asleep. We shot them, just went through twenty, thirty boys it must have been, a bullet in the head, in the chest, some of them woke up and tried to flee but how do you outrun a bullet?' She stared at Wolf through the bars and her eyes—he didn't want to look into her eyes. 'Yes, Judith was dedicated,' she said. 'The rest of us just went along with it but she did it for herself. I never wanted to kill nobody.'

Wolf was aware of the pressure of time, but it was so quiet down there, and all the girls were silent, listening. Perhaps they all had the same story. 'What happened to Judith?' Wolf said.

'She fell in love.' The girl laughed again. This time her laughter rose and threatened to escalate out of control. Wolf tapped the bars again and she stopped, as abruptly as she'd started. 'She fell in love with a nice Jewish boy.'

'A Zionist?'

'I don't even think that he was, that's the funny thing. He was a good comrade, even. Worked at the Ministry of Public Enlightenment.'

'So what happened?'

The girl shrugged. 'He got shot. Everyone said it was Brownshirts who did it, but how many were left by then? Judith was convinced it was an execution. Someone at the Ministry, or a different branch of the Party. She said that even the communists hated Jews. She started talking about Palestine, as if anyone would ever want to go to Palestine. I heard there's nothing there but camels and desert. I wouldn't want to go there. I wanted to go to America. I wanted to be a movie star.'

All the girls were quiet. Wolf waited. The girl said, 'She got her daddy to pay a smuggler to take her out of the country. She told me and I begged her to let me come. She couldn't get the money from her daddy, he said he wasn't a charity. But she took me anyway. Everyone knows the smugglers are Brownshirts, what's left of them. Ex-Nazis. The organisation is still there, only instead of killing people for politics they do it for money. On the border the man who took us made me go on my knees and he put his cock in my mouth. Judith was asleep in the next room, she didn't even know. He said I'd have to work off the debt. When we crossed the border they took all of our papers and drove us in a closed truck with a lot of other people. I thought we would die; we had no air. We drove for hours and hours. Then we were on a boat. We only stopped once, when we came off the boat. I remember smelling the ocean. I think we were in England by then but I can't be sure. A man came and we all got out and lined up in rows and he went and checked each of us against a list. Some of us went away. Some of us went back in the truck. I went in the truck. Judith went away. The truck drove for another long time and then we came here.'

'You don't know where she went?'

'She went to her daddy.'

'I don't think she did.'

'Then I'm sure I don't know.'

Wolf stared at the girl. The case was becoming bewildering—if Judith had been paid for and delivered, then where was she? And if she had been added to the tally of the lost, then why wasn't she here? Had she already been resold? He said, 'That will be all.'

'Don't you want to know my name? My name!' She was close to tears. 'This is my number,' she said. She raised her arm. He could see a number tattooed on her wrist. 'They did that here. He did that here. Do you want to know my name?'

'No,' Wolf said. 'But you can have the God damned keys.'

He tossed them to her, through the bars, and turned away. There was silence behind him. He climbed up the stairs again and stood looking down at the girls' jailer. The man groaned and tried to crawl away. Wolf smiled. He didn't care what happened to the girls but he liked the thought of them coming up the stairs and finding themselves face to face with Klaus Barbie. What was left of his face, anyway.

'Have fun, sweetheart,' he said. He went back through the hatch and closed it neatly behind him and then he left the shop and closed the door softly, so as not to disturb the neighbours.

When I stepped outside the air was cold and the sun was gone. Barbie was a lapdog, a man of no consequence. I left him the way I had as a message to his unseen employer. I rather thought that would get his attention. Somebody ruthless and meticulously organised was behind the trafficking ring, someone I could not help but feel a touch of admiration for. I admired efficiency. And I wondered which of my old comrades it could be.

I began to walk down Whitechapel Road. Soon I had the feeling of being followed again. I stopped. It seemed to me two shadows moved in the distance but it was hard to tell with the bad illumination of the streetlights. I had had enough of shadows, then. My anger and hatred were all the illumination I needed. I faced up to the dark, defiantly. I raised my arms, daring them to come. 'I'm here!' I screamed. 'Come and get it if you think you're tough enough!'

The darkness did not reply and after a moment I dropped my arms and continued walking, feeling deflated. They were out there, nearby, and they were watching, but that was all. Well, let them watch.

I was walking aimlessly. The brown envelope I had taken from Barbie's safe was heavy in my coat pocket. When I came to London Wall I stood there for a moment admiring the ancient Roman architecture. Had I still been painting I would have wanted an easel and brush at that moment. The dying light cast a gloom over the ancient stones and I thought of all that had come before, and of the Greek and Roman emperors I had so admired. Sometimes it occurred to me I had been born into the wrong era. I was Alexander, without a world to conquer.

I was sunk in melancholy thought. Architecture affects me

that way. Too late I heard the soft purr of a car behind me. I turned. It was a black Mercedes-Benz without headlights. It was a marvel of German engineering.

Behind the car came dark shadows: my two men in black.

They came and stood before me. I recognised one as the man from the Charing Cross Road, the one who had claimed to be an American tourist.

'Mr Wolf.'

'Do I know you,' I said.

The American smiled, a little embarrassed, with those even white teeth. 'We ran into each other the other day.'

'That's right,' I said. 'Were you trying to make sure that I saw you, or were you just being sloppy?'

'He was being sloppy. He's since been disciplined.'

The voice that spoke was older, graver. I turned. A rear window had been rolled down. For a moment a stray beam of light caught the speaker's face. He had a well-maintained beard, black woven with a tapestry of white and silver. His eyes were clear and strangely innocent, like a child's. He had a hook nose and a scar under one eye that trailed down like a long tear and finally disappeared under his beard.

'Who the hell are you?' I said.

'You can call me Virgil,' he said.

'Like the poet?'

'If you like.'

'I don't think that I do.'

'Mr Wolf, I mean you no harm.'

'Then why are you following me?'

'Because I have a great interest in the well-being of Germany, Mr Wolf. Please. Let me give you a ride.'

'I'd rather walk.'

The two men took a step forward each. I stood my ground. 'Who do you work for?' I said.

Virgil said, 'The President of the United States of America,' and I laughed. 'America is a racial cesspit,' I said. 'It is a land fit only for dogs and Jews.'

One of the men in black made to move towards me then but his companion grabbed him by the arm. 'Stand back, Pitt.'

I glanced again at the man in the car, this Virgil. 'I can smell spooks a mile off,' I said. 'You give off a special smell, the stench of rats.'

He laughed. He had a rich, deep laugh, the sort a man makes when he thinks how easy it would be to kill you. 'Get in the car, Wolf.' He moved down the seat, his face disappearing from view. 'Pitt, open the door for Mr Wolf.'

'Sir, yes, sir.'

The one called Pitt went and opened the door like a servant. There was resentment in his eyes. I went up to the car. I put my hand on Pitt's shoulder, gently. My other hand reached down and grabbed his balls and squeezed. 'Next time I see you, sunshine,' I said, 'it won't be just your balls you'd need to worry about.'

His companion laughed and made no move to help him. I released Pitt and watched him sink to the ground, his hands covering his testicles. There were tears in his eyes but he never made a sound. It made me feel I may have been wrong about him.

I got into the car. Waited with the door open until the second man came over and closed it. I smiled at him through the rolled-down window. 'Look after your girlfriend for me,' I said.

'Let's go,' Virgil said, beside me. The driver in the front of the car was a shadow in a black peaked cap. He pressed on the accelerator and the car pushed forward as soft as a thief in the night. He was a big man, Virgil, spread out against the seat. He looked like an old tomcat, one who was brought up in the streets and took his punches, but seldom lost a fight.

'Mr Wolf.'

'Virgil.'

He smiled. We were heading south. I could smell the river. The old Roman wall was left behind. The Tower of London lay ahead, with its lame ravens. They reminded me of the soldiers who had returned home broken from the Great War.

'I'd like your opinion of the current situation in Austro-Germany,' Virgil said.

I looked out of the window. 'And what is the American interest in the region?' I said, politely.

'Do you always answer a question with a question?' he laughed. 'You answer questions like a Jew,' he said.

'Are you trying to insult me?'

'Just making conversation.'

'You didn't answer my question,' I said.

He sighed. 'Mr Wolf,' he said. 'My government is *acutely* concerned over the rise of communism in Germany and its neighbours. The German government may pretend it is independent, but you and I both know the decisions come from Moscow.'

'Yes.'

'What is your take on it?'

'I believe war is coming,' I said. He was silent beside me. I knew that I had his attention, then. 'I believe Russia is building up to drastically alter the map of Europe, and beyond. Its neighbours are already under threat. The purpose of communism is nothing less than world domination. A global revolution. They will not sit on their laurels having won the German election. Once communism takes hold it never relinquishes power.'

'A world war,' Virgil said.

'Yes.'

'That is something my government is acutely concerned about.'

'So you said.'

'How would one go about . . . *counteracting* the communists in Germany?' he said.

I turned and looked at him. That coarse face, his hands folded in his lap. He had enormous hands. 'Who, *exactly*, do you work for?' I said, softly.

He chuckled, not in the least put out. 'Just a group of concerned citizens,' he said.

'Intelligence? Sig Int? MI-8? The Treasury Department?'

He chuckled again. 'Your sources are outdated,' he said. 'Let us say concern over a possible second war with Germany has suggested to us some form of consolidation of departments was in order. I work for the Office of Strategic Services. The OSS. Our main concern lies in the former German Republic. A second war in Europe could be disastrous for all concerned. But we cannot allow international Bolshevism to raise its ugly head! No, sir!' His enormous fist punched his enormous palm. 'Mr Wolf,' he said, turning his head and looking into my eyes, 'how would you like to work for *us*?'

We were driving along the river, now. I saw the Tower sinking behind us, and I wondered where we were going. East along the river, east to—where? The docks?

'Am I being kidnapped?'

'Mr. Wolf! Please! We are not *communists*.'

'Then where are we going?'

'I wish to show you something,' he said. 'You are free to leave at any moment. Just say the word.'

'Then stop the car.'

'Bernie, stop the car.'

The car slowed, then stopped. We were somewhere past Tower Bridge. It was dark and quiet. 'Bernie, open Mr Wolf's door, please.'

The driver, still only a featureless shadow, slid out of his seat and came round the car and held the door open for me. The cool air rushed inside and I could hear the cry of seagulls in the distance.

'Well, Mr Wolf?'

I stared out at the quiet street. Turned back and looked at Virgil. He smiled at me. His teeth were large and square like an ogre's.

I gave a tiny nod of assent.

'Start the car, Bernie,' Virgil said. 'We haven't got all night, now, have we.'

The driver shut my door softly and went back to his seat and started the car up again.

'Work for you,' I said, 'work for the United States of *America*?'

'It's the greatest country in the whole God damned world,' Virgil said, complacently.

•

In another time and place Shomer stands naked in the snow, clutching his bleeding leg. It was all Mischek's fault, Mischek the dirty little Russian Jew, the commissar of the latrines. He has an in with the Salonician Jews, those hardened gangsters of the camp: three years those bastards are inside and still alive, their blue tattooed numbers like badges of honour, the low numbers that shame all the others, the latecomers. But it wasn't the Greeks' fault, those black market traders in bread rations and spoons and gold teeth. It was Mischek's, or it was Shomer's own, who was digging in the hard ground, digging when he stumbled and fell and Mischek's spade came down and an ugly bleeding gash opened in Shomer's leg, and the overseer barked an order and work was halted, momentarily; and the others, he knew, were grateful for the respite: whether Shomer lived or died he had bought them a few moments' rest.

Shomer was clutching his wounded leg and biting his lip to keep from uttering curses and for a moment Yenkl's figure, always beside him, grew faded, like clouds or ash, as if he weren't there. And Shomer waited as the overseer studied him, assessing the severity of the wound, assessing this skeletal human shape with its loose skin and sunken eyes, receding hair, receding gums, sores on the feet and lice everywhere else. Assessing him to decide if he is worth conserving, or whether it is cheaper and easier to dispose of him now.

'Go to the infirmary,' the overseer said, at last.

So simple, those words! And yet Shomer gets to live another day. Now he stands naked in the snow, for his old clothes are not allowed in the infirmary block, and only his feet are still crammed into the ill-fitting wooden clogs, until the very last moment he keeps them on, and the queue moves, so slowly, one by one they disappear into the lighted door. He shivers and holds his wound, triumphant. The infirmary! It is like Heaven, spoken of in hushed voices, a place of rest and heavenly comfort, like reclining on clouds. And Yenkl is beside him, how has he ever doubted his friend, Yenkl, who says, 'You call this a wound? When I was a kid, we had *wounds.*' And Yenkl is in full flight and the queue shuffles slowly and the snow starts to fall and Shomer hugs his bony naked arms around his hollow chest and shudders and so Yenkl tells him a joke.

'This one time in Poland,' Yenkl says, 'the people of the shtetl discovered that a Christian girl had been found murdered nearby. Murdered, Shomer! How afraid they were. Oh what will we *do*? they said. Oh what will the goyishe Poles *think*? Surely soon they will come for our blood, oy but we are doomed, surely a pogrom is coming and we will all die!'

Shomer nods and shuffles forward, staring at the square of light, the pearly gates into the infirmary of Heaven.

'The Jews,' says Yenkl, 'have gathered as is their wont in the shtetl's main synagogue, with much wringing of hands and gnashing of teeth. "What shall we do? What shall we do?" Suddenly, the president of the synagogue bursts in through the doors. "I have wonderful news!" he cries. All talk ceases. All eyes turn on him.

"The murdered girl, she's *Jewish*!" the president says.'

Shomer laughs, dutifully. He shuffles forward and at last enters the hut, leaving his clogs behind, standing there as naked as the day God had made him, though far less fat, it must be said. Inside the queue continues, to see the doctor, but it is also warmer, and there is only one bored Polish guard, and so Shomer's mind wanders yet again, and it is drawn inexorably to murder most foul, that hoary old staple of the pulps and of *shund*.

7

The watcher in the dark watched; only watched. He had seen the detective
leave his building for the first time in days but he elected not to follow him.
The detective wasn't going anywhere. The watcher eyed the girls and it was
as if his cloak of invisibility was somewhat worn for he thought they seemed
more nervous now, more brightly brittle, casting their eyes into the shadows
as though searching for the mystery man there. But still they could not see
him; no one ever could. He eyed the half-caste, Dominique. Those long
brown legs bare in the cold, that saucy smile, the eyes that promised much,
the muscled arms . . . she was not like the other girls, she was more dominant somehow, and the men who came for her were different, more affluent
and when she went with them she took a small bag of her accessories and,
once, the bag had opened and the watcher saw the contents inside, though
he could barely comprehend their meaning, a coiled whip and a black thick
object, long and rubbery, which the watcher thought must be a *godemiche*,
that is to say, a dildo. And there were other things there, but he had caught
only a fleeting glimpse and then she had shut the case and climbed into the
john's car; and was gone. But the memory of it kept the watcher awake at

night and when he slept he dreamed of a woman perfumed like a whore who lashed him with a whip, lashed him until he shuddered and came.

In the mornings before going to work he made his father breakfast and hung the bib round the old man's neck and fed him, and listened to the old man tell him stories of the War. The old man listened to the wireless for hours, and cursed Mosley for a weakling and a fool, and spoke of the bravery of the German soldiers he had had to fight in the Great War. After the watcher cleaned up he left the old man listening to the BBC and went to work, which was soothing to him and involved paperwork. It was only when his work was done for the day and darkness descended, and before he had to return to make supper and help the old man wash, that he went to visit the whores, and dream, and plan; and the knife was in his pocket always, and whispering to him, curses and promises, and the watcher knew that he had promises to keep.

•

'National Socialism,' Virgil said, 'is a pile of steaming bullshit on the road-side of history, friend.'

Wolf said: 'I beg your pardon?' The car, German made and German engineered, drove smoothly along the poor English road. On their right the Thames expanded as it flowed onwards to the distant sea.

Virgil laughed. 'Don't get me wrong,' he said. 'It was a *great* con. A great con. *Deutschland über alles!* Eh, Wolf? Promise them the world and blame all their ills on the Jews. That's like blaming it on the weather. Do you know, I was stationed in Berlin in the twenties. Naval intelligence liaison.' He patted his stomach. 'I was slimmer then. Berlin! It was full of whores. The clubs, the jazz, the girls—they called it the filthiest city on Earth and I can't say that they were wrong. Killed a man for the first time in Unter den Linden. Got laid every other day. It was good to be young in Berlin.'

'I don't think you were ever young,' Wolf said. Virgil laughed again. He laughed easily and, Wolf thought, with no more sincerity than a whore. 'OSS,' Wolf said, as though tasting the letters, the shape of them in his mouth. The idea of the Americans involving themselves in the affairs of Germany again was abhorrent to him. It was American intervention in the Great War in 1917 that had finally ended the conflict.

And Wolf ended up blind, in a nerve hospital for those deemed deserters or insane . . .

'The communist threat *must* be contained,' Virgil said. 'America cannot easily afford another war, but we cannot and *will* not tolerate further Russian expansion.'

'So what do you want from me?'

Virgil half turned in his seat. His eyes were bright. His voice was soft. The car was approaching the docks of Limehouse. Here lights burned in secretive little pubs and wharf-side establishments, and furtive Chinamen walked the streets. 'You could go back to Germany,' Virgil said, his voice as slow and treacly as honey. 'You could lead again.'

'Lead?'

'Lead Germany. Resurrect National Socialism!'

'You're mad,' Wolf said.

'The remnants of the organisation are still there. The men retain their loyalty or, if not, are at the very least practical. Nazism has always attracted ruthless, practical men. Listen to me, Wolf. Listen to me!' He grasped Wolf's thigh in his meaty hand, crushing it, and Wolf winced: the American's fingers would leave their mark. 'You could do it. We'll parachute you back, in due course. We have agents in place. Working for us. When everything is ready you'll go in, you'll claim back what was rightfully yours!'

'A *putsch*,' Wolf said.

'An assisted regime change,' Virgil said.

'You can do that?'

'You bet your sweet ass we can! At least,' Virgil amended, with a feral grin, 'we can try.'

'Get your filthy hand off me, American.'

Virgil's squeeze grew even stronger. Then he abruptly released Wolf. The car turned a dark corner into a quayside alley lined with looming warehouses. 'Stop the car, Bernie.'

'Yes, sir.'

'Come, Wolf.' Virgil did not wait for his driver but opened the door himself and clambered out, as big and ungainly as a bear. Wolf remained seated, for just a moment staring ahead. Unseeing.

Could it be true?

It could not possibly be true. To even imagine such a thing was to open himself to the worst agony he had ever suffered.

The agony of defeat.

To offer him the impossible was not a gift but a hideous curse, and he did not trust Virgil, did not trust any American.

Wolf had never trusted anyone: it was why he was still alive.

Wolf thought but only fleetingly of the nerve hospital in Pasewalk and what had transpired there.

Six hundred miles by train from the front to the small hospital near the Polish border. Blind—he had been blinded! As a boy he feared the dark, in the darkness was the ogre reeking of drink, the ogre and his belt whistling through the air, as a boy he sometimes cried, but silently, sometimes like all boys he wet his bed. Then his mother would comfort him, hold him close, and he would breathe in the softness of her, the smell of fresh laundry and apfelstrudel, and all would be better once again.

And then she was gone, and Wolf was on a train, in absolute dark, and he was terrified. Remembering the attack, the whistle of mortar, the gas—the gas! Quick, boys, and fumbling with the straps of the mask, too late, and the light thick as green honey. His comrades fell beside him. 'My eyes! My eyes!' he screamed. The mud welcomed him and he rolled in it but still he could not see, and the pain burned and when they came and carried him away he was still like that, screaming and sobbing and blind, blind, and he thought he would be blind for ever.

He was stoic before the doctor, one Karl Kroner, a Jew.

Sometimes Wolf thought of his life as having two distinct phases: the one before his blindness and the one that came after. Before, he had been a boy, an artist, a soldier. After, there came a man.

He did not understand what the doctor said, whispering to the nurses, the sound of his pencil tap-tapping on the clipboard. 'Hysterical,' Wolf heard. 'Pasewalk,' he heard, and, 'Dr Forster.' Whoever he might be.

Then his orders, which he could not see, invalided out when all he wanted to do was continue fighting, and what did the doctor mean, *hysterical*?

And those long interminable hours on the slow train away from the front and the groaning of the wheels and the murmur of soldiers and the taste of hot strong tea which he never drank but was given anyway, his shaking hands all but spilling the drink, and turning his head, this way and that, helplessly: where was the *window*?

In that slow procession of the train Wolf died and was reborn and died again. Could this really be the end of him? To be just another casualty of the war, another disabled soldier, blinded, lame: never to hold a brush and paint again, never to know the sun setting over a field, the colour of fire or blood, and to become—what? A beggar in the streets of Vienna or Berlin, coins rattling in a tin cup, Spare some change, spare some change for an ex-soldier?

He put his hand against the window, feeling the cold outside. He could not see; and yet could see so clearly.

The future lay ahead like a broken road. He would kill himself, he thought with sudden savagery. Put the gun in his mouth and pull the trigger, no time for thought, a quick ending denied him by the war. No more would he be Wolf, he would be nothing, dust as all men must become dust. And was that so terrible? Was that so wrong?

He must have dozed off, eventually. He was woken to the silence that follows the breaking of a train, the lull between stop and renewed motion. Outside, the other soldiers were gathering their kitbags, calling to each other, doors were opening and slamming, boots on snow, and Lance-Corporal Wolf roused himself to follow, into the cold and the unknown.

Although he did not know it, the future lay ahead for him still . . .

'Mr Wolf?'

Wolf roused himself. 'Yes, yes,' he said, almost spitting out the English word. That sibilant sound. He ran his tongue around his mouth. It tasted sour. He stepped out of the car. 'Yes, what is it?' he said testily.

'Come, Mr. Wolf,' Virgil said grandly. He nodded and, as if responding to his command, the wharf was suddenly bathed in bright electric light. Wolf was momentarily blinded. He blinked back tears. When he opened his eyes again the wharf was transformed and he took a step back unwittingly.

The warship floating down the river was enormous. Its grey hull shone wet and above it rose an armoured citadel, topped by the rising conning tower, with gun-slits like malevolent eyes. It was a marvel of engineering, lying low in the water yet carrying enough firepower, Wolf saw at a glance, to lay waste to a small coastal town. Wolf was immediately in love.

'What *is* she?' he said, awed.

'She's an amphibious HST Destroyer,' Virgil said, with obvious pride. He was like a cowboy out of one of Karl May's Western novels, speaking of his prized cow.

'High Speed Transport?' Wolf said.

'Indeed, Mr Wolf. American born and bred, our USS *Valkyrie.*'

Wolf turned his head sharply, but Virgil seemed not to notice.

'The Chooser of the Slain . . .'

'Indeed, Mr Wolf. You have a knowledge of the classics.' Virgil barked an order and the doors of the warehouses opened as one, and Wolf saw men streaming out. They wore civvies but they were military men all the same, American soldiers in civilians' clothes. Beyond the open doors he saw the warehouses were in fact giant hangars. There were planes inside, crates of ammunition and arms, camouflage netting, an arsenal for a small and private war.

Wolf said, 'Does the British government . . . *know* of your presence here?'

Virgil waved his hand dismissively. 'We are not officially here, Mr Wolf.'

'And unofficially?'

Virgil shrugged. 'Everyone wants to see the Red Menace removed,' he said.

Wolf surveyed the dock, which only moments before had appeared abandoned. The warship floated serenely in the Thames. 'What if I say no?' Wolf said; he spoke low; the words were loath to depart his larynx.

Virgil seemed amused. 'You would refuse?' he said. 'We would make you great again, Mr Wolf. We would put men at your service, arms at your disposal. The offer of the might of the entire United States of America behind you, Mr Wolf, is not something to refuse lightly.'

Probabilities swam in Wolf's mind, futures diverging like roads in a yellow wood. His mouth felt dry. He nodded his head, slowly, uncertainly. 'No, it isn't,' he agreed.

'Good man!' Virgil clapped him on the back, as if all were decided, nearly sending Wolf sprawling. 'Come. Let me show you our little base.' He walked with great purpose, his giant hands swinging loosely by his side. He looked like a great ape then, and yet he walked as though he owned the very earth he stepped on. Wolf followed him with trepidation, and yet with wonder, too. Like a sleepwalker he was dragged in Virgil's wake through the bright unreal glare of floodlights high overhead, and when he moved his hand before his face it was as though bioluminescence had clung to his skin and trailed a ghostly band of colour through the air. Inside the first warehouse he saw men with a military bearing and civilian clothes sitting tensely around a radio receiver; maps of Europe on the wall, dotted with coloured pins; unmarked heavy wooden crates piled in one corner; camouflage nettings in another; an upturned rubber dinghy, a mechanic working patiently with a boat engine between his knees; more crates, one open, showing Wolf the armaments inside, guns oiled until they shone. Then through to the second warehouse where two Cessna light aircraft were sitting at rest, a group of men in overalls sitting playing cards on upturned empty crates. Then last to the water where the destroyer, *Valkyrie*, sat in all her glory, with her silent power, and the men climbing on board her like worshippers at temple, for all that they seemed as small as ants. And more warehouses, on the other side, filled with ammo and guns, tinned food, parachutes, rockets, grenades, bayonets and handguns, an Aladdin's Cave of lethal wonders, not to mention the explosives. Round and round in the empty space before the jetty Wolf turned and turned like a bride whose face was raised to the high sun, round and round he turned as though he'd been dancing.

'All laid at your service, Mr Wolf, and in the service of your country, your Fatherland, to be liberated, made whole, replenished and resplendent once again.'

As in a dream: 'And if I say no?'

'But you won't, Mr Wolf. Why would you?' A paternal chuckle, perhaps that is who Virgil reminded him of: his old man the ogre, dead and buried these many years. 'How could you refuse?'

And, still in that dreaming state: 'But think it over. And Bernie will drop you off wherever you like.'

•

Half-asleep in the infirmary, Shomer listens to the sounds of Jews gossiping.

'I heard he can't get it up.'

Laughter.

The same speaker: 'Not in the . . . usual way.'

'What does that mean.'

'*I* heard . . .' The man lowers his voice. '*I* heard he likes to be . . . whipped.'

A shocked indrawn breath. 'Whipped?'

'Spanked. Like a child.'

'Feh!'

'*I* heard he only has one ball.'

'One ball! Can you imagine such a thing?'

Shomer stirs. Around him there is temporary merriment. In the infirmary no one has to work, there is nothing to do, and nothing to wield but words.

And he thinks of *him*. And pictures him humiliated, gagged, dominated, abused.

'I heard he has a thing for young *shikses*. The blonde, zaftig ones. Good Aryan types.'

'What I wouldn't give to shtup one.' Laughter.

'*I* heard he's fucking that film director.'

'Who, Fritz Lang?'

Laughter.

'No, Leni Riefenstahl.'

'Her? I heard they're thick as thieves.'

'I'd slip her the sausage!'

'What sausage? You mean your toothpick?'

'Screw you!'

'I thought she was good in *The Blue Light*,' someone says.

'She's a Nazi!'

'So *nu*? They're all Nazis.'

A lull. Shomer turns, blinks. Thinks of *him*, in bed: does he ever think of them, in the camp? Does he imagine what they feel, what they miss, how they die? Does he know them at all, beyond the numbers on their arms? And he pictures a book of accounts, filled with rows and rows of endless numbers, a book as large as a world.

'I heard he likes them to . . .'

'To what?'

'No, no.'

'What?'

'No, no . . .'

'Go on!'

'I heard he likes them to, to *piss* on him!'

'*Feh!*'

'Are you *meshuggeh*? Who does such a thing?'

'A wilde *chaye*, a wild beast!'

'I have a bucket here for him, a bucket of piss!'

Laughter.

Then silence, as each man withdraws into his own private cell of the mind. Shomer tosses and turns, restless. From below: 'And what do *you* think, *luftmensch*?'

Shomer almost smiles. It's what they'd taken to calling him: a dreamer, a man with his head in the clouds.

'What I think, boychiks?' he says. He pauses to consider. Says, 'I think what I think doesn't mean a God damn.'

'Putz!'

'After the war I'm only going to buy German-made pens,' someone says. Waits expectantly.

'Why?'

'The ink won't come off!'

Groans all around, then a silence.

'May he die a thousand deaths,' someone says, but quietly.

It was a glorious dream. 'Bernie will take you wherever you want,' Virgil had said. The car moved soft and smooth like a young woman; the whole city glittered that night, its lights burned clean and clear; the very air was warm, enchanted. To be old and in love with an impossible dream is the bitterest thing.

'Where to, sir?'

'Just drive.'

As the docks receded behind us, the dream lost tangibility, the air became colder and thinner, and I felt as though I were waking up.

A dream. It was just a dream.

And I was cursed with greatness, or had been once. I knew when I was being sold a falsehood. Shit wrapped in roses smells no less like shit.

Oh, I had no doubt this man who called himself Virgil was, in his own mercenary way, sincere. And for a moment I had let myself be dazzled by the promise: the grand warship, the airplanes, the guns, the men. For a moment longer I was seduced by the American dream.

Then reality set in.

One ship, two rickety airplanes and a handful of men with guns.

Did Virgil propose to take over Germany with *that*? It would have been laughable if it weren't so heartbreakingly sad. Once I had held all of Germany in the palm of my hand. I had men beyond count, the army on my side. What Virgil was offering me was a group of mercenaries who would not get farther than a Hamburg suburb before they were slaughtered and fed to the local farmers' pigs. What was I saying—that bunch of American cowboys wouldn't have made it as far as fucking *Glückstadt*.

'God damn you!' I said, with feeling. '*Scheisse!*'

'Excuse me, sir?'

'Just drive!'

He must have been told to humour me, for he obliged without a murmur.

Which led me back to my first question, the one I had asked Virgil, and then again: the one he would not answer. What if I turned down his offer?

Virgil wanted a regime change in Germany. What he needed was a symbol, a figurehead to reunite the remnants of Nazism into a resistance force.

I knew better. The communists had put what was left of the Party in prisons and camps, and brutally oppressed any and all dissent. National Socialism was done, finished, its practitioners dead or scattered. My old comrades who had managed to escape were now homeless émigrés, and small-time gangsters in all but name . . .

But the Americans were mad enough to try. Maybe. Not too mad as to provide more than a handful of mercenaries, though. Working without official sanction, maintaining deniability.

If not me, I thought: then *who*?

And somehow answering that was important: more important than I could say.

Who could replace *me*?

Göring was a good comrade, now. He was fat but he was smart: he would sell his own mother if it benefited him and he would have sold the Yanks down the river without a blink. But Göring had gone over to the communists, was no doubt flourishing in the new Germany.

So Göring was out.

Hess? But Hess was in London and comfortable with his émigré

143

club and his principles lost. Hess could have been second only to me, but he had always been weaker, softer: and he corrupted.

Not Hess.

Then who? Goebbels? Himmler?

Whereabouts unknown.

Streicher? Dead.

Bormann? He had been Hess's deputy but I could not underestimate him. He liked to work behind the scenes.

Last seen in a communist concentration camp, though.

Alfred Rosenberg? My ideologue, a man who knew his higher and lower races, and his conversation on the World Ice Theory, the *Welteislehre*, has always been fascinating and erudite.

Dead by firing squad, though.

Albert Speer? A gifted architect. Escaped to South America, or so I had last heard.

Reinhard Heydrich? Wonderful musician, fine Olympic-class fencer, a dedicated Jew-hater. Ruthless. He would be a good choice. I did not know what had happened to him after the Fall. Suspected he survived. He was the sort to survive.

But that same list of—and what were they, suddenly? Suspects? That same list could lead me to the man behind the white slavery ring. The man who controlled Hess, the one who was perhaps behind Judith Rubinstein's disappearance, too. One of my former comrades, my associates, my . . .

The men who had once served under my absolute command.

'Sir? Charing Cross Station, sir.'

'Did I ask you?'

'No, sir.'

'Then shut the fuck up, Bernie.'

'Yes, sir.'

'Drive up Charing Cross Road.'

'Yes, sir.'

'I want to buy a book.'

'Yes, sir.'

I made the young American drop me off outside Marks & Co.

'Goodnight, sir.'

'You take care of that car, young man. That's German engineering you're handling, not one of your Buicks or Fords.'

'You a fan of automobiles, sir?'

'I admire workmanship.'

'You should come visit us, sir. In the States, I mean, sir. I think you will like the cars.'

I felt old just talking to him.

'Where are you from, soldier?'

'Los Angeles, sir. It's a beautiful country. All the sun and sea in the world.'

'And the movies, eh?' I said.

'Sir?'

'Have you heard of Leni Riefenstahl?'

'Who?'

'A great actress and a personal friend of mine,' I said.

'I'm sorry, sir. We don't get much German cinema back home. You know how it is.'

'Yes,' I said. 'Yes, I suppose I do.'

'Goodnight, sir.'

'Drive carefully, soldier.'

The night sky was clearing as I watched him drive away. Moonlight came down through an opening in the clouds and for a moment the world was tinged silver. I went inside the shop. Marks & Co. was a wonderful shop for all that it was owned by Jews.

I was able to spend a pleasant thirty minutes or so just browsing indoors. In the back of the shop, in a section devoted to bargain books, I found a small octavo of Thea von Harbou's *Metropolis*. It was the English edition, showing a sort of mechanical woman against the background of a Bauhaus city. A Jewish form of architecture, and I loathed it both as an artist and as a man.

'The book sensation of Europe,' said the front jacket.

'The great romance of the century,' said the back jacket.

'Prune-faced bitch,' I said out loud. 'And a talentless hack.' I held the book in my hand. The future of Germany stared back at me from its cover, a nightmare land of automaton workers and their Jewish masters. I was not in a good mood. I wondered how much von Harbou had made from the sale of her English-language rights. I had been paid £350 from my British publisher, Hurst & Blackett, but I was in the concentration camp by then. I needed to talk to my literary agent. I had been working on a sequel to *My Struggle* on and off since before my exile, but my creative juices refused to flow. Nevertheless, I determined to get in touch with them, at least to demand a royalty statement.

I replaced the book on the shelf and eventually found a copy of *Max und Moritz*. What charming illustrations! What beautiful rhyme. I found myself laughing quietly as the two fell into a vat of dough while trying to steal pretzels from the baker. How they rolled in the dough! Then the baker came back and baked them in his oven. I was laughing so hard my ribs were hurting.

'Sir? Sir? Are you all right?'

But I couldn't stop laughing. Everything hurt and I couldn't stop, and I stood there, holding the book, helplessly, laughing and laughing and trying to stop until they helped me out of the shop and closed the door on me, softly, with a final clang of the bell.

•

In another time and place Shomer lies sleeping; and he is neither too hungry nor too cold; and in the large block of the infirmary there is a relative quiet: nothing to do but lie there and try to sleep amongst the other sick or dying men; and try not to think in all that quiet, try not to think at all, of what has been, and what there is no more.

•

By the time Wolf reached Berwick Street the hysterical laughter had drained out of him and left in its stead a cold burning fury. It was never buried deep, never too far beneath the surface; it motivated him, it drove him on; anger and hate were the beats of a great primitive drum, of the sort the Germanic tribes had played before marching into battle; they were the beats of the drum to which he, too, marched; always.

There was a car parked outside the Jew's bakery, a white Crossley Sports Saloon with no one inside. Wolf unlocked the side door by the bakery and climbed up the stairs and when he reached the corridor he saw that the door to his office was open.

He went cautiously; he was afraid, perhaps, of another attack.

She was standing in the middle of the room surveying its destruction. Her dress hugged her figure. A slit down the side exposed a flash of long white leg. She was biting her lower lip.

'Did Daddy do this?' she said.

'Get out.'

'He can be so *mean*.'

'I said, get out!'

'It's those two boys of his,' she said, not paying him any heed. 'They do indulge him so. He always wanted a boy, you know.' She turned to Wolf and gave him a quizzical smile. 'After Judith I guess he gave up trying. Instead he tried to make her into the boy he never had but she did what boys always do and left him.'

'Get—'

'Out, I know.' She sighed. 'I have *just* the decorator in mind. You'd *love* him. Sydney. He's a *genius*.' She walked up to Wolf. She was a little taller than he. She touched his cheek with the back of her hand and he flinched. 'Your face,' she said.

'My face? My *face*?' For the first time Wolf's face twisted in open fury. The anger and hate had been building up inside, the fury that in the past drove men to madness and murder. Once he had commanded men not unlike those Jew thugs of her father's, men who obeyed orders without question, who beat and maimed and tortured and killed at his command. 'My *face*?' He pushed her roughly against the wall. She bumped against it gracefully and stayed there regarding him with that same quizzical smile. Wolf fumbled with his belt buckle. The sound of the belt slithering out of its hooks whistled through the air and Isabella Rubinstein bit her lower lip again. The belt hit the floor. Wolf unbuttoned his trousers and with the same hurried gesture pulled his mutilated penis free. It was half erect, and painful. 'My fucking *face*?' He advanced on her, his penis in his hand.

'He did this to you?' If she was afraid she didn't show it.

'You fucking *whore*!' He was screaming, up in her face, strings of spittle falling from his lips. His cock was pressed against her now, this Jewish woman, the source of his humiliation, his pain.

She slapped him.

The sound resounded in the room. For a moment he couldn't believe it. His cheek stung. She had slapped him with force; there was heft in her action. 'Listen to me, you fucking little *worm*,' she said. Her hand reached down and grasped his penis, painfully hard, and he almost screamed. It was the second time in a week that a Rubinstein was holding Wolf by the balls. So to speak.

Isabella leaned close until her face was almost touching Wolf's. 'You think I don't know what you are? Who you are?' She gave his cock a painful squeeze, making him yelp in pain. 'You think I don't know what you *want?*'

'Let me go, you *bitch*—'

She slapped him again. Released his cock and pushed him with both hands splayed open against his chest. He staggered and fell back. He couldn't believe this was happening to him, nor did he know why he felt so weak at that moment. His penis was fully erect now, the unhealed wound burning.

Isabella advanced on him. She knelt, for just a moment, and rose with Wolf's belt in her hand. 'I used to watch you,' she said. 'Watch you on the newsreel when I was a girl. It was only a few years ago to you, a lifetime to me. How we all hated you! Hated and feared you.' Her free hand came down her body, as if it had its own will. She stroked her flat stomach, slowly, and came down lower, at last, to the triangle between her legs. It was pronounced, now. Her fingers grasped, pushing against the material, in between her thighs, as she touched herself. A small moan escaped from her lips, the sound suspended like ice crystals in the cold air of the room. 'You're a monster,' she said, whispered, 'or you were, once. You're a nobody now.'

'Yes,' Wolf said. Isabella whipped the belt through the air. It made a whistling sound and hit Wolf on the chest, the metal buckle nicking his skin. 'Yes. Yes.'

Isabella stared at Wolf's erect penis as though hypnotised. Her eyes were feverishly bright. 'Lie down.'

'What are you—'

She whipped him again. 'Lie *down*! On your back.'

He fell back. Lay down, his eyes on the ceiling, his head on a pile of books about the superiority of the Aryan race. His penis stood erect, at attention like an SS-Sturmführer. Isabella stood and watched him, her chest rising and falling with her breath. Slowly, making sure he watched, she began to lift up her dress.

'I used to sit in the cinema and watch you,' she said, dreamily. Wolf's eyes were fixed on the slowly rising dress. 'Giving speeches, your fist raised in the air. You had that funny little moustache, like Charlie Chaplin.' She laughed. Her thighs were bare. Her dark triangle of pubic hair was wet. 'We all used to hate you so.'

Holding the dress above her waist, she approached him and stood over him. He looked up, staring at her. 'I know men,' Isabella Rubinstein said, softly. She stood over him, one leg on either side of Wolf, affording him a view straight up her engorged commodity.

Slowly, she lowered herself down. She squatted over him until the lips of her cunny were inches away from Wolf's face. He could smell her, could inspect every fold of this most intimate aspect of hers. It had been this way with Geli. Slowly Isabella Rubinstein rocked back and forth on Wolf's face, rubbing herself against him. She rubbed against his nose, his lips, his reluctant tongue, lowering herself, positioning herself at last so that her anus was over Wolf's nose, her vagina over his mouth. The smell and warmth of her threatened to suffocate him. He tried to struggle but she reached and took hold of his manhood and held him still. Pain shot up his body, but he liked it. She tugged on his newly circumcised penis, not harshly, this time, but not gently either. *'Deutschland über alles,'* she murmured, rocking back and forth, back and forth, forcing herself on him. *'Deutschland über alles!'*

Then, quickly, she shuddered over his face and cried out, a high, keening single note. Wolf choked, his mouth filled with the product of her orgasm. She relaxed, sinking lower, crushing his face. Her hand was on his penis like on the rudder of an aircraft.

Then the pressure eased. She pushed herself up and stood squatting over him. Her lips twitched and then a trickle of urine came out, stopped, and then began again with more force. It fell down on Wolf's face and some of it ran down the inside of Isabella's thighs and some of it soaked Wolf's hair and his shirt. Wolf shuddered uncontrollably and shot semen into the air and onto his belly. He bit his lips to stop from crying out from the pain of his orgasm; he bit them until they bled. Isabella finished her toilet and shook the last drops into Wolf's mouth and stepped over him and pulled down her dress. Wolf lay there. Then he too stood up and pulled up his pants and tidied his shirt. He looked at her. She was standing by the window, in profile. She flicked her gold lighter alive and lit a cigarette. She blew a cloud of smoke at the sky and turned and looked at Wolf dreamily. 'We *really* must do something about that ghastly wallpaper,' she said.

8

WOLF'S DIARY, 8TH NOVEMBER 1939

In the morning the bitch was gone and I tidied my office as best I could. I had slept fitfully. I was woken in the night by terrible dreams in which I was a Jew incarcerated in some sort of work camp. My leg was sore and tender with pus forming over a blood-ied wound. In my dream I was a writer but all my readers were dead.

My bruises hurt and the little wolf, too, was sore. I woke early with the sounds of the bakery down below and the smell of the ovens. My mouth tasted of ash. I washed and dressed and grabbed a bite to eat at a cafe down the road and then returned to my of-fice. I cleaned and tidied up but the smell of urine and my own excitement still filled the air and I cursed all Jews as I worked. My painting was ruined. It hurt unreasonably. It was another link to my past that had been severed.

When the office was more presentable I sat myself down be-hind my desk. I took out the fat brown envelope I had taken from Barbie's shop on Petticoat Lane. I slit it open with my letter opener, etched with the image of twin lightning bolts of the old, defunct SS. I took out the papers, carefully, and spread them out across the desk.

Interesting.

They were identity documents. The girl in the cellar, Judith's former schoolmate, had told me they were taken off them once they crossed the border out of Germany. There were all manner of papers, German identity cards, passports from a variety of nations, visas, onward tickets to Palestine or America, a whole plethora of identities, a life in papers. Most were women, but not all, and I found myself staring in fascination at the passport of one Moshe Wolfson.

This Jew was about my age, that is to say, fifty. He had been born in Vienna and worked as a furrier. In his photograph he wore the black clothes of Hasidic Jews. He looked older than me.

Perhaps it was the similarity of the name that gave me the idea. Though I no longer painted, I could still use my skill as an artist. I went out and returned later in the day having visited a photographer and an arts supply shop near Covent Garden. One curious thing happened while I was out: as I walked past the Seven Dials I saw the fat policeman again, Keech. He was just loitering about, and when he saw me his eyes lit up and he approached me, twirling his nightstick like a performing monkey in the circus. 'So, Mr Wolf!' he said. He poked his nightstick at me and I dodged it, restraining the anger that was threatening to make me lose self-control.

'Constable,' I said, coldly.

'Spend time with any whores lately?'

'Not since I climbed off your mother last night.'

At that his fat face lost its fat smile. 'I'd tread carefully if I were you,' he said.

'It's a free country, last I checked.'

'Not for long, sweetheart. Not if your boyfriend Mosley has anything to do with it.'

'Scared, constable?'

That brought the big fat smile back to his face. 'Fucking immigrants,' he said, poking the nightstick at me again, halfheartedly. 'You should all go back where you come from.'

'What about your boss, Morhaim?'

'Morhaim's as British as anyone.'

'I'm not sure Mosley sees it that way.'

'What is your problem, Wolf?' he said. For a moment he seemed almost sincere. 'What is it with you and Jews? Why do you hate them so much?'

I stared into his big fat face in silence. After a moment he laughed. 'On your way,' he said. 'Don't do anything stupid. If that's at all possible.' And, as I began to silently walk away—'We'll be watching you, Wolf.'

I was more disturbed by the encounter than I let on. Was it coincidence? Were the Metropolitan Police watching me, following me? I needed to go about my business without the pursuit of shadows. But that afternoon I gave no one cause for concern. From the photographer I obtained several self-portraits of myself, cut to size, and from the arts supply shop I purchased scalpel and ink, glue and a selection of rubber stamps. So equipped, I returned to the office, where Herr Moshe Wolfson's pitiful face stared up at me from his passport. I wondered where he was, and whether he was dead or alive—dead, I assumed, smuggled out of Germany only for his body to be dumped somewhere in the Alps, his possessions stolen: there was much to be admired in the efficiency of such a system, I thought. And again I wondered, futilely, which man was behind it all; I was sure that I would know him; would I not?

And so I spent a pleasurable hour at my desk, with scalpel and ink and stamps. I began by gently removing Wolfson's photograph from his passport. I set it on fire and watched it burn to ashes and then returned to the document. The passport, I saw, had been used several times in the years before the Fall, with trips to France, Switzerland and Belgium. More intriguingly, it contained a brand-new, genuine Palestinian visa, granted by the British High Commission only a few months earlier. Such visas, I knew, were rare, and I wondered how much he had paid, and to whom, in order to gain one. Next I set about ageing my own photograph and, while it was drying, I put the other papers of the dead or enslaved Jews back into the envelope and into a drawer: I had no further use for them.

I inserted the photograph bearing my own face into Wolfson's document and set about reproducing the official stamp over it. It had been a long time since I worked in such a trade and my concentration was complete. At last I had finished and with a sense of achievement sat there. For a long moment I stared at my new passport. 'Moshe Wolfson,' I said, trying out the name. 'Moshe Wolfson, *ja*. It is a pleasure to meet you, *mein herr*.'

My face stared back at me, severe and mute, from the photograph. It was the face of a Jew.

WOLF'S DIARY, 9TH NOVEMBER 1939

Were I ever asked to offer my professional observations on the art of detection, I would merely note that it is a truth universally acknowledged, that once a detective acquires two concurrent cases, the two must be in some way related.

I call it Wolf's Law.

It is a point of contention with me that I had never, in fact, been asked to offer my professional observations on the art of detection. That big fat oaf Gil Chesterton once said that the criminal is the artist, the detective only the critic. He was a Catholic and a prude and was never shy of a meal or an opinion. In this, as in all things, he was wrong. I *was* an artist, for it is an artist's purpose to make order out of chaos. A criminal defaces; a detective restores. Had I been asked to proffer my observations, I dare say they would have made for a gripping and elucidating read. I had, in fact, been working, on and off, on a sequel to my first, and so far only, book, and in this *Zweite Buch*, or *Second Book*—for I did not yet have a title for it—I intended to set aside a chapter, at the very least, in order to discuss my methods and views on crime, which I believed would make a significant contribution to mankind's understanding of the criminal mind.

Yet the manuscript eluded me; and I did not have a publisher.

My enquiry had led me to combine my twin investigations: these being Judith Rubenstein's disappearance and the question of Mosley's Palestinian assassins. The root of all crime, of course, is the Jew; and so it was only natural that it was in that direction that I next turned my attentions. I needed to understand the Jewish angle.

Jews always had an angle.

The headquarters of the Jewish Territorialist Organisation were in the basement of an office block off the Strand, towards the Fleet Street end. They were dark and dim and did not look busy. It was the sort of place rented in a hurry and abandoned even faster. It was exactly the sort of place I was looking for.

It was Thursday; and I was on the job.

Eric Goodman looked like a con man who'd seen better days.

He was in his mid-thirties, with receding black hair and watery blue eyes that were magnified by his too-large glasses. The collar of his shirt was open and his nails were bitten down to the quick and I didn't like his eyes. They were those of a man who trusted no one and nothing and least of all me. Behind him in the office was a receptionist as old as Napoleon and as attractive, and she was bent over a cumbersome typing machine, pecking desultorily at the keys.

'Moshe Wolfson,' I said, trying out the name. 'It is a pleasure to meet you.'

'Funny,' the man from the ITO said. 'You don't look Jewish.'

'You want funny?' I said. 'Let me tell you a joke. A goy comes to a Jew acquaintance of his. "You Jews," he says, "everyone knows you're smart with money. Teach me how to be smart like a Jew."

'"Well," the Jew says. "It's simple. Go to the market and look for my cousin's fish stall and buy his pickled herring. Once you eat the pickled herring, you'll become smarter in no time."

'The goy, delighted, goes away. The next day, he shows up again, fuming with anger. "You cheated me!" he cries. "I bought your cousin's pickled herring like you told me, then this morning I was at the market and I saw the same fish being sold on another stall—for a third of the price!"

'"You see?" says the Jew, delighted. "You're *already* smarter!"'

I beamed at him expectantly. Goodman looked at me sour-faced. 'You're a regular comedian,' he said. 'You'd be packing them in at the Hackney Empire in no time.'

'How do you get to the Hackney Empire?' I asked him.

'You can take the bus,' he said, and I stopped him in frustration before he could give me directions and said, 'No, no . . . practice!'

He gave an involuntary shudder.

'What exactly did you want again, Mr Wolfson?'

I stared into his ugly mug of a face and considered my response.

'I am interested in the activities of our brothers and sisters in Palestine,' I said at last, with what I hoped was an ingratiating smile.

'Well, then I'm afraid that you came to the wrong place, Mr Wolfson.'

'I'm not sure that I understand.'

He was of the English Jewry, like Morhaim, the prick from the Met. Thinking himself at home on this island and arrogant with it. But earlier, when I had gone down the Strand, the Blackshirts were marching and little old ladies were throwing them flowers and little boys ran about waving the Union flag; and as I passed Charing Cross Station I saw a Hasidic Jew, dressed all in black, propped up against a brick wall as young men took turns beating him about the face and body, until his thick white beard was matted with red blood. His heavy felt hat lay crumpled on the road beside him, as though he were asking for alms. The policemen who were set to patrol the march did nothing but watch. It was not becoming any easier for Jews in this country. But then it never does, for the Jews.

'Mr Wolfson, the Jewish Territorialist Organisation was founded in 1903 by the author Israel Zangwill and the journalist Lucien Wolf—'

An author, and a journalist, I thought. Jews! They were good with nothing but words.

'Following the offer, from then-Colonial Secretary Joseph Chamberlain, of a Jewish settlement in British East Africa.'

A sensible offer, I thought, but didn't say. Stick them as far away from civilisation as possible. 'I take it that did not carry through, in practical terms?' I said, politely.

'The Zionist Congress sent an expedition to British East Africa—'

'You mean Uganda?'

He looked pained. 'That was the name the *common person* on the street referred to it by.'

'I see.'

I would see his face smashed into the naked glass, if I had my way.

'Unfortunately the expedition did not return a favourable report.'

'Too hot?' I said.

'The heat, hostile tribes . . .' He waved his hand airily. 'Details to be overcome, in our opinion. But the Congress voted the offer down.'

'How . . . short-sighted.'

For the first time he expressed real emotion. 'Indeed! Quite right! And so the ITO—'

Why they called it the ITO and not the JTO was beyond me.

'—was established and continued to explore alternative propositions for Jewish settlement beyond Palestine, believing, as we do, not in the need for a return to a Biblical land, but rather for a practical solution to the question of a national homeland for the Jewish people, for—'

'Quite, quite,' I said, cutting him off hurriedly. 'Indeed.'

He sighed. 'Anyway,' he said, 'the Balfour Declaration in 1917 did rather take the wind out of that particular sail. For a while, at least. As you are probably aware, the inherent anti-Semitism of the British, like elsewhere in Europe, has prevented commitment to *any* particular national homeland for the Jews for many years now.'

'So you are considering other possibilities? Besides Palestine, I mean?'

'Of course. Uganda still.' He glared at me. 'I mean British East Africa, of course.'

'Of course.' I grinned at him charmingly. The little *scheisskopf.* 'Where else?' I inquired.

'Argentina, for instance. El Arish, in Egypt. Albania. British Guiana. There are many possibilities.'

'But Palestine amongst them, surely.'

'Well, yes. I'm sorry, I think I forgot your name.'

'It's Wolfson,' I said. Pictured him on the ground being kicked by hobnailed boots. But said, 'That's quite all right, young man. You cannot be expected to remember every visitor's name, surely!'

'So you do understand. Yes, yes, we are quite busy here, I can assure you. *Quite* busy!'

His was the third office I had tried, after the Palestine Jewish Colonisation Association (too legit, engaged in arranging visas and work for Jews in Palestine) and the Council of British Zionists, or CBZ (who seemed to spend most of their time arranging black-tie fund-raisers). The ITO was different. I liked the look of this con man in his too-large glasses. I liked the cut, as they say, of Eric Goodman's jib. I liked the furtiveness of his glances and the disused air of the office and the comatose receptionist. I knew deceit like a lover and here, I thought, was somebody giving out all the right signals for a quick and dirty lying fuck.

'So if there is nothing else I can help you with . . .'

'It's only, you see,' I said, 'that I have recently come into some money and, of course, the Palestinian cause is close to my heart, as it is to the heart of all Jews . . .'

'Is that so?' His demeanour became instantly sympathetic when I mentioned money. He all but beamed at me, like a cat smelling his favourite tinned fish. I hated cats. Cats and Jews. What kind of a name was 'Eric' for a Jew? It was typical of the Jews, to give themselves seemingly Anglo-Saxon names, the better to try and fool the unwary man or woman. No doubt he was a pervert, too, a sexual deviant of some kind.

'If you would like to make a donation . . .'

'Let me think about it.'

He lowered his voice. 'Palestine is not out of the question,' he said. 'In fact . . .' then he shook his head and smiled. 'But I get carried away.'

'No, do go on.'

He looked at me with returning suspicion. 'You're not a policeman, are you?' he said.

'Do I look like a copper to you?'

'I don't know. There is something about you, Mr Wolfson, that doesn't feel quite right to me,' he murmured, raising his head and removing his glasses. I stared into his pale blue eyes. He stared back at me, unblinking.

'I do not need to stand for this kind of treatment!' I said. 'And as for a donation, young man, you can forget about *that*!'

He did not try to stop me. In fact I didn't think he would. I marched out of there and closed the door and walked back down to the Strand and round the corner, never once looking back, not doubting that he'd be following, if only for a little while. If only to make sure that I was gone.

Yes, I liked Mr Eric Goodman, for my purposes. I liked him very much indeed.

It was surprisingly uncomfortable for Wolfson the Jew to walk the streets of London that day. Wolf realised that for all of his recent association with Mosley, he had simply not paid enough attention to the forthcoming elections. The signs for Mosley's campaign were everywhere, his aristocratic face staring down from billboards and posters glued to the ancient walls, and his men, the Blackshirts stood and glared at passers-by like truant schoolboys.

'Enough is Enough!' screamed their signs. 'Fight, Fight, and Fight Again!'—'Stop the Open Door Policy!'—'Say No to Mass Immigration!'—'Vote BU: Putting Britain First'—'Mosely for Prime Minister'— and so on and so forth.

Wolf's strawmen had been the Jews; for Mosley, it was the European refugees from now-communist Germany who must serve—and that included Wolf himself.

It was an uncomfortable realisation.

Equipped with a Thermos of hot herbal tea, and cheese-and-tomato sandwiches, and his raincoat and fedora, he returned two hours later, near closing time, to the little narrow lane off the Strand; and there found himself a sheltered space in a doorway and there he stood, unobtrusively, and sipped his tea, and ate his sandwiches, and watched the door of the Jewish Territorialist Organisation.

At 5:30 in the afternoon the comatose secretary emerged, wrapped up like a large ham, and made her way down to the bus stop. It was already very dark and it had been raining intermittently and dark wet patches covered the pavements.

At 6:30 on the dot the door of the ITO offices opened and Eric Goodman emerged, huddled in a coat, and shut and locked the door. He looked from side to side but apart from a handful of theatregoers lost on the way to the Strand there was no one on the lane. Wolf's Thermos was still half-full but so was his bladder and he needed to pee. His leg ached from the old wound. Goodman turned right and Wolf followed him. Goodman went through Covent Garden and Wolf hobbled after.

They passed the Royal Opera House and came finally to Dryden Street, where Goodman entered a small cafe of the sort reactionaries and penniless artists frequented; that is to say, it was a dive. Wolf waited some moments, adjusted his hat and entered. The place was crowded and noisy, the clientele boisterous and young. Goodman was sitting in a corner with his back to the door. He was not alone. Wolf went into the small water closet to urinate and stared in horror at his circumcised penis before tucking it away again. He went back into the cafe and got himself a fruit juice, and sat two tables away from Goodman. He tried to listen to their conversation but they spoke in low voices. The other man was Goodman's age but there was something hard about him, in his eyes and the shape of his mouth, in the way he held himself. He sat with his back to the wall. Wolf had the impression he was not the kind of man to ever leave his back exposed.

The conversations swelled around Wolf.

'The situation in Europe—my brother says—'

'Those damned Fascists!'

'Revolution by peaceful means. The British people are too sensible to give in to a charlatan like Mosley—'

'—understudy for *Hamlet* at the Theatre Royal, the bastard—'

'Yes, do you like it? A wonderful artist, utterly *wonderful*—'

'Only a matter of time before war is declared, the Americans—'

'I blame the French, myself.'

'Utterly *divine* cakes—'

'Playing Rosenkrantz—well, a job's a job, you know what they say—'

'I didn't like the look of him, is what I'm saying, Bitker.'

'Listen to me, Goodman! You're supposed to keep a clean front—'

Wolf, ears perked, trying to isolate snatches of conversation.

'A shamus, a shamus or a copper is what he seemed to me, Bitker—'

'You simply *must* see *Gaslight* at the—'

'The revolution—'

'Wolfson? But his papers were kosher?'

'Kosher like a bagel.'

'You let me know if he comes again, Goodman. Do you understand—'

'My publisher? Stanley Unwin and C—'

'Nothing can interrupt the plans, Goodman, do you understand!'

Wolf was hunched low but he saw the other man, the one he thought Goodman had called Bitker, shove his chair back, leap to his feet and leave the cafe. He was a big man, this Bitker. Wolf got up and followed.

The man strode across Long Acre. He was wary of a tail: twice Wolf saw him check reflections in shop windows, but Wolf was an anonymous face amongst others and the man did not see him. He hopped on a bus and Wolf climbed aboard too. The bus went down Holborn and Newgate and past St Paul's. The man Bitker got off there and Wolf did too. It had begun to rain again. Somewhere in the distance he could hear a wireless playing Judy Garland's 'Over the Rainbow.' Wolf had seen the film but, had he been the one swept up to the magical land of Oz, he would have raised an army of flying monkeys, stuck the witches in a concentration camp, razed the Emerald City to the ground and executed the wizard for communist sympathies, being a Jew, a homosexual, intellectually retarded, or all of the above.

He did like the tune, though.

He followed Bitker in the dark through the City, abandoned to the night at this hour. The streets were taken up by the homeless and the criminal, and police presence was light. Outside the Bank of En-gland Wolf saw a group of protesters, their faces obscured by scarves, setting alight a vast straw figure dressed in the Blackshirts' uniform. Policemen did arrive then, and the protesters threw bottles and stones and the policemen cursed and advanced on them with their clubs and Wolf walked on, following the elusive Bitker.

The night made Wolf uncomfortable. It was filled with grotesque human shapes, shambling through the narrow streets, their feet bare in the cold or wrapped in hastily torn bandages: some were missing limbs, others had scars from torture or acid, others still carried sharp implements the better to remove a man's valuables or life. All were beggars, the lowest of men, the lost, those who had despaired; refugees, unwanted, undesired, holding on to life tenaciously, hungrily, like beasts. They frightened Wolf, he saw himself bared, ugly in the mirror of their suffering.

Yet Bitker navigated these selfsame streets with ease and Wolf in his wake was left unharmed. They came shortly to Threadneedle Street and descended a flight of stairs to the door of a basement flat. After looking from side to side but missing Wolf again, Bitker knocked three times and waited. Presently the door was opened and light spilled out, illuminating a plain-faced Jewess in a flower-patterned dress. Bitker disappeared inside and the door closed and Wolf was left outside in the darkness. He crouched on the stairs and peered through the lace curtains.

•

The watcher in the dark, too, was watching, but this time he could no longer control the eagerness. He was watching the whores and had missed the detective's whereabouts and only knew that the detective wasn't there. Earlier he had fiddled with the cheap lock on the door and opened it and gone up the stairs and into the detective's office and he sat behind Wolf's desk. It felt so good to be sitting there. It felt so right.

The detective was so *stubborn*, he thought. It was because the man had lost a part of himself after the Fall, and was unable to get it back. It was pitiful, watching him hobble along, this once-great man, this *leader* of men, now like a decommissioned soldier, blinded by gas, a beggarman, a sleepwalker almost. The watcher in the dark wanted to grab him by the shoulders and shake him, shake him so hard and shout, *Wake up! Wake up, you daft old fool! We need you!* but no sound emerged and the detective wasn't there and hadn't been listening so far, but by God the watcher was going to get his attention. You did not just abandon a *destiny*.

Tonight. Soon. He could feel the need and the desire and he knew he could not put it off any longer, he needed . . . he shuddered in the chair and got up, moved softly around the room, not touching anything, just . . .

feeling it. Was this what it was like to have been in his presence, before? In his office with men always coming and going and the sound of hobnailed boots on hard floors, the rustle of stiff leather, the whisper of flags like silk, the smell and taste of *power* so strong it suffused the very air and changed all who came into contact with it?

He left the office regretfully, softly, and picked Wolf's bedsit's lock. Once the door was open he closed his eyes for a long moment and stood there, and when he opened them again it was as though the room was transformed and for just a moment he was standing in Wolf's old bedroom, in the Berlin residence, and the swastika flags were moving in the breeze, and outside the chauffeur was polishing the official car. For a moment he pictured a young blonde woman in the bed . . . she opened her eyes and smiled sleepily, her eyes filled with slowly fading dreams. Her long blonde hair was the colour of the sun and her skin was white as snow, but hot, so hot . . . the watcher was so erect just standing there and he moved with a great effort, looking at Wolf's books, Wolf's *toilette*, his meagre possessions: his razor, his soap, his threadbare blanket and the books, all those books everywhere. The watcher stood over the sink, imagining Wolf brushing his teeth, shaving his cheeks, washing his hands. The watcher looked in the mirror but it was only his own ordinary face staring back at him and that broke the spell. He left and locked the door behind him and went back down to Berwick Street. He had work to do, so much work.

WOLF'S DIARY, 9TH NOVEMBER 1939—CONTD.

It was an ordinary basement flat, sparsely furnished with heavy Victorian high-backed chairs and two tables joined together in the middle of the room, for all that their heights didn't entirely match. A flower-patterned cloth covered the tables. Sitting in the chairs were five men and, entering the room, was the plain-faced Jewess. Bitker trailed behind her.

I'd not seen such an assembly of reprobates since the camp. They were a shifty lot, swarthy and hairy like the *untermenschen* Jews that they were. They sat with no decorum, in their white undershirts, and hairy arms on the table, all but one, and all but one smoking. The ashtrays were filled to overflowing with what the English call 'fags.' I was glad I was outside in the cold clean air. The beasts had not even opened a window. It must have been like an oven in there. Of the five men one was a skinny lad with smooth cheeks and a face like a hooked fish and he wore an over-sized shirt with sleeves that covered his wrists. He reminded me of someone but I couldn't think of whom.

The men were talking animatedly but stopped abruptly when Bitker entered. They all stood up and shook his hand and one or two of them slapped him on the back

I heard his name, Bitker, once or twice but could not hear the discussion, which took place in low voices. The Jewess disappeared and reappeared later with a large tray of tea things. I became convinced this was, indeed, a Palestinian terror group, but could they be the ones behind the assassination attempts on Mosley? I pressed closer to the window, trying to hear, when I felt more than saw a dark shape drop down from the windowsill of the flat above. It meowed at me and, startled, I banged my head against the window.

The voices inside ceased at once. A moment later the lights went out. I pushed the cat away and it hissed at me. I kicked it, feeling a savage satisfaction even as I could hear running feet and the door to the conspirators' flat crashing open.

I ran.

They moved like professionals. They didn't shout, didn't curse as they chased me. They ran quietly and swiftly and with violent determination. My lungs burned and my leg throbbed with old pain and I fled for my life, down narrow alleyways, trying to lose them, my traitor leg hurting and my chest heaving until I thought I would be sick, and as I ran I caught sight of a sign and realised I was on Old Jewry. For a moment I thought I'd lost them.

The God damned cat tripped me up.

It came out of nowhere, streaked between my feet like a spirit of animal vengeance, screeching hideously. I tripped and fell, hard, catching myself with the palms of my hands. I felt skin tear and my knee crack, sending a shudder of fresh pain up my body and I cried out: I could not help it.

In moments they were on me and I could smell the bloodlust on their unwashed bodies. I curled into a ball, trying to protect my head and my genitals as they kicked me.

I think they were shouting questions at me, and the foreigner, Bitker, was ordering them to stop but they had lost discipline. I almost prayed, remembering the old words, my mother's and the priest's. To die like this! Ignobly in the Old Jewry at the hands of the selfsame Jews who once before were evicted out of England. It was too much to bear.

The sound of a whistle cut through the night and my pain. The kicking, miraculously, stopped. I heard running feet and saw the bouncing light of several torch beams. 'Jews! They're Jews!' came the cry.

I opened my eyes. I saw a group of young Blackshirts rushing towards the Palestinian terrorists. 'Fascist pigs!' someone yelled. I saw the blade of a knife gleam but who held it I wasn't, afterwards, sure. In the uncertain light of the torches I saw the face of the smooth-cheeked youth in profile and for a moment I almost laughed, for it was no man at all, it was a woman!

'Hello, Judith,' I whispered, softly.

Then all hell, as they say, broke loose. The two groups, the Jews and the Blackshirts, went at each other. I heard punching, grunting, saw a Jew raise a brick and smash it into a Blackshirt's head, caving in his skull. I saw a Blackshirt choking a Jew by the throat, his thumbs driving into the other man's windpipe. I saw the God damned cat standing a foot to my left, looking at me with a smirk on its dumb animal face. I crawled away, though every movement hurt. In moments they were behind me. In the darkness and the fight no one saw me go but the cat.

I straightened up, eventually. I stood and then walked, away from that awful place. I caught a bus and sat on the upper deck. On my swollen lips, I tasted blood.

'Why are you all on your own, a good-looking boy like you?'

The fat whore leered at him. She was rouged with cheap make-up over a too-pale face. Her jowls shook with her smile. Her teeth were small and uneven. Her tongue was red and she stuck it out at the watcher in the dark. 'You want to fuck old Gerta?' she said. 'You want old Gerta to suck your baby cock?'

Her bosoms were immense. She grabbed her breasts from below and shook them at him, and the pale white flesh wobbled like waves on a sea. The other whores were busy. The street was quiet. The watcher in the dark was ready. His hand closed on the hilt of the knife, the shiny, shiny knife. 'Come here,' Gerta said. She pulled him by the hand and forced his head between the twin mounds of her breasts. 'Give Aunty a kiss!'

She was strong; stronger than he had guessed. She released him and he could breathe again. Her hand tested him down below and she leered again, knowingly. 'Let's go,' she said.

She did not lead him to the alleyway where he had done the other. The girls did not use it any more. She led him somewhere else, past the dirty bookstore and a florist and a haberdashery and a cafe run by émigré Italians, all shut now, and pushed him against the wall near the rubbish bins where no one could see them. His heart beat fast and wild. She raised up her voluminous skirts, revealing pink fleshy thighs and a dark unruly bush of pubic hair. 'No, what are you doing,' he tried to say, 'no, not like that,' and he tried to struggle with her, then, but she was having none of it, she held his neck in a hug that was all but a chokehold, and with her other hand she pulled down his pants and took his stiff cock in her hand and before he even knew what was happening she had guided him inside her, squeezing his buttocks roughly as she pulled him in.

She seemed oblivious to him then. Her eyes were half closed and her lips parted and she made strange animalistic sounds, grinding him against her, over and over. The watcher had never done it before and he felt sick, sick being inside of this grotesque old creature, and only the thought of the knife kept him going until at last Gerta gave a shuddering little laugh and abruptly released him, pushing him off her. She looked down at his now-flaccid member, flopping there in the dark, and gave a little laugh again, contemptuously.

He pulled up his trousers quickly. She was still looking at him but then her eyes changed: when she saw the knife.

'What the hell do you think you're doing—' she said, or began to. He lashed out at her with the knife but she raised her arm and the knife grazed her but he had obviously missed his target. 'You little fuck hole!' she said. She sounded outraged more than scared.

'You disgusting whore!' He stabbed with the knife, again. They were so close to each other, it was as if they were making love, still. She grabbed him, pulled him close and then the knife was sticking out of the right side of her chest and she stared at him in surprise, or shock, clutching him to her, her blood staining the front of the watcher's shirt.

'Just *die!*' the watcher pleaded.

Instead, Gerta kneed him in the balls.

The watcher collapsed. He was still holding the knife. It pulled out of Gerta's chest and it emerged with a sickening, *sucking* sound. Gerta gasped, clutching her hands to the wound. There was very little blood.

'You little *worm*!' Gerta said.

The watcher had never felt such agony before; his body seemed on fire. He backed away from her. Gerta advanced on him like a figment of the watcher's nightmares, gigantic and terrifying. 'You little . . .'

At that moment he could hear footsteps coming rapidly down the street and a voice say, in foreign accented English, 'What is going on here, please?'

•

'What is going on here, damn it,' Wolf repeated. He had been nearly at his door when he heard the sounds of a scuffle. He did not want to get involved. Only fools got involved.

He saw, by the rubbish bins, the fat whore Gerta and a man, but he only knew Gerta from her profile, and he did not know the man. The man turned and ran. Wolf didn't give chase. He went to Gerta. Her face resolved when he came closer. It looked like a ghastly clown's mask. 'Wolfie,' she said. 'Is it really you, dear boy?'

'What happened, Gerta? Gerta?'

She had pulled down her dress and her pale bosoms swung free, and there was a knife wound on the right side of her chest. It was frothing weirdly.

'I'll call a doctor,' Wolf said, alarmed. He didn't want to get involved. He was repulsed by the prostitute's appearance. 'He looked so . . . harmless,' Gerta said. She was breathing heavily. 'It's always . . . the quiet ones.' She tried to leer at Wolf, but just looked pained, and old, and beaten.

Wolf shouted, 'Help! Help!' He was too tired to run any more. Too tired to walk. He just kept shouting until the other prostitutes showed up and, after them, the police. He was sitting next to Gerta by then, both of them coated in blood, their backs to the rubbish bins. He only just remembered to stash the forged Jewish identity document in a crack between the stones before the policemen finally came and arrested him.

•

The watcher was panicked, his breath caught in his throat. He tasted bile. Police whistles tore up the night. In Soho Square he found the bag he had hidden earlier that day. Quickly he stripped off his blood-soaked clothes and changed, the air freezing on his exposed skin. He shoved the clothes into the same bag and continued at a slower pace. On Oxford Street he caught a bus home.

How could it have happened? How could he fail? His mission was a holy one. He *could not* fail. At home Father was asleep in his armchair by the unlit fire. The wireless was on, playing a Chopin étude. The watcher stroked his father's thinning white hair, gently, and the old man shifted but did not wake. The watcher went up to his room and stripped again. His penis throbbed as though it was infected. Naked, he walked into the bathroom and washed. The water was lukewarm and he was shivering. He scrubbed himself and scrubbed himself, scrubbed at the whore's smell on him, her cunny juice on his penis. As much as he scrubbed he couldn't get it off. He sat in the bath and hugged himself, rocking in the dirty water. The blood coloured the water pink.

She . . . she raped him.

The taste of bile was in his mouth still. He couldn't afford to fail again. He had been sloppy. Next time there would be no mistakes. No more mistakes! He got out at last, shivering, and wrapped a towel around himself and brushed his teeth, over and over, until his gums bled and his spit was red. Later he lay in the cold bed and shivered and that smell clung to him still, that disease-ridden old hag's awful smell. Everything had gone so wrong. What if he had caught something? Whores were nasty creatures, they had crabs and the clap and God alone knew what other terrible diseases. He held his penis in his hand, like a child, trying to comfort himself. He was so cold. The knife was in the bedside drawer. The knife was whispering to him, calling him names. He'd cleaned the knife from the whore's diseased blood, he'd cleaned and cleaned and cleaned until it shone. When they'd beat him as a boy he would hide under the covers, later, clutching his penis. Why are childhoods so awful, the watcher wondered, and he remembered suddenly and with aching clarity Mr Woodford, the neighbour, a jolly chap always popular with the ladies of the neighbourhood, he was friends with Father, too, always nice to the kids: and he took him in, once, after a beating, and offered him candy and then took out a gross fleshy thing and asked the watcher to touch it. It was warm and it changed shape as the boy touched it, and Mr Woodford made strange sounds and spurted a milky viscous liquid that covered the boy's hand. But he always gave him sweets, after. Sweets and affection.

For a long time, the watcher blamed himself. It was their secret, his and Mr Woodford's. And you don't tell secrets. You never tell. Mr Woodford had fought in the war; he was a hero. The watcher closed his eyes but in the darkness he could still hear the footsteps approaching, and the rank hot breath of the prostitute, strangely similar to Mr Woodford's.

He couldn't sleep. He took the knife out from the drawer and ran the tip of his finger down the blade, drawing blood. There was comfort in that, a way of asserting control. He cut himself slowly, with great deliberation, running the blade down his ribs, littered with old scars. The blood stained the bedsheets. At last he could sleep.

•

In another time and place Shomer lies restlessly awake. There is nothing to do in the infirmary, no work, nothing to do but think of all that had been and is no more. Outside, the camp goes on its inexorable daily routine, and to the place where the tracks terminate the trains keep coming, carrying Jews. Every day more come to this Auschwitz-Birkenau complex, so vital for the interests of the war, from all across Europe they come, Poles and Czechs, Slovaks and Greeks, Italians and Hungarians, but all Jews, marked with the yellow star, all bound to be processed, quickly and efficiently, children and women and men, and the black smoke rises from the ovens, day and night the black smoke of Jews rises, so many Jews: who would have thought there were so many Jews still left in the world?

Prisoner 174517 is a recent arrival, an Italian, Levi by name. 'And how can we write this rent in the world,' he says, waving his hands animatedly while his voice remains soft. Like Shomer he has suffered a leg wound. 'Only by science, by using a language as accurate and dispassionate as possible can we describe the atrocities, for it is a scientific genocide we are subject to, with gas they are killing us, with charts and lists they record us, and in Mengele's lab they dissect us like animals. And this must be recorded, for future generations, to never forget, and for that the novelist must employ a language as clear and precise as possible, a language without ornament.'

He is not speaking to Shomer but to a veteran of the camp, a Polish Jew with soft sad eyes and curly black hair, skeletal like the rest of them. When asked his name, he says, 'I have no name. They took my name and now I am Ka-Tzetnik 135633, and no more—' *Ka-Tzetnik*, that is to say, 'inmate.' And Ka-Tzetnik says:

'But there you are wrong, for this is no longer the world you knew, the world any of us knew. That world is dead, everything is divided, Before-Auschwitz and the Now, for there is only now, even to think of a life beyond is to indulge in fantasy. But to answer your question, to write of this Holocaust is to shout and scream, to tear and spit, let words fall like bloodied rain on the page; not with cold detachment but with fire and pain, in the language of *shund*, the language of shit and piss and puke, of pulp, a language of torrid covers and lurid emotions, of fantasy: this is an alien planet, Levi. This is Planet Auschwitz.'

And Ka-Tzetnik says:

'We have no names. We have no parents and we have no children. We do not dress the way they dress on Earth. We were not born here and we do not give birth. We breathe by different rules of nature. We do not live by the laws of Earth and neither do we die by them. Our name is a number.'

And at those words the world makes sudden sense to Shomer, for here he is, an astronaut on an alien and hostile world—and isn't everything trying to kill him? 'Death and sex,' Ka-Tzetnik says, but mournfully, 'death and sex,' and he and Levi begin to argue, and Levi says, 'But that is kitsch, and bordering on pornography,' and so they go on until another inmate tells them to shut the fuck up about literature and they lapse into a heavy silence.

'Well, that's another fine mess you got us into,' Yenkl says, cheerfully, dangling his legs from an upper bunk bed, contentedly puffing on his pipe. And Shomer's mind shies from the glare, conjures up a safe haven, a world of mean streets and buxom dames and flat-footed detectives, as if, if only he could open up a secret door, he could be transported there, and be free.

9

WOLF'S DIARY, 10TH NOVEMBER 1939

'Well, well, shamus. Here we are again,' Keech, the fat policeman, said.

'Fuck you, pig,' I said. I wasn't in a good mood. I seldom was, these days. 'What are you holding me for this time? Last I checked fucking your mother wasn't a crime.'

His face darkened and he said, 'You're a right old funnyman, aren't you, Wolf.'

'What do you want, Keech? I'm trying to sleep here.'

They put me in a cell again in Charing Cross nick. This time I rather welcomed it. A doctor had looked me over but had better things to do. I got soup and bread and I fell asleep until the morning without being disturbed. I was aching all over but I would live. I was getting used to being beat up. It was all on a par for this line of work.

'How is the whore?' I said.

'She'll live,' Keech said.

'Is she talking?'

'Do you mean, does she confirm your story?' He laughed, a

short ugly laugh. 'She don't remember much.'

'What the hell do you mean?'

'I *mean* that all Gerta remembers is being assaulted by a man, and that the last face she saw was yours. So why did you do it, shamus? You have a thing for whores?'

'I didn't do it!'

He leered at me, this fat fuck of a pig.

'God damn it, I didn't *do* it, Keech!'

'Scared, Wolf? You should be.'

'But this is absurd! I came to her rescue. Keech, you have to believe me!'

'I don't have to believe shit, shamus. This isn't the church. It's the law.'

'You have no proof!'

He shook his jowled face. 'You won't get off again this easily,' he said. Then he went and shut the cell door on me and turned the key in the lock.

WOLF'S DIARY, 11TH NOVEMBER 1939

'Enjoying your time with us?'

'Are you going to charge me, or let me go?'

'We'll never let you go, kraut.'

I sighed. 'You're walking a dangerous line, Keech,' I said.

'Are you threatening me?'

I stared at him and he laughed, but there was no humour in his eyes. 'Inspector wants to see you.'

'Tell him to go to hell,' I said.

'Oh, play nice, Wolf,' Keech said. 'You look worse than a beat-up old whore, you know. You could do with a friend.'

'Are you going to be my friend, Keech? We could go fishing together up the Thames.'

'How are you feeling?' He was being solicitous and that had me worried.

'I've been worse.'

'Then come along. We don't want to keep the inspector waiting, do we.'

I followed him, stretching. I was beginning to like the cell. Maybe I could finally write that sequel to my book, if they kept me in there long enough. Once again down the corridor and to Inspector Morhaim's small office. He sat behind his desk as if he hadn't moved since the last time I saw him. 'Mr Wolf. Do sit down.'

I took a chair. I saw no reason not to.

'You know Mr Freisler?'

We were not alone in the room. I nodded, politely. 'Hello, Roland.'

He had a long mournful lawyer's face and a lawyer's fidgety manners. The bald dome of his head was bookended by black hair like a wig. He was an anti-Semite and an early Party member and I had met him in Berlin a few times. I hadn't realised he had escaped Germany after the Fall, or that he was still alive. To be honest, I had given the man no thought at all. In the early days he had helped defend members of the SA when they inevitably got into trouble with the law. How he came to be here, now, I had no idea.

'Herr Wolf.'

'What are you doing here, Roland?'

'If it pleases you, sir, I am here as your representative.'

'Are you,' I said. I looked at Morhaim. I could see he had to hold down his temper. He did not like Freisler's being there. 'And who, if you don't mind me asking, sent you?'

'My employer would rather remain anonymous,' the lawyer said.

'I don't doubt that,' I said. He nodded, briefly. 'It is good to see you again, sir,' he said.

'I wish I could say the same. You are not needed, Freisler. You are dismissed.'

'But sir!'

Morhaim sighed. 'Mr Wolf,' he said, 'do you know why you are here?'

'I am unjustly accused of a crime I did not commit,' I said.

'Yes, yes. But since I am sure there are many crimes which you did commit, and of which you have never been accused, don't you think that rather cancels out?'

'I object,' Freisler said.

Morhaim turned mild eyes on him. 'To what?'

'My client is not guilty of any crime.'

'And I am not accusing him of any . . . yet.'

'Is this about the whore?' I said. 'I told your man Keech, I had nothing to do with it.'

'How do you explain being covered in blood? Again?'

'I cut myself shaving.'

Morhaim almost cracked a smile. 'Gerta will live,' he said. 'Though she won't be whoring for a while, I'm afraid. A brave woman, and very spirited.'

'Good old Gerta,' I said, with feeling.

'How do you explain your close proximity to both murders?' Morhaim said.

'I object,' Freisler said again. We both ignored him. 'They were committed right outside my office,' I said. 'You can hardly blame me . . .'

'Yes . . .' Morhaim said. 'It is strangely suggestive, though, don't you think, Mr Wolf?'

'Someone is trying to frame me.'

'No doubt, no doubt. You must have many enemies.'

I had no answer to that. It was true I'd not exactly been making friends, of late. Genius is often lonely.

'I'd like to show you something,' Morhaim said.

'You could show me the door.'

'Very witty, Mr Wolf.' He looked pained. 'Mr Freisler?'

'Yes?'

'You will remain behind?'

'I must represent my client—'

There was something unspoken in the air and I didn't like it. The lawyer subsided. 'He goes free?'

'Do we have a choice?'

'Very well. Mr Wolf.' He nodded to me again and departed abruptly, a dark bird taking flight. I wondered what had spooked him.

'I'm free?'

'I want to show you something.'

'Will it take long?'

'Do you have other plans?'

'Who hired the lawyer?' I said.

Morhaim stood. 'Please. Follow me.'

Once more I was led back to my cell, once more my own clothes were returned to me. I followed Morhaim out of the police station. A wan day, the sun struggling behind grey clouds. Morhaim's car was a beat-up Trojan Tourer, at least a decade old. 'You have treated this vehicle abominably,' I said, unable to help myself. He shrugged, almost in apology.

'Please,' he said, gesturing. I entered the passenger side.

He drove badly. The car's suspension was all but non-existent. I suffered in silence though my bruises had stiffened in my two nights of captivity and the journey was agony. 'Where are we going?'

We were headed west. The cityscape changed, buildings became grander, the make of cars better, the streets cleaner. We came to Hyde Park and Morhaim parked the car. I was just grateful, at that moment, that we'd stopped.

He led me through the park gate, still not speaking. He seemed lost in thought.

'Are we going to feed the ducks?' I said.

He turned to me abruptly. There was something like real agony in his eyes. 'Why do you hate the Jews so much?' he said. 'What have Jews ever done to you, Mr Wolf?'

I felt embarrassed for him. I didn't reply. After a moment he turned away and continued walking. I followed.

We were walking through pleasant green grass, Kensington Palace to our left, a low rising hill ahead. People were out walking their dogs. I missed Prinz and Muckl very much at that moment.

'Where are we going?' I said again. Then we crested the low rise and I saw the duck ponds ahead of us. I saw a police van and men in uniform idling by and I prepared myself for what I'd find there.

'Another dead whore?' I said.

'In a manner of speaking.'

He led me, not hurrying. As we approached I saw a body had been dredged out of the pond. It was a man, lying face down in the mud. A rather majestic swan was preening nearby, calling to a mate.

We stood over the corpse. Morhaim nodded wordlessly and a policeman in thick boots rolled the body onto its back. But even before he did I knew who it was. I stared down at Rudolf Hess's bloodless face. His head was twisted at an unnatural angle, the grass framing it almost gently, like a crown. He was as dead as anyone I ever saw.

*

It was Saturday. As Wolf stared down at his one-time companion the church bells began to ring from across the park, from Kensington and from Bayswater. Beyond their huddled group, people went about their lives, strolling in the park, admiring the trees and the autumn colours, enjoying the brisk chill air. People were on their way to church or to market. Life went on everywhere at once: the ducks stared disinterestedly and the swans preened on the calm surface of the water.

'Who did this?' Wolf said. His voice was low.

'I understand you saw him recently?' Morhaim said. 'There is a club he frequented. Owned, in fact. The Hofgarten on Gerrard Street. I understand it is popular with German émigrés . . . of a certain bent, anyway.'

'I . . . was there, yes.'

'I understand that you had a fight.'

'Please!' Wolf was agitated. 'This is persecution! First the whores, now this?'

'Can you identify the victim?'

'What for? It is quite obvious that you know who it is.'

'Who is it?'

'Hess. Rudolf Hess. He is . . . he was a businessman.'

The young policeman with the thick boots snorted. Morhaim silenced him with a gesture. 'You knew each other before? In Germany?'

'You know that we did.'

'In fact you were in prison together, were you not, Mr Wolf?'

'This is irrelevant!'

'Can you tell me what you talked about? When you last saw him?' Morhaim consulted a notebook. 'November 7th?' he said. 'It was a Tuesday.'

'It was last Tuesday.'

'Indeed?'

Wolf said, 'You are well informed.' He stared down at Hess's lifeless face. 'He was a good man,' he said.

'What did you talk about?'

Wolf waved a hand. 'Old times,' he said.

'Were you close in recent years?'

'We did not see each other often.'

'And yet you saw each other twice in the space of a week? Following which Mr Hess'—Morhaim gestured at the corpse—'was found earlier this morning in a fatal condition.'

'I did not murder Rudolf!'

'Then who did, Mr Wolf?'

'I don't know.'

Morhaim nodded. 'Thank you.'

'Excuse me?'

'I said, thank you, Mr Wolf.' He waited a beat. 'You can go.'

'Is that *all*?'

'I'm afraid we *are* rather busy . . . was there anything else you wanted to add?'

'No.'

'Then goodbye, Mr Wolf. I'm sure we'll meet again.' He gave a faint half-smile. There was nothing warm in it, nothing at all. 'Who knows what we'll find floating in the duck ponds next, eh?'

Wolf stood there, glaring. He wanted to wipe the smirk off the inspector's face. But the man would not look away and, at last, Wolf about-turned and stalked off.

WOLF'S DIARY, 12TH NOVEMBER 1939

On Sundays, London becomes almost bearable. I did my laundry. I saw Martha, the woman who lived down the hall. The corpulent old bitch came and stood in the doorway of the washroom and regarded me with her arms crossed as I washed my clothes in the bathtub. 'You wash like a woman,' she said.

'Don't you have any pigeons to poison?' I asked. She chuckled. 'Soon, ducky,' she said. 'It's a bit early in the day.'

I thought of the families who came to Trafalgar Square to look at the pigeons. At this old woman smiling at the children like a lost aunt, and selling their parents a small bag of seeds; the children scattering the feed in an arc, the grey birds descending. Pigeons were like Jews: as many as you killed there were always more to take their place.

I scrubbed bloodstains out of my clothes. The tub filled with pink swirling shapes. 'Been in a spot of trouble, have you, ducky?'

'None of your God damned business.'

'Heard you was out on the street, night someone took a knife to old Gerta,' she said.

'I didn't do it.'

'No one saying that you did, ducky.'

'A friend of mine died yesterday,' I told her. I don't know why I told her that.

'I'm sorry to hear it.'

I shrugged. Lathered up soap. 'He was weak. The weak die.'

'And the strong survive,' she said. There was a sad note in her voice I couldn't interpret. 'You and me,' she said. 'The pigeons and the whores.'

'He was so loyal,' I said. 'To his last breath, he was loyal. I value loyalty.'

'Heaven knows there's little enough of it to go around,' Martha said.

'Someone killed him. Drowned him in the ponds in Hyde Park.'

'That's nice.' She gave a shuddering, dramatic sigh. 'It's so peaceful there. I went once, with one of my old johns. He liked to do it in nature, you see. He was French.' She shrugged, as if that was explanation enough for everything. 'It must be a nice place to die.'

'I hadn't thought of it that way.'

'Do you ever think how you will die, Wolf?' she said. The conversation was turning morbid but somehow I didn't mind. My mind had been occupied with death, of late.

'I always thought I'd die in the course of my duty,' I said. 'Serving the Fatherland. It hasn't worked out that way.' I thought of the Americans' offer. I wondered if they were still shadowing me. No doubt they could make life difficult for me, if they so chose. To return to Germany . . . it was a dream, a sweet dream, but nothing more. And if, by some insane miracle, their *coup d'état* succeeded . . . what then?

I would become their puppet.

'I would have liked to die peacefully,' I said, 'in my sleep. With a book on my chest and a woman beside me and my dogs at my feet.'

'How . . . pleasant.' There was a rude loud sound and a look of surprise momentarily suffused Martha's face, followed by a bellowing laugh.

'God damn it, Martha, that stinks!'

'I knew I should have laid off them Brussels sprouts,' she said, fanning the air. 'Well, I better go. When is your friend's funeral?'

'I don't know. The police haven't released the body yet.'

'Will you go?'

'I don't know.'

'Goodbye, Wolf.'

'See you later, Martha.'

She left me alone with her stink still in the air. I scrubbed blood off my clothes and watched the soapsuds form in the bathtub, pink and red, pink and red.

On Monday I went back to the Jewish Territorialist Organisation but the lights weren't on. There was no sign of Goodman or the typist and a notice on the door simply said 'Closed'.

I made an anonymous phone call to the police and watched the flat on Threadneedle Street. I ate a sandwich and drank lemonade. The police arrived promptly enough but, as I suspected, the flat was empty and seemed to have been that way for a couple of days. I crumpled the paper I had used to wrap the sandwich and put it and the empty bottle of lemonade back in my bag, to dispose of later. I loathed litter.

I had come so close! That mannish Jew bitch had been all but in my grasp and I let her slip away. It seemed obvious to me now that Judith Rubinstein's escape had been facilitated by her Palestinian comrades. Either they had struck a deal with my former associates or they had known to hijack the shipment of illegals before it was delivered into that loathsome Barbie's hands. Either way I now had no idea where she was, and I had lost both her and the terrorists threatening Mosley.

I had hit a temporary dead end. It was in the nature of such work, and yet I felt angry. I wanted those Jew conspirators caught. I could only hope that the Blackshirts who had unwittingly come to my rescue the night I trailed Bitker had put some of them into hospital.

Hospital!

I returned to my office and set to work. For the next hour I dialled the local hospitals. No luck! Wherever my Palestinian terrorists went, it was not to a public hospital.

'*Himmel, Arsch, und Zwirn!*' I said, with feeling.

'What do you mean Mosley is not there?' I said.

'*Sir Oswald* is not here.'

'Sir Oswald, yes, fine. Where is he?'

'I'm afraid Sir Oswald is unavailable at the moment, sir. Would you care to leave a message?'

'No, I do not *care* to leave a message! Who is this?'

'Thomas Alderman, sir.'

'Alderman? Who the hell are you?'

'I'm Sir Oswald's assistant, sir. One of his assistants.' An embarrassed hesitation on the line. 'We met, briefly? At Sir Oswald's soirée?'

'Did we? Well, Alderman, is Lady Mosley there?'

'No, sir. I'm afraid no one is available. It is the elections, you see. The final push and all that? Sir Oswald is speaking to supporters around the country all week.'

'And Lady Mosley?'

'She is with Sir Oswald, sir.'

'I don't like your tone, Alderman.'

'Sir?'

'Tell him I called. Tell him I expect to hear from him!'

'Of course, Mr . . . Wolf?'

'You know bloody well who it is,' I said, slamming down the receiver.

The sheer arrogance of it all!

'Hello?'

She had the kind of breathless voice that promises sin, that teases you with it. I hated her and wanted her and I didn't lie to myself about it. I never lie to myself. It is the core of my strength.

'Miss Rubinstein.'

'Wolf!' Her voice changed, became a delighted tinkle. I pictured her urinating on herself, surrounded by silk sheets. 'Is there progress on my sister's case?'

'It has become somewhat more complex than I at first anticipated.'

'What does that mean?'

It means a terrorist conspiracy, I thought, but didn't say. And a dead man in a pond. I was trapped in a maze, beset on all sides by those with evil intentions. I alone was pure of thought and deed. Were I ever asked to offer my observations on the art of detection—for which I am uniquely qualified—I would say that a good detective is but a soldier in the universal *chaoskampf*, the cosmic battle with anarchy. Murder is a frustration not just of the individual: it is a frustration of the race. Indeed, I had written several times to the *Private Investigator's Gazetteer*, of Boston, Massachusetts, offering to share my views on detection—on condition, naturally, of receipt of a modest author's fee—but had yet to receive a reply. The impudence of those Americans!

For murder is a simple art—if it can be said to be any art at all—and it seems to me it is merely a question of *scale*. I believe it was that French scientist, Rostand, who wrote that if you kill one man, you are a murderer, yet if you kill millions, you are a conqueror. I would have been a conqueror!

Chaos, all my life I have battled chaos!

Was I the only completely sane man still left in the world?

'Wolf!'

'Yes,' I said, coming back to myself with a start.

'You were saying?'

'I may need your help,' I said, hating myself for it.

'Oh?'

'I am working on a case that may be related. I need access to . . . a part of the Jewish community.'

I heard her laugh. 'You want me to work with you? Solving . . . crime? Like Nick and Nora Charles!'

'Very amusing, yes. But no.'

'Really!' I could hear rustling sounds on the other end of the line. Imagined her rubbing her naked thighs against the sheets. Bit my lip, trying to concentrate. 'You can't manage on your own, Wolf?'

'Let's just say my previous attempt has not been a complete success.'

'I can't imagine why!'

'Listen you horrid little bitch, don't you—'

'I love it when you talk dirty,' she said. 'And I'd be delighted to help—in fact, we may be able to help each other.'

'Oh?'

'I'd like you to come with me to a party.'

'I beg your pardon?'

'It's the event of the season!' she said. 'I'll pick you up, tomorrow, at six thirty sharp. Dress nicely, Wolf.'

'What sort of party? Wait—' but she had already hung up. I sat there staring at the phone and cursing all Jews.

'You look so dashing,' she said. She was standing in my office smoking a cigarette through a silver holder. Her white dress shimmered as she moved around the room.

'*Must* you smoke?' I said.

'Does it antagonise you?' She grinned at me with her lovely white teeth and shimmied to me. Her hand reached down and grabbed me by the crotch, hard. She had no shame; no shame at all. She leaned her head into the crook of my neck, licked upwards. Her teeth nibbled my earlobe. 'Why do I like bad boys so . . .' she murmured.

'You're a harlot,' I said. 'A slut.'

She pulled away from me and slapped me, hard. 'Fuck you, Wolf!' Her eyes flashed. 'Get on your knees,' she said.

'Get away from me, you whore.'

She laughed, a cruel high-pitched sound. 'Get down on your *knees*,' she said. She kicked me, suddenly, sweeping my legs from under me. I fell, painfully. 'That's better.'

I whispered, 'Whore . . .' My mouth was dry. She lifted up the hem of her dress. She wore nothing underneath. She grabbed me by the back of the head and forced my face between her thighs. My mouth was on her engorged lips as they rubbed against my face again. She made strange animal sounds; her intensity was building up too quickly, but then she stopped. She stepped away from me, holding the hem of the dress carefully so as not to stain it. 'Turn over,' she said. 'I said turn over!'

Then she was kicking me, calling me names, terrible names, tearing at my trousers, pulling them down. My behind was exposed to the air and she slapped it, again and again, leaving angry red marks on the white flesh, and she was moaning: the room was a cacophony of animal sounds. I held myself in my hand, I felt her finger slide, coated in her discharge, suddenly and painfully into my anus. I screamed and came, spurting seed over my hands, but careful, careful not to stain the rented suit. She stood over me, breathing heavily.

'We'll be late,' she said.

I stood up carefully, pulled up my trousers one-handed. Isabella wiped herself clean with a monogrammed handkerchief, quite un-selfconsciously. I left her there and went to the bathroom down the hall and stared at my face, shining with her wetness, in the mirror. I washed my hand, watching my seed wash down the sinkhole. I washed my face. When I left I saw Martha at the end of the corridor. She watched me without expression until I turned away.

In my office Isabella Rubinstein was a model of decorum. Her cigarette holder was set between her teeth again. She blew out a cloud of smoke contentedly and smiled at me. 'We don't want to be late, do we,' she said.

I followed her down the stairs when I remembered I had stashed the Jewish identity document behind the bins, after the fat prostitute's attempted murder. 'Excuse me,' I said. I went back down the road and retrieved it: it was still there, in a crack in the wall. Dried blood was still splattered, in dull patches, on the stone. I returned to Isabella. Her white Crossley Sports Saloon was parked outside the dirty bookstore, magnificent and shining like a beacon of wealth. Isabella drove. I sat beside her. The car was filled with the smell of her expensive tobacco and the musk of our hurried sex.

She drove with easy abandon, the way she did everything else. She was young, so much younger than me, yet something inside her was rotten and corrupt, and it withered her from within.

We drove with the windows open and a cold breeze wafting past and the smell of London, of salt and tar from the Thames and urine from the sewers and roasting chestnuts and exhaust fumes and dung from horse-drawn carriages. In what seemed like moments we were by the British Museum. Greek columns rose into the air and a thin drizzle of rain began to fall as Isabella parked the car. A glow of festive light came from behind the windows of Number 40, Museum Street.

I clenched my fists.

These were, after all, the premises of Allen & Unwin, the publishers.

People were spilling out of the open doors of the publishing house. They stood in clumps in the rain, smoking and drinking and laughing, an unruly crowd of artists, writers and painters and their hangers-on. 'Oh, how *exciting*!' Isabella said, weaving her arm through mine. We strolled up to the party; I felt conspicuous in my suit and hat amongst the mob of scruffy bohemians. And yet I was once one of them; I, too, was once a penniless artist, in Vienna, painting bright watercolours of the city's architecture and scenes, selling them to the tourists for a handful of coins. It had felt to me then an honest way of making a living. But that had been before the war, before the blindness and the hospital, before my fate had been shaped to follow a different path: to lead, to rule!

At last, to Fall.

'Managed to insult both of us in the same sentence!' someone said.

'Wolf? Are you with us?' Isabella said.

'Yes, yes, of course,' I said. 'Is that Evelyn Waugh talking to Cecil Forester?'

Isabella shrugged. 'Are they painters?'

'Writers,' I said. Isabella went ahead of me, her arm slipping out of mine. She nodded and smiled, greeting people she knew. 'Who is the Chinese-looking man?' I said.

'That? That's Leslie Charteris!' she sighed as though in ecstasy. 'Don't you just love *The Saint*?'

'Charteris?' I said. 'I thought he was working in Hollywood.'

'He is. There's a company of them arrived in town for filming. But no one's going to miss this party.'

We went inside.

'Wolf!'

I turned to see, without much surprise, the big American,

Virgil, bearing down on me, a glass of wine in each hand. He handed me one without asking. I held it without sipping. I abhor drink, always have. To me, a man must always be in supreme command of himself.

'Virgil,' I said; for a moment I felt like a gunslinger in one of Karl May's westerns, facing a showdown. The feeling persisted.

He smiled at me but his eyes were hooded. 'Have you thought further of my proposition?' he said.

'I have.'

He waited, but I said nothing more. He nodded, slowly and inexorably, the way a mountain moves in an earthquake. 'Don't think for too long,' he said, softly. 'Everyone can be replaced, Wolf. Even you.'

'I have never liked Americans,' I said, and he laughed. He had the coldest, hardest eyes of any man I'd ever seen. 'Cheers,' he said, clinking his glass against mine.

'Are your people still following me?' I said.

He sipped from his drink and shrugged. 'Do they need to?' he said.

'Is that a yes?'

He shrugged again. One had the sense of contained physical threat in every gesture he made. 'I hear you're having troubles,' he said, 'with some prostitute murders.'

'*One* prostitute murder,' I said, 'and I didn't do it.'

'You're not a killer,' he said, sympathetically. 'You're a soldier, like I was, like many of us will be again once war breaks out.'

'You believe war will break out?'

'It's only a matter of time,' he said. His glass was already empty. He looked at mine. 'Do you mind?'

'Not at all.' He took it from me and drank as though he had been deprived of drink for months. 'Yes,' he said, after draining my glass. 'War with Germany will come—war with Russia, I should say, and its proxy, Germany. A European war. Perhaps even another world war.' He put his hand on my shoulder, squeezing. His rank breath blasted into my face, coarse with the fumes of cheap red wine. 'You can help stop that,' he said. 'Do you want to see your country ravaged by war, destroyed by bombs? International socialism *must* be stopped, Wolf. Stopped before it is too late!'

The words sent a chill down my spine. Or perhaps it was the draught from the open door. 'At what price?' I said. 'You want me to serve Germany by turning her into a whore, spreading her legs wide for America?'

He laughed. 'Everyone needs must be a whore sometimes,' he said. 'Would you rather be fucked by the Russians, or us?'

'I would rather my country slit its own throat than prostitute itself,' I said.

'Listen to me, Wolf.' He was standing close, now, his hand on my shoulder reaching for my neck, almost choking me. 'You do not say no to me. No one does. I am America, and America does not take no for an answer. Refuse us, and we will bomb the shit out of your country, kill your women and rape your dogs and burn your houses and piss on the embers. Do you understand me? I said, do you understand me!'

'I understand you perfectly,' I said. I gathered up phlegm and spat in his face. My aim was perfect. The mucus hit him in the eye and ran down his cheek. His face turned red in fury; his grip on my neck slackened. 'And the answer is no. *Nein*. Never!'

'You will regret this, you little shit stain,' he said.

'Get your fucking hands off me!'

'Wolf? Who is this man?'

I felt rather than saw Virgil's hand leave my neck. He wiped his face with a handkerchief. When he turned back his face wore a semblance of charm. 'Just an old friend,' he said. 'I apologise if I was monopolising his time at your expense, Miss . . . ?'

'Rubinstein. *Excuse* me.' She led me away, to a corner of the room. I felt Virgil's glowering presence receding behind us. 'Who *was* that ghastly man?' Isabella said.

'I . . . am not sure,' I said. I had a bad feeling about Virgil: about the possible fallout from my refusal. Could the Americans be better allies than the Russians, in the long run? Could I still somehow use them to my advantage? And his mention of the prostitute murder—if they were following me, could they have inadvertently come across the real killer's identity?

But I had no time to dwell, for at that moment I saw a figure I recognised, and all thoughts of such things fled from my mind. 'Albert!' I yelled. 'Albert! It's Wolf!'

I abandoned Isabella to her own devices and hared across the room. He turned slowly, with a smile of polite inquiry on his face, which disappeared when he saw me. 'Ah, Wolf,' he said, awkwardly.

Albert Curtis Brown was my literary agent. He was originally an American journalist who had then settled and made his home in Britain. He was in his seventies, but still wiry and strong. 'I wanted to discuss with you a sequel to *My Struggle*,' I said.

'Quite, quite. Mr Wolf. A sequel.' Was it my imagination or did a fleeting look of distaste pass across his face like a cloud? But I did not care for Mr Curtis Brown's approval; I cared for what remained of my literary career. 'I have written to you repeatedly,' I said, '*repeatedly*, in the past few months, regarding the manuscript I am in the process of preparing—'

'Let me stop you there, Mr Wolf,' he said. 'I am no longer actively involved with the agency. My son is taking care of all outstanding contracts and the like. Now, if you'll excuse me—'

'Wait!' I said. 'Mr Curtis Brown, I really must insist that the agency treat me with more respect. I have never even received payment of royalties due to me!'

'Mr Wolf, there *are* no royalties.' He sighed, looking suddenly old. 'The manuscript was taken on, from the German publishers, in the good faith that it would be of general interest to contemporary readers as a view of the situation in Germany.'

'Yes? Yes?'

'Well, Mr Wolf, the belief was that National Socialism would win the elections of 1933, therefore catapulting Nazism into the international spotlight. This has failed to happen, and interest in the manuscript, accordingly, waned. I'm afraid there's little to add, really. Interest currently is in material by or about Stalin, or Ernst Thälmann, the current German Chancellor. Your advance never earned out, Mr Wolf. In fact, I believe unsold copies of *My Struggle* will soon be pulped, and the title allowed to go out of print.'

'Out of print!' I said, deeply shocked.

He nodded sadly. 'I'm afraid so,' he said.

'But that is an *outrage*! You must do something!'

'I'm afraid there is little I can do, Mr Wolf.' He patted me on the shoulder, awkwardly. 'History has passed you by, old chap,' he said. 'But look on the bright side. You're only—what? Fifty or so?—you're young enough to start again. Write something new. Not another diatribe against the Jews. That stuff is out of fashion now. Of specialist interest, certainly, but not of a mass market appeal. Why not try your hand at a proper novel, Mr Wolf?' He regarded me thoughtfully. 'Do you know,' he said, 'detective tales are always popular.'

'*Detective* tales?' I said. I was so dumbfounded I could only echo him. 'A work of *fiction*? Mr Curtis Brown, my book is a treatise on politics, on race; it draws from the most distinguished sources, not to mention my own autobiography—do you have any *idea* how many copies it has sold in Germany *alone*?'

'Like I said, I am no longer involved in the day to day running of the agency,' Curtis Brown said. 'I wish you all the best, Mr Wolf. But a word of advice—don't give up your day job just yet.' And with that, and chuckling to himself, he walked off abruptly, joining a circle in which I could only identify Alan Milne, the author of a popular children's book about a talking bear.

The outrage! The provocation!

For a few moments, I must confess, I wandered the party in a daze, seeing faces familiar to me only from their dustjackets' photograph, yet paying them no attention. My book was to be *pulped*? My *book*? *My* book?

It was inconceivable!

Across the large room a makeshift bar had been set over cartons of books, and there I saw Isabella chatting to Lord Rothermere, the owner of the *Daily Mail*.

I needed fresh air.

Instead, as I turned, I caught a hint of perfume, the flash of gold, a breathy voice saying my name, over and over. I turned and there she was, the most real woman I had ever seen, as bright as the star that she was.

'Leni?' I said, in total disbelief. 'Leni, is that *you*?'

•

The watcher in the dark was aware of the other watchers in the dark. There were so many eyes in the night. London was a city of watchers, all watching each other watching each other. It made him giddy just to think about it.

He knew so many secrets! He knew, for instance, that the detective was seeing the Jewish woman, and the shame of it was almost more than the watcher could bear. The detective, with a Jewess! The horror and the disgust it evoked in him were visceral, physical; he almost retched. He thought more and more of the woman, these days. She was a whore, as all Jewesses were. He thought of the knife, safe and hidden in his pocket, and how it might sing as it touched her flesh. He'd seen them, earlier, in her white car, together as they left. The whores on Berwick Street were more careful now. Some had moved away entirely, but not all. Business had to continue and this dark street was a foil for desire and a shelter for the men who frequented such creatures. Evil creatures, succubae. In ridding the world of them he was only easing their pain. And yet he could not lie, not to himself. He was not easing their pain. He was using them, if for a noble cause—using them to try and awaken the detective. Still: the whores were merely a means to an end.

The night was full of eyes and they made the watcher in the dark apprehensive. There were the American shadows, for instance. They were good; he had missed them entirely at first, and he suspected they may have seen him, the way shadows can see the other shadows in the night. He was worried about that. No one should have been able to see him.

He watched one now, young but hard-faced, the way he melted into the night; the way he, too, was watching the detective's office. Earlier the watcher saw him break in, with far more ease than the watcher himself had mustered. The American had slipped in as easily as a ghost. Now that he knew they were there the watcher found it easy enough to avoid them, but he had the feeling they had been there when . . . at the time of that unfortunate incident with the fat whore, and when he ran. He was reasonably sure he had shaken off any pursuers, overt or covert, by the time he changed his clothes in Soho Square, but he couldn't be positive. They might still come for him. Or maybe they didn't care. Or they even thought they could use him, now or later; but in that they were sorely wrong.

The detective was away with his Jew whore but sooner or later he would return and when he did the watcher would be ready. But not tonight. Tonight he only watched, and touched the knife, and he thought, suddenly and inexplicably, of the Alps, in winter, which he had never seen; and of the snow, falling and falling down on the slopes, until the whole world was white and pure.

•

In another time and place Shomer lies on the bunk bed as the snow falls outside; it falls and falls, as if, by its mere presence, it could silence the world. There is no work to be done in the infirmary, no hard labour, only time. And time is dangerous. It is a space in which to think. All is silent, until the doctor comes, walking past each patient, marking in his little black book. The doctor is a tall skeleton, with no face. He is dressed in a long black leather coat that rustles by his ankles as he walks. His pen is black and he examines each man with a cursory glance, checking each man against his number, in his little black book. A cross, a cross. And the men with the crosses rise without a murmur, without a murmur they walk to the gas chambers. The doctor like Death walks the rows of beds until at last he finds Shomer, and he gives him with a cursory glance and his diagnosis, what of his diagnosis? And he nods, once, and says, 'You're fit to leave,' and so with these words Shomer is once again saved; for a little while longer he's saved.

10

'Wolf!' She leaned in to the shorter man, kissing him on both cheeks. She smelled intoxicating to him. 'Darling, where have you *been*? Have you simply dropped off the face of the *Earth*?'

'Leni? Leni Riefenstahl? My God!' Wolf said. He could not take his eyes off her, she was radiant, a star. 'I thought you had been caught behind, in the Fall!'

'You silly man,' she said, laughing, 'do you not read *Photoplay*? I'm in Hollywood now!'

'Leni, but that is incredible! Let me look at you!'

He held her at arm's length, admiring her cool Germanic glamour; she was the most perfectly Aryan woman he had ever known.

'I remember seeing you speak in '32,' Riefenstahl said. 'You were incredible, amazing. The most magnetic man I'd ever met.'

'You're too kind.'

'And *My Struggle*! The book made a *tremendous* impression on me, Wolf.'

'You were always faithful to me, Leni. To the cause. Remember Nuremberg?'

'But of course.' Her face clouded. 'But what a terrible time it's been. I was all set up, mein kleiner Wolf. Ready to film the glorious victory of National Socialism, its inexorable rise to power!' For a moment she almost looked like she would cry. 'I would have called my documentary film *Sieg des Glaubens*, the Victory of Faith. But it was *der Verlust des Glaubens*, the loss of faith, instead. How could Germany do this, Wolf? How could history turn out so different than it should have?'

Wolf shook his head. 'Let us not speak of these things, *meine liebe*. I had thought many things impossible, yet here you are, and here I am—'

'Isn't London wonderful?' Riefenstahl said.

Wolf said, 'I would not say it is wonderful, exactly.'

'But, Wolf, what do you do here?'

'I'm a private investigator, Leni.'

For a moment she looked stunned; then she exploded in laughter. 'A private eye? A shamus? A *dick*? You, Wolf?'

'I believe in law, in order. There must always be order, Leni. There must always be an account.'

'Then you may as well become an accountant,' she said, dismissively. 'Oh, Wolf! You were meant for better things. You were meant to shape the future in your hands, to mould it like clay! You break my heart.'

She was crying. Wolf put his arms round her. People looked their way, then looked away. 'Come, *meine liebe*, come. Tell me of yourself. Tell me of Hollywood!'

'Oh, Wolf.' She pulled away, dried her tears with the tips of her fingers, began to tentatively smile. 'I went to America shortly before immigration out of Germany became impossible. I had friends, a director who wanted to work with me. I'd been offered a job with the studios in the past, but had turned them down. This time I accepted. I work for the Warner brothers now, in California.'

'Warner?' Wolf said.

'Jews,' Leni said. She shrugged apologetically. 'It is an industry dominated by Jews, Wolf. But it is what I do. We must all make a living.'

Wolf briefly thought of Isabella, on the other side of the room; pushed her out of his mind. 'I do not blame you, Leni,' he said. 'It is as you said: we must all make a living.'

'Oh, Wolf.' Her eyes filled with tears again. 'You don't know how much it means to me, to hear you say that.'

'Please! No more tears.' He put his arm round her waist. 'Let us go outside,' he suggested.

She acquiesced. Outside the rain was still falling, but softly, a London drizzle. The poet Stephen Spender was arguing loudly with Christopher Isherwood. Isherwood ceased abruptly and was violently sick on the pavement. Spender held his head gently, encouraging him to 'Let it all out!' to loud cheers from the assembled smokers and drinkers. 'Artists,' Leni said, as though that explained it all.

They had shared a powerful attraction, though it was never more than that; there was never talk of Wolf leaving Eva, for instance. They were two strong and charismatic people and their auras intertwined, for a while, and what they did behind closed doors was nobody's damn business.

'But what are you doing here?' Wolf said. 'In London?'

'You really don't read the film magazines,' she said. 'I don't know why that should surprise me—why should you? It's just that, in Hollywood, everyone knows your business in advance, before even you do. It's a city of hustlers, Wolf. Hustlers with big dreams.'

A small smile played on Wolf's lips. Leni always brought out his softer side. 'One could say the same of me.'

Leni laughed. 'It's a city of dogs,' she said. 'And you're a wolf.'

Wolf was touched. 'But you didn't answer my question,' he said. 'What are you doing in London?'

'We're filming!' Leni said. She saw the surprise on Wolf's face and laughed again. 'It's a wonderful picture,' she said. 'It really is. It's about Germany, in a way, you see. About the war. Everyone in America is convinced there is going to be a war, and soon.'

'Yes,' Wolf said, thinking of Virgil. 'But I hate the idea of my Germany at war, even a Germany fouled and abused by communism.'

'A war for the liberation of Germany,' Leni said. 'Surely that would be a good thing? Communism is an international threat.'

Wolf shook his head. 'I don't know,' he said, slowly. 'But I do not trust the Americans.'

Leni shrugged. She lit a cigarette, blew smoke as blue as a bruise into the cold humid air. 'But tell me about your film,' Wolf said. 'Your . . . your *picture.*'

Like all actresses, she was essentially shallow and self-involved, with the attention span of a child, he thought. She liked bright things and dominant men and an easy life. But she was charming, enchanting, with that ill-defined quality of the movie star about her: as if she could only ever truly exist on the silver screen, beyond the reach of mere mortals. There was something of the *waldelfen*, of the fey, about the screen folk like Leni, something ethereal and strange.

'Do you know the writer, F. Scott Fitzgerald?' Leni said.

'Not personally,' Wolf said.

Leni smiled tolerantly. 'Well,' she said, 'Scott was on contract to Metro-Goldwyn-Mayer, but Jack Warner stole him from them, and to be honest I think they were glad to be rid of him. He drinks, you see. And his health is quite poor as a consequence.'

'A wonderful writer,' Wolf said. '*The Great Gatsby?*'

'Yes,' Leni said. 'Well, it is about Gatsby, you see. Jack—Mr Warner—he's been after Scott for years, for a sequel.'

'But Gatsby dies!' Wolf said, shocked.

'Yes, yes,' Leni said; a little impatiently. 'But it's Hollywood.'

'So then, what does Warner want? You say it's a . . . a sequel?'

'In a way. You see, he's offered Scott rather a lot of money for an original screenplay. Scott originally called it *Everybody Comes to Gatsby's*. He was rather inspired by visiting Europe with his wife, Zelda—a lovely woman— and seeing the plight of the refugees fleeing the communist regime. In the screenplay, Gatsby survives his gun wound from the first book, and after several years travelling the world, working as a gun runner and revolution- ary, ends up a jaded, cynical bar owner in Morocco. War breaks out but Gatsby maintains his solitary existence even as desperate refugees come to Morocco en route to Free Europe. He spends his time drinking and smok- ing and playing complex chess problems against himself. Until one day Daisy Buchanan walks through his door, and everything changes.'

'Daisy? The woman he was so desperately in love with? But she left him, without a moment's thought!'

'Who knows the heart of a woman, Wolf,' Leni said. 'In any case, Jack didn't like the title. He felt it was too long. So the picture is named after the town Gatsby's is in. Tangier. We're shooting some of it here in London. I'm in it, you see, Wolf. I'm the star!'

Wolf stared at her, for once open mouthed. '*You're* Daisy Buchanan?' he said.

'And Humphrey Bogart is Gatsby,' Leni said.

'Who?'

'He's a great actor. Anyway, we've run into some problems with the production, so everyone's a little tense right now. You know how it is in motion pictures. Nothing is ever certain.'

'Like politics,' Wolf said, darkly.

'Yes. I suppose. It's all politics, isn't it, Wolf? Oh, Wolf, I wish things had been different!' She clung to him, fiercely. 'We'll always have Nurem- berg, won't we, Wolf? We'll always have that, at least?'

'Leni,' Wolf said, and then, in a different tone of voice, 'Leni, who is that man?'

'What man, Wolf?'

'There is a man coming towards us, Leni. He seems to want your attention.'

Leni turned her head. A man was indeed coming towards them, yet he did not approach, but waited in the drizzle, his fedora cocked to one side, a cigarette dangling from his lips. He was young and not unattractive, with dark wavy hair. Wolf knew his face immediately; but he did not think the man would have caught sight of his, before.

'Oh, it's only Robert!' Leni said, laughing. 'For a moment there you seemed so intense, I was almost scared!'

'Robert?'

'Robert Bitker. He's with the production crew. A Jew from Poland, but he's in with that Warner lot. Why, do you know him, Wolf?'

'I would like to know him better,' Wolf said, but quietly.

'I could introduce you!'

'Better not. Can you tell me where he's based?'

'Where we all are. The Grosvenor Hotel, by Victoria Station. Why, what's the matter, Wolf?'

'It's nothing, Leni. Leni, he seems to be trying to get your attention.'

'It must be a message from Hal. Hal Wallis? He's our producer. I think we're expected elsewhere. Oh, Wolf! Can I see you again?'

'I hope so. I would like that.'

'Come see me at the Grosvenor!' Leni said. 'We're here for another week. We were supposed to be shooting already but there'd been a problem with the studio, so we're just doing publicity and the like. Party, party, party, Wolf.'

'You seem to hang out with plenty of Jews, these days.'

'Oh, Wolf! Don't be like that. I don't like it any more than you do. It's just Hollywood.'

'Yes,' Wolf said. 'Well, you better go, Leni. I will come for you, soon.'

'Please do.' She kissed him on both cheeks, held him again at arm's length, marvelling. 'You look *tough*, Wolf. You should have been an actor!'

Wolf laughed, the sound startled from his throat. He couldn't remember the last time he'd laughed. He was not a man much given to frivolity, but Leni had a way with her. She was not like other girls. And she had taken his little predilections as something entirely natural, not even worthy of comment. She had been very accommodating in that way. He kissed her on both cheeks and off she went, to that man Bitker. Wolf watched them together. Bitker touched the brim of his hat, briefly, in acknowledgement, then turned his back on Wolf. Could he have recognised him?

But Wolf didn't think so. So the man he had been seeking and thought lost was there all along! A movie man, of all things. It made sense. Hollywood was full of Jews, Bitker must have been their appointed go-between, their bagman to the London cells: the American Jews sponsoring terror attacks on the Fascist leader carried out by their brethren in Britain.

But now Wolf knew where Bitker was. And he would not lose him a second time. And Bitker, in turn, would lead him to Judith. He was sure of it.

He went back inside. The party was picking up volume as drunken authors, poets, artists and their various editors, agents, copy editors and sales reps were polishing off Allen & Unwin's discretionary wine supply. 'Wolf?' It was Isabella, her cheeks flushed, her eyes shining with a mixture of alcohol and excitement. 'I have just met the most fascinating man, a professor of Anglo-Saxon at Oxford. John Tolkien? Apparently he has a novel with Allen & Unwin. Have you heard of him?'

'I've read his book,' Wolf said, grudgingly, though he had enjoyed it awfully. 'It is a trifle, a fantasy for toddlers, as all fantasy literature is inherently for children.'

'You're in a bad mood,' Isabella said, and there was a flash in her eyes, something dangerous and promising at the same time. She pressed close to him; her fingers closed hard on his crotch. 'Do you need to be punished?' she whispered, close in his ear. Her breath smelled of wine.

'Get away from me, you whore!'

Conversation quietened abruptly. People turned, watching them. A trim, energetic-looking gentleman in his fifties approached them. 'Is there a problem?' he said.

Isabella was pale. 'How dare you,' she said. 'How *dare* you!'

'Stay out of this,' Wolf said to the man. Isabella's hand rose to slap Wolf. He grabbed her wrist, his face burning in fury, his words coming out in spittle that hit her face. 'Whore! Foul, disgusting *whore*!'

Suddenly and terribly, Isabella laughed. 'And you like it!' she shouted. She pulled back her hand. Her smile was cruel. She pulled out a wad of notes from her handbag and tossed the money in Wolf's face. The money fluttered in the air, falling down gently around Wolf, settling between their feet. 'Who is the whore now, Mr Wolf?' Isabella said. Her beautiful young face was split by an ugly leer. 'You know where to find me, when you need more.'

She turned and stalked off.

'What do you want?' Wolf screamed, into the dapper gentleman's startled face.

The face hardened. 'I'm afraid I'm going to have to ask you to leave,' he said.

'And who the hell are you!'

'I am Stanley Unwin, sir. I am the owner of this office, and the host of this party. And . . . I don't believe that you were invited?'

'You're Stanley Unwin?' Wolf said. '*You're* Unwin?'

'I don't believe I've had the pleasure?'

'You rejected my *book*!' Wolf said. The man looked blank. 'I did? We receive so many books here at Allen & Unwin, it really is quite impossible for us to publish them all—'

'*My* book! *My Struggle*! I wrote it in *prison*! Do you know what I had to go through, the years of suffering, Vienna, the War, *imprisonment*, and you, you . . . you uppity God damned *Englishman*, you had the *gall* to *reject* it?'

'Like I said, it really is impossible to—'

'It wasn't even a *personal* rejection!'

'Sir, I must insist that you—*sir!* I must ask you to leave the premises immediately.'

'You damned Jew-lover! Don't you know who I am? And him'—Wolf was pointing wildly at the awkward, genial pipe smoker standing by the makeshift bar—'you publish *him*? This . . . this *Tolkien*? With tales of . . . of *hobbits*? I would have changed the world! My book *mattered*!'

'Sir!'

Two of the more burly authors present had materialised beside Unwin and were moving on Wolf, who backed away, his face red with anger, spittle dribbling from his lips in his passion. 'Damn you, Unwin! No one rejects *my* manuscript!'

'Get *out!*'

He wasn't, afterwards, sure who the men who threw him out were: Leslie Charteris and Evelyn Waugh, perhaps, as unlikely as that pairing may have seemed. They dragged him, still screaming and cursing, outside. They didn't let go until they reached the end of Museum Street and there they threw him bodily to the ground. Wolf landed in a puddle, cold rain soaking his coat. The two men stood panting above him, and one of them lit a cigarette while coughing. 'Forget it, man,' he said. 'It's just a God damned party.'

'Everybody gets rejected, sometimes,' the other said. They stood there breathing heavily and watched him; until Wolf picked himself up and dusted himself down, and without another word walked away.

WOLF'S DIARY, 16TH NOVEMBER 1939—CONTD.

When I had arrived at the hospital in Pasewalk, in 1918, I was scared—terrified. I won't deny it, won't lie. I was a ghost of the man I had been, a shadow. I moved in the dark, in a place into which no light was allowed to penetrate. I was frantic with fear.

The hospital was cool and calm and the nurses abrupt but not unkind. I remember being led down a corridor, trying to picture my environment using my other senses—smell and touch and sound. It was terrifying, the noises I could hear from the rooms we passed, the screams and the groans and the mutters of the inmates. I had been plucked off the battlefield and placed in an insane asylum. But I was not mad!

I was the sanest man I ever knew.

That first day, and the smell of disinfectant, of cabbage boiled too long, of the nurses' uniforms, that smell of clean washing. The nurse helped me to my room, to the narrow bed beneath a window out of which I could not see. I was blind! For hours I lay on my back, staring into absolute dark. I was clean, washed, scrubbed. There was no mud, no sound of shells whistling overhead, no cries of the dying, of my people, my people. Germany suffered, and I suffered with her. At that time, perhaps, though it is hazy to me now, I still believed I would be an artist. But how could an artist work who could not see the canvas? I was no longer one thing, but not yet another. I was myself an empty canvas, waiting to be filled with light.

It was only the next day that I met him. The nurse led me to his office and helped me sit down. Before me was his desk; I felt its edges, holding the thick board of wood between thumb and fingers, as though to reassure myself of its reality. I knew him only as a voice then. It was his voice that haunted my sleep, his voice that shaped me.

He said, 'My name is Dr Forster.'

I gave him my name and my rank. He began to question me, noting down my answers with a scratch of his pen on the paper. His voice was gruff, his manners equally so. I felt he was quizzing me, pushing me. He was challenging me, calling me a deserter from the front, a coward, telling me I was shirking my duty! I protested, spoke of my desire to go back to the front, to fight for the Fatherland. I felt him become puzzled as the time went by. I got the impression, never spoken aloud, that many of the inmates at this hospital were just of the nature he accused me of being: faking injuries and mental states to escape the trenches and the war. But I was not like that! And my injury was real: I had been blinded by the gas!

'You must help me!' I said. 'Is there nothing you can do?' and then, when he said nothing, 'Why was I brought here? These people are crazy! Do you say my blindness is not real? That I too am faking it?' My voice rose in pitch and fever. 'You must help me, doctor! I must see again!'

His silence lengthened. At last he promised to speak with me again, later, but I could sense that he was puzzled. I was not what he had expected. I was led back to my room and once again stretched out on the bed. I whiled away hours in this manner, thinking furiously, blaming God though I did not believe in him, blaming my father, blaming the British and even my own leaders, for failing to secure us a victory.

I was then but a boy, a child. I had seen death and destruction of the most terrible kind, but I did not yet appreciate the larger shape of the war, of the world. I cried, I blamed others.

But Dr Forster cured me.

The next day I was called in to his office. We sat in silence. At last he began to speak. His voice was low, gentle, hypnotising. He was a neuropsychologist, I learned later; a decorated, veteran medical officer, and a German patriot. He spoke of his other patients: malingerers, hysterics. The day before he had examined my eyes. Now he told me the worst: what I had suspected was true. I was blind, my eyes irreparably damaged by the gas. I would never see again!

Perhaps I burst out crying. I am no longer sure. His voice kept speaking to me, gently, authoritatively. 'You are not like the others, Lance-Corporal,' he told me. 'You are special. In you I see something of the past glory of Germany. A Siegfried, an Attila, a Wotan!'

'I am blind!' I wailed. 'I am nothing, I am dirt.'

He slapped me. My cheek burned. My pity was replaced with rage. I rose, I swore at him, I kicked away the chair. I stumbled blind and cursing in the dark. 'Yes, yes!' he said. 'You are angry! Passionate! Do not whine like a dog who has been hit! There is a chance yet, Lance-Corporal. Yes! I must tell you, there is one chance.'

His words penetrated my agonised consciousness. 'A chance?' I said, quietly.

'Yes,' he said, 'for you see, you are exceptional, Lance-Corporal; you are nothing short of an *Übermensch*! I believe in you, Lance-Corporal.' I heard him move about the room. Heard a match being struck. He said, 'I have lit a candle. All else is in darkness. Can you see the flame?'

'No,' I said. 'No!'

'Yet I believe that you *can* see it!' he cried. 'Use the power of your mind, Lance-Corporal! Believe yourself great, greater than any who had ever stepped upon this earth. With the power of your mind alone, you can achieve anything! Do it for Germany, do it for the Fatherland, now under threat from its many enemies. Can you do it?'

'No,' I said, 'no, I can't!'

It was lunacy, surely! I had been blinded, physically blinded. How could I heal myself through the power of thought alone? But his voice kept at me, urging me, like a conductor facing an orchestra. 'Prove yourself!' he said. 'If you can see the flame, then you are

212

indeed a great man, an Over-Man. If you can see the light, then you could lead all of Germany, lead our nation to victory! Show me,' he said, 'the triumph of the will!'

I was roused by his speech, by his words. I had always thought myself special, not like the others. I always knew better. Secretly, I believed him. His words made me see the truth at last. I had tried to pass for normal when I was nothing of the sort! And as I thought this, as his words kept running through my mind, my eyes became acutely sensitive. I began to discern a dull flickering light.

Perhaps he could tell as much from the movements of my eyes. 'You are doing it!' he cried. I concentrated—could I really heal myself? Cause organic damage to be replaced by healthy tissue? Slowly, slowly the image resolved, grew in depth and detail. It was a flame! A bright flame in the dark room. I could see the candle now, the wax running down the shaft, its grooves and irregularities. Slowly, the room came into focus, shelves of books, the grand desk. The flame threw shadows on the walls. And there he was, too. Dr Forster.

He had a bespectacled, round face with receding dark hair. He had an intense expression. His eyes shone with fervour, or so it seemed to me in my state then. 'You did it!' he said. 'You can see!'

'I can see, doctor!' I said, overwhelmed. But I was not overwhelmed for long. So many things had suddenly become clear to me then. The truth of who and what I was, and the destiny that lay before me. The boy I had been was dead, gone. A man—an *Übermensch*—had emerged in his place.

I don't know why I recalled my sessions with Dr Forster as I walked back through the rain. I was in a fog of rage. For a moment

I imagined myself an *Übermensch* again, leaping into the sky, soaring over the city as I sought out my enemies with my powerful vision. But events have proven me wrong. The Fall had crushed my dreams. Forster had restored my sight, but he had done so by trickery, by sleight of hand.

For I had seen the details of my file from that time: 'A hysteric,' he had written. In those notes he claimed there had been nothing wrong with my sight. That I had merely suffered a nervous reaction, believing myself blind; but that there was no organic, no physical damage to the eyes.

The foul man had tricked me!

And in the process he had made me into an instrument of righteousness. The man who would lead Germany. Or so I thought, until the Fall; until I lost everything I had once believed in and became, once again, nothing but a man.

How I hated them all!

I was so wrapped up in my thoughts that I did not notice the black car driving past me, slowly, too slowly, until it was too late. I heard the doors open and heavy footsteps and turned and saw the face of an old friend, Emil, the big barman from the Hofgarten. 'I'm sorry, Mr Wolf,' he said. He held a lead pipe in one enormous hand. I was too slow in trying to avoid it. It connected with the back of my head with a dull echoing crack and a burst of blazing pain and then, mercifully, darkness.

'Martini?'

She was a simpering old bitch and always had been, Wolf thought. She lusted after power the way other women lusted after movie stars or the milkman. He grimaced. His head felt raw in a terrible way. 'No, thank you, Magda.'

They were in a drawing room having tea. He thought they were some-where west of the city, Kensington perhaps. It seemed to make sense. His head hurt. He had woken up halfway there, in the back seat of the car, Emil on one side and another man he didn't recognise on the other side of him. They drove without speaking, through the quiet night, arriving at this quiet residential house on a quiet residential street. Briefly Wolf imagined the whole place blown up, airplanes swooping low, dropping down bombs, air-raid sirens wailing, residents running for shelter, but all was quiet and peaceful and clear. Emil helped him out. 'I'm really very sorry for hitting you, Herr Wolf,' he said. 'I was just following orders. You understand.'

They walked in through the gate and the lights in the house came on and the door opened and a shadow stood in the doorway. A neat but rat-like man came forward with a limp, his arms extended, his face plastered with a smile Wolf knew only too well.

'Joseph?' he said. 'Joseph *Goebbels*?'

'Wolf! Wolf, Wolf, *Wolf*!'

They stopped and stood facing each other. Goebbels was small, skinny, lame and dangerous. He had been their propaganda man, before the Fall. His smile turned into concern. 'Are you hurt?' he said. 'What did they do to you! Emil?'

'I'm sorry, Herr Goebbels,' the large barman muttered. He shifted on his feet as though afraid of the much smaller man. 'You said to—'

'I know what I said! Nincompoop! My dear Wolf, I am so, so sorry. Please, come in, come in! It is so good to see you again!'

'You live here?' Wolf said.

'This old place?' Goebbels said, shrugging, as if to say it was nothing, really it was nothing at all.

'You've lived here all this time? In England?'

'I wanted to seek you out,' Goebbels said. 'But Hess told me you no lon-ger wanted to associate with your old friends . . . I did not wish to intrude.'

'I thought the communists had got you!'

Goebbels shrugged again. He led Wolf into the house. The wallpaper was ghastly. 'I survived,' Goebbels said. 'You know how it is, Wolf. The things we do to survive.'

Wolf stopped. He felt the back of his head. His hair was matted with blood. He was tired and hurting. Slowly, he said, 'You cut yourself a deal.'

Goebbels was silent. Outside, Wolf heard nothing. Even the birds were asleep. He felt cold inside. 'You cut a deal with the communists, in exchange for your release. What did you do, Joseph? What did you *give* them?'

'It was all gone, Wolf. We lost. We had to be practical. I only gave them that which they would have already got, sooner or later. Some names, some details. What does it matter, now? Some S.A. beer boys? Streicher?'

'You gave them *Julius Streicher*?'

'His usefulness had come to an end. And the man was a pig, a veritable pig, Wolf!'

'He was,' Wolf said. He began to laugh. 'Joseph, you haven't changed one bit.'

'Wolf.' The gimp-legged man turned to him, and Wolf could have sworn there were genuine tears in his eyes. 'I have missed you. So much have I missed you.'

'It's good to see you, too, Joseph. But you could have just sent a card.'

'I did not mean for them to harm you! Emil, come here.'

'Sir?'

'Close the door behind you, Emil.'

'Yes, Herr Goebbels.'

'Good.'

Goebbels took out a gun from his pocket. He waved it carelessly in the air. 'American made,' he said. 'Do you like it?'

'It's wonderful. You have been talking to the Americans?'

'We have cause to do business together, sometimes. Why not? It is good to have friends. Again, I am terribly sorry, Wolf.' He raised the gun levelly at the puzzled Emil and pulled the trigger. The sound was deafening in the small hallway. From upstairs there came a woman's shriek. Emil collapsed to the floor, half his head now smeared on the wall behind him. His blood soaked into the carpet. Wolf stared down at the corpse.

'I liked Emil,' he said.

'So did I,' Goebbels said. 'But discipline has to be maintained.'

'Are you just going to leave him there?'

'Franz will clean it up. Come. Magda is just *dying* to see you.'

Wolf's ears were ringing. He followed Wolf to the drawing room.

'Magda? Where the hell are you, woman?'

Wolf heard footsteps come down the stairs and halt for a moment. Then a long beat as she stepped over Emil's corpse, before resuming her progress towards the drawing room. She wore a black evening dress and a veil and gloves and high-heeled shoes. 'Wolf!' She ran to him, hugged him. Her hand squeezed his buttock covertly. 'It is so good to see you again,' she whispered, her breath soft in his ear. He pushed her away, but gently. She had always been like a minx in heat around him. 'It is good to see you too, Magda.'

'How long has it *been*?'

'Too long,' Wolf said. But he felt tired, depressed. This was not a social call. The balance of power between them had changed. He no longer commanded the Goebbelses. They had grown apart from him, had changed. He was cautious.

'I will make drinks! Martini?'

'No, thank you,' Wolf said, politely. He turned to Goebbels. 'Where are your children?' he said. The Goebbelses had bred like rabbits, as though almost single-handedly they could populate the Earth with their Aryan offspring. Goebbels had been loyal; a gifted orator; an ardent Jew-hater; and, though he didn't like people to know it, a failed novelist.

'Upstairs,' Goebbels said.

'Asleep,' Magda said.

Wolf thought of the gunshot. They must be some children to sleep through the sound of a shot in their own hallway. But then, for all Wolf knew, such things were not so uncommon in the Goebbels household. He said, 'Speaking of Hess.'

'Were we speaking of Hess?'

But he saw Goebbels and Magda exchange glances, and Magda got up. On her way to the kitchen she looked back. 'Chocolate cake?' she said.

'That sounds lovely, Magda, dearest,' Goebbels said. She disappeared through the door and the two men were left alone.

'Hess is dead,' Wolf said, without preamble. 'I saw him floating face-down in the duck pond in Hyde Park.'

'What a way to go, eh?' Goebbels said. It wasn't exactly a smile. It wasn't exactly a smirk. But it was unpleasant and oily and rat-like all the same.

'Did you kill him, Joseph?'

'Me?' Goebbels said, looking shocked. 'Of course not, Wolf!'

'So who did?'

'Must we speak of Hess?' Goebbels said.

'That's why I'm here, isn't it?' Wolf said.

'You wound me. Is this what you think?'

'I know you, Joseph. All of you. You were mine. You were children I had let run wild. And when the Fall came you ran, and some of you came here, and now you do—what? Pimp out girls? Run numbers? You've become nothing, Joseph. Nothing but common criminals.'

'Some would say that is all we ever were,' Goebbels said, still with that faint, mocking smile. 'You lost your power, Wolf. You lost!'

'I was betrayed!'

They stared at each other. Goebbels was no longer smiling. 'I love you, Wolf,' he said. 'But you have not wanted to get involved. You prefer to play at being a private eye like some grotesquery out of a Fritz Lang movie. Hess was a good man, but he was weak. Weak, and he talked too much. In this business, it's not healthy to talk too much.'

Wolf regarded him without expression. The silence sat between the two men, the threat still hanging in the air. 'Hess talked to *me*,' Wolf said, softly.

It was Goebbels's turn not to reply.

'Who is behind it, Joseph?' Wolf said. 'Behind the smuggling, the whores, the white slavery? It's not you. You're not smart enough, Joseph. You're not ruthless enough. You talk a good talk, and I have to admit you impressed me just now with the gun and that little show of yours, and poor Emil. But it was a waste. It's not—it can't be—you. Then who?'

'Wolf,' Goebbels said. And his eyes were filled with sorrow.

'Yes,' Wolf said.

'It's not good to ask too many questions,' Goebbels said, softly. 'Do you understand?'

And Wolf did. Truly, he did. He knew better than anyone, for had he not written the rules of this dangerous game himself? And he began to say yes; to nod; to say that he did understand. He saw Magda come in through the door with a chocolate cake on a silver tray in her hands. And he saw Goebbels's eyes flicker upwards, to a point behind Wolf's head. And Wolf remembered the second man, the one who was going to clean up the dead Emil; Franz, he thought Goebbels had called him.

Wolf half-parted his lips, began to form a syllable, noticed the look, began to turn his head. Again he was too late. There was a bright explosion of pain in the back of his already tender head and, for a moment, Wolf saw spiral galaxies and interstellar clouds, suns and planets and moons, all drifting past at inexorable speed, growing brighter, converging to become the faces of departed comrades: of Hess and Streicher and Göring and Goebbels, Himmler and Bormann and Speer. And he knew that one of them was behind it all; one of them pulled the strings behind the scenes. The galactic vista sped all about him until his field of vision became the bright light of a supernova, of a dying star, and it suffused him, incinerating every cell and atom in his body, and he was once more swallowed up by the cool and blessed darkness of deep space, of a place entirely outside of time.

WOLF'S DIARY, 16TH NOVEMBER 1939—CONTD.

In my dream I was in a cold, bright place and it was snowing. The earth was hard, frosted over. Men, skeletal men, shuffled all around me. They wore striped pyjamas, and wooden clogs on their feet. I had never seen such men before. They were grotesque, caricatures of men. There were watchtowers and fences holding us in. Blocks of housing squatted on the frozen ground. I saw a bird soar overhead. It was shot by a sniper in one of the towers and dropped to earth, its wings clipped, feathers flying. It plummeted to hit the ground with a splat of blood and tiny breaking bones. I saw one of the men hurry to it, scoop it up and attempt to hide it under his tattered coat. The gun barked again and the man dropped to the snow and lay there. No one came to him. The bird had fallen from out of the shelter of his coat and lay there beside him, a single drop of red blood decorating its tiny crushed head.

Though I knew it was cold I did not feel it. I walked through the throng of inmates like a spirit. They did not see me and I could not interact with them. The light was very strong. The skies were blue and clear. The sun shone in the sky but it was small and a long way away. It was a cold brightness, it provided only stark illumination. It eradicated shadows. I don't know how long I spent in that place. I lost track of time. The sun never seemed to set. The snow hung suspended in the air. The men were frozen in their places, in the act of lifting a weary leg or bending down to dig, bony fingers wrapped round the handle of a shovel.

I thought it must be a model village, populated by waxwork figures. The snow wasn't real at all; it was paper, thousands and thousands of tiny balls of paper all suspended by strings. The sky was painted over canvas, the sun was a splash of yellow paint. I walked through the exhibits marvelling at it all, the amount of detail that must have been required to create all that was staggering. I saw black smoke in the distance. I realised I had been breathing it all along. It rose from a set of chimneys in the distance and suffused the air. It got into my eyes and my nose and my ears. It coated the inside of my lungs. The black smoke was everywhere, rank and yet strangely sweet, but it never left, it clung to me, to my clothes, my skin, my hair. I ran my tongue around my mouth and my gums were raw and painful. I felt a loose tooth. I prodded it with my tongue and it came away entirely and I spat it out. I was suddenly frightened and I didn't know why. I knew it was only a bad dream but even so, I couldn't wake up. When I looked at the back of my hands I did not recognise them. They were like an old man's hands and the skin hung loose, in folds. My clothes felt heavy on me, and I was terribly weary, they pressed me down, they didn't fit me any more. Then I realised I wasn't even wearing them. I was wearing dirty striped pyjamas and wooden clogs that opened the sores on my feet. A band struck a rousing martial tune. I heard a shrill whistle. A man in uniform came to me, shouting. He asked me where I thought I was going. I tried to explain to him it was all just a terrible mistake, that I didn't belong here, but he just laughed. I was so hungry. He began to lead me towards the source of the black smoke. There had been a mistake, I kept saying. There had been a mistake. I didn't want to go. I kept saying no, no, I don't want to go there. We walked and walked, into the black smoke. There had been a mistake, I kept saying. There had been a mistake. It became very dark. I need to open the blinds, I told him, desperately. But he wasn't even there.

11

WOLF'S DIARY, 17TH NOVEMBER 1939

I woke up and proceeded to retch violently, the rancid contents of my stomach burning my lips and tongue, leaving a disgusting puddle on the floor. Light was seeping in through the windows. The blinds were drawn. The room was clean and impersonal. It smelled of disinfectant and my puke. A voice above me said, 'Settle down, now.'

Hands pressed me back down onto the bed. 'You've had a nasty accident.' I blinked as a face came into view, hovering over me like a vision. Her blonde hair framed her pale face. 'I didn't have an accident,' I said, petulantly. 'I was beaten up.'

'I know.' She plumped my pillows. 'I'm so sorry, Mr Wolfson.'

'Wolfson?'

'We found your identity card in your pocket,' she said.

'Wolfson!' I said. 'Of course. I am . . .' what in all hell was it? 'Moshe Wolfson,' I said.

'Do you know who hit you?' she said.

'No.'

'They were probably Blackshirts,' she said. 'We've been treating so many of your people recently, Mr Wolfson. It's best that you rest now.' I saw her reaching for a syringe.

'Wait!' I said.

'Yes?'

'Where am I?'

'Guy's Hospital.'

'Guy's?' That meant I was on the south side of the river, by London Bridge. 'How did I get here?'

She shrugged. 'You need to rest now, Mr Wolfson.' She primed the syringe and I saw the tiny bubble of liquid at the needle's end. 'Wait! My name isn't Wolfson, it's—'

The needle penetrated my skin. A sense of great relief and of peace washed over me, and I sank into the mattress and in seconds I was asleep again.

WOLF'S DIARY, 18TH NOVEMBER 1939

'We're being overrun with the damn Jews,' a male voice said. I could smell pipe-tobacco in the room. 'I keep telling them, we need more staff, we can't cope, they should rein in the bloody Mosley boys until after the elections, at least.'

I opened my eyes. He was about my age, with ample facial hair, round glasses. He left his pipe smoking by the window and approached me. 'Let's have a look at you,' he said. His hand went to the back of my head and I nearly screamed. 'Yes, yes,' he said. 'That's a nasty wound you've got there, Mr . . .'

'Wolfson,' the nurse said. It was a different nurse.

'A nasty wound. It's a good thing you came to us,' the doctor said. At last he released my head. 'We need to keep you for a few days. Is there anyone you wish to call?'

'No,' I said. Then, 'Yes.'

'A wife, a friend?'

'Call Oswald Mosley,' I said, and he laughed.

'Call Oswald! Tell him it's Wolf.'

The doctor sighed. 'Why do they do this,' he said. Again it wasn't clear who the 'they' referred to. 'Keep him sedated for the time being. He needs time to recover.'

'Wait, listen to me! You don't understand!'

But the doctor had moved on to the next bed. I looked up at the nurse. My head hurt terribly. 'Please, call him. Tell him it's Wolf.'

'I thought your name was Wolfson,' she said. She primed the syringe. 'Don't do that,' I said, 'don't—'

Again, the cold touch of the needle. Again, that near-immediate relief. I smiled up at her goofily. 'Call him, tell him I'm—'

'Sleep well,' she said.

WOLF'S DIARY, 19TH NOVEMBER 1939

'Mr Wolf?'

It was dark. In the beds beside mine men were snoring and crying and farting in their sleep. My visitor perched on a chair beside me, an unremarkable young man in an unremarkable grey suit. His face was pleasant, plump, and shiny with a thin film of sweat. 'Who the hell are you?' I said.

'I'm Alderman, sir? Thomas Alderman? We met at Sir Oswald's . . . party? And we spoke on the phone, more recently.'

'Alderman? Who the hell are you, Alderman? Where is Oswald?'

'*Sir* Oswald is on the campaign trail, sir. As the Americans say. He is unavailable but he of course sends his best regards. There seems to have been a mishap, if you don't mind me saying, sir, but you appear to be registered here as a Jew named Wolfson.'

'Don't you worry about that. What was that about the Americans? Did they get to him? Is he cutting a deal? I demand to know!'

'Sir Oswald is of course speaking to many different factions—'

'I knew it! The dirty worm has cut a deal! The man has no moral fibre, he has the spine of a snail!'

'Snails . . . don't have spines, sir.'

'That's what I said!'

The young man looked pained. 'I hate to see you like this, Mr Wolf.'

'Like this? Like how!'

'All frail, like.'

'Frail! How dare you! What did you say your name was?'

'Alderman, sir. Thomas Alderman? We met at Sir Oswald's party—'

'I know who you are! Do you think I have no eyes? Do you think I'm crazy? You tell that slimy Englishman this is Wolf, Wolf he's talking to! Where is Oswald?'

'He's . . . electioneering, sir.'

'Why is he not here? Who the hell are you?'

'I think I should call a nurse, sir. You seem agitated.'

'Agitated? *Agitated?* I could have ruled the world, you know!'

'I know, sir. Let me just say, Mr Wolf, I have the utmost admiration for you. I . . .'

I stared at him, dumbfounded. The young man reached into the breast pocket of his suit and brought out a tattered little book and presented it to me. 'I know this is hardly the right time, but . . . would you sign this for me?'

It was my book.

My Struggle.

I took it from him; held it in my hands. It was the British first—and, if I were being honest, only—edition, published by Hurst & Blackett, useless asses that they were. It was in a plain yellow dust-jacket, like the books published by that Jew, Victor Gollancz.

'I'm . . . touched,' I said. I blinked; my vision had become blurry. A single drop fell on the open title page. 'Do you have a pen?'

'Here,' he said. I accepted it from him.

'What was your name again?'

'Alderman, sir. Thomas Alderman.'

'A good name. You're a good man, Alderman. A good man. We need more like you in this world.'

'Thank you, sir. That means a lot.'

To Thomas Alderman, I wrote. My hand was shaky. *Best wishes*—and I added my signature with a weak flourish. 'Here,' I said, thrusting the book back into his hands.

'Thank you, young man.'

'Thank you, sir. Thank you so much.'

'This is a time of war, Alderman,' I said, sinking back into the sheets. I felt so weary. 'And we're all soldiers, whether we know it yet or not.'

'Yes, sir.'

'Come and see me some time.'

'I'd like that, sir.'

'You tell that Oswald Mosley . . .' I said. But I was too tired. My eyes closed. I felt almost weepy. Like a woman—like a weak woman! 'You tell him . . .'

From a long way away I heard him get up, the scrape of the chair legs on the floor. 'Sleep now, sir.'

'You tell him . . .'

On her sickbed in Urfahr my mother lay dying.

I was eighteen. My sister, Paula, was eleven years old. I had been residing in Vienna at that time, attempting to enroll in the Academy of Fine Arts. I had hurried back home when I received the news from her physician. I returned in October. Dr Bloch, her doctor, was a Jew. I remember him sitting us down, Paula and I. 'Your mother's condition is hopeless,' he said. Paula cried. I myself cried. I am not ashamed to admit it. I only cried like this again when I thought I had lost my sight, in the war. I remember most strongly the smell in her room. Death has a special smell, that slow wasting of a human body. It is a sickly, sweet smell, a special odour that comes off the sick body, a rotting from within. That and, mixed with bodily waste, the smell of constant cleaning, of old carpets, of my mother's perfume which she insisted on wearing to her last day. I slept beside her, in a cot in the corner of the room. The windows were kept closed, as my mother was always cold. The air in the room was stifling. I had to hold her naked body in my arms, washing her, washing her and trying not to cry. The cancer was in her breasts and it had spread: there was no cure. Her hospital stay at the start of the year had cost one hundred Kronen.

Leaving her—going to Vienna—was the hardest thing I had ever done. Returning, I could do nothing but watch her die slowly. For two more months she lingered, becoming light as air; time seemed suspended, each particle and mote of dust froze in the everlasting air; in my mother's eyes I saw past and future meet.

She had become unchained from time. In lucid moments she spoke haltingly in alien tongues. Her eyes were open windows allowing me a glimpse into strange other worlds: in one the very moon was carved with an image of my face, while in another the Earth lay in ruins and corpses filled the seas from shore to shore and the foam bursting on the rocks ran red with blood. My mother's blood was black ichor. Her tears were purest crystal, like those found only on virgin sands. In the night she cried in broken syllables, but more and more she faded, with every passing day there was less of her.

My mother died that December.

Never will there be another woman like my mother.

WOLF'S DIARY, 21ST NOVEMBER 1939

'Damn you all to hell, this food is *scheisse*!' I said. 'Bring me vegetables! *Vegetables*, I said! No, don't tell me to be quiet. Get your hands off of me! I said get your dirty hands off of m— No, don't you dare reach for that syringe! I said don't you dare—'

WOLF'S DIARY, 22ND NOVEMBER 1939

'Enough!' I yelled. My headache was gone, I was hungry, I needed to urinate, and I was sick and tired of being sick and tired. 'I want to be discharged immediately.'

'You have suffered serious trauma,' the nurse said. It was a different nurse again. I was getting sick of nurses, and needles, and what passed for hospital food.

'Then bandage me up and give me some pills,' I said.

'It might not be safe for you out there,' the nurse said. 'It's ugly outside, there are mobs, everything is tense—it's the elections today, isn't it.'

'*Today?* How long have I been in here!'

'A few days. And I really do think you should—'

'Don't you worry about me, *bubeleh*,' I said. Was I really using Yiddish? What was happening to me? 'I have friends,' I added, darkly. 'I have friends in high places.'

'I'm sure that you do. And we could use the bed. But the doctor—'

'I don't need a doctor! I healed my own blindness with the power of my *mind*!'

'I . . . see.'

'Look,' I said, calmer now. Trying to reason with her was like trying to teach National Socialism to a goat. It was an enterprise doomed to failure and bound to disappoint both parties. 'I'm leaving. I want my clothes.'

'This is highly irregular—'

'I'm *leaving*! Don't you know who I *am*?'

'I have no idea who you are.'

'How dare you!'

'Sir, please!'

But I was already standing, tottering on the hard floor. I regained my balance, smiled at her contemptuously. 'It was a minor setback,' I said. 'It's only a matter of time until I'm on top of things again.'

'Sir—'

'Get out of my way!'

I barged past her to the cheering of the other patients, found my clothes folded tidily and carried them to the bathroom where I changed. When I emerged I felt like a new man. I was myself again. 'Goodbye!' I said. I tapped my finger on the brim of my hat and walked away.

She didn't follow.

*

Wolf emerged into a cold November day. A pale sun hid behind clouds. It was raining again, a thin, constant drizzle. The railway arches rose ahead of Wolf, obscuring the river. Men in suits flowed down Southwark Street.

It was Wednesday.

His head no longer hurt. He was rested, he was irritable and he was still on the case, whether anyone wanted him to be or not.

It was time to act.

Wolf hailed a black cab. Settled himself into the back seat. 'Where to, mate?' the driver said.

'The Grosvenor Hotel, Victoria. And step on it!'

The driver chuckled as though Wolf had said something funny. On the other side of the window, grey clouds gathered on the horizon.

The city flowed past outside the windows of the cab. The streets deepened and the sky darkened overhead and the clouds seemed like giant ships doing battle, raising the black flags of pirates and privateers. The water of the Thames churned and Wolf imagined vast spirits underwater, entwined in a battle reflecting the heavens above, great amorphous translucent creatures of some primordial ooze, ancient beyond all imagining, things that were beyond good and evil but merely *were*, from even before the world was formed.

It was possible he was still somewhat under the influence of the hospital drugs.

The Grosvenor Hotel rose before them then like a castle. The driver stopped the cab. Wolf paid the fare.

'Sooner or later,' he thought groggily, 'everyone pays the fare.'

'Pardon?'

'Nothing,' Wolf said. He exited the car. Went up the steps to the hotel entrance where liveried doormen stood like toy soldiers. He went inside and marched up to the reception desk. 'Leni Riefenstahl,' he said. 'Tell her it is Wolf.'

The hotel clerk behind the desk was severe in a beige and cream suit.

His face had the faintly disapproving air of a maiden aunt. He said, 'I'm afraid Miss Riefenstahl is no longer staying with us, sir.'

Wolf took a step back from the desk. He hovered there uncertainly for a moment, looking one way and then the other, helplessly. The hotel clerk said, 'Are you unwell, sir?'

But Wolf recovered.

Wolf always recovered.

'Where did Miss Riefenstahl go?' he said.

'The film crew left two days ago,' the clerk said. 'I believe they went back to America. There were issues with the production of their film that necessitated their decampment.'

His eloquence irritated Wolf. 'She is not here?' he said, shortly.

'No, sir. Are you sure you are all right?'

'I'm fine. I'm fine!' Wolf turned from him. How could it be? He had counted on Leni. She stood for everything he had once believed in, she was Aryan womanhood incarnate. She was loving—uncomplicated—sexually compliant—she was his! And yet even she was gone now, had gone back to Hollywood, leaving him with an aching emptiness, a dull pain. He was hollow inside, and the hollowness was spreading, beginning as a tiny seed, undetectable, and growing through him over the years, replacing healthy cells and blood vessels, bone marrow and muscles and nerves, until he was entirely hollow, until he was lighter than air. He felt as though he were floating, untethered. He no longer knew who he was.

Then movement caught his eye. A man, with a face he had seen before, emerging from the lifts. For a moment Wolf stared, disbelieving, though he didn't quite know why. He had assumed they'd all left with Leni, yet here he was.

It was the Jew, Bitker.

Wolf turned away before Bitker could see him. He observed him through the mirrors fixed above the hotel's plush entrance. Bitker went right past Wolf, heading outside. Indecisive, Wolf stared after him, then broke into a run. 'Herr Bitker!' he said. 'Herr Bitker!'

The Jew turned. A look of polite bemusement filled his face. 'Yes . . . ?' he said.

Wolf stopped, disbelieving again. 'We've met,' he said.

'Have we? I'm afraid I do not recollect, Mr . . .?'

'Wolfson,' Wolf said, thinking quickly. 'We have not been introduced. Unwin's party? You are working with Leni?'

'I am part of the film crew,' Bitker said. 'How do you know Miss Riefenstahl?'

'We . . . I am, was, an artist. I did scenery work on one of her Berlin films,' Wolf said.

'I see. Well, she has gone back to California, I'm afraid,' Bitker said.

'So I understand.'

'I am sorry I can't be of more help,' Bitker said, politely.

'Herr Bitker!' Wolf's voice was desperate; hungry. He put his hand on Bitker's arm. 'Please.'

'What is it, Mr Wolfson?'

'I want to help!'

'Help? Help with the film? The production is halted. I myself only stayed behind for, well, for some other business. I shall be returning to California tonight.'

'No, Herr Bitker!' Wolf lowered his voice, leaned in closer to the Jew. 'I want to help. With the cause.'

'The cause?' For the first time Bitker looked alarmed. 'What cause?'

'Herr Bitker, please! Do not play games with me!'

'This is not the time or place—!'

'I want to help. I am ready to do whatever it takes. Life is intolerable, here, for us Jews!'

'I don't disagree. But I don't see what you think I can do—'

'I want to do what has to be done. I want to join. I know things, Herr Bitker.'

233

'I can see that. Come with me.' Bitker grabbed Wolf roughly by the arm, half-dragged him into the empty hotel bar. 'Who are you and what do you want?'

'I told you, I'm Wolfson. Moshe Wolfson. Here.' Wolf fished out his forged passport. 'Take it!'

Bitker took it from his hands, leafed through it. He stared at Wolf and his expression turned puzzled. 'Have we met before?' he said. 'Not at Unwin's party.'

Wolf thought of following Bitker to Threadneedle Street, of being discovered, chased and beaten. 'No,' he said.

Suddenly a small smile materialised on Bitker's face. He laughed. The sound was unexpected, startling. 'Do you know—!' he said. 'If you grew a moustache, you would almost be the spitting image of—'

'Please, Herr Bitker! Do not joke of such things!'

'No, of course not. My apologies.' Still, some of the man's good humour seemed to return, as if Wolf's superficial similarity to that long-vanished leader had put him at ease. He put a hand on Wolf's shoulder. 'Listen to me, Wolfson. There is nothing here for you. Nothing remains. The election will not go our way. England will become a hell for the Jews. The Americans are closing their borders to our people. Europe remains hostile to us. There is only one place remaining, Wolfson.' He stared into Wolf's eyes with a deep and dark intensity. 'There is only Palestine, now.'

'We must kill Mosley,' Wolf blurted.

'Don't worry about Mosley! That scum will be taken care of.'

'How?' Wolf said. His hands were shaking with excitement.

'I have said too much. Listen to me, Wolfson. There will be a ship, leaving tomorrow morning before dawn. If things go wrong for us here. Greenwich docks. The SS *Exodus*. Now go! You're putting us both in danger.'

'But Herr Bitker! Wait!' Wolf tried to halt the other man but Bitker shook his head.

'Good luck,' he said, softly. He shook Wolf's hand and then, with quick, hurrying steps, disappeared into the grey daylight outside the hotel. Wolf stood staring after him. His brain was awhirl. What had Bitker meant about Mosley? He had successfully caught the Jew off-guard, had extracted valuable information from him. It was obvious there was a threat to Mosley's life, planned sometime soon, planned, perhaps, for that very evening. He had to warn Mosley.

Wolf left the hotel and saw Bitker enter an Austin Tourer. It was an ugly two-seater car with an open top. Bitker sat behind the wheel while, beside him, Wolf could make out a face he knew and loathed.

It was the little sister, Judith Rubinstein.

She was dressed inexplicably in a domestic servant's uniform. 'Wait!' Wolf shouted, but neither heard him. The car's engine came to life with a hacking cough and the Tourer slid away into the traffic. 'Judith!' Wolf cried. 'Judith!'

He ran after the car but the road was clear and the car disappeared. Wolf's lungs burned and his leg throbbed with the old wound.

He stood there with his hands on his knees, breathing hard.

He should warn Mosley, he thought dully. A weak sun momentarily shone from a break in the grey clouds. Wolf felt himself filled by the light, once again seemingly detached of space and time: he felt as if he could just float away, into the clouds, for ever; but the feeling passed and he was himself again, and after a moment he straightened up.

He found a red phone box and went in and shut the door. Reached for coins and gave the operator the number to call. The ringing seemed to fill the air, becoming a flock of dark birds against the cloudy sky.

'Mosley residence.'

'This is Wolf.'

'Mr Wolf! It's Alderman.'

'Who?'

'Thomas Alderman, sir. I came to visit you at the hospital.' There was a note of reproach in the voice.

Wolf conjured up with some difficulty the image of a serious, pale-faced young man, sitting beside the bed in a high-backed chair, asking him to sign a book. Had that really happened? He thought he had dreamed the episode up—they *had* given him rather a lot of drugs at the time.

'I must speak with Mosley. It is of the utmost urgency!'

'I am sure. Sir . . .'

Wolf did not like the boy's tone. 'What is it?' he demanded.

'Sir, I'm most awfully sorry.'

Was he too late? Was Mosley even now lying dead or dying by the side of the road or in some beer hall somewhere, or wounded from an assassin's bullet or mutilated by an explosive device? 'What is it?' Wolf said. The dread rose in bubbles above his head, his speech encapsulated inside.

'I'm afraid—' he could hear the boy swallowing, over the phone. 'Sir Oswald has found it necessary to terminate your employment.'

'I . . . what? I beg your pardon?'

'Your services are no longer necessary. I'm so sorry, I really am, Mr Wolf.'

'My . . . my *services*? What are you—who do you think—how *dare* you! How *dare you*!' Wolf was screaming at the receiver, his lips trembling in rage, his spit flying onto the mouthpiece of the telephone. 'I have important *news*, urgent news for this . . . little . . . fucking no-good wannabe Fascist *imitator*!'

'I truly am very sorry.'

'Sorry? You will be sorry! You will all be sorry!'

The boy, Alderman, said something, 'Can I see you?' perhaps, which would have been an odd thing to say, but anyway Wolf was no longer listening. He bashed the receiver against the phone box, over and over, splintering the casing, wantonly destroying the property of His Majesty's General Post Office. Having done this, at last, and panting heavily, he exited the red phone box like an *Übermensch* awakened and transformed.

•

In a place beyond space and time Shomer stands, his back bent, working. Released from the infirmary he has wandered with a child's gaze back into the camp. Everything about him has been replaced anew: his wooden clogs, his fetching striped pyjamas, his plate, his spoon. All those he knew are gone and he has been placed into a different block with different company, a new capo to command him, two new bunkmates on either side of him, one tall and skeletal and French, one short and skeletal and Polish. Also in the block is a rabbi, or in fact several rabbis, or perhaps only one rabbi and several yeshiva students (it is hard to tell), who in the rare moments of rest at the end of the day after the soup and before fitful sleep sit together and debate issues of the Torah and the Talmud, and did not Rabbi Akiva say—

'Just as the house is proof of the builder,' Rabbi Akiva said, 'and the cloth is proof of the weaver, so is the world proof of its creator, so does the world proclaim the existence of God.'

And it is certainly something to think about, is it not, Yenkl says, cheerfully. They have given Shomer a new job, too: no longer digging graves but working in a factory, a job as though from very Heaven, where it is warmer than outside, though the breath of the men frosts in the air before them as they work on the assembly line.

They make doors.

What the doors are for Shomer doesn't know. There are hundreds of doors every day going round and round, with men to sand the wood and men to polish it and men to attach the hinges and men to carry the doors to the trucks. Large doors and small doors and toy doors and great big thick doors that would stop a bullet, and it is Shomer's job to attach the handles, for without a handle, how can a door be opened, and therefore what good is a door? And for each door there is a lock but never, not once, does he see a key. And every day for hours at a time he stands there with his back bent and his feet throbbing with their new sores and his muscles straining and he attaches handles and every single nail must be accounted for. He sees men die on the assembly line, of accidents and carelessness or for trying to steal from the factory, men shot on the spot and the numbers on their arms carefully recorded. How many numbers, how many names, how many men have died to build this house, to weave this cloth?

One day he sees a plane fly overhead and it is not a German plane. The guards in their guard towers shoot it but it flies past unscathed. And on the secret wireless, the rumour goes around the camp, it says an army is advancing across the winter land, that it is coming closer. And yet the trains still come, the black smoke rises, the gold teeth of dead men collect in ever-growing piles, extracted by those unfortunate few, the *Sonderkommando*. All those corpses, all that gold and the hair harvested and every few weeks a new squad to shave and harvest the corpses of their predecessors on the job—their first assignment.

But Shomer works indoors; how this miracle happened he does not know. And Yenkl keeps him company.

•

In his office the watcher tidied his desk and the papers on his desk and aligned the telephone just so and the pens and the ledgers and he looked around the empty room and he was happy. And then he left and closed the door and locked it and went out in the night, into a darkness whispering promises of blood and murder.

12

I was dressed in my beat-up old raincoat, a suit that's seen better days, scuffed shoes and a fedora that didn't quite fit me. I was shaved but awkwardly. I had a bruise the size of a hen's egg on the back of my head, where I had been knocked out twice in the space of an hour several days back, and I was sober but for the drugs they had given me at the hospital. When I took a piss I held a Jew's cock in my hands. I didn't know how much Rubenstein's house was worth but my guess was plenty. I was calling on Jewish money.

The Rubinstein residence was a three-storey mansion off Sloane Square. It had a white stucco front and a driver in black leather and a black peaked cap washing a black Rolls-Royce parked in front of the house. I did not see Isabella Rubinstein's white Crossley. It was a quiet street in a quiet neighbourhood and the air smelled fresh and clear, as though it had been laundered with money. I went up the steps and rang the bell and waited. A maid in a starched apron opened the door and stood there looking at me. 'Yes?' she said.

'I'm here to see Miss Rubinstein,' I said.

'Miss Rubinstein is not in.' She made to shut the door in my face. I stuck my foot between the door and the frame, prohibiting her from doing so. 'I know she's in there,' I told her. 'I can smell the whore's wet snatch all the way from out here.'

The maid blanched white as a hard-boiled egg. 'I'm going to call the butler!' she said in a rising voice.

'I wish that you would,' I said.

'You repulsive man!'

I watched her disappearing back, pushed the door open the rest of the way and stepped inside. It was a cool antechamber with dark panelled oak and the kind of boiseries to give Syrie Maugham heart palpitations.

I heard hurried footsteps and in a moment a large pink butler in a tight black suit appeared with the maid in his wake. 'Who the hell are you?' he said, in a New York accent. He looked like a goon gone to seed and stuffed like a goose into a suit two sizes too small for him.

'Wolf,' I said. He sneered. 'The gumshoe? You have a lot of nerve coming in here.'

'Where is Isabella?'

'Miss Rubinstein is not accepting visitors,' he said. 'Now scram.'

I tried to push past him but he was having none of it. I heard the maid hurry behind the butler's back. For a long moment we stood facing each other, the butler and I. I had never liked butlers.

'Get out,' he said.

I reached down and grabbed him by the testicles and squeezed, hard. His face turned red and a low slow moan emerged from his blubbery lips. I leaned in close and whispered endearments in his ear. He nodded, once, to signal that he understood. I put my other hand flat against his chest and pushed, and in this ungainly way we progressed into the house, my one hand on his precious jewels, the other navigating him: it was just like driving a car.

We came into a large sitting room and I saw portmanteaus, black travelling bags and suitcases piled against one wall. They seemed hurriedly packed. One suitcase was still part open and I could see feminine toiletries and items of underclothing inside. 'Going someplace?' I said.

'Let me . . . go . . .'

I heard the same hurried footsteps again and the maid reappeared, looking agitated. 'Let him go!' she screamed. She came at me like a demented pheasant, flapping her hands. She was surprisingly strong and I had to release the butler to protect my face from her. He leaned against the wall, taking deep breaths. There was no fight left in him.

'Enough!'

For a moment I couldn't tell where the voice had come from. Then I noticed an odd instrument, like an ear trumpet, placed high in one corner of the room, close to the ceiling. I knew the voice. The maid stopped abruptly and stood very still, breathing heavily.

'Show him into the conservatory,' the voice said.

The maid glared at me. The butler slid to the floor and remained there clutching his testicles and moaning faintly to himself. He was as red as a cockerel's hood.

'Would sir please follow me,' the maid said. I grinned at her and, when she turned, I pinched her rear and heard her squeal, then swear in a very unmatronly way. I followed her through a corridor and a turn and to a door that she opened. Warm humid air wafted from within and it was dark. The maid said nothing. The whole house was silent, pregnant with anticipation. I suddenly did not want to go in. It seemed to me, irrationally, to be like the entrance Dante had described into the circles of Hell. My palms were sweating. It was too warm in there, too quiet. The maid stared at me with hate-filled eyes, her lips curling into a cruel mocking grin, but still she said nothing. The air smelled of death. I clenched my fingers into fists. I imagined fires, the sweet cloying smell of burning bodies, the hiss of gas. The maid was as still as a statue. I stared into the dark hot room, paralysed with indecision.

Dominique, too, was staring at the darkness. She had never got used to the dark. One of her strongest memories, the one she carried deep inside of her, wrapped and carefully hidden, was of a summer when her mother and her father were still together, and they had gone to visit her mother's old home in Abidjan on the Ivory Coast. Dominique remembered her mother in her summer dress, purchased on the Champs Élysées, her father's cool linen suit, made for the tropics. They had been so happy. In the memory, her father held her small hand in his, and they walked on the sands, on the banks of the *lagoon n'doupé*, and the air was so still, the water shimmered like a mirror, reflecting an immensity of sky.

It had been a good time.

Then came her mother's illness, her father's bursts of anger, the alcohol which took hold of him like a serpent and squeezed, squeezed until one day his heart had burst. She was a nothing after that, a girl of mixed blood abandoned at her father's final posting, somewhere in the Lebanon. Her father's relatives disowned her, her mother's were in faraway Abidjan or scattered. She was alone.

She had never got used to the darkness, not truly. Not on the ship taking her to Paris, not in the dark hold, with the grunting men, nor on the streets of the city nor later, following a handsome cavalry officer to London, more fool her.

There were times when she didn't have sex with clients. There was more money in specialising, and she had learned during her time in Paris: the art of the *dominatrice*. There were men who liked to be controlled, humiliated, abused, in a mockery of giving away power while still controlling her with their money. She had her kit, whips and chains and dildos, but there had been so many girls who came to London after the Fall, so many refugees, and competition was fierce and so she found herself once again on the streets, once again turning *triques*.

Now she watched the darkness, with an anxiety she hid well. Gerta was still in hospital; her whoring days were over. The young German girl, Edith, was dead. There was a devil out there, out to kill and mutilate. She did not understand such hatred. That strange symbol carved into Edith's chest—she had seen it before, the swastika. But why anyone would want to cut it into a woman's flesh she couldn't comprehend. She hugged herself against the cold. Would the killer come tonight? The night after that? She did not like this cold, this city. Footsteps in the dark, unhurried, almost awkward, shy. She put on her professional face. Would it be him this time? There were so many watchers in the dark, eyeing the girls with a terrible beastly hunger. Her fingers closed on the knife in her handbag. A face came into view as he crossed under the streetlight and she sighed with relief. He seemed so harmless, almost earnest, really. A clerk from a nearby office, perhaps, at last tempted by the girls he must have observed, covertly, so often. She smiled, revealing even, sharp white teeth. She knew the effect her smile had on the men. The other girls catcalled to the boy—the man—but he had eyes only for Dominique.

She knew his type. Her smile widened. She'd once been told there was a predatory quality to her smile, by an old French-Lebanese orange trader who had kept her for a time, when she was sixteen. She hadn't known what he meant, exactly. There was something about her that men found both frightening and exciting. And this man—he was really not so much more than a boy. And so nervous!

'Good evening,' he said. His face was pale, his eyes wide. Dominique let him look her over. The boy's gaze was drawn to her brassiere. He licked his lips, unconsciously.

'Shouldn't you be at school?' Dominique said. The other whores crowed with laughter.

'Can we talk somewhere more private?' the boy said.

'About what?' Dominique said. She stepped closer to him. He seemed to radiate such heat. She leaned her cheek against his. 'What do you want to talk about, *boy*?'

Her hand went down to his front. He was so hard, his whole body shivered when she touched him. 'I know what you like,' Dominique said. 'Don't I.'

'Yes, yes,' the boy said.

'The other girls, they don't understand,' she said.

'No . . .'

'You have money?'

The boy reached into his pocket. Brought out a handful of notes. It was more money than Dominique had seen in a long time. The notes were crumpled, in disarray. She took them from him quickly, before the other girls could see. She put the money in her handbag, feeling inside for her instruments. Her hand closed on her favourite *godemiché*. She could bugger him with it, bugger him until he cried for mercy and came in the dirt. He would be quick, they always were, the eager ones.

The boy reached for her with clumsy hands. She pushed him away, laughing. 'Not here, love,' she said. She could tell he loved her accent. His eyes were so feverish-bright. She shivered.

'Where?'

'There's a hotel not far from here,' Dominique said. The boy shook his head. 'No. I have a place.' He took her by the hand, almost gently, and pulled her away. The other girls were no longer interested; they had new marks to entice, burly men who had spilled out onto the street from some nearby pub—dock workers or labourers.

'It's my friend's place,' he said. He was so tense. His whole body seemed to vibrate, like a single note, a single string holding mad music inside. The door was right there.

'I don't know,' Dominique said, doubtfully. The boy stood there and looked at her. She thought of all the money he'd given her. He opened the door. She stared into the darkness beyond.

•

How Wolf made the transition, how he had crossed the threshold, entered from the lit world of the house into the dark one of the conservatory, he didn't, afterwards, know. He remembered no conscious step, no movement. One moment he was standing before the door; in the next, the door was behind him. It shut noiselessly. He stood still and breathed in the rank odour of the air. It was very hot, very humid. The conservatory had once been the back garden of this London townhouse. It had since been roofed over with glass and now provided a tropical atmosphere. Dim red lights provided the only illumination. Wolf heard the drip-drip-drip of water and the buzzing of insects and the thrum of a water pump. He felt nauseated from the smell of the flowers.

'Orchids,' a voice said. Wolf started; he had half-fallen asleep on his feet. 'Did you know there are thousands of different orchid species? They're beautiful, don't you think?'

'They smell disgusting,' Wolf said, and the other chuckled.

'I didn't have you pegged as a gardening enthusiast,' Wolf said. There was movement ahead and then he saw him, approaching: Julius Rubinstein, banker, gangster, loving father. Hatred swamped Wolf. He blinked sweat from his eyes. It was on his lips. It tasted of salt and blood.

'You have a lot of nerve coming into my house,' Julius Rubinstein said. He spoke without haste or seeming anger. It was more of an observation.

His body was open, his arms at his side, his face exhibiting nothing but a sort of puzzled curiosity. It was this that offended Wolf's sensibilities most of all, perhaps. The man had not even taken notice of him, had mutilated him and then dismissed him as though he were of no consequence at all.

It was a cold ruthlessness Wolf could almost admire.

'I have unfinished business with your daughter.'

'You have *no* business with my daughter!' With this, the genial look disappeared from Rubinstein's eyes. For a moment he seemed grotesque, demonic, a great shadow towering over Wolf. Then the impression subsided and Wolf saw him more clearly: a man no longer young, and for all his presence small, almost slight, with greying hair and tired eyes. 'What will it take?' Rubinstein asked. 'What will it take to make you leave my daughter alone?'

He turned his back on Wolf and walked deeper into the dark jungle of the conservatory. Wolf followed him, unbidden. Though the distance between them was small it seemed huge to Wolf; it seemed to him that he walked miles and yet the shadow before him never grew closer or farther away but always remained at the same distance, never turning, and that he could dawdle or hurry but the shadow would always be there, awaiting him; and that sooner or later it would consume him.

But really it was merely a few steps. And Wolf saw that, in the middle of the conservatory, Rubinstein had built himself a makeshift office. He had a wide oak desk and a comfortable chair and a makeshift bar. He reached for a bottle of scotch and two glasses and put them on the desk and then poured. Wolf said, 'I don't drink.'

'You'll drink.'

He handed Wolf the glass and Wolf accepted it. He didn't know why the Jew had this power over him. He put his lips to the glass. The rank smell of the alcohol nearly choked him.

'I said drink!'

Wolf sipped. The alcohol burned his lips, his throat. He coughed and Rubinstein smiled. Wolf said, 'I am still on the case.'

'The case!' Rubinstein laughed, an angry or bemused bark. 'Who do you think you are?' he said. His hand fluttered up and down, taking in Wolf from his beat-up old fedora down to his scuffed shoes. 'What *is* this? At least I knew what you were before. I have no idea what you are now.'

Wolf's composure abandoned him; packed up its suitcases and left. 'I'm a private detective!' he shouted. 'A shamus, a gumshoe, a flatfoot, a peeper, a snoop, a sleuth, a, a . . .' words abandoned him momentarily. 'A dick!' He waved his finger threateningly in Rubinstein's face. 'This is all I have *left*!'

The silence left was like a vacuum; it demanded to be filled. Rubinstein laughed again. He laughed and laughed, holding his belly in, his entire body convulsing, shaking. 'You . . . you . . . !' he couldn't speak. Wolf watched him, hatred burning. He smashed the glass with the scotch against the desk. It broke into pieces and the rank stench of the alcohol filled the air, worse than the orchids. Wolf attacked the still-laughing Rubinstein. He caught the man by surprise, pushed him to the ground before Rubinstein could act. He landed one good kick in the Jew's ribs. It felt so good, so right! But Rubinstein only grunted in pain and then pushed himself up, easily. He stood on the balls of his feet like some street-brawling, bare-knuckle pugilist. Wolf launched a fist but Rubinstein deflected it easily. Then he slapped Wolf.

It was a slap the way you would administer a slap to a woman or a child. The way Wolf sometimes had to keep Geli in check. 'Punch me!' Wolf screamed. Rubinstein slapped him again, and the sound of the slap was swallowed into the foliage of the conservatory. Rubinstein reached for a desk drawer. Wolf tensed, expecting a gun. But all Rubinstein came out with was a wad of crumpled money. He threw the money in Wolf's face. 'Here,' he said. 'Take it. I said take it!' He slapped Wolf again, grabbed him by the neck, forced him to bend and catch the falling notes. His face was close to Wolf's own, breathing alcohol in Wolf's face.

'She's mine, not yours,' Rubinstein said. 'She has always been mine.' He said it gently; almost sadly.

He pushed Wolf away and stood there watching him, until Wolf left.

He walked away wordlessly; with each step he felt lighter and lighter. The maid waited for him outside the conservatory. She escorted him to the door. He passed the pile of suitcases. He thought he saw a figure standing at the top of the grand stairs, watching him. When he raised his eyes he thought he caught momentary sight of a pale beautiful face, heard the rustle of a summer dress, but then it was gone, perhaps had never been. A mocking final laugh, trailing into nothing. Outside it was dark and the clouds were amassed low on the horizon. The driver was still cleaning the car. He seemed to have been at it for hours. 'Noticed the bags in the hallway,' Wolf said. 'Going someplace?'

'Airport, mate,' the driver said. 'Flying?'

'Makes sense.'

'You know where?'

'What's it to you?'

Wolf sighed. 'Nothing,' he said, tiredly. 'It's nothing to me.'

'California,' the driver said, unexpectedly. He spat on the ground. 'Jews, right. Know it's over for them here. Whereas me, I got to find another job. Didn't tell the missus yet. What would I tell her? Got a small one at home, a lad. Still got to drive them to the airport tonight, don't I. Who did you vote for?'

'I didn't vote.'

'You should have.' He smiled, exposing his teeth. 'I voted for Mosley. Got to do what's right. Not a Jew, are you?'

'No.'

'Well, you look a bit Jewish, mate. No offence.'

Wolf glared at him. He'd had enough.

'Well, have a nice life and all,' the driver said.

'Yes . . . you too,' Wolf said. He walked away. Behind him, the curtain on the second-storey bedroom window might have twitched as she maybe watched him go. But he never turned to check.

WOLF'S DIARY, 22ND NOVEMBER 1939—CONTD.

I was out of work. I was out of luck. I had two cases and I lost them both and I hadn't been too happy about either to begin with. Like the Rubinsteins' driver, I needed another job. Things bothered me, things I couldn't quite put my finger on: who my old comrades were working for, for instance. Hess had only been a link in the chain. Goebbels was another, higher up. But someone was above them all, in the place I had once occupied. Someone had pulled the strings to put me in hospital.

But who?

And where was Judith Rubinstein now?

I felt light-headed from the alcohol, but still, almost supremely, in control. My anger was hot, coiled inside me. I walked for a while. There wasn't much rain. The air felt expectant. It was quiet in Belgravia but in the distance I could hear shouts, chanting. I found an open garage.

'My car,' I said apologetically. 'It stalled. I think I ran out of petrol.'

'No problem, mate.' The mechanic wiped his hands with a dirty cloth and filled a bottle. The wireless was on and the BBC was reporting live from Trafalgar Square, where Mosley was speaking to an audience of thousands. When the mechanic wandered off to put the money away I stole the cloth. I daresay he wouldn't have missed it. I also swiped a half-empty box of Swan Vestas. They were matches you could trust.

I felt very calm. I retraced my steps. Townhouses towered over me each way. It was very quiet: in this neighbourhood there were special employees just to walk the dogs. The Rubinsteins' house was dark. I didn't see the driver though the car was still parked outside. I uncapped the bottle of petrol and twisted the mechanic's cloth and soaked it in some of the petrol and then jammed it into the mouth of the bottle. I stared at the house. A light came on, on the second floor. I wondered what she was wearing. I struck a match and applied it, carefully, to the soaked cloth. It flamed brightly and for a moment I saw myself standing on the street, holding the makeshift bomb, reflected in the black gloss of the Rolls-Royce.

The bottle arced through the air.

It hit the window and smashed through into the house, flaming petrol exploding in a wide pattern over furniture and carpet, paintings and wall.

A whoop of flame billowed out of the broken windows.

Wolf heard a scream. Heard a man swearing. The flames climbed higher. He hid in the shadows and watched them come tumbling out from the house, smashing open the door in their haste to escape. The maid was wobbling and the driver was cursing and swearing to quit and damn them all to hell, he was going home, and then came Julius Rubinstein with a shotgun in his hand and finally Isabella.

She wore a sheer silk nightgown and her feet were bare. She looked young and scared. Wolf almost wanted to reach for her, in some perverse way he couldn't quite define she reminded him of Geli. Then Julius Rubinstein fired the shotgun into the air and Wolf jumped. Isabella laughed, a high-pitched, crazy sound that filled the night. Wolf saw her father's hand come to rest on her shoulder, pulling her close to him. Julius pulled open the passenger-side door of the car. He pushed Isabella in and shut the door on her and got in himself on the other side. Wolf couldn't see them inside the car. The house burned and the flames were reflected on the car's hood and there were sirens in the distance. The Rolls-Royce growled to life, then accelerated away. Wolf tracked it with his eyes. It moved fast, took a corner with a screeching of tyres, and was gone. In front of the burning house only the maid remained, too shocked to move. The box of Swan Vestas rattled between Wolf's fingers. He let them drop to the ground as he walked away from the flames.

HERR WOLF—

She was waiting, as though she always knew I would come. She would have haggled over the price but I gave her money to silence her. It was a lot of money for a whore. I led her by the hand to the door—your door. The bakery was shut, and it was but the work of a moment to unlock the door in the dark, when no one was watching. I don't know, she kept saying, I don't know. We stole up the stairs. I broke into your office. Here? she said. To me the place was enchanted. In the darkness there was the presence of you, in everything I touched there was magic. To her it might have seemed a blight, a place of decay, but she did not under-stand what you and I have.

Get on your knees, she said. She pushed me down. Her hand reached into her bag and came out with a black whip. It whistled through the air. I said stay down! She slapped me, rocking my head back. Is this what you want? she whispered. Is this what you want?

Yes, yes. Everything was a fog. Take off your shirt, she said. I threw it in a corner, and shivered as cold air touched my exposed skin. Have you been a bad boy. Yes, yes! She lashed me, once, twice, and I cried out.

Is that what it feels like for you, too?

I knelt before her. But I needed, wanted, more. When she lashed at me next I raised my hand and grabbed hold of the whip and wrapped the leather around my wrist and pulled. I caught her off-balance and she stumbled and I caught her, rising. My cockerel was on her skin, rubbing in an agony of pleasure. I wrapped my arm round her neck. She smelled so sweet. Listen, bitch, if you struggle it will go worse for you, I said.

I didn't know she had a knife!

The whore stabbed me.

You fucking bitch! I yelled. I released her with the pain and stepped back, confused. I stared in horror at my own blood. She had stabbed me in the ribs. I raised my eyes and she was standing with the knife in her hand, and she was smiling.

You like that, do you? You like that? I shouted. I lunged for my coat, for the knife hidden there. She slashed at me with her own sharp little knife, missed. I tried to get my blade out but my hands were shaking. The coat was crumpled in my hands. She kicked me, catching me on the side of the head

with her heel. I lost my balance and landed on my
buttocks, hard. She began to kick me, viciously,
and her heels tore chunks out of my skin. I tried
to curl into a ball to protect myself. I was lying
on the coat and I felt something cold and hard and
my hand closed on the handle of my knife. Then I
felt calm again, in control. I stood up with the
knife in my hand.

13

Wolf was in a cheerful mood. He was humming a popular song with-out quite paying attention, then realised it was Marlene Deitrich's 'Falling in Love Again.' He continued humming and adjusted his fedora at a cocky angle. His cases were finished with, but so what? He had been paid. Who cared where the stupid Jew bitch Judith Rubinstein had got herself to? To-day was the first day of the rest of his life. He came to his street but there was no one about. Even the whores were gone. Beyond he could hear shouts, see fireworks rise over the rooftops from the direction of the Thames. The hordes were out there, in Leicester Square and Trafalgar Square and Picca-dilly, and thronging the Embankment and the wine bars and pubs. He went to his door and found it unlocked, the lock in fact jammed, inexpertly, and his good cheer evaporated. He pushed the door open and went in.

It was dark and he climbed each step with a slow and careful footfall; each step was like another level he was climbing, on top of some ancient and enormous pyramid, a once-grand edifice now reduced by centuries of neglect and misuse. The air smelled metallic. His shoes on the faded carpet made no sound. It was so very quiet. He could hear his own breathing, but nothing else. Nothing moved. He came to the landing and stopped. The door to his office was open. The taste of rust was in Wolf's mouth, on his tongue and in his gums. He pulled the door open all the way.

He went inside.

He saw it in snatches, not quite forming a full picture. The faint light from outside rippled on the walls and on the carpet, ancient light that had been traversing space for untold millennia and new light, born from the mysterious electrical processes housed within the streetlamp outside. The light illuminated the room in a chiaroscuro where shadows danced like the naked savages studied by Ernst Schäfer on his expeditions to prove the origins of the Aryan race. Arcs of bright fresh blood decorated the walls of Wolf's office. Some reached as high as the ceiling, some criss-crossed each other in strange hieroglyphs, a language of death and blood. A raincoat had been tossed to the corner of the room. There were dirty red palm prints on the floor around it.

Wolf watched the toes. The toes were long and slender and the nails were painted a fuchsia colour. Furniture had been overturned in the room and one chair was broken. A woman's high-heeled shoe lay on its side. Wolf couldn't see the other one. A woman's handbag, a bag he recognised, was upturned by the window and spilling out of it were dildos and a whip and makeup, blusher and lipstick, a wad of notes, keys, prophylactics, half a sandwich wrapped in wax paper, of the sort Herr Edelmann occasionally sold in the bakery downstairs.

There was a concavity in the floor where her head had been bashed, repeatedly, with cold fury, and he saw her hair, clumped with brain matter and blood, in delicate bunches like the stems of flowers. She was not like the first girl, cleanly arranged. She had struggled, had inflicted her own violence on her attacker, and was silenced, at last, for her transgression, for the crime of being a woman, or a prostitute, or for just being. Her murderer had lashed out blindly, repeatedly. Her head on the floor barely resembled something human.

There was the fading smell of semen, like wet mushrooms.

Having done this deed the killer had tidied himself up, had become a man amongst men once more. He had tidied his clothes and straightened himself and then he had dipped his finger in her blood and he had drawn a swastika on the wall, and then, beside Dominique's head, he had left Wolf a toy: a tin wind-up drummer.

Wolf picked up the toy. Idly, he wound the little key. He set the drummer on the floor and watched it march past Dominique's body, the tiny hands moving mechanically up and down over the drum, beating out a funeral dirge. It was the only sound in the room. He watched it go. It marched and marched.

On the desk was Wolf's typewriter and in the typewriter was a sheet of paper, neatly inserted. Wolf went round the desk and sat down in his chair. The keys of the typewriter were smeared in blood. He pulled out the piece of paper and read.

It began, *Herr Wolf.*

He read the letter, holding it at a distance and squinting at the hard black letters on the page.

The letter was a confession of a sort. It ended with a simple entreaty for the two of them to meet.

On the desk next to the typewriter was a ticket for the revue show at the London Hippodrome, dated for that night. Wolf picked it up, looked at it, turned it over, put it back down. As an afterthought he turned the typewritten page over in his hand.

Written on the back of the paper in an unsteady hand, with the same ink that only a scant time before had run through Dominique's veins, was a single word in the murderer's hand.

Run.

The door downstairs crashed open. The sound, unexpected and terrifying, made me jump. My heart beat fast in my chest.

Could it be the killer, coming back?

A madman, I thought, dazedly. I was dealing with a madman. Not for the first time I wished I had a gun. A gentleman killed with bullets, the state with gas. Only a madman used a knife.

I listened to footsteps come labouring up the stairs. Stray light from the window bounced off an object thrown beyond my desk. It was a blood-covered knife. It must have belonged to the girl. It was the weapon she had used on the killer. I picked it up and sat behind the desk again, waiting. The footsteps reached all the way to the landing and stopped.

'Oh, it's *you*,' I said.

'Well, well, well,' Constable Keech said. 'What have we got here, then?' He stood in the doorway, his fat face covered in a sheen of sweat. When he grinned his big square teeth looked like coral reefs buried under a murky sea.

'I would like,' I said, 'to report a murder.'

Keech bellowed a laugh. He laughed genuinely, with big heaving breaths, his face turning redder and redder, his hands supporting his weight on his knees as he almost keeled over on himself. 'Would you now, shamus,' he said. 'Would you now.'

'I didn't do this, Keech.'

'Of course you didn't.'

'I didn't do this! You have to believe me!'

'Don't insult me, Wolf.' He straightened up, glanced at the corpse, lost his good humour. 'Jesus, Wolf. What did you do to that poor girl?'

'Someone is trying to frame me.'

'Well, they've done a bloody good job, then, haven't they! Get up. You're under arrest.'

'Fuck off, pig!' I was feeling panicked. 'How did you get here?' I said. 'How did you *know*?'

He shrugged. 'I got an anonymous call at the station,' he said.

'I'm being *framed*!'

'Come along, Wolf. You can explain everything at the station.'

'Is it that inspector again? Morhaim.' I spat out the name. 'The filthy Jew has been after me from the beginning.'

'Inspector Morhaim is no longer in the employ of the Metropolitan Police. And another word from you about him like this will get you some broken teeth to complain about.' He took out his nightstick and ran his fingers along its dark shaft almost lovingly. Still I didn't move from the desk. Hidden from Keech's view was the dead girl's knife.

'What happened to Morhaim?' I said. I was, genuinely, surprised.

Keech spat on the floor. 'He quit. It's not like he was popular with the men. And well, with your boy Mosley headed to Downing Street, I don't think it would have been long before he was pushed out anyway.'

'Now, are you going to get up from that chair there or do I need to make you?'

'Make me, pig.'

'Oh, I'll make you all right!' he said. He advanced on me, the nightstick raised. 'Look!' I said. I waved the killer's letter in my hand. 'It's all but a confession, it's proof I didn't do it!'

'Proof?' His stick came down on the desk, shattering the cheap wood. 'Proof?' He snatched it from my hand, looked at it, his fat lips moving as he read. 'You typed this.'

'No!'

He scrunched the killer's confession into a ball and tossed it in the corner. 'You're sick in the head,' he said. 'You know what they're going to call you? The greatest murderer since Jack the Ripper. You're not right, mate. You're not right at all.' And he brought his stick down once again, right on the typewriter, smashing it to pieces.

Keys flew in the air; a semicolon hit me in the eye. 'Damn you, Keech!' I said. I rose from the chair just as he strode past Dominique's head and reached for me, his stick descending a third time. I slashed him with Dominique's knife. The knife missed his face, grazed his chest. The nightstick caught me on the arm and a terrible numbing pain spread through me and I could barely breathe. The knife fell from my hand. I screamed, '*Scheisse!*' and raised my knee sharply, catching him unawares between the legs. Keech made a high-pitched hissing sound and fell, slowly. Somehow he was still holding the stick and he swung it as he went down, hitting me on the shin, the pain so excruciating that I screamed and went down, too.

For a moment both of us were on the floor facing each other like two lovers at the end of an intimate moment, looking deep into each other's eyes. 'I didn't do it, Keech. I didn't kill them!'

'I will . . . fucking kill *you*,' he said. He spoke with difficulty. He reached for me, those huge meaty hands, his fat fingers closing on my throat. Their weight was terrible. His thumbs found my windpipe and began to press. I reached desperately for the fallen knife, scrabbling for it, panicking, the pain growing impossible, my breath departing. I tried to fight him off; we were entwined on the floor, slick with the dead girl's blood. His body pressed on mine; he was so heavy I couldn't breathe. I thought, what a way to die. Then miraculously my fingers scrabbling in the blood on the floor found the sharp edge of the knife. It sliced the tip of my finger, and my blood mingled with the girl's. Slowly, slowly I moved my fingers until I found the handle of the blade. I was so weak I could not breathe, but I could do this, just as I had cured my blindness with my mind. The power came to me, for one last desperate act, and I thrust the knife into his neck; just so.

The blood came out of the wound hot; it spurted out of him. And still he pressed on my neck, and for a moment I blacked out.

I came to, only moments later. The pressure on my neck had eased—was gone. I could breathe. The air tasted so sweet. I blinked back tears. His face swam into focus. His hand was pressed to his neck, holding back the blood, but it spurted out of him nonetheless, running between his fingers. His eyes stared into mine, and I was terrified of him. I scrambled to get away from him, from the blood. It was everywhere in the room, his blood, my blood, the girl's blood, the murderer's blood. I slipped and fell in it. Typewriter keys were pressed painfully against my flesh, an A and an H. Keech said nothing, just watched me, the blood still pouring out of him. I pushed myself up until I stood, supporting myself against the desk, looking down at him. The knife was on the floor. I think Keech smiled. I think he said, 'Now they'll get you.' I walked backwards until my shoulder blades hit the wall and I stopped and stood there, breathing deeply, looking about me at the room and the dead whore and the dying policeman.

Keech was right, I realised, with dread.

I was a marked man, now. And there was no escape.

I watched him die. He died well. I will say that much for him.

I picked up the ticket for the revue show off the desk. I took one last look at the room. My office. I had been almost happy there, for a while.

One dead copper, one dead whore. I was getting too old.

Everything hurt. I would miss my books most, I thought. But books, like people, can always be replaced.

. . . And so into the night Wolf went, and a thousand lamps glimmered in the dark, and the ancient light of a thousand stars fought through the cloud cover to be changed forever by the hard surfaces of the city; within its narrow twisting alien alleyways Wolf walked like an explorer on the surface of a foreign hostile world, an invisible umbilical cord stretched from his past to his present, stretched until it finally broke, unable to hold him anchored any longer; and so he felt light of gravity, and floating, like an astronaut in one of those glorious, colourful American pulps. He pictured men on the moon, proud Aryan *raumfahrer*: spacemen, voyagers. Pictured capsules of aluminium floating through space, men inside them; pictured a lunar landing, a man stepping out onto the alien dust, planting a swastika flag where no man had gone before. Wolf walked through the city that night as a man with no purpose, a man whose life had taken the wrong turn, around whom history had flowed a different way, taken a different course and left him stranded in an island of unreality in the midst of that great river that was time. He felt untethered. He did not know who he was or what he would become.

On Shaftesbury Avenue the last theatregoers had come and gone and the theatres were shut though their lights shone on. The pavements were crowded with a festive restless mass of people, shouting, drinking, waving Union Jacks and the cross of St George. Wolf was swept up in the current. His fate was no longer his own. He was carried by the tide of these English citizens the way a spectator may have been in one of his own rallies, in the old days. Down Shaftesbury to Piccadilly where a Blackshirt rally was in progress, a full military campaign, and the men in their futuristic outfits no longer looked ridiculous but serious and deadly. He was carried along through the throng down Haymarket and on to Pall Mall, where

he saw a ring of policemen blocking the road and a clash between Union-
ists and Blackshirts spilling bloody and awkward across pavement and
road, men with makeshift weapons of bricks and piping smashing at each
other, blindly, in a rage, but silently, or so it seemed to Wolf, in a primitive battlefield such as between Spartans and Persians, and the cars in the
street jammed against each other and were savaged, too, and he watched
the battle escalate, drivers trying to escape, windows smashed, glass shards
spilling on the road, skulls cracked, a vehicle set on fire, policemen shouting, someone firing a gun in the air, a stampede where men were trampled
underfoot. Somehow he managed to get away, swept again in the tide,
down to Trafalgar Square.

From just down the road, along Whitehall, a sudden silence spread out
as Big Ben began to strike the hour. The first and then the second heartbeats of the old clock went almost unnoticed, at three the sound began
to penetrate, at four and five the massed crowds quietened, at seven and
eight the silence grew; at nine it was entire. Nine and then ten heartbeats
Big Ben struck and they echoed over the ancient city, old and new, old
and new like the harbingers of a new dawn. Time hung, suspended. On
the podium by Nelson's Column, Oswald Mosley waited, his face sweaty,
his black uniform replaced for this one occasion by a dignified three-piece
suit from Savile Row. Two other men were waiting in the wings, only one
of whom Wolf would have known, but Wolf stood a way away, at the
Whitehall intersection, listening to the clock strike the hour like a drum.
Eleven, old Ben struck, and the second stretched and stretched and in its
expectant silence Wolf saw the city as he had never seen it, rising before
him like a metropolis dreamed of by Fritz Lang: huge shining buildings
rose amidst the squalor of old London, by London Bridge a shard of glass
taller than the pyramids pierced the sky. From the City of London there
rose a phoenix egg of metal and glass, and a giant wheel spun and spun
on the south bank of the Thames like a mandala. This city of the future
was brighter, brasher, awash in an electric glow which faded as he watched,

the ghostly outline of this futuristic could-have-been slowly washing away. Wolf held his breath and Big Ben tolled, twelve, and one day ended, and a new day began.

WOLF'S DIARY, 23RD NOVEMBER 1939

The night erupted in a shower of fireworks. The air filled with the repeated sounds of explosions, playing out a moment after the formation of bright shapes in the air. The smell of cordite, magnesium and sulphur stung my nostrils. In the sky were the fabulous shapes of spinning rings and diadems and tailed chrysanthemum, crossettes and hearts and palm-shell fireworks. A band began to play, rather incongruously, Gilbert & Sullivan's 'He Is An Englishman.' The crowds around me cheered, faces red and teeth yellow and skin sickly white; they were cast in the lights and shadows of the exploding colours overhead. Demonic grinning faces all around me, a nightmarish vista of skulls seen through translucent skin, moving skeletons clad in sacks of blood. I hadn't even thought of how I must look, bruised, battered and covered in blood, mine and others', but I didn't think anyone even noticed. I pushed my way towards the steps of the National Gallery. I had to batter my way through people and every moment I half-expected a policeman to find me, to blow the whistle, raise the alarm. But no one would find Keech and the dead girl, surely, I thought, not until the morning at least. What I would do then I didn't know.

I watched the stage. Watched Mosley come on, smiling, waving at the crowds, his arm extended in a Blackshirt's imitation of a Nazi salute. The man was nothing but a cheap copy.

'Victory!' he called out. The crowd erupted in cheer again but I could hear booing coming from the distance and turned my head to see a group of union demonstrators trying to push towards the podium and being repelled.

'Britain belongs to the British people once again!' Mosley's voice echoed over the crowd. 'We've won! This is the beginning of a new dawn! This is a new day for Britain—and for the world!'

Cheers. Boos. Fireworks exploding overhead, the booms coming a moment later, disorientating me. I felt sick and dry-heaved. I had not eaten in I couldn't remember how long. On the stage Mosley assumed a serious, studious expression. His voice took on dulcet tones. He said, 'His Majesty the King has asked me to form a new government and I have accepted.'

Silence. Overhead the last fireworks burst and died.

'I would like to discuss some of the challenges we are now facing.

'I believe we need a strong government, a stable, good and decent government that I think we need so badly.

'It has been more than six years since the Fall of Germany to international communism. Communism with its method of madness is making a powerful and insidious attack upon the world today. It seeks to poison and disrupt, in order to hurl us into an epoch of chaos.

'It has flooded our country with refugees. We have opened our borders, our arms, our homes to them, in friendship. And they came, in their thousands, and thousands of thousands. Our cities reek of their cabbage! Their children speak foreign tongues in our schools. They are draining our country of its resources, they are taking the very bread from our own people's mouths!'

Cheers. Fists raised in salute. I felt a cold chill I could not explain. And yet it was almost as if it were my own words he was using against me.

'I think the service our country needs right now is to face up to our really big challenges, to confront our problems, to take difficult decisions, to lead people through those difficult decisions, so that together we can reach better times ahead.

'Germany is not our enemy. Communism is. That, and the bankers behind it all. I think you know their real name.'

'Jews!'—'The elders of Zion!'—'Shylocks!'—'Yids!'

'We must help Germany in its time of need!' Mosley said. 'Yes!'

'Get the foreigners out!' someone shouted. Mosley smiled. The smile faded. His eyes gazed out coldly over Trafalgar Square.

'This is a testing time,' he said, gravely. 'I have news, news we could not share before with you. At nineteen hundred hours today, Germany, with Russian help, has invaded Poland.'

Gasps. Shouts. A wave of shock running through the crowd.

'It is true.'

He waited. Drew out the silence.

'Our bilateral agreement with Poland dictates a response,' Mosley said.

'It is my first duty to you as your prime minister, to let you know that we are at war.'

Gasps, but also cheers. The mood was turning ugly. They were enthralled. They relished the idea of war.

'I would like to introduce you to an old friend of mine!' Mosley said.

I began to make my way through the crowd, up towards Leicester Square, but now I paused. Turned back.

'Germany *will* return to its former glory,' Mosley said. 'This I promise. We will fight for its release from the shackles of communist oppression!'

This was less joyfully received.

'I would like to introduce you to the head of the newly formed German Government-in-Exile: a man who loves his country, who wants to return the refugees from our streets to their rightful homes. A former member of the National Socialist party, the rightful winners of the last German elections.'

Somewhere behind that stage the American, Virgil, would be standing, smiling like the cat who drank all the cream. Somewhere there, waiting to make his entrance, would be the man behind it all, behind the white slavery and the people-smuggling rings, one of my old comrades, I was sure.

My replacement.

My fingers tightened into fists. Who could it be? Hess was dead, Goebbels ruthless but lame.

Himmler? Bormann? Heydrich?

'Together we will change the world!' Mosley pumped his fist in the air. 'Please welcome the rightful Chancellor of Germany—Mr Adolf Eichmann!'

'Who?' someone beside me said, bewildered.

'Who?' I screamed. A tallish thin man with a vulture's face and thinning hair came onto the stage and solemnly shook Prime Minister Mosley's hand.

'Who the fuck is Adolf Eichmann!' I said.

'Thank you, Prime Minister. You do me a great honour.'

'Eichmann? I have never even heard of this Eichmann!' I screamed. Heads were turning. 'Who . . .? How . . .!'

'You may not know me,' the man on the stage said. 'I joined the National Socialist party in '32, only a year before the Fall of Germany. Some of you may even remember our one-time leader, the man we called our Führer—'

'God damn you, Eichmann! Who is this imposter, this swindler!'

'But he was weak. And I shall replace him.'

'No one can replace me, do you hear! No one!'

More heads were turning my way but I didn't care. I did not

know this man! He was nothing, a nobody! Did Dorothy feel this way when she finally discovered the great wizard was just some man behind a curtain?

'Germany has been taken over by Jews!' Eichmann said. 'But I have a solution! A final solution to the Jewish question. Mr Prime Minister?'

'Indeed,' Mosley said, smoothly. 'Mr Eichmann has some innovative and creative ideas, and we shall be discussing them thoroughly in the coming days. And for now—' he took a breath and looked mournfully at the assembled hordes. 'I regret to inform you that as of this moment I am declaring limited martial law. All non-registered foreigners will be collected and deported. All Jews will be designated hostile aliens and rounded up, to be either deported or placed in internment camps. We must cut out the cancer eating away at our society! Together we can do this! Together we are as one!'

'Together we are as one!' They all raised their fists in the air. They were saluting him, his power. A woman beside me whimpered, her thighs rubbing together as she climaxed herself to an onanistic orgasm.

This should have been *me* up there! The mood was ugly, and I was a foreigner alone and undocumented in this crowd of blood-thirsty British pigs. I had to get away!

I began to push again, to try and edge away, but the crowds closed on me and on the stage Mosley was speaking, shouting, cheering, and the band struck again, that ridiculous song from *H.M.S. Pinafore*, and a second bout of fireworks shot into the sky.

In the general confusion, at least, I began to make headway in my effort to escape, pushing through the crowds at last to reach Charing Cross Road. Bands of drunken men were forming into impromptu search parties, seeking out foreigners to round up and beat. Communists and agitators challenged them and fights broke out and policemen appeared like mushrooms and the whole thing was threatening to become one huge riot. Then I saw it.

The Hippodrome.

The club sat on the corner of Leicester Square. Charlie Chaplin had played there once, that vile man. It was a grandiose building, once home to a travelling zoo, from which it got its name; then it became a music hall and then a revue. I remembered the ticket in my pocket. The building was shut now, of course. I was being pushed closer to it by the turning tide, people fleeing the melee. The main doors were locked and I was shunted sideways, into Leicester Square, where a battle was commencing between Blackshirts and a group of belligerent, drunken Austrians. My people. I could have wept!

At last I came to the back of the building, and found the service entrance to the Hippodrome.

The chain holding the doors fast was broken.

It was dark inside the Hippodrome and quiet, the noise from outside abating almost instantly when Wolf shut the door. Metal surfaces gleamed in the dark. Pots and pans hung in orderly rows. All he could hear was the soft tap-tap-tap of water drops hitting the bottom of a sink. He tried to listen for movement, for signs of life, but there was nothing. The entire building felt oppressively *empty*. Wolf tiptoed through the kitchen. Somewhere inside the building, he was sure, a killer was lying in wait.

In a kitchen drawer, wide as the span of his arms, he found an assortment of sharp knives. He equipped himself with a chef's knife. The sound the drawer had made when he pulled it sounded very loud to him, and so did the rattling of the knives, and he went hurriedly on, through the service doors and into the theatre proper.

It was a magnificent place, though desolate in its abandonment. No players moved upon the stage. There was no magician to perform his tricks, no comedian to tell off-colour jokes, no dancing girls to flash a glimpse of thigh, no jugglers to astound with feats of the impossible, and no audience to applaud and laugh and gasp and jeer, as could be demanded by the occasion. There was nothing but a great barren silence. The wide stage stood to one side, draped in red velvet curtains, which were raised now, and before it the floor was set with tables for tomorrow night's diners. Overhead, the auditorium rose in four tiers, all sparkle and velvet and dark wood, steep stairs rising on each side. But all the seats were empty: there was no one in the house.

Wolf moved cautiously, quietly through the aisles. He stopped and listened, but still there was no sound. Was the killer waiting, watching? He stumbled against a chair in the dark. It fell over with a loud crash. Wolf said, '*Scheisse*,' softly.

He heard someone moving, high overhead. Craned his head upwards. Sudden white light hit him in the eyes, blinded him. He turned his head away. A spotlight illuminated Wolf, alone in the theatre. It fell on him from high above, from the gods. Wolf moved, and the spotlight moved with him, and he heard someone laugh; high above the world.

'Show yourself!' Wolf cried.

'I have been waiting a long time, Mr Wolf.'

There was something familiar about the voice but it was distorted, amplified. Wolf climbed onto the stage. He stood facing the empty theatre, one hand protecting his eyes. At last he thought he caught movement, but all he could make out was a shadowy figure in the gods.

'What do you want?'

Wolf moved. The spotlight followed. He paced the stage. His patience was being exhausted. He had had a bad night, a bad month. The whole of November had been a bit of a washout, really.

'I wanted you to see.'

The speaker sounded plaintive. As though Wolf had somehow let him down. 'See what?' Wolf snapped. He edged to the wings and then slipped off-stage. The spotlight tracked him but it couldn't follow him beyond the curtains. 'Where are you?' the shadow said.

Wolf crept behind the scenery. A magician's sawing-a-woman-in-half trick box, a clown's red nose hanging from a hook, a pastoral village scene with cardboard cut-out cows that looked good-naturedly at Wolf as he passed.

'I don't like this, Mr Wolf. Really, hiding won't make any difference. I mean you no harm. On the contrary, I am your friend.'

A prop gun, a mask like something out of a Venetian dance. Ah, there! A set of hidden stairs behind the stage, twisting and turning away, leading up. Wolf raised his head. It was a jumble of unsteady construction as far as he could see, hanging sandbags and rickety gangways suspended from the ceiling. But the stairs looked solid enough.

'Don't you *see*? This isn't who you are! When I first saw you I was in awe, I could not believe it was really you, but then I watched you, I observed, I am the watcher in the dark—'

The watcher in the dark? How ridiculous! Wolf thought. He climbed the stairs quietly, cautiously. They rose up, a service passageway that ran parallel to the paying customers' stairs that mirrored them. The man—this *watcher*—was somewhere above. Probably he would be in a technician's box somewhere. The spotlight moved across the empty stage, still searching for Wolf. The man was all the time talking, talking: Wolf wished he would shut up.

'. . . Fallen,' the watcher said. 'Reduced, debased! You who were the greatest of all men, now playing out the role of the lowest: a shamus, a private dick? I could not believe it, I was outraged. You had a *destiny*!'

What do you know about destiny, Wolf wanted to shout, you stupid little man. What do you know of real pain?

'And you just gave up! You were like a man who is sick, I finally realised.

A man out of his senses, a man in shock. I had to wake you. I had to make you see. To face yourself again. So you could become the man you were always meant to be.'

There. The voice was close. Wolf could see the limelight now, and the vague outline of the man behind it, moving it. He gripped the knife tightly. He would make this fast. He was an orderly man and he was settling up all of his accounts.

'That's why I killed them,' the watcher confided; his words floated down to the empty seats, the unserved tables, the stage on which no clown or magician performed. He had an audience of one, this watcher, and he seemed intent, Wolf thought, on boring him.

How he abhorred bores!

'They were whores, they didn't matter,' the watcher said. 'Diseased prostitutes, you said so yourself. In your book. I have read it so many times. It changed my life. Where do you get your ideas from?'

Wolf crept the rest of the way up, low on the metal stairs. The man was just behind the wall of wood. *Where do you get your ideas*? Really? It was the stupidest question Wolf had ever heard.

'I needed you to see. I need you to wake up!' He sounded desperate. 'Don't you *understand*?'

Then he stopped speaking and Wolf, too late, tried to rise with the knife but he was, of course, too slow. A young man in a shabby suit stood on the other side of the divide, holding a gun which he aimed at Wolf. It was a Parabellum M17, a German pistol. Wolf remembered when it was first produced, in the closing years of the Great War.

'Drop the knife. Please.'

Wolf dropped the knife. They were suspended high in the air. Below them the theatre stretched in tiers, all lifeless, all expectant. It was quiet. So quiet.

'My father brought it with him as a memento from the war,' the young man said. 'The pistol, I mean. He always had much respect for the German soldiers. He said the German army was the best in the world, but it had been let down by its leaders. It's good to see you again, Mr Wolf. I am glad to see you well.'

'Oh, it's *you*,' Wolf said.

A small smile played on the boy's face. 'Yes,' he said, softly.

'I'm sorry, I don't quite remember your name.'

The smile disappeared. The gun wavered. 'It's *Alderman*! Thomas Alderman! We spoke on the *phone*! We met at Sir Oswald's party!'

'Mosley's man, right! I wondered where I knew you from.'

The boy's face was pale, his eyes too large, bloodshot. His clothes were covered in gore and he held himself as though he were wounded.

'I visited you at the *hospital*!' the boy, Alderman, said.

'I wondered if that really happened,' Wolf said, softly. 'It seemed rather odd, at the time. I assume the nurse did as I asked her, and got in touch with Oswald?'

The boy looked genuinely confused. 'What nurse?' he said.

'How did you know I was at the hospital?'

'I looked for you everywhere! I was frantic with worry when you never returned to your office. I have been watching you. It's what I do, I watch, I listen, and no one sees me, no one suspects. No one *sees* me!'

'Alderman.'

'Yes!'

'What do you *want*, Alderman?' Wolf said. He was so very tired.

'I just want you to *see*!'

'I'm looking,' Wolf said. 'Put the gun down, Alderman. You're not going to shoot me.'

The gun wavered. 'I don't know . . . I don't know if I will or not. You can't tell me what to do! Don't you understand?' he said, pleadingly. 'I did it all for *you*. I killed them. *I* did it. So you won't have a choice but to become what you were meant to be. I didn't *like* to do it—well, not much.' An expression that was part sly smile, part grimace rose and fell on

Alderman's face. 'And it worked, didn't it?' he said. 'The police, they will be coming for you. For the girls, and that fat policeman. What did you do to him?'

'I killed him.'

'You see!' the boy shouted in triumph. 'There is nowhere left to run! Admit who you are! Say it!'

The whole thing was grating on Wolf's nerves. 'I know who I am, Alderman,' Wolf said. 'I have always known myself. Now give me the gun, boy!'

'Say it!' Alderman screamed. 'Your name, say it!'

'Wolf.'

'No! Damn it, don't make me shoot you, I won't—'

Wolf stumbled against the low wooden door. It swung open into the box, catching Alderman on the knees, knocking him back. The boy lost his balance and his gun dropped from his hand. He tottered on the edge of the box, above the dark chasm of the stage. His face was beaded with sweat, white and grotesque. 'Help me!' His hand reached out in a mockery of a Nazi salute. Moved by compassion or some other, more nebulous emotion he could not quite name, Wolf reached for him; for just a moment the tips of their fingers met, touched. The boy's eyes shone wet. 'Adolf . . .' he whispered. And then he said, '*Heil* Hitler,' and, for just a moment, Wolf thought he smiled. Then he lost his balance and fell.

Wolf watched him fall. Alderman fell like a trapeze artist, sailing with a grace he had never possessed on the ground. Then he hit the railings of the lower circle with a wet sound and rolled ungainly downwards until he smashed through a table already laid out for tomorrow night's guests, crushing the china, scattering the silverware and coming to land, at last, in a broken heap on the Hippodrome's floor.

'Wolf. Adolf. It's the same fucking name, you dolt,' Wolf said. He turned off the useless spotlight. It was still shining, on the wrong spot, on somewhere where nothing had happened. Everything was clearer in the dark but not for Wolf, not any more.

He saw the gun lying on the ground and tucked it into his waistband at the small of his back. Then he stepped out of the box and began to descend the stairs, going slowly.

Back on the ground he went and looked at the boy. He stood over him for some time; what remained of him. He felt like a match, burning. A hot hate suffused him. 'I'm Hitler!' he screamed. He kicked the boy, and again, and again, his foot slamming into the soft unresisting flesh of the corpse. 'I'm Hitler! I'm Hitler! I'm Hitler!'

The dead ruined face stared up at him with mocking blind eyes. Wolf's own voice came back to him reedy and thin, lost in the high ceiling of the Hippodrome. He was no one. He was nothing.

'I'm . . .' he said. The theatre was quiet. The seats were empty and silent with disuse. There was no one to see him; no one at all. There was no one to hear him, no one to respond. There was no one to acknowledge him; there was no one to march to his tune.

'I'm a Jew,' he said, and laughed; but like Wolf himself, the sound meant nothing.

14

In another time and place Shomer builds doors; endless doors come down the production line: small doors, big doors, house doors, prison doors, dollhouse doors and cage doors, and oddly shaped doors that fit no blueprint Shomer can imagine. A row of skeletons work on the production line, skeletons bent over in the cold emptiness of the factory, skeletons still clutching their soup bowls and spoons between their legs so that they are not stolen, like some nebulous proof of their vitality, of their existence. Men die like smoke. Time ebbs and congeals like dirty, slushy snow. Suns rise and fall, days turn to nights, trains come to a stop, men die. Across this vast camp children still clutching their dolls are escorted to showers from which no water comes but gas and gassed they are taken out in wheel-barrows, arms soft and flaccid, eyes glassed, their mothers and fathers lifted up and placed before the *Sonderkommando* whose job it is to extract their gold teeth, search their cavities for hidden valuables, to shear their hair for the war effort, to strip the corpses clean.

It is the job of the *Kanada kommando* then to sort through the items retrieved, piles and piles of gold teeth, shoes, rings—for Canada is the land of plenty; it is the promised land, so much wealth piled up, so many dead, but if only you can steal the occasional item you could trade gold for an extra slice of bread, a bowl of soup that came from the bottom of the vats and not the top, for down in the depths there could be lurking a cube of grey meat, a speck of potato. But all that rich food runs through you, constantly, and it is the job of the *Shiessekommandos* to clean up the latrines, every day wading in so much liquid shit, an endless sea of it, running and dripping and collecting in great oceanic puddles, but there are worse jobs.

In the camp's various Joy Divisions, what we may also term *Lagerbordell* or camp bordellos, the women are branded with *Feld-Hure* on their chests, field whores they become in service of the guards and some favoured inmates, man after man they must satisfy, relentlessly, and any failure means immediate dismissal, and that in turn can mean only the ovens, preceded of course by the showers and the gas.

Women die like air. They are consumed like oxygen. They are as transient as breaths. And in what was once fields, men dig mass graves into which they themselves will fall.

And so Shomer builds doors, while Yenkl stands beside him, watching, as insubstantial as smoke. Moons traverse the sky from horizon to horizon and fall and rise, the planet turns, the trains arrive, and Europe is slowly running out of Jews.

And so Shomer builds doors, until his entire world is contracted into one rectangular shape, always hovering before his eyes, calling out, an impossible promise, until he reaches out to the handle just attached, and pulls.

The door opens, and Shomer steps through.

•

Into a house at rest. A hushed Shabbat calm descends when he enters. Avrom in his starched white shirt, Bina in her Friday dress look up at him across the table where the Shabbat candles burn. Fanya at the oven straightens with the loaf of bread in her hands, and smiles. '*Nu?*' she says. And he takes his place amongst them like a man still dreaming—already the details of that other place, that other time, are fading. And he blesses the wine as though in a dream.

And Shomer goes to the sink and fills a cup with water. He transfers the cup to his left hand and pours on his right, three times. He then transfers the cup and repeats the process, until his hands are washed clean. Returning to the table he ruffles Avrom's dark locks, kisses Bina's porcelain cheek. Touches the back of his wife's hand, briefly. '*Baruch ata adonai,*' he says, 'Blessed be, God, king of the world, for bringing bread out of the earth.' The cobwebs clear from his mind with the prayer. He tears a piece of cholla, dips it in salt, takes a bite. Tears more pieces, dips them, passes them on, to his children and his wife.

They eat.

Peace descends on Shomer; it engulfs him; almost he wishes to leave the dining table and go to his sanctuary, his little office where the typewriter waits, to feel once more the keys beneath his fingers.

The children chatter. Fanya brings out chicken and potatoes from the oven. The smell makes Shomer's mouth water. He carves the chicken and Fanya distributes potatoes to the children. '. . . But *I* want the thigh!' Bina complains, and Avrom says, 'No, I want the thigh!' and Fanya tells them to hush. Shomer thinks of a book he was going to write, something new and full of light. When they are done he sits back and the candles flicker and cast shadows on the wall and one shadow, disturbingly, resembles a door. 'Look, Papa!' Bina says, pointing. She pushes back her chair without asking, her little face lifted in excitement. 'No, no,' Shomer says, an unknown fear makes him tremble. 'No, Bina—'

But she doesn't listen and the shadows deepen and etch on the wall a door. Shomer jumps up, his chair crashes to the floor, Fanya and Avrom are shadows at the table. 'No, don't—'

But his little girl reaches for the handle and she *pulls*—

The door opens and Shomer throws himself at her, knocking her away from the shadows, for a moment this place feels to him as warm as an oven. He stumbles and loses his balance. He totters on the threshold of this shadow door. Only darkness beyond.

He falls.

. . .

And steps into the streets of a city at peace. It is silent, he is somewhere in an English town, London, perhaps, in the deep time of night. To his left is a river. On the ground are buntings, beer bottles, discarded cigarettes, flags, the remains of fireworks, yesterday's newspaper in yesterday's grease, some chips still left poking out cold and oily.

He picks up the newspaper. 22nd November 1939. The *Daily Mail*. 'Mosley Projected to Win Election.' Shomer looks at it in wonder, lets it drop again. A cold wind. He walks along the Embankment. No, he thinks. This isn't it, either. He spots a door ahead and opens it.

. . .

Emerging into a wide corridor lined with unmarked doors on all sides. He opens one and finds himself in another corridor. He tries another door, walks through into another corridor. Another door and another corridor, and another, and another: Shomer is opening and shutting doors.

'No, that's not it. That's not it either.'

In this other time and place, Shomer searches for an exit.

•

Dawn found Wolf at the Greenwich docks. How he got there he couldn't say he knew. He walked aimlessly, had walked for hours through the night as Big Ben ticked away the hours, the sound growing fainter and fainter until it disappeared altogether and with it the outline of the city, too, had been erased, and Wolf found himself in a liminal space, a twilight world of ship hulls, boatyards, shuttered pubs and empty streets, the river first on his right, before he crossed, it must have been at Tower Bridge, though he could recall nothing of this transition from north to south, only the call of ravens, ancient stones, the passing of a barge laden with refuse from the capital, down below, as silent as a ghost, with ghosts in its wide wake.

The Thames on his left as London was abandoned behind and he entered a land less populated, empty pastures, factories silent in the pre-dawn dark, chimneys rising like admonitions into the sky, the river widening, the Isle of Dogs in its midst, the call of seagulls and the sour tang of tar, boats looming in the fog, a whole flotilla of them.

And as he walked he was no longer alone. Wolf was joined in that ur-moment between night and dawn by others. Silently they appeared, walking beside him, behind him, ahead: silent haggard figures, faces pinched and drawn, carrying suitcases and holdalls and babies and things: the detritus of lives, hastily packed together; and everything that couldn't be carried was left behind. In a sombre, ugly mood, they flowed along the banks to Greenwich: to the place where the meridians start. All about him they congregated and the fog parted before them, these exodii, and Wolf amongst them, one of them now: one of us, one of us.

At last then they came to Greenwich and through the sleeping town they went like the coming tide, flooding the narrow streets until they came at last to the river bank again and there, in silhouette against the sky, were the ships.

The largest of the ships was named the *Exodus* and it was a packet steamer, almost one hundred metres in length. Its name had been hastily changed: stencilled underneath the lettering was her old name, the SS *President Warfield*. Beside it were two smaller ships: the *Salvador*, flying the Bulgarian flag, and the *Taurus*, flying the Greek colours. The *Exodus* itself flew the Honduran flag, blue and white. There were men and women in uniform clothing waiting for them by the quayside and they guided the crowd as best they could, and all in silence, families with their luggage and their life at their feet waiting in the cold dawn of the docks to flee this island with a hope that had no guarantees. Amongst the officials Wolf saw a familiar face: Eric Goodman, the man from the Jewish Territorialist Organisation. Next they were divided into queues, though not in an overly ordered way. Wolf saw men of His Majesty's Immigration Branch standing around, and port officials, and sailors smoking and eyeing these refugees with pity or disdain or indifference.

For refugees is what they had become, Wolf realised, as is the way of their people, and he in their midst, a wolf amongst the sheep, such as it were. Slowly the line progressed, in a makeshift booth before each ship there stood one man, one woman, each one holding clipboards and pens, slowly, slowly the line moved on.

Dawn came, the sun rising sluggishly, the fog like spider webs melting in the morning air. The honk of a steamer cut through the morning, the call of gulls, a baby cried nearby and was shushed.

Wolf shuffled forward with the rest. A little boy with a Jew's pinched, hungry face sidled up to him. He pulled at Wolf's sleeve. Wolf looked down. The boy wore overalls and a mop of unruly ginger hair. 'Mister, mister,' he said. 'Are we going to Palestine?'

'Fuck off, you little twerp.'

The boy grinned, revealing buck teeth. 'You ain't nothing, mister,' he said. 'You ain't worth shit.'

Wolf went to clout him but the boy hared back up the line, grinning cheerfully as he went.

The queue shuffled on. At last Wolf reached the makeshift booth. 'Your papers?' the woman said. She was short and stocky and had long brown hair in a bun. Wolf took out the identity document. 'Wolfson,' he said, emptily. 'Moshe Wolfson.'

The woman carefully wrote down the name in her list. She had neat, small handwriting. She noted the date and country of his birth. Smiled at him distractedly. At last, gave him a ticket, a grubby piece of cheap paper, stamped hurriedly with ink that had already begun to run. 'Good luck,' she said, softly. Wolf nodded. Then he followed his fellow Jews up the ramp and on board the *Exodus*.

SHIP'S JOURNAL, 23RD NOVEMBER 1939

We left for sea at 10:25 at high tide. The *Exodus* led the way while the two smaller ships followed. A damp, unpleasant breeze. London receding in the distance. I won't miss the damn place much.

The ship overcrowded. Thousands on board. Number of latrines limited. The river opened on all sides, the banks seemed as distant and exotic as those of some unexplored land, filled with danger.

We move so slowly. No one has attempted to hinder our progress but the river is filled with traffic. Listened to the wireless, Mosley taking office at Number 10. The damned man has been nothing but a nuisance.

So many people. It is hard to breathe. Sat on the deck watching England roll by. It rained, then stopped. Played cards with a group of men, friendly enough. There are all sorts on board this ship, a Babel of Jews: black-clad chasidim mix with East End roughs and German refugees, and genteel English Jewry looking bewildered at this sudden change. I won three shillings. We all carry our money on our person at all times. Many children running around; they seem to regard this as a holiday.

SHIP'S JOURNAL, 24TH NOVEMBER 1939

Friday. An odd thing. When darkness fell many of the men were gathered in an impromptu minyan, the women grouped separately, praying and welcoming in the Shabbat, or *Shabbos* in Yiddish. Cholla bread was divided amongst us by the committee. These are the men and women who are behind all this. It is a well-run organisation, the plan must have been in preparation for a long time. They wear blue shirts to distinguish them from us passengers. Listened in on a Hebrew class. '*Shalom. Shalom.*' It means hello, or welcome, or peace.

Yesterday we cleared out of the Thames Estuary into the North Sea. We sailed along the coast, going past Margate to Dover, then made the crossing to France across the Channel. Now we sail hugging the coast still, the French countryside on our left, the Celtic Sea beyond.

I have been given some clean, though not new, clothes to wear. My blood-caked clothes are being washed. No one said anything. I was not the only one bloodied that night, evidently. Dozed below decks as the night was very cold.

SHIP'S JOURNAL, 25TH NOVEMBER 1939

Bay of Biscay. The *Salvador* and *Taurus* chug behind us with their own cargo of Jews. I miss my books. I thought of Alderman and how he seemed so impassioned about his cause. It all feels very distant now. Played cards but lost this time: two shillings.

Hebrew word of the day is *tapuz*. This means the orange fruit, which we are told is plentiful at our destination.

Seen by a doctor. Expressed surprise that I was still alive, considering the various bruises. I explained it has been a difficult month. He nodded sympathetically, patted me on the shoulder and moved on to his next patient. I took that as a good sign.

It's the Shabbat. Strangely peaceful. Several of my fellow passengers had brought a book or two each with them, and a makeshift library was organised. Success! Obtained Agatha Christie's *Death on the Nile*.

SHIP'S JOURNAL, 26TH NOVEMBER 1939

'I can't believe Jacqueline was the murderer!' I told the man who came to borrow the book after me. 'I did not see that coming at all.'

He glared at me and snatched the book from my hands. 'You bloody bastard,' he said.

How rude!

The steamer is making good time. We have passed the French coast and entered Portuguese territorial waters. No way to escape the ship—we dock nowhere.

Last night a woman gave birth to a baby boy; the whole thing carried out quite garishly in the open. I miss having a dog. Food is uninspired but adequate: we have supplies for two weeks. Air is clear. There is something peaceful about the movement of the ship, lulling me into the first instance of calm I have felt in years.

Masturbated last night on my bunk thinking of Isabella Rubinstein.

SHIP'S JOURNAL, 27TH NOVEMBER 1939

Approaching Gibraltar. The air feels warmer. Spain on our left, Morocco on our right. Tangier. Made me think of Leni and whether she ever finished making her film. It all seems very distant now. A strange day, the mood subdued. Towards lunchtime I took a constitutional on board deck and, skirting a pile of thick rope lying quite dangerously in my path, I thought I saw a face I knew. It was only for a moment, across the crowded deck, so I could have been mistaken.

I hope for both our sakes I was!

SHIP'S JOURNAL, 28TH NOVEMBER 1939

. . . 'I thought it was you,' he said.

The Mediterranean. Weather continues to grow warm and rather pleasant. Crossed Gibraltar around midnight. I was on deck, at the stern. A clear night, black-blue with a myriad of stars.

Soft footsteps. I had been anticipating them. I turned, affected a smile. 'Morhaim,' I said, with loathing.

'Wolf.'

We stood regarding each other in silence. The deck quiet, we were obscured by upright pipes, carrying the stench of the sleepers down below.

'So,' I said, at last.

'I won't ask how you made it on board,' he said. 'Or, in God's name, why!'

'Why are *you* here?' I said.

He gave a short, bitter laugh. 'Where else would I go?' he said. 'My country has been devoured by vultures.'

I shrugged. 'We've all got problems, Morhaim.'

'You shit. Tell me something, *Wolf.* Did you kill them?'

'Who?'

'The girls.'

'You know damn well I didn't!'

'How many people *did* you kill?' he said, softly. 'How many *would* you have killed, had you been elected to office?'

'You want to play what-ifs, Morhaim?' I said. 'You Jews spend far too much time in your own imagination.'

He laughed. 'Us Jews,' he said. I did not like his tone, or what he was implying.

'So?' I said, again. *'Nu?* What do you want, *Inspector?'*

'Do you know who did it?' he said.

I shrugged. 'Some boy.'

'What happened to him?'

I didn't say anything and he laughed again. I don't think there was any real joy in his laughter. It was as if he had forgotten how to laugh. I looked at him and saw only a bitter, tired old Jew. He had no power any more.

'Don't,' I said.

He had a gun. It was aimed at me. I remember the night; it was so clear and, for a moment, quiet. A lone seagull flew in a parabola overhead. 'Give me one reason why not.'

My hand edged to the small of my back. 'I'll give you two,' I said.

SHIP'S JOURNAL, 29TH NOVEMBER 1939

Wonderful weather! Passing Sardinia. Hebrew word of the day is *sof,* meaning ending. Also *aliyah,* which means the immigration of the Jews to Palestine. Played cards, lost two shillings. I am beginning to smell—we all do. In the latrines an argument over who is a Jew, some suggestion not everyone on board may be kosher. 'Easy way to tell,' I said. Pissing against the wall in a row, we all had a good laugh. I looked at my Jew dick in my hand almost in affection.

Read Conrad's *The Secret Agent*. Have read better, by worse.

SHIP'S JOURNAL, 30TH NOVEMBER 1939

Listened to the BBC World Service on the radio in the afternoon. Disturbing news. Third assassination attempt on now-PM Oswald Mosley: a bomb hidden in Number 10. There is no confirmation yet if Mosley is dead or alive. Not that I care, much. Mutterings on board, concern for those Jews left in England—we lucky few represent but a small fraction of the whole.

Taurus keeps apace but the *Salvador* is flagging behind. Past Sicily, approaching Greece. Weather is balmy. Hebrew word of the day is *ley'da*, meaning birth.

SHIP'S JOURNAL, 1ST DECEMBER 1939

Greece. A lot of small and rather pleasant-looking islands. We are heading towards Cyprus. Heard on the wireless that Mosley is in critical condition in hospital. Palestinian terrorists sought in connection with the bombing. A cheer on the deck. Saw the ITO man, Goodman, talking intensely to a woman who bore a strikingly familiar face.

'A Jewish woman sought in connection with the bombing

worked as a maid at Number 10 under an assumed identity. The police appeal to the public . . .'

Went past Goodman and the girl. She had a humourless face, her father's cruelty. I smiled at her politely and doffed my hat as I walked past, with the sense of an ending. 'Judith,' I said.

'Do I know you?'

'No,' I said, and walked away.

Hebrew word of the day is *machaneh*, meaning camp.

SHIP'S JOURNAL, 2ND DECEMBER 1939

Skirted Cyprus. Palestine full steam ahead.

•

. . .

Opening and closing doors Shomer tumbles through half-worlds and fraction-worlds, 'No, this isn't it,' falling down trapdoors and out through endless corridors, 'No, this isn't it, either,' for how long he cannot tell, for there is no time here, where there is no space, until:

He opens the door and steps onto a beach. The sand is yellow, coarse. Dust fills the sky. The air is humid, warm, scented with citrus trees and late blooming jasmine. On the horizon the first star appears: Venus, which in Hebrew is called *Noga*, meaning light.

The night is quiet, peaceful. He looks up, to the darkening sky, as more stars come into being overhead. And for a moment it seems to him a woman and two children hover there, outlined in light, and that they're waving: but he can't be sure and in another moment they're gone.

The sea is calm. In the distance, the lights of a town. Shomer stands still, breathes in this wondrous air. 'This must be it,' he says to Yenkl; but Yenkl is no longer with him.

Shomer stands on the shore of that sea on that ancient land and looks out over the water. He sees a ship gliding into safe harbour as the sun fades in the east.

He stands there like a man suspended. Or, perhaps, like a man released.

The *Exodus* arrived in Jaffa as the sun was setting. They waited on board ship until officials came. An argument broke out. On the shore people gathered, waiting for them. At last something was decided, small boats came towards them in a fleet, shouts in Hebrew, Yiddish, Polish, German and English, a scramble to get off, along the wharves sacks filled with oranges awaiting export, stamped JAFFA.

On the shore they formed again into queues and there again waited their turn with the officials. The man waited in line meekly. When it was his turn he handed over his documentation and after careful examination a stamp was placed on the page. The man smiled his thanks.

'Welcome to Palestine,' the official said.

. . .

In that other time and place, the camp prepares to wake for another day of work and death. Beyond the walls, perhaps, the war continues. There is a rumour that the Red Army is advancing on the camp, intent on liberation, but will it be today, tomorrow, in an hour, in a year? The camp prepares for waking as it has done every day, in every block the inmates rise preparing for inspection. The prisoners rise but for the ones who had expired in the night. Slowly they shuffle, these skeletal men. Ka-Tzetnik wrote of Auschwitz, 'It was another planet,' but later in life he went back on himself. 'Auschwitz was not created by the devil,' he wrote, 'but by men, like you, or me.'

. . .

In the morning they came for Shomer, but Shomer wasn't there.

HISTORICAL NOTE

In 1888, the leading Yiddish novelist Sholem Aleichem launched an extraordinary attack on the *shund* writer whose pen name was, simply, Shomer. This remarkable document, *Shomers Mishpet* ('Shomer's Trial'), ran to many pages, and categorised Shomer's writing as being 'ignorantly composed, poorly constructed, highly repetitious [and] morally bankrupt.'

Why Sholem Aleichem—the leading writer of his time—should feel the need to launch such a bitter attack on a humble purveyor of *shund*, or pulp fiction, is perhaps a mystery. Whatever the cause, Shomer—at the time a prolific author of hundreds of novels and plays—is now all but unknown, while Sholem Aleichem's place in literature remains assured.

This Shomer died, peacefully, in New York City in 1905. Thankfully, he never saw the Holocaust that was about to erupt some three decades later.

How does one write the Holocaust? In Chapter 8, two prisoners briefly discuss that question. Prisoner 174517 is, of course, Primo Levi, whose *If This Is A Man* (1947) remains one of the defining works of Holocaust literature. His 'opponent', prisoner 135633, wrote under the name Ka-Tzetnik (a word which means 'concentration camp inmate'), including the infamous novel *House of Dolls*, which first described the Nazi 'Joy Divisions,' or camp brothels where women were kept as sexual slaves. Where Levi is cool and dignified, Ka-Tzetnik burns with the clear-eyed madness of a *shund* writer. His books were 'often lurid novel-memoirs, works that shock the reader with grotesque scenes of torture, perverse sexuality, and cannibalism,' noted David Mikics in *Tablet* magazine, adding: '*House of Dolls* is, unavoidably, Holocaust porn.'

During the 1920s, Adolf Hitler used the *nom de guerre* of 'Wolf' ('Adolf' means, literally, 'Noble Wolf'). Though countless books have been written about him, so much yet remains uncertain, shrouded in rumour and misinformation and propaganda. Certainly, it seems clear that he was an abused child; that his experience as a runner in the First World War led to that extraordinary scene (described in Chapter 10) where his blindness was seemingly cured by the psychiatrist, Edmund Forster; and that, though women were powerfully attracted to him, his relationship with them was far from simple.

Kershaw, in his vast, two-volume biography of Hitler, is surprisingly reticent about the question of Hitler's sexuality. While discussing the experiences recounted by Hitler's friend August 'Gustl' Kubizek (in *Adolf Hitler, My Childhood Friend*, published in 1951), Kershaw concludes that 'Later rumours of Hitler's sexual perversions are similarly based on dubious evidence. Conjecture—and there has been much of it—that sexual repression later gave way to sordid sadomasochistic practices rests, whatever the suspicions, on little more than a combination of rumour, hearsay, surmise, and innuendo, often spiced up by Hitler's political enemies.'

Indeed, in their highly entertaining and scurrilously gossipy *Hitler and Women*, Ian Sayer and Douglas Botting note that 'Investigating the private life and sexual inclinations of Adolf Hitler has been like trying to work one's way through an Elizabethan maze built on a tidal mudflat.' They go on, however, to discuss Hitler's 'copulation business' with some considerable, if often suspect, detail.

Many erstwhile Nazis weave their way through this novel. Of these, Josef Kramer (Chapter 2) was a ruthless concentration camp guard who was eventually put in charge of the gas chambers in Auschwitz, and later became the commandant of the Bergen-Belsen death camp. He was executed by hanging after the war.

Ilse Koch (Chapter 2) was known as 'The Beast of Buchenwald.' She was notorious for acts of violence and sadism against prisoners, and was accused of taking mementos off the corpses of her victims—including using their skin to make lampshades. She committed suicide in prison in 1967. She was also the inspiration behind the 'classic' Nazisploitation film *Ilsa, She Wolf of the SS* and its sequels.

Klaus Barbie (Chapter 6) was known as 'The Butcher of Lyon', where he was the head of the local Gestapo. He was known for torturing prisoners, including the use of electroshock and severe sexual abuse. Some prisoners were skinned alive. He was behind the deportation of some 14,000 Jews to the death camps. After the war, Barbie worked for American intelligence in its battle against communism. He emigrated to South America, and while there it was rumoured he was behind the eventual capture and murder of the revolutionary Che Guevara. He was finally extradited to France in 1983, and was convicted for war crimes in 1987. He died in prison.

As for the higher-up Nazis in this book—Hess was Hitler's long-time deputy; Göring, the founder of the Gestapo and commander in chief of the German air force (he was a decorated World War I ace fighter pilot); Goebbels his propaganda minister. Adolf Eichmann, whom Wolf fails to recognise in the novel, joined the SS in 1932. He rose quickly through the ranks, working for the Jewish Department of the SS. He was the recording secretary at the Wannsee Conference, in which the Final Solution to the Jewish Question was first formulated, and became the effective administrator of the Jewish genocide. He escaped to South America after the war but was captured by Israeli Mossad agents in 1960. He was put on trial, in Jerusalem, and executed in 1962. The author Ka-Tzetnik (revealed at that time as Yehiel De-Nur) famously testified during the trial, collapsing unconscious after delivering a short statement. He did not resume the stand (see Chapter 8 Endnotes).

One unexpected by-product of the Eichmann trial was the short-lived flourishing in Israel of 'stalag' novels. Published as pulp paperbacks during the 1960s, and featuring garish, lurid covers, they began with the infamous *Stalag 13*, by a 'Mike Baden': the cover portrayed two female guards in skintight leather, cut to expose a great deal of cleavage, as they torture a male prisoner of war down on his knees. A string of such books—which featured sexual domination and torture of POWs by sadistic Aryan 'nymphomaniacs'—was published, available under the counter. They sold in unprecedented numbers, perhaps enabling many Israelis, for the first time, to talk openly about the great taboo that was the Holocaust. The pulp novels were themselves possibly inspired by Ka-Tzetnik's 1955 novel, *House of Dolls*, which was considered canonical, and became a part of the Israeli high-school curriculum. Whatever the causes, the relationship between desire and dominance, coupled with the power of taboo, continues to exert a fascination to this day.

In the margins of history one comes across, from time to time, remarkable yet obscure figures. Robert (Boris) Bitker (Chapter 8) was a militant Zionist, a Polish immigrant who worked in the film industry in Hollywood, fought in both China and Palestine and died in 1945 in San Francisco. In contrast, Leni Riefenstahl was famous as the golden girl of Nazi cinema. A close personal friend of Adolf Hitler, she created Nazi propaganda films such as *Triumph of the Will* (1935) which chronicles the triumphant Nuremberg victory rallies of the previous year, and *Olympia* (1938), which details the 1936 Olympic Games held in Berlin under the Nazis. She was never convicted of a crime and died of old age in 2003, when she was 101 years old.

Oswald Mosley, an admirer of Hitler, founded the British Union of Fascists in 1932. His paramilitaries, the Blackshirts, wore one-piece jumpsuits designed by Mosley himself. They are perhaps best remembered today for the Battle of Cable Street, in 1936, when they attempted to march on—and were repelled from—the mostly Jewish East End. By 1940 the organisation was outlawed: Mosley and his wife spent the majority of the war in London's Holloway Prison. His second wife was Diana Mitford. They married in 1936, at the house of Joseph Goebbels. Adolf Hitler was the guest of honour. Diana's sister, Unity, was a fervent devotee of Hitler, and for a time competed for his affection with Hitler's mistress, Eva Braun. She remained in Germany as part of Hitler's close circle for five years before the outbreak of the war. She attempted suicide in 1939, returned to Britain, and died in 1948 of complications relating to the bullet still lodged in her head. She was 33.

The *Exodus*, *Salvador* and *Taurus* were all ships used by the Mossad Le'Aliyah Bet to illegally bring Jewish refugees from Europe to Palestine. The *Salvador* was wrecked in the Sea of Marmara in 1940, carrying some 300 refugees. The *Taurus* was the last refugee ship to operate during the war. It sailed in 1943 from Romania, carrying some 900 refugees. They arrived safely in Istanbul and from there caught the train to Palestine. The *Exodus*, famously, was stopped by British forces at Haifa harbour in 1947, and its cargo of some 5,000 Holocaust survivors sent back to camps in Germany. My own mother came to Palestine on board a similar ship when she was two years old: she was born in a refugee camp near Munich after the war, to parents who had each survived Auschwitz. The majority of my family, on both sides, died in the camp.

Adolf Hitler finally married his long-term mistress, Eva Braun, in a private ceremony on the 29th April 1945 in the Führer's bunker in Berlin. They committed suicide, together, one day later, and their corpses were carried to the garden outside, placed in a bomb crater, doused with petrol and burned.

NOTES

Chapter 1

5   '*She had the face of an intelligent Jewess*': Wolf is possibly echoing here the words of the crime novelist Raymond Chandler (1888–1939). We know he was fond of popular, or 'pulp' crime novels, though they comprised but a small part of his extensive library. See *The Big Sleep* (1939).

8   '*The Jews are nothing but money-grubbers, living on the profits of war*': See *My Struggle*.

9   '*I was so cold, and it was going to be a cold winter*': Wolf isn't wrong—the winter of 1939–1940 was the coldest in 45 years, with record temperature lows. Frost and fog were common in London. By January snow storms had hit Britain and the Thames froze for some eight miles between Teddington and Sunbury.

9   '*The painting on the wall showed a French church tower rising against the background of a village, a field executed in a turmoil of brushstrokes*': The painting is, possibly, *The Church of Preux-au-Bois*, a large water-colour dating to Wolf's time in Vienna before the Great War.

9   '*a personally inscribed copy of* Fire and Blood, *Ernst Jünger's memoir of the Great War*': *Feuer und Blut*'s nationalistic ideology was an early inspiration for the nascent National Socialist movement. It was first published in Germany in 1925.

12   '*One could tell by the number of darkened windows how trade was going*': The incident is similarly recalled in the memoirs of Wolf's friend, August 'Gustl' Kubizek.

13   '*Whores. How I hated whores! Their bodies were riddled with syphilis and the other ills of their trade. The disease was but a symptom. Its cause was the manner in which love itself has been prostituted*': Wolf expresses a similar sentiment in *My Struggle*.

Chapter 2

24   '*Sometimes he thought he would drown in words, all those words*': 'Books, always more books!' recalled Wolf's childhood friend, Gustl. 'Books were his world.'

29   '*[The Jews] were a parasitic race, preying upon the honest portion of mankind*': See *My Struggle*.

33   '*Wolf liked his women cute, cuddly and naïve, or so he liked to say at his more expansive moments back in Munich: he liked little things who*

were tender, sweet and stupid': Wolf's friend Gustl quotes a similar sentiment in his memoirs.

Chapter 3

47 '*I respected my father, but I loved my mother*': Wolf says much the same in *My Struggle*, though in that earlier book he does not delve as deeply into the matter of his childhood and his father's subsequent death. That Elois was a violent drunk, and that the young Wolf felt freed by his passing, however, there seems little doubt.

Chapter 4

63 '*And yet worse was the time we had been approached in the street by an older man, on the corner of Mariahilferstrasse-Neubaugasse*': This incident is indeed also recounted in Gustl's memoirs.

64 '*There was this, too, about Gustl: he was a compulsive masturbator. At any given opportunity, in his bed, in his wash, behind his piano, sometimes at his desk in class or even on the corner of the street, his hand in his pocket, Gustl would relieve himself the way I had denied myself*': Wolf is perhaps being unkind here. Certainly Gustl had the normal impulses of a young man, and in his memoirs he recalls that Wolf, himself, did not seek physical release in this way. Perhaps, for Wolf, any kind of masturbatory impulse would have seemed excessive.

64 '*as the personification of the devil, the symbol of all evil, assumes the living shape of the Jew*': Wolf expresses a similar sentiment in *My Struggle*.

72 *"Marxism must be destroyed," Mosley said. "It is the poisoned ideology of the Jewish race"'*: Perhaps unconsciously, Mosley is here echoing Wolf's own words (see *My Struggle*).

Chapter 5

80 '*In 1917, Lord Balfour wrote a letter to Baron Rothschild, in which he asserted British support for the establishment of a Jewish homeland in Palestine*': 'His Majesty's government view with favour the establishment in Palestine of a national home for the Jewish people, and will use their best endeavours to facilitate the achievement of this object, it being clearly understood that nothing shall be done which may prejudice the civil and religious rights of existing non-Jewish communities in Palestine, or the rights and political status enjoyed by Jews in any other country.'

80 '*[Palestine was] then still in the possession of the Ottoman Empire*': Palestine fell to the British forces, commanded by General Edmund Allenby (1861–1936), by early 1918.

85 '*"You were always steadfast in your hatred of them, Valkyrie"*': Wolf is perhaps thinking of this letter to *Der Stürmer*, in which Unity wrote: 'The English have no notion of the Jewish danger. Our worst Jews work only behind the scenes. We think with joy of the day when we will be able to say England for the English! Out with the Jews! P.S. please publish my name in full, I want everyone to know I am a Jew hater.'

96 '*The alcohol hit me like an uppercut from Max Schmeling*': Schmeling

was a German boxer and heavyweight champion of the world 1930–1932.

Chapter 6

113 *'One day walking down the street he saw one of their number in the black Hasidic garb and he was plain bemused: was this a Jew?'*: Again, much the same instance is similarly recounted in *My Struggle*.

117 *'"Put a tenner on Bogskar for us, will you?" he said'*: A good bet, as Bogskar went on to win the Grand National the next year. However, he was an unexpected winner, with long odds of twenty-five to one, so perhaps the tall man simply knew something the bookies didn't.

124 *'I was sunk in melancholy thought. Architecture affects me that way'*: Though Wolf aspired to become an artist, he was rejected twice by the Academy of Fine Arts in Vienna, with the recommendation that he study architecture instead. Wolf, however, lacked the necessary academic credentials. He also lacked the money, and for a time lived in a homeless shelter, before settling in the men's dormitory on Meldemannstrasse 27.

Chapter 7

144 *'his conversation on the World Ice Theory, the* Welteislehre, *has always been fascinating and erudite'*: Also known as *Glazial-Kosmogonie* (Glacial Cosmology), the idea came to the Austrian engineer Hans Hörbiger in a dream in 1894. It suggested bodies in the universe were composed primarily of ice, and was adopted by National

Socialism as an antidote to 'Jewish science,' such as the theory of relativity.

146   *'I had been paid £350 from my British publisher, Hurst & Blackett'*: *My Struggle*. London: Hurst & Blackett, 1933. By 1939 the small firm had been subsumed by the larger publishing firm, Hutchinson.

148   *'It was the second time in a week that a Rubinstein was holding Wolf by the balls'*: Various sources have claimed over the years that Wolf was in possession of only one testicle; but that has never been conclusively confirmed.

Chapter 8

156   *'That big fat oaf Gil Chesterton'*: G. K. Chesterton (1874–1936), was indeed a large man—he was over six feet in height and weighed some twenty-one stone. He converted to Catholicism later in life, and is best known as the author of the Father Brown detective stories.

158   *'"The Zionist Congress sent an expedition to British East Africa— . . . Unfortunately the expedition did not return a favourable report"'*: For further details, see *Report on the work of the commission sent out to examine the territory offered by H. M. Government to the Zionist Organisation for the purposes of a Jewish settlement in British East Africa* (London: Wertheimer, Lea & Co, 1905).

175   *'"We have no names. We have no parents and we have no children"'*: Ka-Tzetnik's testimony during the Eichmann Trial in 1961 lasted

just 2:50 minutes before his collapse. He did not resume the witness stand. He said:

> '*It was not a pen name. I do not regard myself as a writer and a composer of literary material. This is a chronicle of the planet of Auschwitz. I was there for about two years. Time there was not like it is here on earth. Every fraction of a minute there passed on a different scale of time. And the inhabitants of this planet had no names, they had no parents nor did they have children. There they did not dress in the way we dress here; they were not born there and they did not give birth; they breathed according to different laws of nature; they did not live—nor did they die—according to the laws of this world. They were human skeletons, and their name was the number "Ka-Tzetnik."*'

Chapter 9

178 '*He had a long mournful lawyer's face and a lawyer's fidgety manners*': Roland Freisler (1893–1945) Nazi lawyer and judge. An officer in the First World War, he joined the Nazi party in 1925 and indeed, as Wolf notes, served as defence counsel for Nazi party members.

188 '*Murder is a frustration not just of the individual: it is a frustration of the race*': Wolf is, perhaps unconsciously, echoing Raymond Chandler again here, in an essay ('The Simple Art of Murder') written some time after the events depicted here.

189 '"*I am working on a case that may be related. I need access to . . . a part of the Jewish community*"': It is not clear, in view of later events, what Wolf was planning. Perhaps he was hoping to use Isabella Rubinstein's wealth and social influence, such as they were, to try to gain access again to the Palestinian networks, thus working the Mosley case. But he does not, unfortunately, record here the details of his plan.

189   '*"You want me to work with you? Solving . . . crime? Like Nick and Nora Charles!"*': Nick and Nora Charles were a mystery-solving husband and wife team in Dashiell Hammett's 1934 novel *The Thin Man*, and in a subsequent series of films.

195   '*Albert Curtis Brown was my literary agent*': Albert Curtis Brown (1866–1945) was indeed Wolf's literary agent in the UK, having taken on representation of *My Struggle* from Wolf's German publishers, for the English-language market. He founded Curtis Brown Ltd in 1899, representing Steinbeck, Faulkner and Mailer, amongst others, and growing the agency into one of the largest in the UK.

Chapter 10

201   '*"Leni? Leni Riefenstahl? My God!" Wolf said*': Leni Riefenstahl (1902–2003), German actress and film director. She was a committed National Socialist; Wolf had always been an ardent fan of hers, and the attraction was mutual.

208   '*"It wasn't even a* personal *rejection!"*': Stanley Unwin indeed received a copy of Wolf's book—but turned it down—around 1926. Wolf obviously bore a grudge.

214   '*The foul man had tricked me!*': Professor Edmund Robert Forster (1878–1933) was much as Wolf describes him here. A Berlin neurologist and decorated war medic, Forster was put in command of the Pase-walk hospital, in charge of treating soldiers from the front diagnosed with being hysterics—what we would probably now call posttraumatic stress disorder (PTSD). He had little patience for the

soldiers in general, seeing them as 'shirkers' from their duty. Treatment for such 'hysterics' sometimes included electric shocks and total isolation. Forster confined himself to a harsh, almost bullying attitude to his patients—an attitude which often worked. He treated Wolf during October–November 1918, successfully restoring the young soldier's vision with the method Wolf indeed mentions above—as unorthodox as it may seem.

Chapter 11

227   *'It was in a plain yellow dustjacket, like the books published by that Jew, Victor Gollancz'*: Victor Gollancz (1893–1967) was a British publisher and well-known socialist. He was born to an orthodox Jewish family in North London. In 1927, he founded Victor Gollancz Ltd, publishing works by George Orwell amongst many others. The yellow jackets were a distinctive brand choice for the imprint, which had existed for many years. It is quite possible Wolf's publishers had simply copied the design. The imprint continues to this day, though mostly publishing popular fiction, primarily science fiction and fantasy.

228   *'On her sickbed in Urfahr my mother lay dying'*: A small village near to—and now a suburb of—the Austrian city of Linz.

228   *'I had been residing in Vienna at that time, attempting to enroll in the Academy of Fine Arts'*: As noted previously, Wolf was not accepted into the academy.

231   *'"The Grosvenor Hotel, Victoria. And step on it!" The driver chuckled as though Wolf had said something funny'*: It seems probable Wolf's

English tended to incorporate elements of slang borrowed, sometimes inappropriately, from the kind of books he was reading. 'Step on it'—referring to a driver pressing down on the gas pedal of an automobile—dates some twenty years back and is probably of American origin.

Chapter 12

239 *'I was dressed in my beat-up old raincoat, a suit that's seen better days, scuffed shoes and a fedora that didn't quite fit me . . . I didn't know how much Rubenstein's house was worth but my guess was plenty. I was calling on Jewish money'*: Wolf is again, here, and perhaps unconsciously, echoing the words of the writer Raymond Chandler, specifically the opening scene of Chandler's debut, *The Big Sleep*. It is possible Wolf read the novel on publication—it had come out in the UK, published by Hamish Hamilton, in March of 1939.

240 *'the kind of boiseries to give Syrie Maugham heart palpitations'*: Syrie Maugham (1879–1955) was a leading British interior designer; with her penchant for white, airy rooms, she probably would not have approved of the boiseries (ornately carved wainscoting) Wolf mentions.

Chapter 13

266 *'"Who the fuck is Adolf Eichmann!"'*: Adolf Eichmann joined the Nazi Party in 1932 as a member of the General SS. As such, he would have been unknown to Wolf at the time.

Chapter 14

289 *'"Auschwitz was not created by the devil," he wrote, "but by men, like you, or me"'*: See Ka-Tzetnik, *The Code* (1987).

ABOUT THE AUTHOR

LAVIE TIDHAR is the World Fantasy Award–winning author of *The Violent Century, Osama,* and many other books. A past winner of both the British Fantasy Award for Best Novel and the World Fantasy Award for Best Novel, he grew up on a kibbutz in Israel and in South Africa and currently lives in London.

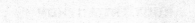